TENSILE TOWN

A NOVEL

RS PERKINS

Published by Innovo Publishing, LLC
www.innovopublishing.com
1-888-546-2111

Providing Full-Service Publishing Services for Christian Authors, Artists &
Ministries: Books, eBooks, Audiobooks, Music, Screenplays, Film & Curricula

TENSILE TOWN
A Novel

Unless otherwise noted, all scripture is taken from the King James Version of the
Bible. Public domain.

Holy Bible, New International Version®, NIV® Copyright ©1973, 1978, 1984,
2011 by Biblica, Inc.® Used by permission. All rights reserved worldwide.

Library of Congress Control Number: 2022908427
ISBN: 978-1-61314-836-5

Cover Design & Interior Layout: Innovo Publishing, LLC

Printed in the United States of America
U.S. Printing History
First Edition: 2022

Has God called you to create a Christian book, eBook, audiobook, music album,
screenplay, film, or curricula? If so, visit the ChristianPublishingPortal.com to
learn how to accomplish your calling with excellence. Learn to do everything
yourself, or hire trusted Christian Experts from our Marketplace to help.

Thank you, Nick & Rachael, for encouraging me.
Thank you, Bart, for saying yes.

A Special Thank You

My life has most certainly been blessed by love, first from
The Almighty Creator God the Father, The Son Jesus, and The Holy Spirit.

Then, my mom, Betty, and my grandfather, James Homer, who planted
the seed of Jesus in my fertile heart when I was ten years old; my wife,
Elizabeth; my children, Cheyenne, Asher, and Gabe; and my sisters,
Bethany and Sandi.

It was my older brother, Phil, though, who inspired me, in his early
days of performing live music before he became a successful business
owner, to spend my life making music. Lovingly, Phil included me in
those formative years, allowing me to see firsthand what it takes to go
from the imagination into the real world. I am a dreamer, and he is a
doer. With Tensile Town, *I was inspired once again by my brother after*
reading his first novel. Phil's "doing" was the boot on my backside that
finally motivated me to put this story on paper (or pixels).
Thank you, Bro.

"When lives intertwine, there forms a fibrous human rope tested for fortitude and merit. It can be a lifeline to share with others who are in need, but if not protected and cleansed, friction and dirt weakens the bond and the rope becomes unreliable. The results are only a matter of tension and time."

— Daniel Mosely

"We know that all things work together for good for those who love God, to those who are called according to his purpose."

— Romans 8:28

CHAPTER ONE

It is six o'clock in the morning and five, youthful hikers are abuzz in the Reed's two-car garage, all packed and ready to roll. There is Sam Reed, the oldest hiker and the appointed leader. Barry Meade is the son of the county's most trusted pediatrician and lives across the street from the Reeds. The large and rough Jeff Lindor has a humor as dry as snakeskin and is the catcher on the school's baseball team. Danny Mosely is a lover of words and lives with, and was raised by his dad Walter who lost his wife and Danny's mother when Danny was a baby.

The group of friends is rounded out by Danny's best friend and Sam's younger brother King Reed (that's right, King) who is a free spirit and who loves rock and roll music. These boys are close and, some, have been best friends since Elementary School. *"Unbelievable!"* Gordon Reed, father of Sam and King, shouts as he enters the garage. "I would have bet money that at least one of you would be late. I am happy that you guys are so excited," he says, smiling and shaking his head in pestering disbelief as he opens the trunk to the big-but-sleek 1963 Pontiac Bonneville.

Sam and King's mother, Eleanor, asks Sam if he found the extra sleeping bag so that Jeff will be as comfy as the rest of the boys. It is unfortunate common knowledge, among the hiker's parents, that Jeff's mom has not been as attentive to her son's needs since her divorce. "Yes, Mom, it was up in the attic," Sam says with a yawn that displays his tonsil area. Sam looks over at Jeff as his yawn is ending, squints his eyes and says in an early morning Karloff spooky voice, "Probably full of spiders." For even greater effect, Sam adds the wiggling of all ten of his fingers in Jeff's face.

"There are no spiders in our attic, Samuel Reed!" Mrs. Reed says emphatically, making it clear to everyone that her house is clean.

The hiker's diversities and similarities, extreme as they are, are the glue that binds four of them together, with Sam too old to truly relate. The parents of the four younger adventurers knew they could trust Sam to make good decisions, beyond his nearly eighteen years, and watch after their sons. Sam is, certainly, more mature than the other boys. He is tall and sinewy with a swimmer's body, dark brown hair and thickening sideburns stopping at the bottom of his ears. Though it is the swinging year of 1967, Sam keeps his hair properly trimmed and combed over and back, held with the steadfastness of Brylcreem, the hair product that all the "men" wear to get that professional look.

Sam is the captain of the basketball team, the Flint High School Pumas, and a silver-tongued Debate Team star. It has become obvious that Sam is destined for law and, possibly, politics. His peers love him and so do his teachers. The girls flirt with him and the guys want to be seen with him, but Sam is focused and gobbles up life, spitting out the parts he does not like. He knows that dating, in any regular way, will just distract him from his goal of attending college and becoming an attorney. As far as his parents know, Sam wants to pass the Ohio Bar and then, and only then, he will open his heart or simply pick someone to marry. Today, though, because of his age and his ownership of a compass, Sam will lead the hike gang out of their natural habitat and into the unknown.

King Reed is named after his mother's favorite singer, Nat King Cole. Nat sang many great songs, but Eleanor's favorite was and is *Nature Boy*. Known as Ellie by her friends and family, she was lauded as an excellent vocalist before she was Sam and King's mom. As a teen, she would sing with her two sisters in tight Andrews Sisters-style harmonies. The Sparks, the name of their trio, being that their last name was Sparks, were so fetching that they received an invitation to perform on local Appleton radio as contest winners, and that ignited a flame in Ellie that flickers to this day.

The audience applause and excited radio DJ only amplified the dream that had been forming in Ellie's teenage mind. Ellie would spend hours in front of her dresser mirror, pretending that she would someday sing at Carnegie Hall in New York City in front of an orchestra. Her imagination was vivid and placed her appearance as a starlet, standing in the spotlight in a flowing, pale pink chiffon dress, her auburn hair pulled up above her ears. Always, she could see Virgil Thomson, of the

Herald Tribune, furiously writing tomorrow's announcement of a new star found.

But Ellie Sparks met the love of her life in her small town, the dashing yet poised and stable Gordon Reed. From that day forward, Ellie's dream was graciously and generously traded for motherhood and singing in the shower. Her audience changed to two, fidgety, small boys that she would not trade for a truckload of Carnegie Halls. She would sing whatever the radio was playing that year or an old favorite *I Love You a Bushel And a Peck*, but it was the song *Nature Boy* that Ellie would sing to King every night before bed when he was a small boy. She would probably still sing it to King if he were not staying up later than she these days. Secretly, King would love to hear it, too.

Gordon was not thrilled about the name King for his second son. Samuel, or Sam, is a strong but unassuming name and the name of Gordon's best buddy while fighting Japan in WWII, but King was a bit too "royal" for Gordon's red, white and blue American blood. He could already imagine the ridicule and jokes his son would receive with such a "distinct" name, but Gordon loved his wife, he loved her singing and she loved Nat. So, King it was, and the son was crowned with a light blue sock hat the day he was born, March 7 of 1953.

Like his older brother, Sam, and his dad Gordon, King grew into a square jaw and a nose like Tyrone Power. His hair grew white as a toddler and finally has settled on rusty blonde, similar to his mother Ellie's hair color. Perhaps it is the three-year age difference or just the fact that they are two different people, but unlike Sam, little brother King spends no time in front of a mirror. He knows his mother will use her lovingly licked palm to settle down the hairy madness on his head as he exits their home on his way to the school bus. King likes The Rolling Stones, especially Brian Jones. So, he grows his hair as long as he can to copy Mr. Jones before Gordon reminds Ellie that King needs to go with Sam during Sam's regular trip to the barber.

Mr. Reed throws the last backpack into the trunk and motions to the boys to pile in. Sam and King kiss their mom and tell her not to worry (as if that will bring her instant comfort). The Pontiac fires right up, and it glides backwards out of the garage and down the driveway to Marigold Road, the artery that runs up the middle of their community, Marigold. Mr. Reed points the boat of a car toward their starting point, the top of Marigold Hill.

Marigold Hill sits proudly at the center of the universe, in the middle of all the other hills. The Great Lakes created her when their icy glaciers melted and pushed the earth south. Northern Ohio was flattened by the immensity of the melt, but the mighty push stopped just north of Marigold, creating a terrain that resembles a pug's skin. Now, glistening with morning dew, shimmering like a Christmas tree ornament, Marigold Hill looms large over the Shawnee arrowhead-littered valley. Marigold nestles itself quietly, right up to the ancient girl's voluptuous bosom.

No doubt, the community is named after the marsh marigold flower that covers the damp, wooded areas throughout the valleys and moist ravines of this part of the world from April through June. The scattered, abundant patches of this dainty perennial can be an emotional sight, forcing the viewer to define them as either temporary groundcover or an invasion of spring, bursting with new life.

Marigold Road was designed and engineered to provide safe and scenic delivery of clean living for those who had enough of the fast pace of Appleton. Marigold Road cuts a mostly straight three-mile path through the valley, with houses, creeks, churches, a neighborhood grocer, and a community pool lining its sides. Ever so slightly, under its three vainglorious miles, the road gains altitude until you are at the foot of Marigold Hill, where the Reed's comfortable house sits. There, Marigold Road begins to take a nicely rounded left and then a more tightly rounded, well-banked right turn. It snakes its way up the nine-degree grade, three hundred and ten feet through the woods, flint rock and sandstone, to its very top. Once on top, one can see all the way over the river valley to the West Appleton hills, probably five or six miles to the west, but that view is only possible later in the day, after the fog burns off and if the skies are clear.

Ellie waves to the boys until they are out of sight and then hurries back into the basement out of the cold. She shuffles upstairs and into the kitchen where she puts on another pot of coffee for Gordon and herself to sip on through the highly anticipated morning of rare quiet. The Zenith Hi-Fi that Gordon bought for her, when they moved into their Upper Marigold home five years earlier, is Ellie's next destination on this rare morning of freedom.

Mom and Dad's records are not played much these days, now that King and Sam have taken over the console. Covers for the records by The Beatles, James Brown, Jimi Hendrix, and The Rolling Stones, strewn on top and underneath of the entertainment Goliath, do not allow room for the parent's collection. So, Ellie takes great delight in digging out her old, and a few new, favorites like Mr. Cole, Sinatra, music from Breakfast at Tiffany's with the beautiful Mancini/Mercer penned *Moon River*, and Peggy Lee's *Big Spender*. Ellie carefully stacks them on the spindle, record-by-record, and twists the start button. Down the spindle drops Nat, and the house pulsates with silky sounds.

Ellie stands there listening and staring out their big bow window at the Meade's chimney across Marigold Road. Her fire flickers for a few seconds before she places the morning's Appleton Times in the seat of Gordon's favorite chair to welcome him home. She heads back to the kitchen, while singing every beautiful note recorded on Nat's album as she walks and begins breaking eggs for a relaxing breakfast with her husband.

The climb up Marigold Hill is quick in the Bonneville, and there is a turn-around at the top where so many people have stopped to look at the beautiful valley below. That is where Mr. Reed drops off the boys and unloads the trunk. "Be very careful, all of you," Mr. Reed says in a way that might be showing that he wishes he were going. He hugs his sons, and King's best friend Danny, while the others grab their gear and walk over to the old service road entrance. "I want to see you by noon tomorrow, right?" Mr. Reed says in a mockingly stern voice while seated behind the wheel again, with the window rolled down.

"Right!" all the boys affirm as Mr. Reed waves and starts back down the hill.

"Are you bunch of ragamuffins ready to roll?" Sam barks in an imitation drill sergeant growl and with his arms akimbo. Then, in his best Wagon Train voice (Sam loves that TV show), Sam yells with his back to the gang and one arm in the air "Head 'em up! Mo-o-o-ove 'em out!" With that command, Sam's arm points forward up the old dirt grooves of the service road and the Marigold five are off to conquer the hills of five misty ranges.

In addition to their sleeping bags that each young man has packed, or asked his mom to pack, is his favorite lunch that will not spoil. Of course, there are the old faithful peanut butter and jelly and peanut butter and banana sandwiches. Jeff packed a hot dog that was left over from last night's Thanksgiving dinner. Baby Ruth, 5th Avenue and Pay Day candy bars are abundant. Barry's mom wrapped a few carrot sticks and put them in her son's bag along with a fresh muffin for each boy. There are turkey and ham sandwiches from the more proper, though not more appreciated, Thanksgiving dinners and most of the boys brought a thermos of hot soup or hot chocolate and a canteen of water.

Along with food, their dads' old olive-green canvas Army backpacks also carry some supplies like matches, flashlights, and batteries. Danny's dad let him bring a heavy-duty military flashlight that is made like a tank and is heavy, but it is dependable and the light can shine for fifty yards. He hopes he will get a chance to use it for peering into an old, dark cave, if one presents itself. King's mom packed a substantial first aid kit and Sam is going to wait until the last minute, to tell whoever needs it the most, that he is in the possession of . . . toilet paper!

They are all looking forward to when they stop their hike for a lunch break, but right now, they are taking in the grandeur and glory of the sun-drenched rolling hills of their homeland. From their vantage point, along this first ridge, they can still see parts of Upper Marigold. Danny points out King's and Sam's house that looks the size of a Monopoly game piece. "My house must be right in there somewhere," Barry Meade says with genuine excitement as he waves his arm in the general direction across from the Reed's.

Some members of the group may have taken their bicycles exploring up one or two of the various old trails throughout their neighborhood, but this is a whole new perspective. There are no houses, streets or cars up here for as far as they can see. The grand view reminds King that he had heard a song on WROR last night just as he was falling asleep. With the song fresh in his mind, he sings the first lines with expression. They all recognize the song *I Can See for Miles* instantly and agree with the sentiments of which King is referring. At the top of their wonderfully free lungs, from the summit of Marigold Hill that gives the view to the entire valley below, they all sing the super catchy hook line just like the song. Then, as if rehearsed, King and Barry lean their heads in toward each other and ear-to-ear sing "oh ye-e-ah" to finish the chorus like The Who.

"You guys really need to get your band going. You know, the one you've talked about for a year?" Sam yells back to the troop behind him. "King! You could borrow the drum set from the school jazz band, I bet?"

"I'll check with Mr. Wiggins on Monday, Sam. That's a good idea. I didn't want to ask Mom and Dad for a drum set, at least until we see if the band is going to do anything."

"You could get a job, you know? Some of us work for what we want." Sam yells back half-jokingly.

"Funny guy." is all King can say because he knows it's true.

Jeff lights up a Camel, spits out a piece of tobacco that has stuck to his tongue, and urges "I hope we can get started, soon. I'm tired of playing guitar in my bedroom and Danny's TV room. Maybe we could each pick five songs and learn them before Diana Peterson's birthday party in February. Maybe she'll let us play. Danny, you're going to play bass, right?"

"Yeah, man, that'll be groovy. I'm just not sure where I can get a bass. My dad is not exactly a Kennedy or anything. I think my church will probably let me borrow theirs."

"What kind is it?" asked Barry.

"I think it is a Gibson. It's kinda old but they just bought a nice, new Fender Bassman amp from Klein's Music."

"What about you, Barry?" asked King. "What will you play? You can't drag your big piano around."

"For your information, Mr. Reed, I've saved a bunch working for the club and for my dad on some weekends." Replies Barry. "I'm sure I have more than enough to buy a Vox Continental. I think I like those better than the Farfisa. A Farfisa sounds too San Fran-y and I really like all the draw bars on the Vox. I can get more sound variations out of it. I can't wait to show you *Light My Fire* on it. Let's definitely do that song! That is number one in my top five. When do you guys want to rehearse?"

"Man! Slow down," Jeff says as he blows out smoke while grinning and everyone laughs. "Are we all available next Saturday?" asks Jeff.

"Where?" Danny and Barry say at the same time.

King hesitantly offers a meek "I will ask my mom if we can do it in the basement." Everyone agrees that, if it's OK, the Reed basement will be a great place and the four agree on two o'clock. This is after Danny concludes his weekly job of cleaning the church for the Sunday service. Jeff usually works Saturday mornings at Charlie's grocery store, as well, but agrees to come straight from work, if there is a rehearsal.

As the young men of Marigold find their pace walking along the ridge, with Sergeant Sam in the lead, the crew are not talking a lot. Now and then, Barry will let out a howl just to hear it echo through the valley. King and Danny are singing *Time Has Come Today*, shouting out *"time!"* with every eight steps they take toward their destination. Sam is mostly walking ahead by himself, but while there is a bit of a clearing, Jeff double-times it up next to him and asks Sam what he plans to do after he graduates this spring.

Sam is quiet for a few pregnant seconds and then proceeds to unfold his vision. "Well, my friend," Sam begins. "Of course, I will go to college." Jeff moves his eyes off of the leader and looks down at the ground while shaking his head as if to say, *Of course, I knew that.* "I really hope to go to Ohio State and then Moritz or, maybe, Case. However, because of Nam, I was kinda thinking about West Point."

"*West Point?*" Jeff blurts out. More quietly Jeff elaborates, "Man, you're signing your own death certificate if you go there 'cause you know they'll ship you over to fight the VC or even worse, *you'll* be sending boys over to die," Jeff stated matter-of-factly and then continues, "Man, I know you're a smart guy and all, but please think twice or three times about joining up. Our guys are coming back in pieces or dead or crazy and you can do anything, Sam. You don't need to be a soldier." Jeff's pleading words fade off as he looks away in the other direction.

Trying to calm Jeff, Sam tells him, "Mom and Dad haven't heard that I'm considering West Point, yet. I'm just thinking about it, and you and King are the only ones I've said anything to. I haven't applied, so I may be too late anyway."

Jeff Lindor is a stocky sixteen-year-old who always has a joke and an unfiltered Camel cigarette. His straight black hair is actually long, past the bottom of his ears, and he is constantly scraping it back out of his face with his left hand or moving it with a head-sling to the right. Jeff can get into trouble, sometimes, and is not a favorite of the other boys' parents, but his peers love his heart and wit.

Susan Lindor, Jeff's mom, and dad Carl divorced when he was eleven, and his mom still over-compensates with her parental duties, trying to do the job of both parents. Susan is very hard on Jeff which just pushed Jeff away in those fragile early years after his parent's split. Jeff misses his dad, who drives an eighteen-wheeler cross-country and who can typically be away from Jeff for weeks at a time. When they were all together as a family, the special time of the week was when Carl would call collect from the road. The call would come, as promised, on Wednesday nights at eight o'clock in the Eastern Time zone. Susan and Jeff would meet at the phone in the hall and would toss a coin to see who was the lucky one that would answer the call. The phone would get passed back and forth, sometimes while Carl was in mid-sentence. There was laughter and excitement and, what seemed to be, love.

Nowadays, in lieu of phone calls, Carl will try to have something special from some far-off state. Maybe a bear carved out of rock by the Lakota Sioux or real Texas cowboy boots. Carl loves his son with all of his heart but was refused guardianship by the court because of his travel and, according to the court, children should be raised by their mothers. Carl would have set his son right next to him in his cab if he could have had it his way, but Susan was bitter because she began to conjure up paranoia, believing her husband was having affairs while away. There was nothing to back up her theory other than the tongues of friends spewing doubt and conjecture.

One gift presentation, and far and away the grandest to date, was a Fender Jazzmaster electric guitar and a Fender Princeton amplifier. Jeff's dad could not deliver the instruments on his western run because the crate was damaged and there was a slight gash just below the pick guard of the guitar which caused the instrument to be unsaleable. Mr. Lindor offered the owner of the music store in Santa Fe fifty dollars for the damaged guitar and another fifty for the amp. It was a deal.

When Jeff opened the carefully disguised box, he could not believe what his dad was giving him, and the gash was of no concern to the boy. If anything, it made the present more special and unique. Jeff could not keep his hands off of his new love offering and learned to play the instrument very quickly, taking a few lessons from a neighbor. Jeff Lindor has become an accomplished and respected picker in the neighborhood. He cites Jeff Beck, guitarist for a band called The Yardbirds, as his muse, and he works hard at reproducing Beck's piercing tone and those peculiar and wonderfully indescribable sounds, as well as Beck's fluid speed and finesse.

"I have to pee," King announces to the pack, perhaps hoping to change the conversation up front.

"Yeah, let's take a little break," Sam yells back. "It looks like we're getting ready to go down to the valley which only means we will need to climb up to the next ridge and that is gonna hurt. Let's eat a snack for some energy and then get moving and be sure to drink some water so you don't dehydrate. Maybe we can eat lunch on top of number two ridge?" Sam points over through the trees to where the sky meets a jagged line of rocks and trees. He is good at setting goals and going for them.

As Barry takes his canteen away from his dry lips, he asks Sam, "We've been on this ridge about an hour and a half, right Sam?"

"Um . . . yes, I agree with that," Sam answers thoughtfully. "I think you're probably right, Barry, and we should be able to reach the next ridge in another hour and a half."

Barry runs around in a circle with his arms straight up and his hands waving while he yells in almost a sing-song tone, "I love to be free – I love to be free."

"That boy's far out" says Jeff, making everyone chuckle. "Where does he get his energy?"

Barry stops, looks at everyone and spills out, "You guys just don't know what it's like being Roy Meade's son. He's a good man and I love and respect him, but he really pushes me hard and freedom is not part of my life. You really have no idea what it was like just getting to do this hike. I had to beg and plead and promise I would do extra work at Dad's office. I just hope I'll be able to rehearse next Saturday, but I will one way or another."

"Oh, he just loves you, man," Danny says soothingly. "He just wants the best for you, I think. Don't you think that's all it is?" asks Danny.

"Yes, that's what it is, in his own weird way, but what he thinks is best for me is, maybe, not what I think is best for me. It's more like what's best for him."

"What do we know about what is good for us at our ages?" Jeff asks rhetorically. "Right now, I just want to be a rock 'n' roll guitar player like Jeff Beck, but do I really think little ol' me from Marigold, Ohio, for crap's sake, is going to hit the big time? I just hope I graduate from high school at this point. Then, maybe I can get on at the Mill."

"Your guitar playing is outasite, Jeff," says Sam. "Who knows what you could do if you put your mind to it? Don't be afraid, man. Dream *big!*"

"Thanks. I appreciate that, Sam. I'm not giving up or anything. I just sorta take it a day at a time. My Mom and Darren are driving me crazy because they are either yelling at each other or in the bedroom with the door closed. My Dad should be back next week, and I will be able to stay with him a few days. It's so much better there than with my mom."

"Wow, sorry, man," King says sincerely. King then says to everyone, "Let's just have some fun on this hike and air out our brains. We're all good friends, and I've been really looking forward to hanging out with everybody. Let's leave our hang ups down there in Marigold for a couple of days."

"Sounds good to me," Barry says positively. "I'm ready to get moving again. Whaddya think, Sam?"

"I'm ready." Sam replies as he stands up from the fallen tree he had parked on. "Is everyone ready to make the next ridge?" Sam barks and a resounding "yes sir" rises up from the pack as each young man re-positions his backpack and starts the long descent into the valley below.

Barry Meade and his younger sister Kay, live with their mom and pediatrician dad and their statuesque Tobiano American Paint horse named Precious. Precious was a gift to the children on Kay's twelfth birthday at the beginning of summer. You've probably heard it before.

It seems to be in the elusive Mother's Manual: "Now, we know it's Kay's birthday, but Kay sweetie, you must share with your brother," Mrs. Meade said kindly with high eyebrows and a smile on her face while giving the gift. It is Kay's horse, without a doubt, but Barry really does not mind. Horses are not his thing, though he does ride Precious on rare occasions, when he wants to hang out with his sister.

When Kay is outside with Precious and her mother is upstairs doing whatever she does up there, Barry plays piano. The instrument is a mahogany baby grand piano, and it sits in front of the shallow alcove of long-paned windows that look out onto their well-manicured front yard. It is a perfect setting in their home, but Barry got to know this fine work of art at the fresh and innocent age of three years old, when the piano was in his Grandfather Meade's home. The toddler would reach up to the keys, with his eyes fully round, to see what was making the sound. Barry would not bang on the keyboard like so many three-year-olds, but instead, he would find notes that excited him, and he would do that for an hour.

Piano lessons started for Barry at five years old, paid for by his father's father Pops, and after many successful recitals and performances, through the years at charitable events, Barry finally stopped his lessons. High school homework and a job playing piano at the Appleton Country Club, during dinner, started ruling the night. Besides, Barry could play better than any of Marigold's or Appleton's teachers by that time. Also, nobody was teaching any songs by current artists, like The Animals or Stevie Wonder. Let's face it, no one was going to bring the sheet music of the new song by The Doors, *Light My Fire*, and set the metronome. No, Barry teaches himself those songs and many more just by listening to them once or twice, no sweat.

The Meade family live almost directly across Marigold Road from the Reed's, but that does not mean the Meades and the Reeds can see each other to wave each morning. Their area of Marigold Road is called Upper Marigold where the modestly sized but well-built houses rest regally in the middle of their acreage. It is more about the land at the foot of Marigold Hill than the size of the house, and the Meade's house sits the distance of about four football fields from the Reed's front door. When the Reeds want to visit, which is not often, they walk down their hill, across Marigold Road, through the horse pasture, across a swift-but-shallow creek and back up another hill where the Meade house, and its small barn, stand.

Though Kay is pampered and stroked by her father, when her father is home, Barry, son of Roy, must be perfect. If not, he will taint the name of Doctor Roy Meade who has worked and studied hard after the war. Barry must bring home straight As or Barry knows his social life will be null and void for the next six weeks until grades come out again. Barry *will* be getting his education from Harvard Medical School. Kay will attend a fine college not far from home where the choice of husbands will fortify the Meade family tree.

Doctor Meade's expectations for Barry are hard to attain and a heavy burden for the teen, but Barry has help from a friend named Benny. Benny is the nickname for a small prescription pill called Benzedrine that Barry steals out of his father's big bottle found in the bottom drawer of the good doctor's office desk. Barry believes he is neither a thief nor a reckless youth. He simply does not want to disappoint his father and goes to any extreme to please him. Barry loves and respects his father, but he has cold sweat nightmares about fulfilling his expectations, and it has been this way since elementary school.

A young Roy Meade became familiar with Benzedrine while fighting in WWII when, as a student doctor, he was ordered to hand out Benzedrine-soaked inhalers to the troops to give them extra energy. Because the arrival of injured soldiers did not follow an easily regulated timeline, student doctor Meade found the inhaler to be a valuable stimulant, allowing Meade to attend to the wounded all night, if need be. Fast-forward to the current highly educated and very successful Doctor Meade, known throughout the county as one of the finest and most acclaimed pediatricians to have ever served the community, and you will find he has an addiction to Benzedrine. He believes he has it under control and it is just a part of his illustrious life.

Again, Barry doesn't spend much time with his (Kay's) horse Precious, but Kay cannot stand being away from her beautiful and powerful friend on school days. When Kay's Marigold Middle School lets out and the bus finally makes it, stop-by-stop, to Upper Marigold, Kay is the first one out of her seat and waiting at the sliding bus door. When the bus stops and the door opens, Kay leaps off the bus and gallops down the gravel road and up the long driveway to the barn. Her mom stands watching her daughter run up the drive and waits until Kay is finished hugging and petting Precious before she calls Kay in to change her clothes. Mrs. Meade wants to hear all about Kay's school day and find out if she has homework.

There is rarely a school or work day when Delores Meade hasn't whipped up freshly baked muffins or cupcakes. They are, conveniently, left sitting on the large, pine wood kitchen table for the family to enjoy after their long day away from home. The baked goods fill the warm and cozy Meade sanctum with a heavenly aroma, and after letting Precious know how much she was missed, Kay runs up the back porch steps. In her excitement to be home, she slings open the wooden and windowed back door, lays her books on the kitchen chair and sinks into her mom's waiting, loving arms.

For the hikers, who are well on their way to new horizons, it is not even eight o'clock in the morning yet.

CHAPTER TWO

The sun and the steady walk are keeping the boys warm, but the farther down the hill they go, the darker it gets and the more slippery the terrain as the dew lingers. Gloves, taken off during the snack break, are put back on for warmth and protection from the damp foliage that had not been so prevalent along the ridge. Up near the ridge grow peaceful, soft ferns sprinkled about, mixed in with the dead and decaying trees and tree limbs that have fallen through the years. On the descent, however, the growth is getting thick and stubby. The walking cadence used earlier has been replaced with a clumsy sideways bounce, with the right foot stabilizing. The left hand is touching the ground, finding roots and growth to slow the pace of the steep slope. The other hand is up in the air for balance.

"Stop!" Sam shouts. Sam normally has complete control of his tone and pitch, but the urgency in this command was immediately noticeable and not one more step was taken. "Guys, Listen up! In about five more steps we will be heading toward the valley in the fast lane. It looks like this part of the hill has been washed away." All five of the hikers baby-step their way close to the edge and strain their necks to peep over without getting too close.

"Whoa! Far out!" King exclaimed "That's a long way down!"

Sam begins to direct "Ok, let's back up about ten or fifteen feet and then it looks like we should walk to our left and go around". Everyone turns and grabs a tree or root, anything to help them shimmy back up the hill fifteen feet, just as their leader recommended. Going to the left will take the five back toward the ridge from where they just came. The natural contour of the topography, though, sends them like a slow sling shot back out to where there is some sunlight.

"I don't think this kind of thing was figured into our time estimate, Sambro," King says as they climb up the hill.

"I hear ya. I just need to keep focused on what is ahead even farther up. I may start running up ahead when I can't see around the bend, so, if I'm not joining in the conversations or the music, please forgive me."

"Sam, we love ya, man. You are our fearless leader! Bwa-a-a-a!" Jeff salutes Sam as he speaks in his best Boris Badenov Russian accent.

King joins in the Rocky and Bullwinkle theme just for fun. Speaking to no one in particular, King imitates Bullwinkle Moose as if he is rehearsing and perfecting his voice, saying, "Hey Rocky!" King clears his throat for another try "Hey Rocky! Watch me pull a rabbit out mah hat! Nothin' up mah sle-e-e-eve. No doubt about it, I gotta get a new hat." The gang responds with a less than enthusiastic mix of chuckles and moans.

Back up front, Sam has found a way down the hill that has plenty of sight distance, but it is steep. Some of the boys are allowing themselves to run down the hill for twenty or thirty feet, passing Sam on the way, and then catching a tree trunk to slow or stop themselves. Jeff and Danny, however, are taking their time and enjoying it. Jeff finds one of those sandstone stages and pretends he is playing in the Yardbirds, mouthing the guitar part to *Smokestack Lightning* from the Rave Up album.

Danny sings the first verse then, surprisingly, with a burst of air heard through the valley, bouncing off the two hills on either side, Danny sings Keith Relf's harmonica part note-for-note with perfect intonation: "Wa-a-ah – wa-wah wah-wa wah wah wah wah." Each of the other four catches himself just standing, facing Danny, jaw dropped and astonished.

"Who knew?" Jeff says in a most unaffected way, and the troops hike on.

At the bottom of ridge number one, there is frozen mud and a cold running creek. Sam strongly suggests that everyone stay out of it as best they can so as not to get their feet wet because they would probably freeze before they would dry. The sun is just not sending its loving, fulgent beams all the way to the bottom of the valley. "It looks like we can get around the wet parts through here!" yells Sam, making sure everyone hears him. "It's almost nine o'clock, so let's keep moving. Going up this next hill will be a bear. Anyway, so if you need to stop to rest your legs, just say the word. I'm used to running up and down the court every day for games and practice, but some of you pampered boys who think playing piano or drums is enough, or maybe you smokers who have the lung capacity of a chipmunk, might need to stop more than I would."

"Oh, thanks for the reminder, fearless leader," Jeff says as he lights up another Camel.

Barry says, "Let me have one of those, Lindor." The other boys' eyes go wide.

Jeff digs out his pack again and shakes it one time at Barry, neatly projecting three cigarettes from the corner of the pack. Barry takes his glove off and reaches out his thumb and skinny pointer finger, pulling out an unfiltered Camel. Jeff has his stainless-steel lighter, freshly filled with lighter fluid, out and ready to light Barry's cigarette as soon as it hits Barry's lips. Barry has never smoked an unfiltered cigarette, though, and his somewhat moist lips stick to the cigarette paper. He pulls the cigarette off his lips, but it is tricky.

"Thanks. How do you smoke this thing without it sticking?"

Jeff turns sideways toward Barry. "See, you don't lick your lips. Make sure they're dry and then you kinda roll your lips around your teeth so your dry upper part touches the fag." Then Jeff puts his own cigarette on his dry lips to provide an example with his directions. He then blows out multiple perfect rings of smoke to show off. "You're going to get some tobacco on your tongue once in a while, but you just spit it out like so." Jeff finishes his lesson with a quick mini-spit by sticking the end of his tongue out between his closed lips and drawing it in with a fast snap while blowing out a short burst of air over the top of his tongue.

From the creek, the hill begins a steep incline very quickly. The valley was more of a crease than anything substantial but that just seems to make the hills on either side steeper. Even Sam is having a bit of trouble as he slips backwards during a few lunges. The others are huffing and puffing very soon after they start up the hill. The two smokers have ground out their nicotine friends on the cold and wet forest floor and are slow to ascend. Barry turns a little green after inhaling so much unfiltered smoke into his lungs and leans on a tree for a moment.

"You guys keep going," Barry tries to yell to Sam, Danny, and King, but he doesn't quite have the strength or air to make it audible, and his voice just trails off.

Jeff is fine and yells, "Keep going, everybody. I'm going to nurse Barry back to life. We'll catch up."

"Ok." the three non-smokers respond, and Jeff tells Barry to sit down for a minute.

"Jeff, man, my head is spinning and I feel like I'm gonna barf," Barry says right before he produces breakfast and his recent snack.

"Crap, man, you weren't kidding."

"Sorry," Barry moans. "Just let me sit for a few minutes."

"Ok, but the others are pretty far up the hill, now. I think we'll be alright for a few minutes, but then we gotta roll."

"Those unfilters are strong, brother. I smoke Marlboros every now and then, but I was not ready for that." Barry lies flat out on his back.

Sam was right about this climb being a bear. It seems almost straight up as the hikers have yet to land any other part of their foot but their toes on the ground. At least there are plenty of dead trees and grapevines to use for pulling oneself forward, especially if you are a bit green around the gills. Sam, King, and Danny are far ahead of the smokers, but they still have at least an hour before reaching Ridge Two.

After Jeff helps Barry recover by sharing a few saltines to settle Barry's stomach, the two are actually making good time. At one point, the hill is so steep that Jeff starts to fall backwards. He reaches out and misses the grapevine in front of him, but Barry grabs Jeff's Puma sweatshirt with his right hand, having a firm grip on a small sapling with the other.

"Whoa! Climbing this thing is hard enough, and I certainly didn't want to climb it a second time. Thanks, my friend," Jeff says with a swoop of his hair.

The three hikers above have stopped to let the other two catch up. "We're over here" yells King after hearing their voices carry up the hill. "I have burs all over my socks. I hate these things." King says, not really caring if anyone is listening.

"Yeah, mine are covered, too." Danny joins in and then asks Sam "How much longer to the top, Sam? I'm starting to get pretty hungry."

"I bet only twenty to twenty-five minutes, Dan Man, and I'm getting hungry, too. Can you see the other two?"

King answers, "I hear them shuffling the leaves down the hill, unless those are really big squirrels."

Saying that reminded King of a time in his childhood. "Sam, do you remember when Pa-paw took us hunting rabbits? What a great shot he is, but I just couldn't take seeing all those little bloody bunnies lined up inside his coat. I don't think I could be a hunter, although I wish I could shoot like that."

"The bloody bunnies didn't really bother me," Sam says. "But I just got kinda bored. I thought his hound dog was really far out, though. As soon as Pa-paw said 'get it' right after the shot, the dog would run into the high grass for a minute and then re-appear with the dead bunny. Sometimes, remember, Pa-paw would just throw a rock into the bushes where he thought there was a rabbit and sure enough, out bounds a rabbit at full speed. Pa-paw would lower his rifle or shotgun, whichever it was, so quickly and pull the trigger. *Pow!* Yer dead."

"Jeff! Where are you guys?" Danny's voice rolls down the hill to Jeff's and Barry's ears.

"I think we are close to you!" yells an out-of-breath Jeff. "Say something again so I can get a bead on your location."

"Something again!" More than one boy answers with this inane retort.

"You are so funny. Keep talking!" an out-of-breath Jeff fires back.

Danny sings "Bringing In the Sheaves," adding a pinched nasal sound to his southern Ohio accent. He offers one elbow, and King takes the cue as he locks his arm in the opposite direction with Danny, singing the song twice more while trotting around in an Irish-style jig. The leaves on top that have dried float up as the jig gets more intense. Sam is obviously looking through the two dancers with something else on his mind.

Suddenly, two heads show up like fishing bobs from a lower part of the hill, and the gang is back together as a unit. With a half-smile and one eyebrow raised, Sam looks right at Barry and asks "Would you mind not smoking Jeff's Camels again while we are hiking? You'll be free to puff away on any brand that suits you tomorrow afternoon." Then to everyone, Sam brings the focus back, saying, "We have about twenty more minutes to Ridge Two if we don't have any . . . interruptions." He glances again at Barry. "If everyone is ready, we can stop and eat an early lunch. Remember, we can't hike after dark so we really need to make two more ridges today so that there will only be one more in the morning and then we hike down to where there *should* be John Chapman Boulevard, if my calculations are correct."

Cheers rise from the four other hikers and various shouts of "let's take this ridge" or "lead on, Sam" or "I'm hungry" and off they go, climbing the steep northern side of the hill.

After about thirty minutes of some grueling side-stepping, Sam's eyes are the first to peer up over the ridge, and his glance is met by a glorious fall sun. Its rays are warming, and the ridge leaves are dry compared to what they have endured for the previous two hours. One-by-one, each friend stumbles to level ground at the top of the hill, and one by one each friend strips off their backpack and sprawls out on their backs to rest their weary bodies. "I need to pee so bad, but I just don't wanna move," King confesses. "This sun feels so good."

Taking in the sounds of the path less traveled, no one says a word. The leaves rustle when a light breeze whips up or when a chipmunk runs close by. An acorn drops from a mighty oak and a red-bellied woodpecker, in search of food, hammers a hole twenty feet away.

"This is heavenly," Sam says quietly. "I don't think I've ever really listened to life in the forest before. It's pretty cool." Then, another even longer round of silence until it is shattered, with perfect timing, by Jeff's ten-second release of methane.

"Thanks for the jolt of reality there, buddy," Danny says dryly as he rolls to one side and reluctantly pushes himself up to an orthostatic position. "I was kinda drifting off into a world where you didn't exist. You probably scared the squirrels." Everyone except Jeff is chuckling and moaning at the same time, again, as they all follow Danny's lead.

He has no desire to change positions so soon. Jeff digs into his jacket pocket and pulls out his pack of Camels and lighter, shakes out a fag and lights it up while still flat on his back.

"Now we're living." he says with a triumphant gloat.

King walks a little way away and finds some targets on the ground that are begging to get drenched. Steam rises up as the warm body fluid hits the cold ground. Everyone follows suit except Jeff and then Sam suggests they eat at this place. That makes Jeff sit up. "I already saw what you had for breakfast, Barry. Whatcha got for lunch? And, let's try to keep this meal where it belongs this time."

"Who wants to ride around America in a van with Jeff, raise your hand?" Barry says, watching no hands go up.

"I will, Jeff," King says with his bottom lip hanging down in mock empathy.

"King, you wouldn't last a day with me in tight quarters." Jeff says.

"You best be quiet, Mr. Lindor," King says, shaking his pointer finger in Jeff's face while closing one eye and squinting the other. "Or I'll sic your buddy Darren on you."

"Oh, man . . . not funny. I don't want to think about that good-for-nothin' while I'm up here away from him. He drives me crazy, and I know we're gonna have it out someday soon. He treats my mom like crap, and she just takes it."

Sam, seeing that Jeff is getting serious, steps in, saying, "OK, let's change the subject. Stop it, King."

"Don't be my dad, Sam," King shoots back.

"Don't be a brat, then, King. You know Jeff has a really hard time with Darren. That was a low blow, man."

"It's OK. I know he was kidding," Jeff intervenes, seeing trouble brewing between brothers. "I can deal with it."

A new boyfriend of Jeff's mom, Darren has, for all intents and purposes, moved in to the Lindor home. He pretends to be a father-figure for Jeff even though he has no interest in him. Darren seems to always meet Jeff at the bathroom door on school mornings, usually snipping "sorry kid" as he nudges Jeff away from the door opening. Darren closes and locks the bathroom door, takes a shower and runs most of the hot water out before Jeff can take his. Every day, the shower delay causes Jeff to not be ready in time for the bus to school. This forces him to either wake up far earlier than his body wants to so that he can catch the bus, or ask Darren for a ride. Jeff has his driver's license, but there is only one car and that is his mom's, and she needs it to drive to work in Stewartsville each day.

Darren will allow Jeff to climb into his filthy, dented, rusty, stinky, smoky 1961 black Ford Falcon with last night's beer bottles rolling under the seat, but Jeff will be dropped off about a mile from school before Darren veers toward his work destination. It never fails, though, that Sam or Barry, driving their very own cars for which they have worked hard, will see Jeff and rescue him, getting him to school on time and into a better mood.

"I'm starving, boys. Let's eat, and we'll all be wearing a happy smile!" Danny says. They all know that King is a sensitive person – moody, even, and that Sam will, sometimes, take advantage of that difference in their personalities. Sam's sharp, award-winning tongue can slice a person up like a surgeon's scalpel, and it can get him into trouble at home and school.

The sound of backpack flaps being opened and wax paper being unwrapped is soothing in the nearly midday sun, and the group is quiet as they begin to take in the incredible view of the Scioto Valley. The panorama is stunning from this vantage point as the ridge slants just slightly downward toward the valley. None of them have ever laid eyes on this part of *their* valley before. It is similar to the view from atop Marigold Hill, but this is more primitive. No houses, churches, or moving vehicles. No yards or fences. It is as if they are pioneers discovering new territory, and this is really why the boys wanted to hike these hills. There is no conversation at first while the entrees are being prepared and assembled, but soon food is being swapped and the friendly repartee returns.

Danny seems a bit overwhelmed by the beauty. "This is sort of how I feel at church. Sometimes, Pastor Pete asks everyone to just be silent in prayer and absorb the greatness of God. God created all of this, everything we see. Wow."

Danny Mosely will be sixteen tomorrow, November 25, and is a sophomore this year at Flint Township High School. He brings a positive spark to most situations and loves to write poetry and lyrics to the music he and his friends write, as well as his own. Danny's appearance reminds people of Peter Tork of the hit Rock group The Monkees that Danny watches every Monday night on TV. The young poet's words are unusually introspective and mature while still being easy to speak or sing. So much so that his church Music Minister, Mr. Blanton, an Ichabod Crane-looking man with Coke-bottle lenses for glasses, has applied some of Danny's poetry, the ones that speak of spiritual matters of redemption and forgiveness through Jesus Christ, to familiar Christian hymn chord changes.

Mr. Blanton has mimeographed and paid for three hundred copies of Danny's lyrics and directed the entire congregation to sing the completed songs in a number of Sunday services. "You glorify the Lord, Danny," Mr. Blanton will bluntly state while looking right into Danny's eyes. Mr. Blanton's eyes are magnified to twice their size as he tells Danny, "And He loves that you use the talents He has given you in that way." Danny has attended his church since before he can remember, and the members have become like family to him and his dad, Walter.

"That's cool, Dano," Barry remarks sympathetically while chewing a muffin. "I know that place means a lot to you and your dad. Church, I mean."

Jeff quickly speaks up as if he'd been holding in his thoughts about religion all of his life. "I'm glad you find comfort there, Danny, but I really have a hard time believing in a god that lets so much crap happen to people. How could God, if he loves us so-o-o much, let Vietnam happen? And millions of people died in World War Two. Where's God when all that shi-i . . . crap is happening?" Jeff immediately takes a bite of his cheese sandwich as he finishes his question, wondering if Danny will have anything in response.

"God does love us, Jeff. That's a heavy question, man, and here's the Truth. I can find comfort there because I know that the God of all creation, the One who created all this that we see and you and me, loves me and is with me all the time, even in the bad times. Vietnam is evil, as was World War Two. The communists who are trying to take over South

Vietnam have no god. Their government doesn't allow religion. Their moral compass points to themselves, and as you know, humans, be they American or Vietnamese, don't make very good decisions because we're egged on by sin. Without God, killing and aggressiveness may as well be the same as deciding what TV show you want to watch. The VC may feel God's seed in them and know that killing is not right, but they have no avenue. No outlet is allowed for fighting the evil that Satan brings. So, they easily give into sin.

"Oh no. We're gonna talk about the little red, horned guy too?"

Danny smiles at Jeff and continues "World War Two was a little different in that it was started by an evil man who twisted religion, specifically Christianity. The swastika is a twisted cross. Evil is persuasive if you don't have any hope, and Germany was at a time of struggle and little hope. Hitler used that weakness of the masses and slowly took over their weak minds but created a Christianity that sounded right to a country that had not worshipped well through their struggle. Some German Christian leaders even fell for it and cozied up to Hitler's version of their faith because it sounded close to what the Bible says, but just a little different. They didn't want to get hanged or shot as well, so they went along with the crazy little guy."

"I kinda don't blame them," Jeff says as he lays his head down on his arm with faux disinterest.

"Christians don't change their beliefs to save their lives. Our lives are kind of a win-win 'cause we're either here working for Christ or we're there with Him. Anyway, America was right to help defend against that evil aggression, and we helped save millions of lives, but only by God's divine providence. He has a plan, and we are too small to see it. It's like looking out a window. All we can see is what the width of the window allows, but God sees the whole big world outside."

"Why, tell me more, Reverend," Jeff antagonizes with his eyes closed and a small hint of interest.

"Well, I guess we Americans need to be careful because we won the war and are rich beyond belief. Those are all wonderful gifts and blessings from God, but we're getting soft and comfortable, and because we are so successful, our nation is believing that we don't need God. It's like 'Hey, look what *we've* done' instead of giving God the credit and worshipping Him for those blessings. Johnson is letting the sin of pride run his life and using the sons of America to prove he can win that horrible war. Everyone is still trying to figure out who shot JFK, but the real war is spiritual and being fought above us in the heavens. Satan pulled that trigger, more or less. He loves to put us in chaos and wants our souls, but God will not let him have the souls of those who love His Son. We need to make the decision, though."

"Oh? What decision is that?" Jeff teases.

"Until we accept that we are washed in the blood of our Savior Jesus Christ, we are just doomed to Satan's whims and cannot fight the sin that is within us, and our world is headed for destruction."

"Oh, how cheery."

Barry jumps in. "I don't feel like I've quote-unquote sinned today. What do you call sin, Danny?"

Danny looks Barry in the eyes. "It isn't what *I* call sin but what God calls sin. You know, uh . . . some examples would be . . . oh . . . pride, like I mentioned . . . uh-h-h . . . jealousy, revenge, bad thoughts about people . . . uh . . . wanting more than what we have as if God doesn't give us enough. Any of these and more are sinful things, and it is super hard to not fall into their traps. You're going to laugh at this one, Jeff."

"I'm sure I will, but go on. I'm all ears! Was Barry's barf a sin?" Jeff mocks drolly.

Ignoring Jeff, Danny says, "I was headed for hell from the moment I was born, as we all are, but I began to understand what Jesus did for me and the whole world. I had some good guidance from knowledgeable Christians like Pastor Pete. Anyway, because Jesus' dad . . . you know, God the Father? . . . His Father, our Creator, loves us so much and wants to have a relationship with us that His Son Jesus left His *really groovy pad*" – Danny says with a smile – "in heaven, came down here and squeezed all His beautiful Spirit and light into a confined, breakable, fallible, stinky earth suit. He entered our time zone through the usual human way, with all the feelings and emotions and temptations that all the humans experience. Jesus, though, was perfect and never sinned.

"He was here for one purpose, and that was to give His life as a ransom for many in obedience to His Father, to be a light in the darkness and to serve and not be served. He wanted and still wants us to know that we no longer need to fear death. He knew He was going to die and defeat death three days later by being raised up out of that dark tomb, and He was and lives today at the right hand of the Father."

Being Danny's best friend, King had heard much of this before or a version of it, but King decided to ask Danny a tough one. "So, was Jesus God or the Son of God or the Son of Man? Who was He or *is* He I guess *you* would say?" King's grandfather, his mom's dad named Homer, is an ordained, foot-washing Baptist minister, but they don't see him that often because King's family doesn't go to church, and Homer is always out visiting the needy in and around Appleton. King loves talking with Pa-Paw Homer when they can see him and has enjoyed Homer's story about how he was saved.

King was not unfamiliar with Jesus at all, but he was too interested in other worldly things to give it real thought.

Danny thinks for a moment. "That is one of the most difficult things to grasp, and frankly, I don't believe anyone with a little human brain can grasp it fully, especially me. There is definitely the Father, God. The Son, Jesus, and the Holy Ghost or Spirit who doesn't get talked about much, but who is an integral part of that mysterious union we call 'The Trinity.' Some things are just too huge for us to understand or describe, I guess, or maybe God doesn't want us to know right now, I don't know. I do know that He was one hundred percent divine and one hundred percent man. In John 17, Jesus prays, and it is incredible. We should read it together sometime, King."

"That sounds good, my brother," King replies to his best friend with a calm, sincere voice.

Danny continues, still with amplified energy. "Jesus was perfect, the only perfect person to have ever lived and was and is always obedient to His Father in heaven. Therefore, Christians try to be obedient, too, and use Jesus's ways as what we should strive for. We aren't forced to be anything, like some religions that force their people to believe. We are free and just do what Jesus says out of our love for Him because of His deep love for us. Because we know He wants the very best for us."

Shoving the last bite of his sandwich into his mouth, Jeff jumps back, still bubbling over with skepticism. "Obedience? Who in the world wants to be obedient to a myth or at best, somebody who died two thousand years ago?"

"Ah, but His Word still lives in the Bible, man, and we Christians believe He is alive in heaven right now and will return one day. Also, Jesus gave us the gift of The Spirit, who lives in us Christians."

"Oh, good grief. Is He right next to my cheese sandwich?" Jeff says irritably.

Danny smiles again. "Because of that, we are saints. We still sin, but we are not sinners anymore. We are not defined by sin, I guess I should say. Look, Jesus doesn't love us because we're obedient. Christians *want* to be obedient because we love Jesus so much because He loves us so much."

"You said that already," Jeff quips.

"I know, but it's a big, beautiful circle, and it has nothing to do with who we are or what we do. He came to Earth to save our souls simply because God, His Father, loves His creation and wants to have a relationship with us. God does not associate with sin, though, so we needed to be cleansed by the sacrificial blood. It's not like joining some club where you have to wear a green tie or else you can't get in. You just need to love Jesus with a real love from your heart, you know what I mean? We must put ourselves last and have a relationship with Him and confess that we are sinners."

"A relationship?" Jeff raises his eyebrows up under his bangs.

"That's right, Jeff. If we were standing together and a car was headed right for you, but I pushed you out of the way and was hit and killed by the car, wouldn't you love me for the rest of your life? Wouldn't you want to tell people what I did for you so that they can see what true love is? Then, that similar kind of love we have for Christ is strengthened through prayer and reading His Word. The Apostle Paul says we should be in constant prayer, not on our knees all the time, but just walking down the street or in your desk at school. It's not easy to follow Jesus, and He warns us about that, but Jesus loves the meek and the needy and asks us to cling to Him. Luke wrote in chapter nine . . ."

"Luke? Who's Luke?" asks Barry.

"A doctor. Funny you should ask. He was a Greek believer in Jesus and sort of a journalist, who wrote some of the most detailed stuff about Jesus and the early Christians, as if he were studying the human body. You know, very detailed. Anyway, Jesus knew and wanted His followers to know that the Christian life is not easy. Jesus told His disciples that 'Foxes have dens and birds have nests, but I have no place to lay My head.' That's not King James, probably, but close enough. He just wanted to help His disciples and us know that it ain't easy."

All these things Danny is saying roll off his tongue with a strength and confidence he rarely exhibits, as if someone was speaking through him. Barry takes a long drink of water out of his canteen and asks Danny how he knows so much about Jesus.

Danny chuckles shyly and says, "Ha . . . you may have noticed I don't sleep in on Sundays, and I work at a church, not to mention I just spend a bit of time reading ye olde Bible and talking to other Bible readers. I really *like* reading it and finding out about Jesus and how to live my life. It makes sense to me and helps to make sense of the world and all those things.

Like wars and stuff that you were mentioning, Jeff. Just to finish my thought, if you will sincerely believe in Jesus and follow His word in the Bible, life won't necessarily get any easier, as I said, but you can be sure of an eternal life when you pass from this life to the next. Any sacrifice or suffering we incur while living on earth is nothing when you consider living an eternity with Jesus in all His glory. He took all our sins, past, present and future, with Him to the cross, and they were nailed there with Him. So, that brings we Christians a great amount of peace in wicked times. Christians held Bible studies in Nazi prisons because His Word, and the good news, brings comfort to those who believe. He bought our ticket to heaven and all we have to do is pick it up at the window called faith."

In frustration, Jeff sits up, raises up his cigarette hand and pushes the air forward saying "Please! Stop! Do you hear yourself, Danny? *This is life!* Right now! Not after we're dead. Key word there is *dead!* There is nothing after we are dead, Dan man."

"How do you know that? How can you be so sure? I think I like my way of thinking better because if I'm wrong, I've still had a great life and then I'm, as you say, dead. If I'm right, though, your best day on this planet will be a million times less groovy than what I will experience in eternity, and you'll need a bunch of Coppertone 'cause it's gonna be pretty hot where you'll be."

"I don't know. I think you've been smoking hippie pot," Jeff says as he lights yet another Camel to calm himself down. "That's some pretty far out stuff. I'm not knocking what you say but come on. Maybe there is a God who made everything, I don't know, but I feel like I'd be wasting my life believing in some guy who lived two thousand years ago. That's just a hard sell for me. Besides, you grew up in a church. I've done way too many bad things and had wa-a-ay too many bad thoughts. Take Darren for example. I guess I'm just boogie-man meat."

"I know it's not an easy thing to accept," Danny fires back in a sympathetic tone. "Only by the grace of God, I have seen people transformed, really changed, after giving their lives over to Jesus. Alcoholics who just stop drinking after they start believing and filled with the Spirit. . . ."

"Yeah! Pa-paw said he was a drunk until he was saved, and he said it was the grace of God that allowed him to quit and never take another drink."

"Right, King! Or men who have been creeps to their wives become great husbands or visa-versa."

"My Ma-maw said Homer was mean as snot before he was saved, but then he was the best guy ever. Really loving and all. Thankfully, I never knew the mean-as-snot guy."

Danny confirms King's testimony, saying, "I've seen God at work, man, and I have faith in Him. He worked on me and still works on me every day."

"Well, I'm glad you have faith," Jeff says in a cloud of smoke. "But I'm going to put my faith in me 'cause that's all I have."

"I'll pray for you, guitar friend," Danny says.

"Whatever makes you feel good. Here comes Christopher Columbus. End of sermon." With that, Jeff gets up to relieve himself.

Sam returns after wandering off to survey the area so that the hikers can make good time after their rest. "Let's pack up and get moving. We have about five hours of daylight and two ridges to climb. It's going to be close, especially if we run into any trouble or detours. We're not in Kansas anymore, boys. Who knows what lies ahead of us?"

"Lions and tigers and bears, I suppose," quips Barry with Danny and King offering the "oh my" to complete the quote. Jeff returns to the fold, and everyone finishes up what they're eating, re-fastens their backpacks, and slings them over their shoulders, rolling their muscles and bones until the mobile suitcase and bedroll are sitting on their back where it is most comfortable.

CHAPTER THREE

T he noonday sun is warm on the boys. They shed their coats and tie them around their waists or stuff them in their backpacks. Small beads of sweat form underneath Jeff's bangs and wispy mustache, but he simply pulls the tail of his flannel shirt up and wipes his face in mid-stride. There is no rhythm to their descent as all the boys go gliding, running, shuffling down the ridge to the next valley.

Songs do pop up, however, such as King's version of *Brown Eyed Girl* by Van Morrison and *My Little Red Book* by Love or Danny singing The Monkees' *I'm a Believer*. Jeff sings about "raising the roof" in *Little Bit of Soul* by Mansfield's own Music Explosion, and Barry croons *Whiter Shade of Pale* by Procol Harum. It is as if they are auditioning for their future band. King leads the whole bunch, even big brother Sam, in the catchy chorus of *Happy Together* by The Turtles. They are like a human jukebox giving promise to next Saturday's rehearsal. Hopefully they will be able to play their instruments at the same time.

Each boy has spent many hours to himself when parents have been away or pre-occupied or merely by choice, but this expedition away from the world is something new. Simply put, they don't know what is around the next corner or tree, not that there is anything spectacular ahead, but they are happy to hang in suspense. Of course, Sam has traveled to many more places on his own, in Appleton and Ohio and surrounding states, than King or Danny. The age difference creates this distinction. Sam is not quite as enthusiastic as the younger conquerors. However, Sam is having a blast just letting his hair down, which is as rare as a Beatles concert these days. He has built into his life a rigidity that can be unforgiving and sometimes iron-fisted, but Sam has looked forward to this weekend.

Even though the others are a bit younger (Barry being only seven months and one grade behind Sam), Sam enjoys these guys and may be somewhat envious of their bond. Sam, by choice, doesn't have many, if any, true friends. He has his basketball and debate team colleagues with whom he takes company, but they are tactlessly disposable when Sam finds himself getting soft. This hike is a challenge with deadlines and strategic maneuvers, so Sam told Sam it was OK to break from the routine because he may learn something. He is ever-so-slightly feeling the freedom, too, as they stroll deeper into the hills and farther from home. On the other side of that coin, Sam is more aware of his parent-appointed position of leader, and he welcomes that rank. Leadership is part of the fiber of Sam.

No school bus trip to Columbus for the state basketball championships is this quiet and friendly. No car ride to Athens for a debate tournament is as dangerous as falling a hundred feet into a shallow creek. As he ventures forth, Sam is absorbing and analyzing the elements and the earth under his boots, and he thinks about Vietnam. He knows it is ugly and brutal over there, and the terrain is full of deadly traps. He knows the Communist North doesn't fight like our boys, but that kind of challenge and stripped-down, bare-nerved reality excites the stony young man. He fancies himself a Ulysses who could concoct a clever and ambitious stratagem that would finally and without mercy defeat a very communist, non-English, slant-eyed Polyphemus.

Of course, on the other end of the human personality spectrum, King absorbs the sounds of birds singing, squirrels rattling leaves, a tree branch cracking and all of his friends and brother bringing their silliness and seriousness to the grand canvas. Sometimes King just stops and stands with his head back and eyes closed, capturing the sun's penetrating rays. He loses track of every man-made boundary until one of his mates yells for him to "come on, King" from a hundred yards ahead, and yet, that does not jolt him out of his sensitive bliss. Instead, King slowly opens his eyes with a smile, takes a deep breath and starts a slow trot toward the familiar voice as if he is re-uniting with time and space.

King is truly an enchanted boy. A little shy and sad of eye, for sure, but his mother already knew this from the day he was born. Perhaps Ellie was hoping to associate King with the subject of her favorite song and masterfully mold him during his malleable, nascent years. Odds are, though, King is a true original, and mom simply enjoys the generous gift of her second son. Ellie will show favor toward King, much to Sam and Gordon's disapproval, but King's genuineness has completely permeated Ellie's quintessence. This is not to say that King rules over or manipulates his mom. On the contrary, he is most at home when he knows she is near. King warms to her tone and touch and even misses her, sometimes, when he is at school, but Ellie is no Jocasta. A sensitive son can have an attraction to all the feminine traits of his mother without it being twisted by sin with which we are born.

Mothers are the natural way for sons to learn about women without the complexity of a romance. Couple that with a dad who treats his wife as if she is the treasure he claims she is, and both boys should enjoy and prosper from their future love lives. King is quite healthy and will no doubt bring these appreciations of womankind into a loving and sound marriage someday, possibly with a woman quite like his delicate yet rock-steady mom.

The tribe is heading downhill, again, toward a wider valley. The drop is steep, but not nearly as extreme as the previous crease in the earth they experienced almost three hours earlier. They have to make good time, now, to make their fourth-ridge-by-sundown deadline. Sam's toilet paper surprise has been a hit, but whoever needs to stop, stops while the others keep moving forward. Everyone understands the importance of meeting their deadline, and the pack of rock and rollers are working well as a unit. Going downhill forces them all to move quickly, but it will be the climb up the third hill that will test their mettle. This descending part of the second hill is cleaner-looking than the last, almost like some very large person with a very large rake pulled all the scrubby underbrush away. There is plenty of space between trees, and the sun is keeping its shining face in full view, and that should be the case for the rest of the afternoon, as the valleys and ridges all face west.

The last fifty yards of hill number two has a graduated slope, so all the boys are just about running at full speed, laughing all the way as they get close to the edge of the valley floor. Just as they level off, they find themselves quickly coming face-to-face with dense underbrush, thorn bushes galore and burs again.

"Oh, fearless leader! How do you picture getting through this?" Barry yells because he cannot see Sam over the cattails and other tall foliage.

Sam answers from an unknown location, "I'm not sure, yet. I think I'll go back and take a look from up the hill a ways. Surely we can find a way to go around without back-tracking."

Sam trots along the edge of the high grass and then turns and runs backwards, scanning the wide, flat valley as he goes. Barry follows Sam and stops when Sam stops. It is a valley as wide as five football fields and the floor seems to have a strip of the high grass running east to west. Twinkling in the distance, cutting the valley floor in half, they see another creek reflecting the afternoon sun rays. The twinkle makes Sam think the creek is running quickly, and he wonders how deep. Sam and Barry agree that they will either need to head west, which would take them down even further in altitude and toward Route 43 or keep going east and up. Neither of them wants to see a four-lane highway after feeling like they have discovered America, and they certainly do not want to add any more feet to their next hill.

Sam yells to the other three, "Let's go east, young men."

As they re-group, King whines, "Man, I had just finished picking off the last bur from my socks, too. Wow, that creek is pretty big. Pretty wide, I should say."

They have a good view of the valley from where they stand, but Sam looks east and, with conviction, says, "Let's keep moving. We're beginning to run out of time." Without discussion, they walk clumsily along the rim of hill number two, heading for number three. "This was a good idea. If it doesn't make one of our legs shorter than the other, this ridge has got to run right into the next hill," Sam says. "I'm just not sure about that creek, though. I really don't want to get wet feet, and I have boots on. Jeff's Chucks will get soaked."

The temperature is beginning to drop noticeably, but they still have three and a half to four hours left before sunset. No one has put his coat back on yet, and the pace helps keep their bodies warm. There was still a fairly steep slant to the rim, which makes their hips ache as they keep pounding their right legs into the dirt and rock as a stabilizer. Up ahead of them, they can hear an unusual sound, as if someone is running a washing machine. "Do you guys hear that noise?" Jeff asks.

"Yes! How weird is *that*?" King says with guarded fascination. Being the youngest, he did not want the others to think he was scared.

"Watch. We'll probably hike right into a neighborhood," Jeff drolls on with campy sarcasm as he throws his hands into the air in mock frustration.

"Yeah! Like Twilight Zone or something," Barry exclaims and then continues with fertile imagination in a Rod Serling voice. "As the five young men approach the sound that is drawing ever nearer, what will they find? Might the sound be the pulsating waves of a Martian space craft, or simply someone's Sears washing machine? Next stop . . . the Hiker Zone."

"Not bad, except you needed to take a long drag off a fag," Jeff says as he takes a long drag off of his Camel.

"No thanks!" Barry shouts as he puts his hand on his stomach. "Do you want me to share more of my inner-self with you?" Immediately, the whole group begs for Barry not to repeat his earlier lapse in good judgment, knowing he would not fall for the Camel unfiltered temptation again.

The sound is loud enough to discern, now, as Sam has moved ahead fifteen or twenty yards. "Boys, unless our Martians really had to take a leak, I would say we have a waterfall up ahead."

"Wha-a-a-a?" is the collective response.

"Man, how far out would that be. I mean, that would be so cool to find a waterfall in these hills. Who knew?" Danny says. He begins to move quickly ahead as the terrain has leveled off to some degree. He catches up with Sam, stretches his head forward and cups his ears trying to get confirmation. "Wow, I can hear it. It sounds kinda big too, don't you think, Sam?"

"It definitely has some size to it. I just can't imagine what the water source is, though," Sam says as the whole group has caught up. "Let's go toward it, but be really careful guys because the ground near it might be loose or slippery. I'll go first, OK? Don't run ahead of me." The rest agree, and they continue their trek toward the sound.

The rim begins to get steep again, very quickly, and Sam warns the others in that rare, excited voice that they have to move up the hill. "If there is a waterfall, then that means there is a long drop. Just make sure you are holding onto whatever you can grab as we move toward the falls." Sam has no doubt it is a waterfall now. They are close but still cannot see it. Then, suddenly, Sam is standing at the edge of a short cliff, maybe eight to ten feet high. Below is a steady stream of cold water, about ten feet across, on its way to the drop. It is certainly not a river, by any means, but a body with some force and speed. As Sam studies the lay of the land, he continues to warn the others not to stray too far away.

The sides of the notch cut into the earth are made of sandstone, slate, and other rock and dirt. Some foliage grows out from between various layers and jagged rocks rise above the depth of the water. Sam figures the water's depth at about eight to ten inches, and the rocks that the boys have begun throwing into the water create a deep concussive sound. They don't bounce off the bottom.

"I want to see the waterfall!" Danny says with urgency, practically pleading with Sam. "I'm just blown away that there is something like that up here. It feels like we're the first ones to see it."

"I just wish I knew where this comes from," says Sam, as if he did not even hear Danny's remark. "I have a feeling that our altitude is about the same as Saunders Creek. That is a pretty wide and fast-moving creek, and it has to go somewhere. It could have followed the natural separation of the ridges and found a nice little passage of rock to make its way down into the valley where we were."

"Man, how are we going to cross this thing without getting wet?" Danny asks.

"Well, we could build a bridge of sorts through the water, stacking up tree limbs and rocks, but then we would still need to scale the other side, and that doesn't look easy," King remarked with thoughtful observation.

With a bit of dread in his voice, Sam says, "We could hike upstream for a little ways. I would just hope this large crevasse doesn't go on and on. If we go backwards for long, we will really be behind our schedule."

"Is there any way we can see the waterfall? It just seems like no eyes have ever seen it and I want to be the first. You know? Like an astronaut," Danny says as he puffs himself out, trying to mimic someone wearing a space suit.

"Danny! Really, man?" Sam barks with Sam's version of tender understanding. "This isn't a game, right now. It's getting late, and we *must* keep moving. If there is any way, once we are on the other side, we will try to see the waterfall. I want to see it too, but our safety and schedule is foremost on my mind. The sun waits for no man." As he is the undisputed master of the English language, Sam tries to end his diatribe toward Danny with a tone that mocks his own seriousness. Sam does not want to stress everyone out, but Danny's litany of reminders that he wants to see the waterfall has been noted, filed, and ready to be voted on in the future.

Jeff tries to help Sam by acquiring the duty of putting the most unpopular and inevitable option into action. "Come on, everybody. Let's head upstream and see how it looks. We're getting nowhere standing here." Everyone agrees with fewer moans than expected. Danny doesn't say a word, showing his support by not mentioning the waterfall. Jeff fires up another Camel and Barry washes down his secret friend.

"Who knows Alice Engel?" Jeff continues to deflect the pain of trekking away from their destination.

"Are you kidding?" King exclaims.

"Oh, man! Alice is so groovy! She has the prettiest reddish-blond hair," Danny says.

Alice is so prominent in their school, even Sam has noticed her. "She's the only sophomore I would ever consider dating. Why, Jeff?"

"Well . . . if we ever make it home from the hills, I'm gonna ask her out. She is in two of my classes and study hall, and we've gotten to know each other a little bit. We have some great conversations." The hikers are speechless.

Alice Engel is the daughter of one of the wealthiest families in Appleton/ Marigold. The family is of German descent, her grandfather fleeing Hitler's rising regime in the mid-thirties with Alice's very young dad in tow. Her father owns the premier shopping destination Engel's Department Store in downtown Appleton. Engel's has gotten so successful and well-known in the state, that they are creating two more locations, one in Columbus and one in Cincinnati. The Engels own the largest house in Marigold, which sits atop the hill just north of Marigold Hill. Its property line runs all the way down the southern side of the hill and meets the back of the Reed's property. The gargantuan home overlooks the entire Marigold valley community and beyond.

Alice is a straight A student, a cheerleader, a candy striper, and a very fashionable young woman, being able to see all the newest trends first through the store. Alice is well-traveled, having accompanied her Aunt Charlene to Europe and India on buying trips for their current and upcoming store locations. Her dad wanted Alice to go to private school, but Alice wanted to be a part of her community and begged her dad to let her attend Scioto County schools with the assurance that she would continue to be enriched by her travels with Aunt Charlene. To top it off, Alice drives a 1957 Leland green, Triumph TR3. It was a gift from her father on her sixteenth birthday this past spring.

With all that said, Alice also loves to smoke Jeff's Camel unfiltered cigarettes when she doesn't have her own Gitanes. Alice began smoking when her Aunt Charlene gave her one from her own pack on a trip to France. "You can't understand the French way until you smoke Gitanes," Aunt Charlene would tell Alice. This was when Alice was thirteen, but she had already acquired the habit of smoking Pall Malls, and it was no secret from her aunt. Sometimes, Alice fancies herself as the tambourine yielding Gypsy woman on the front of the pack, but in Marigold, she is what Marigold boys' dreams are made of.

"Jeff . . . if you get a date with Alice Engel . . . I will freak out!" Danny says with no thought of the waterfall and enough covetousness to start a fire.

"It's not if, it's when, my friend," Jeff says as he takes a long draw off his cigarette.

"Where would you take her, man?" asks Barry as he pushes a tree limb out of his face.

"Cream is coming to Huntington in May. I figure I will see if she will go to the movies and some smaller dates first and then ask her to go see Cream. I think her birthday is around that time, so I could make it a birthday present."

"Not a bad plan, Jeffrey," Sam says.

King joins in. "Why not do it, man? That would really be far out if you two become a couple. I've always heard rich girls like bad boys, and even though we all know you're a pussycat, you would qualify as that to her, I'm sure."

"Shoot! She's not quite as nicey-nice as you might think. She gets pretty raw, sometimes, and can drop some four-letter words when she wants to. Surprised the crap out of me the first time I heard that come out of her pretty face!" Jeff says with the confidence only possessed by one who knows.

"Sam, do you see any change in the scenery?" Barry finally brings the focus back. "We need to decide soon, or we will be so far out of our way, we won't get home until tomorrow night. I'm going to climb this tree and see if I can scope out a way to the other side."

"Yeah, it's my birthday, tomorrow, you know," Danny reminds everyone with a simulated tantrum. With honesty, he continues, "I'd kinda like to get back fairly early because I think my dad is going to do something for me, and I don't want him to be let down or anything." Sam assures Danny they will be back in plenty of time while he helps Barry reach the first limb of the tree by putting Barry's foot in his hand and giving Barry an alley-oop.

Barry climbs up nearly to the top, and because there are no leaves, his view is unobstructed. "What do you see, Barry?" asks King.

"I think I see where the walls get short. Sort of a summit before it starts down the hill. It's about a hundred yards, I guess."

"What are we waiting for?!" shouts King. "Let's go!"

Barry shimmies down the tree, jumping five feet to the ground as he reaches the bottom limb. Everyone is running in the direction Barry pointed out. Sticks are breaking, leaves are flying, squirrels are scampering. It's a mad dash with Barry being the first to find the crossing after passing Danny, Sam, and King. Jeff is still back at the tree, heating up the creek and lighting a Camel at the same time. "Cross up here, Jeff! Come on!" Barry screeches.

The creek is about four inches deep at the crossing with a few boulders and fallen trees to aid in their safe passage. Barry flies across as if he had hopped the rocks before. Sam jumps each step one at a time, nesting both feet before he jumps to the next, and Danny is right behind Sam, studying his moves. King is waiting for Jeff who is taking his time. Jeff can run and has been the school's catcher on the baseball team the past two years. However, since his dad gave him the guitar, he spends most of his time tucked away in his room learning how to play it. It is what one has to do to achieve greatness, spend time at one's chosen craft, but when one combines that inactive activity with smoking, one tends to get out of shape very quickly. He's not sure if he will try out for the team in February when practice begins.

As Jeff catches up to King, King starts across the boulder bridge shouting directions back to Jeff and singing *Help I'm a Rock* by The Mothers of Invention. Jeff laughs out loud and sings a bit of the guitar riff to back up Zappa's repetitious lyric line on which King has sunk his teeth. Then, Jeff decides to ask, at this rather random time, why King wore such groovy clothes for a hike. "These aren't my *groovy* clothes, man. These are my clothes. They are what I wear every day. The sixties fashions just finally caught up to *my* taste."

"Couldn't you have worn regular boots instead of those moccasins? I mean, they can't feel good on the bottoms of your feet," Jeff says.

King looks Jeff in the eyes. "I would imagine you might ask one of our kindred Shawnee brothers about that. I think they hiked up here a lot more than me while wearing moccasins. I have no other shoes, anyway, except my black leather knee boots, which I only wear to parties and things and will wear in our band if we get any jobs. I have a pair of Chucks and some work boots too, but I don't wear them much"

"What about the Nehru collared shirt? You didn't have a sweatshirt or a flannel shirt?"

"I am kinda diggin' flannel shirts these days, but I haven't bought one, yet. The Nehru shirt is warm, and I have this wool vest that feels great underneath my coat." All along, as King discusses fashion, his mind cannot undo the image of the incredibly beautiful Alice with Jeff Lindor, and he sends the conversation back in that direction. "That's really cool about Alice, man. You know we're all gonna bug you to death about your dates, but we love ya," King says with a pucker on his lips.

"I know. I knew that when I made the announcement. It would be weird if you'uns *didn't* say anything. Anyway, I haven't even asked her, yet, but we do talk really well. We even get deep, sometimes."

"That's far out, friend. Come on, let's catch up to the others."

CHAPTER FOUR

The five young men are finally going downhill and along the opposite side of the creek. The steep walls have returned, and the waterfall is loud. "Danny?" Sam shouts. "Since we need to go this way, anyway, let's see if we can see that waterfall."

"Far out, Sam! Thanks, man!"

Sam tips his wool team Puma toboggan to Danny's gratitude but warns, "If it takes us out of our way or we see a clear path toward our destination, then you're gonna have to come back on your own someday."

"Ok. I hear ya. I just bet it's really picturesque. One of God's great creations."

"Sam, we're not going to make it to ridge four before it gets dark, are we?" Barry probes with a small amount of dread in his voice.

"I don't know for sure, Barry. This waterfall is the last tourist destination before we start deadheading it to the fourth ridge. Once we leave this creek, I think we will be able to make ridge three fairly quickly, if there are no surprises, but we will only have a couple of hours left to hike."

Sam stops talking and picks up the pace, pushing aside branch after branch. The grasses and briars are getting more plentiful as they descend and a scared fox runs right across their path. Sam is not distracted, though, and stays steady as he closes in on "Danny's" waterfall. "It has to be right up here, guys. Be very careful. The terrain may change quickly near its drop."

Like stealthy Shawnee, they watch their collective steps and head for the sound. Louder and louder is the sound of water rolling over rock, and wider and deeper becomes the source that is headed west next to them. The creek has to be twelve inches deep by now, and a force to respect.

With no warning, the trees and earth stop, and Sam is standing at the edge of a magnificent precipice with solid rock jutting out at its top, overhanging the valley eighty feet below. At its drop, the creek is about ten feet wide and flowing beautifully over the rocks. It is obvious from this vantage point why the group could not see this powerful, ancient life-source earlier, when they were facing the briars and high grass below in the valley. The creek takes a distinct turn to the northwest after falling before it heads due west for the Scioto River, first passing unnoticed under Route 43. The jagged clef is tucked into the rock just enough to be hidden if you approach it through the hills from Marigold to the north. There are enough small rises of earth along Route 43 to obscure the view of this part of the valley from drivers headed north. The knolls and rises were probably made by bulldozers when constructing the busy connector route.

Danny and King have stepped to the side of the jutting rock and are able to see under it. It appears that there is a cave or at least a dugout behind the waterfall and a second layer of flat rock situated like a floor to the cave. The falling water is not hitting it, but the mist keeps the rock floor damp and slippery. There is not a path, per se, to the lower-level cave but there is enough of the hill to slide down. The only problem is, there is only one five-inch-in-diameter tree to hold onto before the hill stops and air begins. If someone were to lose their grip, it would be time for a parachute.

"Don't even think about it on my watch," Sam belts out sternly to Danny and King. "We really need to keep moving, and you've had your chance to see the waterfall."

Danny hears Sam, but the temptation is too great to turn around. Danny leans forward toward the lone tree that stands between him and the valley sky. "Wait, Dan," King says softly, "Let me hold your belt until you find out if that tree has roots."

King takes hold of Danny's belt and finds an exposed hazel alder root with his free hand. Knowing there is no way to talk Danny out of his desire to know what lies behind the wall of water, Sam rushes to his little brother and holds onto his arm while using his other hand to hold the trunk of the Alder tree. Barry and Jeff move in next to Sam, ready to become links in the developing human chain.

Danny pushes forcibly on the over-hanging tree to test its stability, hoping it will allow him an unimpeded field of vision if he leans on it. The sapling seems well-rooted and is flexible. That will project Danny out from the cliff, providing a ringside seat for the highly anticipated look at the natural den. He seems to pay no attention to the eighty feet of air beneath him, turns to King and says, "Here I go!" And with that, Danny is suddenly perched out over the valley, three or four feet from the waterfall and looking straight back into the lion's mouth. "It's at least ten or fifteen feet underneath the creek. It's really amazing!" Danny yells over the rushing water.

King is being stretched from one hand to the other and has Danny only by two fingers after his others pulled away upon Danny's thrust. "Come on, son, let's go. It's getting late!" Then, the sapling gives under Danny's weight and in a blink of an eye he is dangling from the bent sapling next to the waterfall, so close he can feel the spray. He is holding onto the small tree with both hands, but the spray is causing his grip to slip. Everyone is yelling at him to hold on, and King is inching closer to Danny after his grip was ripped away.

Everyone looks over to see that Barry has changed positions and is lying on the flat rock just above where the sapling is rooted. On his stomach, Barry reaches for Danny, but he is about five inches from Danny's waist. "My hands are slipping!" Danny yells to anyone, though not in a panicked tone.

"Sam and Jeff, grab my ankles, but let me creep out slowly," Barry barks out in full, focused command. The two biggest young men do as they are told without hesitation. "Danny. I am going to get a firm hold on the waist of your Levi's. You are going to have to trust me when I tell you to let go because I will sling you toward the bank, but if you don't let go, my pull might cause you to just drop, and I don't know how long I could hold you that way. You might just pull me over, too. King, get in position so that you can grab him when he hits the bank. His arms and hands are going to be weak, and he will need you to pull him up to safety. Ok?"

"I hear you!"

King moves into position, making sure his feet are firmly planted in the small ridge under the rock slab. They all knew there was no room for error with such a narrow, slimy ridge on which Danny will hopefully land. Barry and Danny's timing has to be flawless, or else Barry will be holding all of Danny's weight by the waist of his jeans, and the mist was making things slick. "I will say one, two, three and then on four is when we will make the move. It's just like counting in a song. We all need to come in at the same time to make this song sound beautiful. Are you ready, Danny?"

"Yep."

"Don't let go of my ankles, boys, but I'm going to inch out and get a good hold on his waist now, Barry says as he begins to worm his body toward Danny.

First his upper chest clears, and he has about an inch to go. With both hands reaching out, Barry slithers to Danny and grabs Danny's waist band on his jeans. "Are you ready, friend?"

"Uh-huh!"

"Ok! On four! One! Two! Three! Four! And with that last number, the choreography begins. Danny lets go as Barry is swinging him toward King. Even though they knew it was coming, the sudden extra weight surprises Jeff and Sam. Barry shoots forward, but the two anchors' grips sink into Barry's boots for dear life. This causes Barry's ribs to cascade over the edge of the hard rock slab, generating great pain that goes unnoticed as they perform their ballet.

For a brief second, Danny is actually hanging eighty feet above the rocks below by his pants, attached to Barry's not-so-Herculean upper torso. With all his might and with great precision, Barry rolls right, yelps in pain and throws Danny backwards to his left, with his lower ribs rolling over the edge of the slab at an angle. Danny flails as he heads toward the sliver of a bank, reaching for whatever he can grab. King's fingers roll around Danny's arm as Barry watches with arms fully outstretched in paralyzed apprehension of Danny bouncing off the ridge and down into the valley. Sam and Jeff pull Barry backwards until he is fully on the slab but rush over to King and Danny, grabbing any piece of Danny that presents itself.

With King having a firm grip on Danny's left arm, Sam tugs at his brother with Jeff securing Danny by the jean's back pocket, pulling him and the explorer up the little ridge to solid, flat ground. As soon as Danny is safe, the four boys collapse in a heap while Barry lies in immense pain on the cold slab of slate. Nothing is said for what seems to be minutes. All one can hear, over the steady low roar of the waterfall, is very heavy breathing and Jeff pulling out his pack of Camels. "That was fun." Jeff says as he takes a long drag off his cigarette.

Sam is not amused, though. "Danny! Everybody! Please don't make this hike any harder than it already is. Are you OK, Danny?"

"Yes, Sam, and thank you all. Especially Barry." Danny sees Barry curled up in a fetal position. "Hey, man, are you OK? What's wrong?"

Barry has multiple bruised and/or broken ribs and is not breathing well due to the pain that increases as his rib cage expands. He tries not to make a big deal out of it, but it hurts and there is no hiding it. Danny is first to rush over to Barry. "What hurts, man?"

"I think I probably broke a rib or two on the edge of the rock. I am having a hard time breathing." The others have circled around Barry, and Danny recites what Barry told him.

Sam puts his hand on his chin, trying to remember reports on sports injuries that he's heard. "As far as I know, there is nothing much we can do for broken ribs other than wrap them up tightly."

"I brought an extra t-shirt. Would that work, Sam?" Danny asks with urgency. "Yeah, I think so, Danny. Let's try it. Barry, I know it is going to hurt, but I need to take your shirt off to wrap up your chest and ribs."

"That's fine," Barry says in an airy whisper.

"I imagine your body is in shock, and I'm sure your lungs are not injured." Sam says calmly, trying to ease Barry's mind as he carefully strips Barry of his shirt and t-shirt. Barry tries futilely to hold back groans and onomatopoeias of pain while his friends, as a group, turn him from side-to-side, as tenderly as they can.

With no humor in his tone, Jeff says "That's what ribs are for, to protect those lungs. That was really impressive how you handled all that, Barry." While he holds his breath, Barry wrinkles up his nose, shows his teeth, squints his eyes, and forces out a mid-throated thank you.

"You saved my life, Barry," Danny says with a bit of a squeak. "All of you, I can't believe what you did for me."

Jeff smiles. "I was kinda wanting to watch you hang there for a while. Maybe throw acorns at you."

"Please, Jeff, don't make me laugh," Barry ekes out his plea with a sad little laugh.

With crystal clarity, Danny scans the group to ensure he has their attention. "He can't finish this hike. I am going to help him down this hill and out to 43. I'm sure it isn't that far through the valley, and then I can flag down a car. He can't be out here when it gets dark and cold.

"I'll be OK. Just let me lie here for a couple more minutes, and I should be able to carry on with our journey."

"Yeah, and I have the new John Lennon sings Ethel Merman album . . . volume two. Barry, old boy, you are busted up, and I agree with Danny. You need to, well, see your dad," Jeff states confidently.

Sam acknowledges his brother with an inclusive, "Do you agree, King? King?"

"He walked up the creek that way, Sam. Maybe you should check on him." With Jeff's suggestion, Sam turns immediately in King's direction and starts his brisk walk toward him.

As he approaches King, he can see King is weeping without restraint. "What's the matter, K? Did you want to finish the hike?"

"No. We almost lost Danny. He almost died. I don't know what I'd do if Danny had fallen and died."

"Hey, he's OK. You were pretty brave there on that little patch of hillside."

"Shoot, if he'd slipped, I would have held on and gone down with him. I mean it! I never really knew how much he means to me until now. I'm not saying I'd do any less for you, Sam, but you know? Danny's about as close as you can get to being my brother without having the same mom and dad." After clearing his phlegm-filled throat, King suggests they create some sort of cot and try to carry Barry down the slope to the valley.

Sam puts his arm around King. "Good idea, brother. Let's get back to everyone before the sun sets. We still have to hike a while to get to 43."

While Sam was away with King, Jeff and Danny wrapped Barry up tightly and re-dressed him for warmth. Barry doesn't seem to be in shock, but the pain is real but under control with the wrap. He takes short breaths to reduce the pain, and then Sam, the toilet paper man, remembers he brought a few aspirins, too. He gives two to Barry and asks Danny if he needs any after the escapade, but Danny says no thank you. Danny wants to suffer a bit for his bad decision and helps complete the primitive-but-sound travois-style cot. Danny's coat will be Barry's bed for the trek, and Danny has asked to be the first "horse" to wear the cloth harness while transporting the damaged hero hiker.

Thankfully, the way is fairly clear down the hill, sans a few broken trees and stumps. The sun is in their faces in the west, and they probably have forty-five minutes to get across the valley and out to the busy highway, *if* it is where they think it is. They know if they head toward the sun, the highway has to be there. The valley has several small rocks along the floor, which tend to shake Barry around, but the pain in his ribs has settled with the medicinal help of Sam's aspirin. Unfortunately, Barry's breathing pattern has now been form-fitted to the injuries and do not amount to much.

Danny has dragged his friend the whole way, as if he were dragging the cross to Calvary, stopping on occasion for water and to straighten up the harness. Danny is beginning to shiver without his coat, but he doesn't even realize it. It is just above freezing now, and the sun begins to perch itself in its southern Ohio nest of western hills, but the work of carrying his friend keeps Danny heated.

"Do you want me to take Barry the rest of the way, Danny?" King asks earnestly.

"No, thanks, King man. It probably isn't that much farther." After a few more minutes, Danny has obviously been replaying the waterfall scene in his mind and again solicits forgiveness from everyone for his stupidity.

Jeff slaps him on the back. "Shut up with that, Dan old man. You were excited, and you went for it. You didn't mean to almost kill us all, I'm sure of it."

Danny feels relieved, finally, and actually chuckles at Jeff's absurdity.

"Look back behind you, Danny. You can see a sliver of the waterfall glistening in the sun. That thing is pretty amazing. I feel like we're in Brigadoon or something," King says, but Danny just keeps moving forward. He does not want to see the beast that tempted him into foolishness, and he knows there is only a little time left. The terrain drops a bit, and the sun seems to have vanished.

"Wow, that was a quick sunset," Danny yells to Sam, who has gone up ahead to scout the best path out of the valley.

"I don't think it's set, yet. Probably because of that little hill in front of us, and that little hill tells me we are near 43!" Sam shouts back to Danny full of hopeful excitement.

Sam runs farther ahead and climbs the small, man-made mound. "I see headlights! The highway is about fifty yards, boys." As Sam runs back to his friends, he tells Danny to take the harness off and let two people grab each end of the travois. It will be easier to carry Barry up the hill and to the highway rather than Danny dragging him. That makes sense to Danny, and he gives up his cross as King takes the front and Jeff the back of the cot. King and Jeff do double time behind Danny and Sam up the scrubby hill and down the other side. One more embankment will put the troupe up onto the shoulder of the northbound lane of Route 43.

With his future vision, Sam tells Barry that he is going to need to get out of the cot when they reach the shoulder so they can get Danny's coat and Jeff's t-shirt that was used for the harness and throw the travois back down the hill. "People are less apt to give us a ride with a guy in a stretcher." Sam cracks a small amount of his semi-occasional humor, but it is enough that Barry begs Sam to not make him laugh.

"Whoops. Sorry!" Sam says with his eyebrows raised and a fake smile on his face. Danny has put his coat on and is already waving down cars, but no one wants to stop. "Let's walk toward Marigold while we try to get a ride. Maybe there will be a house or business along the way." Sam continues to lead. "Are you able to walk, Barry? Are you warm enough?"

"I'm warm enough. I think I can walk a bit. You guys did a great job wrapping me up."

The dusky sky is now a violet blue fading up into black, and the group is an odd shaped moving form. A mere silhouette to the northbound drivers. No one seems to want to pick up a group of faceless humans. The motley group may want to rob them or force them to drive somewhere they do not want to go. It is five-thirty traffic, thick with tired employees of the various Appleton establishments, no doubt a few Engel's clerks headed for the Marigold exit and beyond. City employees with headaches might be in the mix after they have dealt with Appleton's problems, but they are probably off for Thanksgiving. The mill has a three o'clock shift, so they will not be rushing by.

The boys are hoping a sheriff will come along when two headlights pull off onto the shoulder ten feet from the boys. The boys shield their eyes from the bright lights shining directly into their faces and then they hear a raspy, male voice say, "Do you need a ride?"

The entire group yells out affirmative answers and King shouts "One of us is hurt. Can you take us to Marigold? His house is near the entrance."

"Get in," the voice says welcomingly, and the gang walks slowly toward the vehicle. Being careful not to bounce Barry around, they wonder, with a bit of apprehension, who their driver is going to be.

The driver's vehicle is a station wagon, probably a 1958 Country Squire, perfect for transporting Barry. "You boys put the injured one in the back with another one of you back there with him. The others can climb in up here." The five young men do as they are told, and Danny stays in the back with Barry in a car that is surprisingly clean. The automobile is warm and so is the driver. He is a man in his early seventies wearing a hat with ear flaps turned up. The man's hands, now wrapped around the steering wheel, are gnarled-looking, probably from arthritis, and he has on a one-piece, gray work overall with a zipper from the waist up to the neck.

The old man's face is hard to make out because he is, now, the one in silhouette. The radio station the man has chosen is playing The Ink Spots, and his half-smoked cigar is resting, fully lit, in the car's over-flowing ash tray. "May I smoke, sir?" Jeff asks politely.

"Yes, son, you may, although they ain't good for ya. So, our destination is Marigold, huh? I think we can do that. What happened to the hurt boy?" the driver inquires.

"We think he may have broken a rib or two after wrestling with some rocks up in the hills. We were on a hike." King seems talkative now that he is headed home and feeling comfortable with their driver.

"Ouch! That hurts. I've broken a few ribs along the way. In the first war, I was young and held up pretty well, but when I had to fight Hitler, my body took a beatin'."

"You were in both world wars?"

"Sure. I was born in eighteen ninety-four, so I was prime age when Wilson put us in the mix of Allies. I guess I was almost twenty-two when I joined to fight the Germans the first time. They kept trying to sink our passenger ships and such with their submarines, so Wilson just signed us up. What's your name, son? My name is Nobel Doucet. I suppose my grandfather's owner was from Louisiana, but my folks moved to southern Ohio after the Civil War. What's your name?"

"My name is King, sir."

"King? That's a cool name. Why'd they name you King? Your mom and dad that is."

"My mom loves Nat King Cole and wanted to name me King if I was born a boy, and I was."

With a big, ragged laugh, Nobel says "Yes, you were! I love Nat, too. What grade are you in? I'd say about a sophomore?"

"Next year I'll be a sophomore, sir. What do you do, Mr. Doucet?"

"I have worked at Appleton Rope and Pulley since they opened in nineteen and twenty-five. I started out doing anything they needed: sweeping floors, doing some electrical work, building office walls. I got to be real good friends with Mr. Drummond, the owner, and he started putting me on the assembly line. Then I kinda worked my way up through the ranks after Mr. Drummond paid for me to learn to read. He was a real good man to me and to everybody there. He'd always give us Christmas bonuses and that whole Christmas week off. A real nice man."

King seems legitimately interested. "What job are you doing there, now?"

"I lead the UTS department with a couple of young college kids and a good older fella named George Masters helping me."

"What do you do in the UTS department?"

"That's where we test the strength and elasticity of the rope we make. Some ropes are made to withstand stretchin', you know, being pulled on by tension and some needs to be tested for compression or bein' pushed together real tight. The tensile strength machine pulls on both ends of the rope and measures how strong it is before it fractures or breaks. That is important to construction work so they know how much weight they can lift. The core of the rope needs to be without blemish and then the fibers are wrapped around it forming the strength needed to do its job. I kinda liken it to life, with our Lord Jesus being the core without blemish with all of us being the fibers wrapped around Him. If one of us is weak or gets dirty, you know, turnin' away from Jesus, then the rope can't stand up when it is tested by hard times. You couldn't depend on it unless Jesus is at the core. Then you know the rope has been cleansed. Ol' Solomon said, 'A threefold cord is not quickly broken.'"

"Yes sir, that's heavy. We need to turn into Marigold right up here, if you don't mind," King directs his driver, not wanting to pass their entrance.

Danny had been tuned into what Nobel Doucet was saying about Jesus and he belts out an "Amen". Then, in a state of deep, poetic thought, he applies Mr. Doucet's analogy about Jesus being the core of relationships to each one of his close friends, now riding together in Nobel's car, as the fibers of their own human rope. Danny truly loves each friend with what he knows as an agape love, a Greek word Danny learned in Sunday school. Nobel Doucet's analogy will never leave Danny Mosely's mind.

CHAPTER
FIVE

Nobel Doucet enters Marigold and drives parallel to Route 43 on Old River Road, passing the turn onto Marigold Road, until he reaches Danny's driveway. "Just pull in here, Mr. Doucet, please," King says as he points to the left. Danny's dad is not expecting anyone, so when he hears a car engine and sees headlights in his driveway, he turns on the porch light and opens the front door to see who it can be. Walter Mosely does not recognize the vehicle and waits until he sees King jump out of the front passenger side.

"King, what's wrong? Why are you here tonight? You weren't supposed to come back until tomorrow. Where's Danny? Is he OK?" All the boys begin to step out of the old station wagon. King assures Danny's dad that his son is fine and in the back of the old station wagon but informs Mr. Mosely that Barry may have broken a rib.

Sam is first to the back of the station wagon and lifts up the back door. Mr. Doucet gets out and introduces himself to Walter and tells him the story of picking them up on the side of 43. Walter gushes with thanks and invites the old gentleman into his home for coffee, but Nobel declines so he can get home to the missus. "Please let me pay you for gas or something. I'm so grateful for you, sir. Thank you so much for stopping and God bless you!" Walter concludes emphatically.

"Yes sir. I enjoyed talking with King, and I pray the other boy heals up quick. It was real nice meeting you, and you have a good evening and you be blessed, sir." With that said, Nobel Doucet backs out of the driveway, beeps the horn and disappears into the night.

Walter turns to the hikers, puts his arm around his son and says, "All you boys had better call your parents before I take you home so that you don't scare anybody. Come on in and have something to eat. Barry, we'll get you home as soon as you call and let your parents know you are coming."

"Yes sir, Mr. Mosely. I appreciate the ride."

"We think a rib or two may be broken, Dad. His breathing is really shallow because it hurts so badly." Danny provides some detail to his attentive dad.

"We were clowning around and got stuck on a little cliff-type thing, and Barry laid down on a rock with a sharp edge and held onto a couple of us until we could get hold of the bank again. The weight sort of pulled his ribs over the edge of the rock, but he kept holding on." Sam presents a fuzzy version of the story to keep Danny's innocent exuberance from being the reason for Barry's injury. Danny meant no harm, and there was no reason to paint Danny as the instigator.

While the boys make their calls, Walter fixes them all venison sandwiches leftover from Thanksgiving, each with a side of heated turkey dressing. They devour their small feast and wash it down with a glass of milk. The Reeds decide to get their boys so that they can continue to Appleton to pick up Sam's car waiting at their unaccomplished destination. King is not happy with that news because he desperately wants to take off his bur-covered socks. The free-loading hitchhikers are hanging from his moccasin fringe, as well, and that is not cool. Sam, on the other hand, is looking forward to having his baby safely parked at home, back in Marigold. "Please tell Mom to bring me some more shoes and socks, Sam," King begs.

Darren answers Jeff's call and hangs up after a very disgruntled "great." Barry's dad is at the country club and won't be home until late, but Mrs. Meade and his sister, Kay, will be right down to pick him up so that they can nurse his wounds as soon as possible. Danny turns the TV on, and he and Barry watch while waiting for Barry's mom and sister. Mr. Mosely takes Jeff home where Jeff is greeted by an inebriated Darren with a very unpleasant "what the hell happened? Why are you home tonight?" followed by, "Hurry up, you're letting the cold in."

"Can I get you anything, my brother?" Danny asks Barry.

"No, but it is really starting to hurt again."

"I'm sure it will hurt for a while. I hope you can come down here to my birthday party. I don't want gifts or anything, just time with my friends and you're on the top of that list." Danny responds sympathetically.

"Who's coming?"

"Well, hopefully all you guys and Rhonda . . . Steve, Phil . . . uh
. . . Bill and Mike. Uh, Brenda and a couple of guys, Nick and Adam,
and a girl named Hannah from church that I hang out with, sometimes.
They're real cool. You'll like 'em. Let's see . . . oh yeah, I almost forgot
Shannon. You can't invite Rhonda without inviting Shannon. Last
but not least, Diana Peterson. We'll ask her if we can play her party in
February. Shoot, I wish we had a song or two worked out to show her,
but we'll just have to dazzle her with our brilliance and stunning good
looks."

"Ow-w-w! Please don't make me laugh. I'm sure my dad can fix me
up good enough to come down. What time is it, again?"

"Four, and Dad is going to grill some chicken if it isn't raining. I
think I hear your mom."

The doorbell rings, and Danny helps Barry up from the comfortable
chair. They get Barry's coat and open the door. "I'm sorry your hike was
cut short, boys." Mrs. Meade says sincerely and lovingly.

"Are you OK, Barry?" says Kay nervously.

"It hurts, baby sis, but I'll be OK. When is dad going to be home,
mom?"

"Probably late. I'll take a look at your ribs when we get home, and
hopefully you can climb into a warm bath. There is not much that can
be done for broken ribs. Your Uncle Brian broke two when he was about
twenty, and they just put tape around his chest and gave him some Bayer
aspirin."

"Let's go, Mom. I'll hopefully see you tomorrow, Dan man."

"Tomorrow? What is happening tomorrow other than it was when
you were supposed to return?" Mrs. Meade asks.

"It's Danny's birthday party at four."

"Oh. I knew that and happy birthday, Danny. We'll have to see
how you are feeling, but I hope you can come. Thank you, Danny, and
thank your dad for me. Where is he?"

"He took Jeff home and there he is now."

"I better move our car. Bye, Danny. Help your brother, Kay. Hi
Walt!"

Walter Mosely blinks his lights to say hello and waits for the Meade
family to back out of his concrete driveway, cordially beeps his horn
good-bye, and pulls the car all the way to the back door of the house.
That's where Danny is waiting for his dad and where they hug for a solid
ten seconds. "Are you OK, son?"

"Yes sir. It's my fault that Barry is hurt, and I feel so bad. It was a great lesson, though, Dad. God can surely get our attention, can't He?"

"He's really good at that! You didn't mean it, Danny. You have a good heart, and we all mess up, sometimes. I'm sure you've talked to the Lord about it, so He wants you to move on. Just be sure to call Barry in the morning and check on him."

"I will, first thing."

As they walk in the kitchen door, Mr. Mosely reminds Danny "We have a lot to do tomorrow, but at least you get to sleep in your own bed tonight. You are going to work at eleven, right?"

"Yes, I need to make that money."

"Do you want money for your birthday? I really don't know what to buy you, Mr. Sixteen-Years-Old."

Danny looked off to the side. "Money would be really nice. We are going to start a band next Saturday, so hopefully I can make extra money and stop bumming it from you. I need to start saving for a car 'cause I'll be *driving* soon!" Danny dances around the kitchen floor with his hair hanging in front of his eyes.

"Believe me, son, I know," Mr. Mosely says with a loving grin. "I am thankful you have good friends, but I am so glad you are home with me tonight. You're going to be out of the nest more and more, so I value our time together more than ever. Hey, guess what?"

"What?" Danny asks with a sheepish smile, knowing what's coming next

"I love you so much I can't stand it."

"I love you, too, Dad of dads."

***

On the other side of the moon is Jeff's home. As usual, Jeff has walked into a drunken fight between his mom and Darren, and Darren is waving his gun around. Jeff has never heard him fire the gun, but Darren loves to intimidate people with it. He holds it up and points it at drivers who cut him off in traffic, or he cleans the chamber while watching TV when Jeff's friends visit. They do not visit often, usually just for support for their friend.

Tonight, Darren is pointing his gun at Susan, and Jeff loudly tells Darren to put the gun away. Jeff's intensity gets Darren's attention. Darren makes a crude and rude comment toward Jeff but then takes the gun out of Susan's face. Jeff goes upstairs, slams his door, and plays his guitar, first *I Feel Free* by Cream then *Dirty Water* by The Standells. He finally settles for working on the intro to The Yardbird's *Over Under Sideways Down*. Playing guitar always takes Jeff to a better place.

Sam has been worried about his Cragar wheels getting stolen and is happy to find his car in one piece, shiny and ready to roll. King wants to ride with his brother and Gordon and Ellie don't mind at all.

"We're going to go to the A&W if you want to follow us. You must be hungry," Ellie tells the boys before they get in the Belair. Sam and King look at each other, shrug and accept their mother's invitation completely forgetting about the venison sandwiches they just ate. The A&W has the very best root beer floats and cheeseburgers, and the waitresses are usually cute. Cute waitresses, good food and Dad is paying? It's a no-brainer on a crisp, southern Ohio evening. Sam fires up his car and turns on the radio just in time to hear *I'm a Man* by the Spencer Davis Group.

King swoons as he lays his head back and closes his eyes. "Man, help me remember to put this on my learn list for rehearsal on Saturday. This thing is so groovy."

After a very restless night's sleep, Barry meets Benny first thing on an overcast Saturday morning, still in a lot of pain. He can hear his dad coming up the stairs to his room, so he quickly puts Benny away. Doctor Meade taps on his son's door and opens it slowly. "I hear you have some sore ribs. Let me take a look at them." Barry unbuttons his pajama shirt, and his dad immediately squinches his face as he gets a look at the damage. Barry's whole chest is bruised and skinned raw, but now the good doctor will need to poke and prod to find out the extent of the injury.

In between Barry's groans and moans with each poke, the doctor tells him, "I can't be certain without an X-Ray, but I'd say you have cracked two or three ribs." With his stethoscope, the doctor listens carefully to his son's lungs to be sure there has not been a puncture. "The lungs sound undamaged, but you need to breathe with big breaths. You will get pneumonia if you continue to breathe like you are. What happened?"

Barry tells the story without putting anyone at fault, and his dad pats Barry's left cheek. "You guys did the right thing last night. I went to the office this morning and got this elastic bandage, but first, I want to shoot some Bactine on the abrasions and cover them with gauze so the elastic wrap does not stick. Raise your arms up while I douse you with the antiseptic."

The medicine is cold and stings a bit on the new wounds, but Barry does not flinch. The gauze coverings go on and then the elastic wrap, which is actually comforting. "You will need to have it loosened every couple of hours, and it will take a month or so until it heals completely. I am leaving for some house calls, but your mom can help you wrap it. You need to breathe deeply, Barry, remember that. No more shallow breathing. I have some Numorphan for your pain, and I want you to take one every four hours."

Dr. Meade hands Barry an unlabeled bottle of the narcotic. You will think you are all healed when the pain pill takes effect, so *do not* overdo it today. Just take it easy and do something productive like study for your exams that are coming up in, what, two weeks?"

"Yes sir. I have studied every night until Wednesday just before Thanksgiving."

"There is no reason you can't get As on those exams. You're a smart young man. Oh yeah, you were a hit Wednesday night. When I was at the club last night, everyone was talking about how well you played. You have lots of fans, even though they are old like me," the doctor says with a grin. "Ok, go ahead and take one of your pain pills now." Barry dutifully goes into his bathroom, runs a glass of water from their crystal-clear spring water well, and downs the pill with the whole glass of water to follow.

Dr. Meade says goodbye to his son and walks downstairs and out the kitchen door to his car, with a whistle and spunky intention. The bandage helps, but Barry decides to wait until he gets ready for Danny's party before he gets fully dressed. He pulls out his satchel to get his schoolbooks and finds a Playboy he forgot about. Barry flips through it to put the images back into his mind once again and then puts it away. Kay is always snooping around, and he doesn't want her to see what some girls will do. There is a small market near the office downtown where the cashier will allow Barry to purchase the magazine even though the cashier knows Barry is a minor. After getting to know him in a small way, Barry has, in turn, given the cashier some Benzedrine on a couple of occasions and that generosity seems to have secured future Playboy purchases.

Back at Danny's house, after a solid night of sleep, Danny dutifully rises to his dad's call up the staircase. He showers and eats his dad's bacon and eggs and gets to work by eleven a.m. His transistor radio is tucked into his shirt pocket, and he listens to WROR with his earphone so as not to disturb anyone who might be in the office. Danny always cleans the toilets first because he does not want to end his workday with this less-than-enjoyable chore. Danny feels privileged, though and considers all of his work a service to his Lord. He would do it for free if the church did not insist on paying him forty dollars a week. As far as the church is concerned, it is money well spent, as Danny does his work flawlessly and without complaint.

As he passes a window, he notices that there are more cars in the parking lot than other Saturdays, and he wonders what could be so important. Danny vacuums the lobby, then the sanctuary and soon starts up the hall to the offices. For so many people attending to business today, the office area is dark, and Danny wonders if he will need to change a light bulb this morning. He stops the vacuum, and it is very quiet. Maybe there is a special Christmas meeting in one of the Sunday School rooms in the basement. He continues up the office hallway toward the dark office. Danny stops at the door and flips the switch to the *on* position which, to his surprise, turns on the light. At that very second, at least twenty staff and friends pop out from behind the various pieces of furniture and shout, *"Happy Birthday, Danny!"*

Danny's dad is standing next to Pastor Pete and his wife Annie, along with Mr. Blanton and Danny's three friends Nick, Adam, and Hannah, who will be attending his home party later today. "Were you surprised, Dan?" laughs Nick.

"Oh man, was I ever. My heart just about stopped. That was amazing that all of you were so quiet. Thank you all so much for thinking of me," Danny says, almost in tears.

"Come on, Danny, we have some fried chicken and potato salad and birthday cake. I think everyone is hungry. We love you, Danny, and you bring so much to this church, honey," Annie Boggs says, giving him a side hug.

Pastor Pete puts his arm around Danny. "It is hard to believe you're sixteen years old and have become a fine young man,"

Annie, as well as a few other women from the church, is the mother that Danny never had. Walter Mosely cannot imagine how he would have raised Danny had it not been for these selfless women. He believes in God's providence and knows his son has a relationship with Christ because of the loving kindness shown by the people of his church. "I am excited to give you your gift, son. It was not easy to find."

"What in the world is it, Dad? I can't wait!"

Walter smiles. "Oh no, no way! First, let's share this excellent meal with those who made it just for you."

"Deal." They all move into the office lunchroom to enjoy their time together.

As the meal winds down, Walter goes back to the office area and returns with a not-so-masterly wrapped present. He hands it to his son and says the obligatory "I hope you like it." Danny just shakes his head in a way that tells his dad that he did not need to give him anything other than the daily love he already gives.

"It feels like a book. I know I have mentioned a few to you, but I wonder why this one was hard to get?"

"Stop talking and open it, son."

"Yes, please open it!" everyone else joins in. "We want to know, too." With that rousing plea, the paper is ripped off and in Danny's hands, are two books of poetry by Charles Causley, *Farewell, Aggie Weston* and the poet's newest *Johnny Alleluia*. Danny looks up at his dad in disbelief and then proceeds to jump up from his chair and dance around the room.

"How did you remember, Dad? How did you remember? I couldn't find these at Engel's Annex or the library. Nowhere! I can't wait to start reading them."

"I had a nice lady at the Appleton library help me. She made several calls to New York and then found where I could buy them. She recommended these two. Are they alright?"

"Perfect, Dad. Perfect."

After Danny thumbs through the books for a few seconds or so, Annie holds out an envelope and says "Danny, this is from the church. We all pitched in." Danny looks a bit confused and just stares at her outstretched hand. He looks up at his dad as if asking if this is a joke, but his dad sweeps his eyes toward the envelope and says "Go ahead, boy. You are loved."

Danny slowly reaches out his hand and takes the envelope. He sits for a few seconds just looking at the unopened envelope. "Open it, Dan!" Nick yells out. "We don't have all day!" Nick's honesty receives a round of laughs and a few friends chanting "open it – open it."

"Alright, alright." Danny shouts as he raises his right hand, playfully asking everyone to calm down. He slides his index finger under the flap that is glued to the envelope and pulls out a card. On the front of the card is a drawing of a young man worshipping at the foot of the cross. Danny opens the card and something falls out. He looks down at the floor and there around his feet lay ten twenty-dollar bills.

Oddly, at such a festive moment, Danny puts his head in his hand and tears roll down his cheeks. He does not pick up the money. Walter makes the first move toward Danny, but quickly the whole crowd is around him, laying their hands on him, kneeling and rubbing his arms. "Why is God so good to me?" Danny blubbers out with a thick tongue and milky voiced whisper. He reads to himself what is printed on the inside of the card . . .

Every good gift and every perfect gift is from above, and cometh down from the Father of lights, with whom is no variableness, neither shadow of turning. (James 1:17)

Danny reads it twice and just stares at the scripture verse to absorb it. His friends pick up the money that has fallen at his feet and put it in Danny's hand. Walter digs out his unused handkerchief and waves it lightly in front of his son's lowered head. Without looking up, Danny reaches out and takes it and immediately dabs his eyes. "Why are you giving me so much money?" Danny asks. This is a lot of money."

"We want you to use it for a car, Danny," says Pastor Pete. "Sixteen is an important birthday, and this is what the church wanted to do for you."

"Here, Dad, please. I'm scared to hold it. But first, I want to give ten percent to my church. I have to, please," Danny says this with a grin and hands the card and envelope over to Walter, minus one of the twenty-dollar bills that he will lay on the secretary's desk.

"Well," Danny begins, "there is work to be done. I guess I better get back to it, and of course, I really just don't know what to say. Pastor, I would like to thank the church from the pulpit tomorrow, if you don't mind."

"That will be fine, Danny. You can do that at the beginning of the service right after we make announcements. Does that sound good?"

"Yes, sir, that would be great." With that, everyone picks up cake plates and brushes the crumbs into their hands from the table, transporting them to the trash can that Danny will empty as soon as everyone leaves.

Hannah gives Danny a long hug and a kiss on his cheek, and she and Nick and Adam assure Danny they will see him at four o'clock. Danny receives hugs or handshakes from everyone who leaves, and he sincerely thanks each person. Walter waits so that he can hug his son without interruption, and he does so with great warmth and pride. "If I had to design a son, he would be just like you, my boy." Danny buries his head into his dad's chest as he has done all of his life, except now he has to bend down a bit, as Danny is closing in on his dad's six-foot frame.

CHAPTER
SIX

D anny is home by one o'clock and goes immediately upstairs to take an hour nap before he helps his dad set up for the party. As soon as the clock reaches two, the phone rings, which confuses Danny for a second, because he did not remember setting the alarm. Walter answers the downstairs phone, and Danny can hear his dad tell the caller he is sleeping. "I'm awake, Dad, if it is for me."

"It's Jeff, son."

"I'll get it up here." Danny goes out into the upstairs hall and picks up the phone, which signals his dad downstairs to hang up his phone.

"I got a favor, my friend," Jeff says with some excitement in his voice.

"Sure, shoot."

"I just saw Alice at Charlie's Market."

"Alice shops at Charlie's?"

"I guess so, and she asked me what I was doing today after work. I told her about your party and asked if she wanted to come. She said yes. I didn't think she would, ya know? Is it OK?"

"Are you kidding me?"

"No."

"Of course she can come to the party, you dog you. That's far out! Are you picking her up and everything?"

"No, I told her your address and the time and all. She said she will probably drop by between four thirty and five. I'll be there at four, though."

"That is really far out, Jeff. Alice Engel and my buddy Jeff Lindor together. Is she going to drive that cool car?"

"I don't know. I guess so. We're not 'together,' Dan man, and don't blow this up too big, please. She is just coming to a friend's party."

King Reed has slept all day and is now lying in his bed listening to the radio. He thinks about yesterday and how fun and exciting it was. Except for the burs on his socks, he loved the whole experience and was thankful Danny was not hurt, but he is concerned about Barry. He knows he needs to get up and start getting ready for the party, but the bed feels cozy and the house is quiet except for some muffled conversations now and then. King rolls over, picks up the phone next to his bed and calls Barry. "Hello?" Barry's mom answers the phone.

"Hi, Mrs. Meade, how are you today? This is King."

"I'm fine, King, and thank you for asking. I'm just making a pineapple upside down cake so Barry can take it to Danny's party. I think it is Danny's favorite, if I remember correctly."

King's stomach growls. "That sounds yummy. I think I can smell it over here."

King's boyish humor makes Delores laugh. "I bet you want to talk to Barry instead of me, right?"

"Well, I enjoy talking with you, ma'am, but I guess I did call to talk with your son."

"He is studying for his semesters, and I hate to disturb him, but it is getting pretty close to party time, and he needs to get ready for work at the club tonight. Hang on."

Barry picks up the phone on his desk and makes a howling sound right into the mouthpiece. "What goes on, my friend," Barry says happily.

"How ya feeling, Barry?" asks King.

"Pretty darn good! My dad thinks I cracked two or three ribs, but he wrapped me up like a Christmas present and gave me some pain pills so it wouldn't hurt so bad while they heal."

"That's cool. What time are you going to the party? I hope to get there at three to help set up.

"Yeah, I'll just go at three, too, and you can ride with me."

"Oh, perfect, Manfred Mann! I'll eat something and take a quick shower and you just honk the horn when you're outside."

After hanging up from his call, King rolls the other way right out of bed and immediately goes downstairs for breakfast. It is cold outside and overcast, but Ellie has made a fire in the great room fireplace, and she already has King's bacon frying after hearing him talking on the phone.

Scrambled eggs and bacon with a short stack of pancakes will give King the fuel to make it through the day. Breakfast is usually King's biggest meal each day as he doesn't want to take up time with eating once he gets going. He may make an exception today because Mr. Mosely is grilling chicken with his special barbecue sauce.

Fed and showered, King throws on his black knit turtleneck sweater, a pair of tight, lime green, wide-rail corduroy bell-bottoms and his black Italian leather knee boots pulled on and fitting nicely under the legs of his pants. He has not looked in a mirror, either out of confidence or disinterest, and has no desire to waste the time. Barry's horn honks out front. King grabs Danny's birthday present, the brand-new Cream release called Disraeli Gears, which contains the hit song *Sunshine of Your Love*, and runs down the basement stairs where his mom is washing clothes in the part of the basement that is not walled-off as the boy's "play" room. He gives her a quick kiss on the cheek and goes out to the garage.

King raises the garage door and is greeted by the grill of Barry's turquoise 1965 Valiant Safari wagon. The car is roaring James Brown's *Cold Sweat* on WROR, and King slides into the passenger side where he slaps Barry's palm to say hello. Barry has to wear his suit pants, tie and dress shoes for work, but he is sporting a multi-colored paisley shirt that covers up his rib swathe. "Nice shirt." King says, giving his approval as he lays his wrapped album on top of Mrs. Meade's covered cake. Barry's gift, which is Forever Changes by Love, lies wrapped under the cake. "How's your ribs?" King asks.

"It hurts, but Dad told me to keep breathing deeply so that I don't get pneumonia. He gave me some pain pills that take the pain away pretty well. I just took one again, so it should kick in, in a few minutes. What album did you get?"

King and the other future bandmates knew Danny was getting a stereo record player from his dad, and Mr. Mosely asked the boys to buy a record if they wanted to give gifts. The stereo will replace the 1959 blue and white portable Music Master High Fidelity record player Danny has used through his youth. It was not stereo, but it still introduced him to the genius and talent of The Beach Boys, The Temptations, Marvin Gaye, The Beatles and The Monkees, among many others.

His dad would use the Hi-Fi occasionally to listen to Tennessee Ernie Ford, Porter Wagoner and Howard Perkins, but the radio in the kitchen is what he likes to listen to most. He likes the DJs because they give the weather and other local news. Walter's friend Norman, who is a department manager at Sears, was able to get Walter a discounted price on the stereo for Danny, and he cannot wait to give it to his son. As Barry backs out of the Reed's driveway, King can see Kay outside riding Precious with her similar-aged cousin from Cleveland who has come to visit with his family for Thanksgiving. Barry beeps his horn and Kay returns the exchange with a peppy wave.

As soon as the clock strikes three, Jeff rushes home from Charlie's Market and finds his home unoccupied. His mom and Darren have gone to dinner at Frisch's Big Boy before they head into Appleton to the Southern Theatre where Hour of the Gun, with Jason Robards and James Garner, is playing. Darren loves anything that has to do with guns. The space and silence are ideal because Jeff's stomach is starting to get a bit tight when he thinks about hanging out with Alice, and he needs the space to contemplate and play the Yardbirds. He puts on Rave-Up and turns up the record player until the speakers beg for mercy. Jeff grabs a towel and leisurely strolls to the bathroom where there is no Darren. The hot water soaks his thick dark hair and rolls down his stocky body. That body had stopped runners cold as they tried to score a run for their team. No one could touch Jeff Lindor's home plate.

Jeff starts to shave his face, but then he considers that Alice has gotten to know his disheveled look and does not seem to mind. The school has not warned him, yet, either. He still splashes on some Dante and then picks out a perfect-fitting pair of Levi's, a white shirt with one-inch black polka dots and pulls on a gray V-neck sweater over the shirt. Before he goes out, he slides into his white, low-top Chucks. All of this primping and consideration is far more preparation for Danny's party than had Alice Engel not accepted his invitation. Jeff turns on the porch light for either his mom or himself, whoever arrives home first. He locks the front door and starts walking toward Danny's, which is only about a mile and a half away, passing the market at the half mile mark. It is a nice afternoon for walking, and he daydreams that he will be brought home in a Leland green TR3.

Danny and his dad begin firing up the coals and hickory wood that have been shoveled and tossed into the pit beneath the grill. Walter is anxious to try a new barbecue sauce called Salt Lick that Carl Lindor found while travelling through Texas. Carl bought it specifically for Walter because he knew of his love for a good barbecue. Carl found the taste to be like nothing he had tasted before. The sauce has a wonderful blend of sweet and tangy and that special sauce "forced" Carl to eat quite a bit more than he should have on an otherwise boring run through Texas. Danny turns up his transistor radio and laughs out loud when the DJ plays Fire by Jimi Hendrix. As he stokes the coals, he starts doing a crazy dance along with the fast music. His dad looks out the kitchen window while preparing the chicken and ribs, grinning at his beautiful son.

Barry and King roll up in the Valiant but park on the street so that Barry does not get blocked. Unfortunately Barry will not be able to eat the special birthday dinner with everyone, but little does he know that Walter has prepared a barbecued chicken breast for the piano prodigy, and his son's guardian angel, in the house oven. It will not be as tasty as what will come later, not having the hickory smoke laced in with the Salt Lick sauce, but it will be appreciated nonetheless.

"Hey, Barry! How are your ribs, my brother?" As King goes back to the car to get the presents and cake, Danny is very attentive to Barry, leaving the fire stoking duties for a minute while he gets a padded chair for his protector.

"Oh, thanks, Dan man. My ribs hurt a lot, but I am taking some pain pills my dad gave me."

Danny is overcome and moisture wells up in his eyes. "I am so, so sor . . ."

"*Stop right there.* You would have done the same for me. I am no hero, it was just what needed to be done, and I am not going to leave my friend hanging, please excuse the pun." Danny laughs, telling Barry that he will never forget it, and gets back to pushing the coals around and throwing on more hickory logs.

With presents in hand, King enters the house through the front door, instead of walking around back, to deliver the gifts to Mr. Mosely.

"Just set them on the dining room table, King, and thank you for your thoughtfulness. Are you giving Danny a record?"

"Yes, sir, and I can't wait to hear it on the new stereo! Barry bought him one, also," King says.

"You boys could play records all night, but we need to get up for church at seven thirty. If you could help me, we need to close up by ten o'clock tonight, OK?"

"I'll start playing some Perry Como at nine thirty. That will run 'em outta here," King says jokingly.

Walter continues the joke saying "Whoa, now, they may never come back if you do that. We would be the least *groovy* house on the block."

Walter and King hear the front door open and shortly after, Jeff turns the corner into the kitchen. "Good afternoon, Mr. Host-with-the-Most and King my friend."

"Welcome, Sir Jeff." Walter replies as he holds up his saucy hands. "I would shake your hand, but uh . . . ."

"No, no. That's fine, but man, does it ever smell great in here."

"This is that new barbecue sauce your dad brought me from Texas. When is he due in town, anyway? I want to tell him about this cookout tonight, if everyone likes the food."

"I have no doubt everyone will like the food, and I think he will be here Monday night. I can't wait to see him."

"I bet you can't, Jeff. He's a good man, and he sure does love you."

"I know, and I sure do love him."

"Did he ever get a phone put in at his place?"

"Yes, sir, he did. I will write down the number for you."

Jeff knows exactly where the Moselys keep their note pad and pencils. He reaches into the drawer, and writes down the number. "Thank you, Jeff. You boys go on out back and just lay that present on the table, there. Oh, Jeff, before you put the pad away, please make some sort of sign that says 'please' – and please say 'please' – 'go around back' and then get some tape out of this drawer and tape it to the outside of the front door. Then close the front door and lock it so that the guests will know to go around back. Turn on the porch light, too, please. It will get dark soon." Jeff does exactly as he is told and then goes out the back door to meet the others.

While he talks with Barry, Danny has dragged the ladder out of the garage and is running a string of light bulbs from the garage to the plug on the side of the house, held up high by a friendly, outstretched tree limb. Jeff comes out the back door and smells the hickory smoke.

"Far out! I love it when your dad barbecues!" Jeff shouts without reserve.

"Here, plug this in and welcome," Danny shouts from atop the ladder. Jeff takes the plug end of the string of lights and plugs it into the outlet on the outside wall of the house. All but two of the bulbs illuminate.

King offers to go get some bulbs in the garage and Danny steps down the ladder and moves into place for the first bulb replacement. *Pop!* Danny drops the bad bulb he has removed from the string, and it hits the hard ladder instead of the soft ground leaving pieces of broken glass all around the drop zone. King looks at the mess as he delivers the new bulbs, looks at Danny as if to say a sarcastic 'great job', then dutifully turns around to get the broom out of the garage. Upon his return, King starts sweeping as Jeff picks up the big pieces. "It's a good thing it's your birthday, Mr. Sixteen," Jeff says.

Car doors are heard and then Hannah and Nick round the corner. "Happy birthday, Danny . . . again! Wow, does it ever smell good back here."

"Hey, friends! There are folding chairs from church up against the garage over there if you want to sit down. Otherwise, it's good to see you and thanks for coming. Hey, this is Jeff, Barry with the cracked ribs, and King. Jeff, Barry and King, you know Hannah but please meet Nick. Each say hello to each other, Nick asks Barry about his ribs and then the obligatory question is asked. "King? Oh, I have been waiting to meet you. Danny talks about you and your friendship a lot. How'd you get that name?"

"It's a long and boring story," King replies with the bottom half of his face presenting a phony smile and the top half providing no expression whatsoever.

"Well, I think it is interesting, and we have all afternoon," Hannah responds quickly. "I am assuming it is not a nickname."

"You are right, Hannah." Jeff walks a few steps over to the barbecue pit and lights up a Camel, knowing the story all too well.

"My mom loves Nat King Cole, and voila!" King says as he bows in mock pomposity.

"Well, that is an interesting story, and it is a pleasure to finally know it, King. Is your dad inside, Danny?" Hannah asks as she walks over and hugs Danny around his waist while burying her head in his chest. Danny hugs back and kisses Hannah on top of the head.

"Yes, he is in the kitchen preparing the food. I know he would love to see you if you want to go in." Hannah lets go of Danny, announces she will return soon, and heads for the back door. Nick and Jeff have hit it off (Nick smokes, too) and are discussing The Yardbirds. King takes the broken glass he has swept up into the dustpan and dumps it in the trash can where Jeff has unloaded his big pieces.

Barry is not saying much as he drifts in and out of a drug-induced false reality. The pain pill is doing its job, but sitting and staring off into space is not Barry, so he reaches into his jacket and pulls Benny out of his pocket. He pops one into his mouth and swallows it without water. Soon, Barry will regain his other, much more alert drug-induced false reality, which should prepare him for his long night of playing *Autumn Leaves*, *Moon River*, and other hits and standards.

The southern Ohio sunset is about forty-five minutes from consummation, but the trees along the Mosely property line, even though leafless, provide a filter. Behind them, one can see a glimmer of light bouncing off the Scioto River that winds through some of the most fertile soil in the world, just on the other side of Route 43. In the early spring, the Scioto will flood and then recede, leaving the silt for farmers to grow their crops.

The string of lights has become meaningful now, and in a few minutes, a flood light powered by a twenty-five-foot husky and weather-resistant extension cord, run from the back porch, will be put into service over the barbecue grill. It is as if it is Walter's stage. Right now, though, Walter has waved Jeff and King into the house and asks them to make sure the stereo is working. He wants to give it to Danny early so that all of Danny's guests can enjoy the stereophonic sounds.

It is about four thirty, and the guests seem to roll in all at the same time. Mike and Bill walk into the backyard with Shannon and Rhonda. "Did you guys come together?" asks Danny.

Bill answers "No, we just met up out front after we parked. Is it OK if we parked in front of your neighbor's house?"

"Yeah, that's fine. They know we're having a party and might come over for some of dad's barbecue."

"Oh, man. I forgot he is barbecuing. Yummy!" Mike says, rubbing his hands on his rotund stomach. Mr. Mosely comes out of the back porch with a large cooler full of ice and different kinds of pop, especially root beer, his son's favorite. He pulls two bottle openers out of his back pocket, says hello to everyone, and asks them to please not lose the openers or else they will get mighty dry.

Danny can see people up in the screened-in back porch, but he is not sure what they are doing.

"Come up here with me, Danny. I want to show you something. Come on, Barry," Walter sheepishly requests. Danny knows it must be a cake, and he is right, but as soon as he opens the screen door, Hannah, Jeff, King, and Mr. Mosely yell happy birthday and Jeff drops a brand-new stereo needle down on *Hey Grandma*, the opening track of the first Moby Grape album that Danny thought he had worn out. Danny stares at the two speakers that pull away from the turntable, looks at his dad with confusion on his face and yells over the Grape, "Dad, you did not buy me a stereo, right? It's just a loaner for tonight, right?"

"I hate to tell you, son, but it's all yours, and I wanted to give it to you early so everyone could enjoy it with you. Now blow out the sixteen candles Hannah took the time to light."

Danny blows out his candles and stoops down to the best listening position and cannot believe what he is hearing. "I have never heard that guitar part before and all those vocals. That is heavy." Everyone chuckles and then King just starts singing the happy birthday song over top of *Mr. Blues,* and everyone joins in.

"Can we give him our presents, Mr. Mosely?" asks Barry.

"Yes, now would be a great time for that." Danny's three close friends present their square, flat gifts to the birthday boy.

"Oh, so I bet Dad told you guys . . ."

"Yep, and I can't wait to hear the one I got you on that outasite player. That thing sounds so groovy!" King gushes.

Danny unwraps the three albums and loves them all. "We will eat cake after dinner, kids, and we will eat about six o'clock. Does that sound good?" Everyone responds with enthusiastic affirmation and file back down the steps and into the dimly lit yard.

The light over the garage is on as well, and the back porch light helps. Mr. Mosely tells Barry to come inside and eat his specially prepared chicken before he leaves. Barry thanks Mr. Mosely and tells him he will be in in a few minutes, but he is not really hungry. Benny has hijacked his stomach and food doesn't appeal to him just now. Walter asks Jeff and Hannah to help him carry the trays of barbecue chicken breasts out to the grill. Hannah jumps up, but Jeff stands for a few seconds just looking up the driveway toward the street. He is hoping he sees a little green sports car pull up soon.

Barry holds the back porch door open for the would-be caterers and then runs in to where the stereo is residing. Side one of Moby Grape has just finished, and Barry pops the plastic on Love's *Forever Changes.* He takes Moby Grape off and carefully returns it to its rather controversial cover, puts side one of this brand new, never-before-played album on the new system, and the sound is breath-taking. There are strings on the song, and Arthur Lee's voice is mixed with Bryan MacLean's to project a dark and imposing tone.

It's beautiful, and Barry creates a dining spot in a chair between the speakers so that he can absorb the music before he needs to leave for work, which will be in about twenty minutes. There is no preparation needed for Barry, once he sits down at the Country Club baby grand piano. He knows all the songs without music, so he usually comes in about two minutes before start time.

Just to be kind, Barry goes into the kitchen and finds a covered plate filled with barbecued chicken, baked beans and two rolls. He picks at the chicken, but his taste buds are just about non-functional. Two bites of baked beans and another bite of chicken, and Barry slides the rest of what is on his plate off and into the trash. He goes to the bathroom and washes his hands, swishes some water around in his mouth, and goes out to the backyard. "Thank you for the dinner, Mr. Mosely. Very good, as always."

"You are very welcome, Barry, and I am glad you were able to enjoy some of the party."

Barry says goodbye to his friends in different parts of the yard as he makes his way to his car. Jeff is the last guest he sees. "What are you doing up here by yourself, Jeff?" Barry asks as he walks toward his car.

"Oh, just waiting for a friend. Plus, I can smoke more freely up here. I'm not sure if my friend knows where we are, you know."

"Sure. I hope they arrive soon so you don't miss the party."

Barry gets into his car, starts it up, and notices headlights behind him as if the driver is waiting for Barry to leave, which he does promptly. The headlights slide right into the vacancy Barry created, but the car does not shut off immediately. The radio is set on WROR, and the night-time DJ is playing *What a Wonderful World* by Louis Armstrong. As Satchmo's raspy croon puts the song to bed, the car is turned off, the small door opens, and a thin female leg covered in saffron-colored, wide-rail cords, gets out. The leg just hangs there as the person attached to the leg leans over and drops a Gitane on the road and squashes it out with a dark brown suede ankle-high boot, shod with a low heel.

Jeff has walked up closer to the party, not realizing a new car had pulled into the parking space. As the sun is setting, the temperature has dropped to a very cool thirty-four degrees. With his back to the street, Jeff pulls out another Camel, but as he fishes in his pocket for his lighter, another lighter flashes in front of his face. "Is this what you need?" says a familiar, friendly voice. Jeff coolly touches the carefully packed end of his cigarette to the flame.

When the lighter lid snaps shut, Jeff's eyes settle on the prettiest face he's ever seen. "What great timing and welcome." Jeff sounds surprisingly confident and in control as he greets his friend, but he is not sure if he should hug Alice or not. "I guess my directions were OK. Come on into the backyard so I can introduce you to everyone." Completely at ease,

Alice takes Jeff's arm and allows herself to be led toward the light, voices, and music.

Danny sees her first and yells a big welcome to the party's new guest. "It's almost dinner time, Alice. I hope you are hungry." Alice just waves and shines her insanely captivating smile. She is southern Ohio's version of Jean Shrimpton with honey-blond hair, and she knows that. Alice does not play down her stunning beauty, but she does not flaunt it either, at least not in a vulgar way. Just showing up at Danny's party says something amiable about her character.

Those who may have had a begrudging thought about the rich girl on the hill, who receives all the attention when cheerleading at the school for the Pumas just might be able to stop fighting their natural urge to like Alice. Sure, Alice's thigh-length suede, sheepskin, shearling Afghan coat doesn't exactly blend in, but Alice has never wanted to blend in. She loves fine clothes and dressing to impress, and the true beauty of Alice is that she wants others to enjoy those finer things with her. She would give that three-hundred-dollar coat to a stranger if that was what was needed at the time.

Mr. Mosely is just making his last trip from the house to the grill and sees Alice. "Well, another dinner guest. Pardon the apron. I am Danny's dad, Walt Mosely. What is your name?"

"Alice, sir. It is very nice to meet you and thank you for allowing me to invade."

"You are welcome here any time, Alice. I hope you enjoy the party, and I hope you are hungry." As Mr. Mosely walks toward the grill, Jeff leans his head only a short distance down to the five-foot eight Alice's ear. "The fruit doesn't fall far from the tree." It is just a cute comment about both Danny and his dad saying "I hope you are hungry," and Alice gets it with a chuckle.

Jeff had not been that close to Alice's ear at school, so he had never had the pleasure of experiencing her chosen fragrance, which does for the nose what her beauty does for the eyes. "What perfume are you wearing?" Jeff asks as if he knows something about perfume.

"It's called Climat by Lancôme. I was given a bottle when we were in Paris last June. You know, they wanted us to buy some for the stores. It's not too strong, is it?"

"Oh, no! No. It's just right, believe me."

"Why, do you like it?" Alice asks with a playful grin as she fans her hands toward his nose. Jeff just smiles and pulls his friend into the backyard where he begins to introduce Alice to the various friends of his and Danny's scattered throughout the backyard. As she and Jeff walk through the crowd, Jeff finds that Alice can have a conversation with anyone about anything, and it doesn't sound phony.

The music has stopped, and Jeff jumps at the chance to play *Over Under Sideways Down* by The Yardbirds featuring Beck on all the tracks. The drums and bass guitar on *Lost Woman* start rolling out of the new stereo speakers like Jeff has never heard them before, and his senses are ignited with passion as he hears his favorite guitarist while the most beautiful girl in the city, at least, waits outside for him. Some of the guests are dancing, but most are talking as Jeff returns to the backyard. He looks around and does not immediately see Alice. She is over by Mr. Mosely and Hannah, helping cook the dinner. Jeff smiles and shakes a lowered head, not really believing what a truly groovy night this is.

King is a bit taken aback by Alice's presence and punches Jeff on the upper arm. "She's fantastic, Jeff. How did . . . when did . . . did Danny invite her?"

"No, man. I saw her at Charlie's and asked her if she wanted to come by, not thinking she'd say yes, but she did. I called Danny as I was leaving work and asked him if it was OK if she came."

"Amazing. That's truly outasite, especially for a fink like you." Jeff reaches out a playful fist toward King's face. "I can't believe she shops at Charlie's." King continues his gush of admiration. "She seems really nice. I mean, she's over there helping Mr. Mosely already. I guess she doesn't care if she gets barbecue sauce on those fifty-dollar pants."

Jeff laughs. "I guess not. She probably has a key to the store and can just go in and get another pair."

The rest of the evening is spent dancing, talking, laughing, and eating Walter's barbecued chicken, of which there were few leftovers. The new sauce is a hit, and Walter cannot wait to call Carl Lindor on Monday evening to thank him. The highlight of the evening, though, is near the end when Danny, King, and Jeff pull out Danny's guitar and sing a few songs together, passing the guitar to whomever knows the song best.

King and Danny have played through several songs during visits to each other's homes, but one could not label those indifferent road tests in front of the TV as rehearsals. Jeff has only added fancy hot licks whenever he joined the movie nights, but the lack of collaboration is hardly noticeable as the three mesmerize the guests with *Mushroom Clouds* by Love and *No Reply* by The Beatles (King beats on a chair with Walter's spatula).

Both songs are complete with more than decent three-part harmony, but when Jeff starts picking the opening notes to Simon and Garfunkel's *Sounds of Silence*, audible gasps hang in the cold night air. This reaction is a signal to the new band that they are cool, *very* cool. So much so that Diana Peterson rushes to the three stars of the night, after their song is finished, and asks them to play at her birthday party in February. "Even if it's only just a few songs," she begs the three musicians. Danny, King, and Jeff look at each other, turn, and accept the offer.

CHAPTER
SEVEN

King, Jeff, Hannah, Danny, and Alice all help Mr. Mosely clean up the remains of the party, finishing right about ten o'clock. "Barry should be here any minute to take me home," King says. "Is it OK if I wait out on the front porch, Mr. Mosely?"

"King, stop it. Of course, you're welcome to wait for Barry but wait in here. It's cold out there without a crowd of people."

Hannah gives Danny a cozy hug and rubs Mr. Mosely's hand as she thanks the two before she heads out to her car. "See you tomorrow, fellows." she says sweetly as a gentle reminder to get some sleep, soon. She does this so they can worship without head-bobbing in the morning.

"How cool! Barry just pulled in. Perfect timing, so I will see you Monday at school, Danny, if not before. Great night, everyone, and happy birthday my friend!" King certifies as he runs out the door, not to keep Barry waiting.

"May I walk you to your car, madam?" Jeff says to Alice with a hokey-sounding French accent, resembling Pepé Le Pew much more than Maurice Chevalier.

"I believe I am a mademoiselle, and yes, that would be lovely." Jeff and Alice thank the Mosely men, and Jeff tells Danny he is really looking forward to Saturday's rehearsal.

Danny closes and locks the front door behind the two. "The food was fantastic, Dad! The night was perfect. Thank you so much." Danny hugs his dad for a long time, and Walter hugs back with loving warmth that could heat their home. Danny ends the hug with "let's get some sleep."

Jeff and Alice have made it to her car. "Oh, wow! I wish I could see this baby better. Are you going to ride with the top off?"

"Yes, and you are going to ride that way too, unless you would rather walk home."

"Well, if I have a choice, I think I could suffer through a ride in a TR3 with a pretty girl." Alice laughs and thanks Jeff for the compliment. She tells Jeff to get in as she turns the key that ignites the sensationally cool-sounding engine. She opens the thermostat wide for the topless winter ride and then reaches across Jeff's lap and into the glove compartment where she pulls out her half-smoked pack of Gitanes. "I noticed you didn't smoke all night. It would have been OK, you know."

She accepts Jeff's light, and Jeff lights his Camel, too. "I'm a cheerleader. I would be off the team in a second if I outwardly smoked. Coach Freel doesn't really care that we are smokers, but the rule is no public smoking, and I don't want to get the boot, as John Lennon might say. You want to ride around for a while? It seems so early."

"Drive on."

Alice shifts into first and pulls out onto Old River Road, quickly finding second and third gears. Jeff can tell she is headed out to 43. Feeling light as a feather, he puts his head back and absorbs every ounce of what is happening at this moment in time. He is in disbelief, but somehow very comfortable. Alice reaches fourth gear on the four-lane highway and asks Jeff to flip the switch for overdrive. He is not sure which switch is his target, but without belittling the male beside her, Alice simply points out the toggle, and Jeff performs his duty as co-pilot.

"That was an outasite party, wasn't it?" Alice says.

"Yes, it was. Danny has the best dad ever, and all of Danny's friends are really nice, too."

"What happened to his mom?"

"I'm not sure of all the details, but she died when he was very young, and Mr. Mosely just never remarried. He works really hard to give Danny the best life he can, and their church has really helped them, too. Danny loves his church and cleans it to earn money."

"That's nice. I believe Hannah said she goes to church with Danny."

"Yeah, that's right."

"That is sad about his mom, but he seems to have turned out well."

"He's a great guy. Real dependable, but he'll talk your ears off about Jesus if you give him half a chance."

"I could probably use a dose of that conversation. My family does not go to church, and sometimes, I do wonder about it."

"Well, Danny would be the guy to talk with, then."

Alice takes a quick turn off 43 onto the road that runs in front of the school. "I love taking this car over Ox Tail Hill. She's at her best, and I love the way she handles. It might get a little fast around the curves. Are you OK with that?"

"I would love to see how both of you take these curves. Let's go."

Alice takes the sports car to the stop sign and turns right without stopping. The nighttime Grand Prix has begun. The hill starts its ascent quickly as Alice shifts the car into third gear. There have been only minor curves so far, not even worth a down-shift. Jeff lights a Camel and sits back, watching the road that is illuminated by the headlights.

WROR is playing *Jackson* by Johnny and June Carter Cash, and both sing along as if they were on a talent show while Alice maneuvers the TR3 through its paces. The road levels off some, but the curves are worse. There is jagged rock on the left side and a steep drop on the right and they are traveling at a high rate of speed, but Alice shifts through each turn like a pro. This hill is a third again higher than Marigold, and the road is narrow and winding, not as well maintained. Like a roller coaster, Alice takes the last rise that is followed by the descent.

Jeff knows this road well, having traveled it many times to teammate's homes after baseball games. Like Marigold Road, people use this road to cross over to the main Route 159 that will eventually take one to Paradise Park. Ox Tail Hill is just a little farther north. Jeff is familiar with a curve that is coming up that bears sharply to the left and then back again. Too many people have run right off the edge and traveled halfway down the side of the hill, earning it a guard rail and the usual 'Dead Man's Curve' moniker, but the guard rail is crumpled by those too inebriated, too sleepy, or just too slow to make the turn. Alice tries to keep her car in third as much as possible down the hill, letting the British design keep it on the road. Jeff can see the guard rail in the headlights, and it is coming up fast.

Just twenty feet before the curve, Alice finally shifts down to second and successfully turns the wheel left making the first part of the dogleg, but in a quick second she sees a medium-sized animal with white stripes on its back crossing the road and swerves over to the on-coming lane, which is aiming the car at the rocky hillside. After passing the animal, she tries to pull it back to the right to follow the road, but when she does, the backend of the TR3 decides to take the lead, and they are in a noisy, rubber-smoking spin.

The tail goes all the way around, and the two inside the car are not sure if they will take flight or plow into the rocky face of the hill. Alice stops the spin by breaking and steering into the spin perfectly, but the car is still in motion aimed at the rocks. Alice straightens the car out, and it hops sideways to a stop just inches from the rocks that would have put a nice sized gash in her baby, not to mention her head if the edge of one of the rocks was just a little lower.

"You really know how to make an otherwise ordinary night very exciting, Alice," Jeff says calmly as if nothing much is happening.

"I am so sorry, Jeff. Are you OK?

"Of course. What a great driver you are. You kept all three of us alive."

"Three?"

"You, me, and the skunk." After rumpling up her face and playfully hitting Jeff on the thigh, Alice puts the car in first and gets over into the right lane while Jeff lights a Camel. She continues down the hill at a safer speed but still takes the curves without braking.

"Do you want a fag?" Jeff asks.

"No, I'll wait until we're at the bottom. I like how you use that British term, fag. Short for fagerette." The WROR nighttime DJ thinks it is a good time to play *I Think We're Alone Now* by Tommy James, and the two teens in the sports car speed off down the hill and onto the flat, less curvy road. "Let's go all the way into Appleton and back around to 43 to go home, OK?"

"Well, let me check my calendar . . . . You are in luck, young lady. I see no conflicts. Let's go."

"What about that late presidential dinner?"

"And miss a trip around town with Alice Engel? Balderdash! Lyndon can wait. Onward!" Alice laughs out loud and gets a little rubber as she turns south onto Route 159. She does not exceed the speed limit, knowing all too well the Appleton boys in blue love to catch Marigold teens speeding and/or drunk.

It's a crisp and starry night as they enter the last hour of Saturday and neither seems to want the day to end anytime soon. The DJ furnishes a lush backdrop with a song by The Moody Blues called *Nights in White Satin* as the TR3 passes the entrance to Saunders Hollow Road that would have taken the two over Marigold Hill. Jeff asks if his driver would like to stop at the US Diner for a late-night bite to eat. "Perfect!" says Alice and she continues on with Marvin Gaye and Tammy Terrell tearing up *This Precious Love*.

The US Diner is the only twenty-four-hour eatery in town, and it is crowded on a Saturday night in Appleton. There is a table for two in the corner next to the kitchen doors, and Alice and Jeff land there. They both order breakfast for dinner from a lady in her fifties wearing a white apron and then begin to tell each other about their lives. Jeff is guarded about Darren because he doesn't consider Darren to be a part of his life. Darren is a menace, but Jeff does talk excitedly about his dad coming home on Monday. "You love your dad, don't you? I love the way you talk about him," Alice says warmly.

"He's always been a truck driver, gone a lot, but I still miss him in my house. Still, I get to stay with him when he is here, which usually lasts only four days at the longest. I'm really glad you came to the party tonight. You got to go slummin'," Jeff quips.

After a ten-second hour of Alice looking down at her plate, she looks up and right into her friend's eyes. "Jeff. Don't *ever* say that to me, again. I had a wonderful time, tonight, with good and fun people, and there is no price for that. *I* am not rich; my dad is. Yes, I have a fancy little car and groovy clothes, and I love having all those things, but helping Danny's dad get the chicken cooked and served and sitting here with you tonight is what is truly important to me."

Alice stops for a few seconds, continuing to look Jeff in the eyes to emphasize her unfeigned honesty. "I could have gone to Sherbrick Academy, ya know, but I pleaded with my dad not to send me there. I never wanted to be a Sherbrick girl. I *am* really happy my family has a bunch of money and thankfully they are not snobs, but I don't want to believe you think that way of me. I'm just like you, Jeff. Don't you see that?"

"I'm sorry, Alice, but you *are* rich, and you are *not* like me. You don't have divorced parents and a foul drunk living in your house beating up your mom. Please don't pretend you are like me. I wouldn't wish that on you, anyway."

"Are you with me tonight because you think I'm rich or because you enjoy my company?" Alice looks down at her plate.

She nervously finishes her meal, and they both light cigarettes from their own packs. Jeff finally speaks, and does so with thoughtful composure. "I have enjoyed your company and our conversations since the beginning of the school year. I was surprised that you would talk to me or be seen with me at all."

"Why would you *think* that?"

"Well, you can have any guy you want for conversations or dates or whatever, even seniors or probably college guys. I'm a river brat from a broken home who loves to play rock guitar. Not exactly the catch of the day."

"Please don't describe yourself that way, as if there is some part of it that is unattractive. I talk to you because you are funny and smart and interesting. We are more alike than you think, Mr. Lindor, and all I know is that I have had one of the best evenings out that I can remember. You're a good man, Jeff and thank you for inviting me to the party and spending time with me tonight."

Alice takes Jeff's left hand that is resting on the table and uses her other hand to push his long, dark hair back out of his face. Jeff is staring at Alice with a face that conjures up the boy he used to be before Darren and Camels and divorce. His eyes get moist as he finds solace in Alice's beautiful face, but he quickly catches himself and sits way back in his chair. "Whew, we need to get going. It's after midnight, and I don't want your dad to get mad at me." They put their cigarettes out in their plates, and Jeff pays at the cash register. He brought money hoping for a night like this, and God heard Jeff's prayer, even if Jeff does not believe there is a God who loves him.

The ride home is quiet, with some small talk, a few laughs, and WROR. Jeff guides Alice through Marigold to his house where they stop across the street. The porch light is not on, and the blue light of a black and white TV's test pattern beams through the dark night. "That was fun, Alice, even if you did almost kill us." Jeff grins.

"It was a wonderful evening, Jeff. I mean it, and I hope we can do it again soon."

"I know I will see you at school on Monday, right? I hope you have a good day tomorrow, and I hope I didn't keep you out too late."

"You didn't. You have a nice day tomorrow too, and I'm excited for you to see your dad on Monday."

"Thanks! I'm excited, too." Jeff leans over and gives Alice a kiss on the cheek and squeezes her hand that rests on the stick shift ball. Jeff opens the door of the TR3 and lifts his big body out into the street.

Jeff waves from his waist, flicks his hair out of his eyes, and walks toward his house. He listens to the sports car rev up and roll from the gravel on the road's shoulder to the blacktop and away into the night, headed for the house on the hill. Judging by sound, Alice is far enough away that she will not see him, so Jeff turns to watch the taillights fade out of view while simultaneously digging a Camel out of his pocket.

He lights it and embraces the calming effect of the nicotine like an old friend. Jeff stops on the front porch steps and ponders whether she will ever have a desire to see him again. Jeff has not had the best example of what and who a woman should be, but he tries not to let that taint his honest feelings for someone who has started excavating his heart.

Alice Engel is more special than Jeff had imagined, but he is not the type to be putty in her well-manicured hands. Without warning, he is confused and perplexed. Alice is no longer just a friend, so how should he greet her on Monday? Headlights are coming down the street as he takes his last drag off his fag. He stands to go up the steps of his porch when the headlights stop. He hears a familiar sounding engine and a car door close while the engine continues to run. A silhouette walks toward him until he sees Alice in whatever light has made its way to the street. Her last few steps are quick, and then Alice Engel buries herself in Jeff Lindor's broad chest with her arms thrown around him tightly as if they are never to be pried loose.

Jeff wraps his arms around her shoulders and puts his hand on the back of her head. He lays his cheek on the top of Alice's head with his hair falling over her face and just rests there. They stand for what seems like a solid minute, just comforting each other and speaking in a whole different language. Jeff finally pulls back slightly, cups Alice's beautiful face in his husky hands, leans down and softly touches his lips to hers. Alice presses in with fiery passion, and the two kiss for at least a minute.

Alice slowly and reluctantly stops the kiss, looks up into Jeff's eyes and whispers, "I need to go now. I will see you Monday." Alice turns and runs toward her car as if her feet are not touching the ground. The car door closes, first gear is engaged, and off she roars into the foggy night. Jeff doesn't want to move, but his stomach is jumping, and his heart is racing. Then, without any desire to control it, Jeff jumps straight up into the air and leans his head back on his clasped hands. He knows he will never be the same after tonight.

Reality screams in Jeff's face as he enters his home and finds Darren puking in the bathroom. Jeff starts to ask him if he is OK, but Jeff's feelings for Darren are so bitter and encrusted with distain, he walks directly upstairs and into his room, closing the door and locking it behind him. Jeff doesn't work until one in the afternoon because it is now Sunday, and the local laws require no businesses be open until one p.m. other than vital services. He strips down to his briefs and puts on his softest t-shirt for sleeping. Jeff stares up at his ceiling while his mind runs through the previous seven hours like a movie, and with those sublime images secure, he drifts off to sleep not to wake until late morning.

As the sun shows itself in the valley of Upper Marigold, Barry did not sleep well due to the pain and is having his ribs re-wrapped by his dad after a warm bath. Benny has helped Barry get started this magnificent Sunday morning because he needs to work the after-church lunch at the club, which starts at noon. The club does not adhere to the local laws because they are a private organization, and well, most of the lawmakers are members and want their lunch at noon on Sundays after church.

After Dr. Meade finishes the wrap, he reminds his son to take the pain pill he gave him as he helps Barry put on his white shirt. "See you downstairs for breakfast, son. I think your mom went all out this morning. I smell bacon and biscuits. Hurry down, and I want you to get a haircut tomorrow. I know the kids are wearing it longer these days, but we don't want people to associate you with those hippie kids."

"See you downstairs in a few minutes, Dad, and thanks for the wrap."

Barry happily takes his Numorphan with the water that had been beside his bed all night. He pushes his hair back so that it does not look as long to his dad and heads downstairs trying to prepare his tight stomach for his mom's breakfast feast. Barry hears his mom calling Kay in from the barn announcing that breakfast is ready, and he and Kay meet at the table at about the same time. "How are your ribs, my poor brother?" his sister asks lovingly.

"They still hurt a lot, sis, but Dad wrapped them up again, and I took a pill for the pain. I will be very glad when this is all healed, that's for sure." Delores interrupts her children's conversation to ask them how they want their eggs.

Back down Marigold Road, Mr. Mosely and Danny climbed out of bed at about seven and are now at church early where they have greeted their brothers and sisters in Christ. Danny goes directly to the pulpit platform in the sanctuary where he says a cheery "good morning" to the organist Mrs. Myrtle Harlan. He, then, takes his acoustic guitar out of its case and straps it on over his shoulder. Not that many hours ago, this very same guitar was being passed around by his friends and used to entertain a backyard full of people with popular rock songs of the day. This morning, however, Danny will prayerfully pour his heart into strumming the chords to the songs chosen for the service by Minister Blanton. Danny and Mrs. Harlan will play the beautiful old hymn *How Great Thou Art*, recently recorded and released by Elvis.

With Christmas on its way, Danny is excited to find he will play guitar and lead the congregation in singing *O Come O Come Emanuel*, a song of which he is very familiar and loves to sing. Danny feels at home on this platform with these people and with guitar in hand. While he stands holding his guitar, and Mrs. Harlan familiarizes herself with her sheet music, he bows his head to give thanks to Jesus for the ability to serve Him musically and to inspire a room full of people to love the Lord as he does. Mrs. Harlan is probably around fifty years of age and a well-trained organist. She loves the old hymns and fills the sanctuary with beautiful music each Sunday, but she does not hesitate to help Danny arrange any song that he writes or anything new that Danny might find exciting and glorifying to the Lord.

"How does it feel to be sixteen, Mr. Mosely?"

"My beard grew four inches, last night after midnight, and my voice got lower," Danny says with a pseudo-serious face.

Mrs. Harlan laughs from her belly. "Are you playing bass on How Great, Danny, or guitar?" Mrs. Harlan is considering the voicings she will play on the organ. There is no need for foot pedals if Danny is on bass.

"Well, if I have a choice, I *would* enjoy playing bass, if that doesn't mess you up, Mrs. Harlan."

"Oh, not at all, Danny. It will give my old feet a break."

They both chuckle as Danny takes off his guitar and reaches over to the back of the amp head to switch on the new Fender Bassman. As he tunes the four fat strings of the cherry red Gibson bass to the piano, which is sitting in between him and Mrs. Harlan for easy access, Danny listens closely to the clarity of the notes vibrating through the new bass cabinet. "You had better turn it down, my boy, or they will run us out of here this morning," Mrs. Harlan warns last night's rock star.

After a minute of tuning, listening, and thinking about the caution prescribed by his organist, Danny looks up and over at her and expresses a thought that has been brewing for months. "Mrs. Harlan, there is a pretty big group of teenagers here these days, and there are so many temptations in the world. Those kids, and me being one of them, need to know the Word of God, but I think they aren't really listening. It's kinda like the church is not speaking their language or something. I have friends at school who don't mind hearing me talk about Jesus, but they don't really want to come to church because they say it smells like old people. Sorry, but I'm just being honest."

"That's OK, Danny. Go ahead."

"I wonder if Pastor Pete and Mr. Blanton might be open to a couple of ideas I have, not to be disrespectful or anything? I've been wondering if the teens would sing along more if the music *sounded* like the stuff they listen to Monday through Saturday, except with the Lord's words as lyrics? I guess it would be sorta like hymns with drums."

"That's a good question, and it sounds like the Spirit is at work in you, young man. Maybe you could do something in the teen room someday, with Pastor Pete's approval, of course."

"Yeah! Like, a worship service with a modern feel that doesn't stray from the truth. I'll ask him if he would set aside some time to talk with me about it."

"I am sure he will, my boy. You truly have the Spirit in you, Danny. You are a breath of fresh air to my ears."

"Thank you, Mrs. Harlan. You've sure inspired me to play my best and to not settle for mediocrity. It's always good to rap, I mean, talk with you."

"Oh my. It is always good to *rap* with you, too." Both faces beam with joy.

***

In Upper Marigold King opens his eyes from a long night's sleep. It is eleven o'clock, and King immediately turns on his radio. The last half of *Ode to Billie Joe* plays out while King lies in his bed and listens. He does not enjoy jumping out of bed unless there is something very special happening or school beckons, but this song is perfect to wake up to on a late autumn Sunday morning. The song tells its story through a lethargic, unaffected but effective female southern drawl.

The DJ has been up for hours though and follows the slow tale of Billie Joe with the lively and eternally soulful *I've Been Lonely Too Long* by The Rascals, which helps King raise himself up on both straight arms to look out of his windows. It seems that gray and brown are the only colors that ever survive the onslaught of cold weather, and that palette does not excite the sensitive young man. In fact, King becomes quite melancholy after very many days without the sunshine.

In a flash, a ray of light bursts into his mind as he remembers that Ed Sullivan has The Beatles featured on his show tonight. The last time they were on, the performance was just a movie of them singing their songs, but he hopes it is them in the flesh in the CBS Studio 50 Theatre tonight. This is enough to get King out of bed and downstairs to hug his mom and sit in the big oversized chair with his dad as he reads the paper and a magazine or two. Sam has gone to the school to run laps on the track and take himself through various other body-sculpting exercises. He will meet some friends for lunch at one o'clock at Fran's Cafe in Marigold, located on Route 43, with an entrance from Old River Road as well.

"The Beatles are on Sullivan, tonight, Dad. You wanna watch them with me?"

"Uh, we'll see. They're not my favorite musical combo, but I might listen in. Tell your mom about it though. I think she likes some of the new bands." As if on cue, Ellie enters the room with a tray full of quarter-cut ham salad sandwiches.

"How about finger sandwiches for my boys?" Gordon and King immediately reach their hands in for the pre-lunch treats, thanking Ellie profusely. "What are you guys talking about this morning, or is it guy stuff?"

Gordon looks up from his paper. "King said The Beatles are on Sullivan tonight, and I told him he should let you know because you like them, right?"

"Yes, I think I do, my dear. Their music is everywhere these days, and I can't really help hearing them more and more. I suppose I've really grown to like them. I'm not sure what they are singing about sometimes, but . . . let's see . . . *Eleanor Rigby* and *Yesterday* are really pretty songs. Is *God Only Knows* one of theirs, as well?"

"No, Mom. The Beach Boys sing that song."

"How about *Homeward Bound* or *We Can Work It Out?*"

"Ding, ding, ding! *Homeward Bound* is by Simon and Garfunkle, but The Beatles sing *We Can Work It Out*. Not bad for a mom," King says with a huge grin, and Ellie laughs.

"Garfinkle? What kind of name is that?" Gordon quips for fun.

"It's Gar-*funk*-el, old man, and he's a really good singer. I bet you would like him, Dad."

"Maybe. Let me know when I can see them, and I will watch with you."

"Ok, and we'll turn it up real loud," King jokes as he uses two hands to turn an imaginary, oversized volume knob to the right. Gordon tends to enjoy softer music, and King knows his dad might actually enjoy Simon & Garfunkel because they are one of the softer new bands. King just likes to pick fun at his dad, and Gordon loves it when he does.

"Oh, man, I'm glad I remembered this. Is it OK if we have a band practice in the basement on Saturday? We were talking about it on the hike. I'm going to bring the drum set home from school, and Jeff and Barry and Danny and I are going to start a band. Diana Peterson already asked us if we would play for her birthday party in February after she heard us last night."

Ellie's interest is piqued. "You played last night? Where? At Danny's party?"

"Yes, and they loved us, Mom. Barry wasn't there, so we'll sound even better when he adds his parts, but everybody thought we were outasite!"

"I'm so proud of you, King. That is going to be really fun for you, and you will learn a lot about the music business."

"I bet we will. I hope we start making some money. I kinda want it to be my job. I'm not really big on lawn mowing or packing grocery bags."

"Yes, I've noticed." Gordon scowls playfully, looking over the top of his readers at King with one eyebrow raised.

"Gordon. Not every son has to take that path and maybe this will lead to an income."

"I am certainly outnumbered here with two artists against me." Gordon retreats into his comfortable chair with one arm around his son's shoulders.

"Anyway, we won't charge Diana anything, but maybe we can play some school events and things."

"That's really exciting, King. Your dad will need to give the OK for a rehearsal though. I'm sure it won't be quiet."

Gordon ventures into the murky waters and asks sullenly "What time, son?"

"We were thinking about two, and then it would take a little while to get going."

"What time would it end?"

"Ummmm, we haven't talked about that. What time would you like for us to stop, if you let us do it, I mean?"

"Who are you? Eddie Haskel?" They all laugh at Dad's joke, probably because of how close to the truth it is. "I would like for the noise, er . . . I mean music, to stop by six when the news comes on."

"Oh, wow! Thanks, Dad! That should be plenty of time. Barry will need to leave before then. So, I can tell the guys?"

"Sure. I think it will be fun to hear the birth of a band," Ellie says.

"Alright! Cool! Thanks, guys!"

CHAPTER EIGHT

The school week after Thanksgiving is surprisingly reasonable. Carl Lindor is back in town and his son is over-the-moon excited to see him. He will pick up his son to take him to school on Tuesday morning and, later, meet at Fran's for dinner after Jeff gets off work that evening. Carl's 'economically' decorated apartment showcases an oversized couch in the front room. This relic is where his son finds peace and quiet and an uninterrupted night's sleep. Relic or new, the couch and black and white TV will be happily embraced by Jeff until Friday morning when Carl leaves again.

To make the departure less painful, Carl delivers his son at school in his eighteen-wheeler on his way out of town. All of Jeff's friends love to see Carl maneuver the huge vehicle through the school parking lot. Carl is scheduled to be away his usual two weeks, but after that, he will be off and sharing life with Jeff until Christmas afternoon. Jeff will spend the entire holiday living at his dad's apartment, and he could not be happier.

As much as Jeff wants to spend every minute he can with his dad, he is a teen, and his mind has become preoccupied with Alice, now. After a long Sunday without seeing or talking with each other, Alice and Jeff still play it cool on Monday at school. Neither one of them wants to field all the questions, friendly advice, and warnings from classmates yet. Their feelings for each other are strong, but they are optimistically cautious until they know what is going on within themselves.

They are well aware that their worlds are galaxies apart, but that is part of the fiber of their relationship already. So, for now, they manage to smile as they pass each other in the halls and stand close to each other whenever possible. Chance-taker that he is, Jeff manages to grab Alice's hand for a couple of brief seconds as they enter science class. She giggles, and he quickly uses the same hand to wave at Danny across the room after letting go of Alice.

Monday evening though, they take the TR3 into Appleton and try to study at the city library. Alice has never received less than an A in any class through her ten years of school, but she cannot concentrate now that Jeff has entered her life. He is a distraction in the most wonderful sense of the word, and she finds comfort at the big wooden table simply laying her teenage head on his shoulder as he attempts to study. They promise each other that, while Jeff's dad is in town, they will see very little of each other.

The two discuss their upcoming week's activities. Basketball season is ending, soon, and Alice will need to practice with the team after school. Jeff will toil at Charlie's Tuesday through Thursday until eight o'clock each evening then head to dinner with his dad. Alice is so proficient at cheering; she is quite able to dream about she and Jeff and cheer at the same time. Jeff wants to make good grades too so he won't have to hear the coach remind him that he cannot put on his uniform if his grades are not up. After much thought, he is sure he will join the team again this year.

***

As the week moves too quickly, the church is buzzing on Wednesday evening. Danny wants to talk with Pastor Pete alone about his music idea for the youth if he can find him. Lillian, the pastor's assistant and hub of the church, tells Danny that the pastor is meeting with someone at the moment but should be free in ten or fifteen minutes. Dinner starts in twenty-five minutes and then youth studies begin, so it is now or never. "Yes, please tell Pastor Pete I just need ten minutes. I don't want to keep him from eating."

"You are a smart young man, Danny. No one wants to tangle with a hungry Pastor Pete," Lillian jokes. "I heard from Hannah that your party was a real success on Saturday. You attract nice people, Danny."

"Thank you, ma'am. I really appreciate you saying that, and it was a blast."

"Hey, I think I hear the pastor now. Let me go tell him you need to speak with him." Lillian steps into the office area.

Danny hears a short conversation and then the Pastor's invitation to come back to his office. Danny wastes no time, and as he turns the corner to Pastor Pete's area, there the man stands with a big hand stretched out to shake Danny's. "How does it feel to be sixteen, my boy?"

"Oh, about the same as fifteen, I guess, sir, but I know I am of age to drive now. That is beginning to sink in. I've had my learner's for a few months, but to think I can just take off when I need to is very freeing."

"Indeed, it is, and with that freedom comes great responsibility."

"Yes sir. I know, but it never hurts to hear it again. Well, I don't want to keep you, and I have something on my mind that has been bubbling for weeks, and I would like to have your input. It does involve the church, so it would need your blessing, too."

"My, it sounds grand. Let me hear it."

"Whenever I am up on the platform singing the hymns and I look out at the youth, they all seem so disinterested. Disconnected or something. Our lives as teenagers are filled with temptations and distractions and the biggest distraction from Christ, it seems, is music. We listen to music constantly. It is always on our minds, but the messages in the songs they play on WROR are far from a Christian message. The messages we sing here are what we need to hear, but the music is not what they listen to. I love the hymns, but I grew up with them, and they mean a lot to me. Some of our teens are new members of the community, and they look like they are getting their fingernails pulled out or something."

"Ok, Danny. So, what do you think should happen?"

"I'm not exactly sure, but what if I put together a kind of band that would play the hymns and songs we know but have a sort of rock beat to it?"

"On Sunday mornings?"

"No sir, not yet anyway. I was thinking maybe we could have a service in the youth area on Wednesday nights and worship in our school clothes and stuff. It would be pretty much like a Sunday service, only more like our teenage lives. Last night, my friends Jeff Lindor, you know King, and I were playing together at my party. All the kids loved it, and they just sat there all around us and listened intently, as if we were preaching to them, but we weren't, and that made me a little uncomfortable. I loved playing, but I wanted to sing about Jesus instead of darkness being my old friend."

"Are you sure this isn't about you, Danny instead of the Kingdom? I mean, you have learned that we are not to be conformed to the world, but to be transformed by the renewing of our minds, you know, Romans

12:2. I'm not sure if my job, or yours as somewhat of a leader here, should be in the business of putting on a show just to get bodies in the room. I know I am to deliver the Word of God, to feed my sheep, to care for my flock. I throw out the seed each Sunday, and I don't know what kinds of soil they find."

"Don't we all go through seasons, though, Pastor? Maybe it is not the season for teens to hear the Word but being here at Christ Fellowship instead of in some friend's basement smoking grass or sneaking beers is an alternative. The more someone spends time in the Word, or just hears it from a friend, the better. I think we need to offer an alternative to the teens at least, so that they don't stray or stop coming altogether. A place they can sort of call their own, I guess. You know, Paul was all about changing his ways to fit the listener."

"Yes, that is true, Dan."

"Your words on Sunday mornings go right to my heart, Pastor Pete, but so many of the teens aren't hearing you. I believe, and I've prayed about this a lot, that if I told them there was going to be a band that would lead us in worship, I think they would come the first time anyway, just to see what was happening. Maybe not all of them, but Lord, if we can help bring one soul to true salvation, there would be a party in heaven. I just kinda keep coming back to Philippians 4:8: 'Finally, brethren, whatsoever things are true, whatsoever things are honest, whatsoever things are just, whatsoever things are pure, whatsoever things are lovely, whatsoever things are of good report, if there be any virtue, and if there be any praise, think on these things,' and I have been thinking about a room full of young people praising the Lord. God would bless it; I know it."

"Danny, your enthusiasm rubs off, that's for sure. Listen, the true Christian heart can't be about conjuring up a warm and fuzzy feeling, my son. A service that is designed just for me tends to not be for Christ. We gather to worship Christ Almighty, our Savior according to His Word: to be a sweet Christly aroma offered to God the Father. Also, the heart for Christ cannot be made just by knowing the Word. Satan knows the Word, after all, and he uses it as a weapon. He twists it and invokes doubt about what God *really* says. Some of the teens in the room are not chosen by God but will imitate what they see and may even proclaim Jesus as their Savior. They may go on mission trips and serve beside you. The same is true for adults in my service each Sunday. Your idea may just be a way to keep kids out of trouble and that is not necessarily a bad thing, but it should not be confused with worshipping God our creator. I want to meditate on and pray about this."

After a few seconds of thought, Pastor Pete continues, "The church changes, for sure. We don't do everything like the first century church, and maybe your idea is God working through you via the Holy Spirit. The Spirit dwells in you, my young friend, and it sounds like Him, but I need to be sure, and the way I do that is to pray and pray some more. We are in a war with the world and with the flesh and we need to discern whether this is our loving God speaking or a clever Satan. Even Peter was rebuked by Christ when Peter wanted to protect his teacher and friend, Jesus, from the cross. Jesus, being the Almighty Son of God, knew it was Satan because the Father had not told Him that He needed protection from the one reason He was sent.

"I will let you know as soon as I know God's will about this. I really appreciate your loving and sincere heart. I would like to pray with you, now, Danny."

"Yes, please do."

The Pastor takes Danny's hands in his and, with sober reverence, begins talking to whom they both believe is the God of all creation: "Dear heavenly Father. You are the Great I AM who knows all, sees all and who sent His Son to deliver us from darkness. Praise You, our Lord and Your Son and the Holy Spirit. Danny and I come to You in humble prayer asking for Your guidance on this matter of how we deliver our music and message to the youth of our church. Danny is a godly young man, and I have witnessed his growth in the church and his heart for You and for spreading your message, but we both need You to tell us clearly Your will about this matter. We wait for Your word to shine a light in our unknowing. We ask only that Your will to be done for we have no desire to live outside Your will, oh Lord. We pray these things in Your Son's name, Jesus Christ. Amen."

They both raise their heads and look into each other's eyes, and while his mouth forms a peaceful smile, Pastor Pete breaks the righteous silence as only he can. "Now, let's get to the dining hall before my belly rebels. We've put this in the Lord's hands, and I have a class to teach, you know." The Pastor stretches his arm around Danny's shoulders as they walk out the door and turn off the light to the office. Danny is relieved he has shared his vision with the Pastor and knows he will begin deep prayer after he studies about the world tonight.

***

Friday night is high school basketball and that means Alice and squad will cheer their team to a hopeful victory. It is an away game, so the team and cheerleaders load the bus for the long ride to Adams County, an hour one way with the Friday night traffic. The game will be a nailbiter as these are the two best teams in the area, though each team lost important members to college or Vietnam after last year's graduation. Jeff borrows his mom's car, with plans of going to the game, but first he must deliver his amp and guitar to King's house. Jeff needs to arrive at Charlie's bright and early and will work until rehearsal time, hoping Danny's dad will pick him up as they make their way to Upper Marigold.

When Jeff arrives, King is listening to records, choosing his favorite five songs for tomorrow's rehearsal. He is having a hard time because he can hear in his mind many songs he would love to play in front of an audience. Ellie tells Jeff where he can find King, downstairs in the basement, but he tells King's mom that he has his amp and guitar and asks if he can just bring his equipment in through the garage. That works out well for Ellie who would rather Jeff not track up the house and possibly bang the walls.

She pushes the talk button on the intercom to the basement and tells King to open the garage door for Jeff. King jumps up and runs through the laundry room and out into the garage where he raises the big door. "Guitar man!" King says with his arms wide ready for a brotherly hug.

"Thanks for letting me do this tonight. It would be a real juggling act trying to arrange getting my stuff and coming up here tomorrow after work. I just hope Danny's dad can pick me up."

"I'm sure he won't mind since he's coming anyway." King grabs the guitar, leaving the amp for its owner.

As they walk into the living area of the basement, Jeff sees the school drum set assembled and ready to go.

"Man, I'm having a hard time picking my five songs," King admits. "So far, I know I'd like to sing *I'm A Man* and *Mr. You're a Better Man Than I*. Uh, *Around and Around* and *Under My Thumb*. Oh yeah and maybe *Little Black Egg*. There are so many songs that I love, so I will have probably a list of ten. I'd really like to sing *Omaha*, and you would play it so well."

"Thanks, and I think I'll pick ten too, just in case. I don't know the chords to all those you mentioned, but it shouldn't take me long to figure them out."

"We're going to have to get some sort of PA system. Probably not for tomorrow, but we should all scout around for one. I don't know. Maybe school has one. I should have checked when I got the drum set after school."

"Did your mom pick you up or something?"

"No, my dad was home, so he came up to school. He drove around back, and we brought the set out the back door."

"That's really nice of Mr. Grafton to let you use them."

"I know. I hope he'll let me borrow them again for our next rehearsal."

"Whoa, partner. Let's see how the first one goes before we start planning the second."

"Oh, it's gonna happen. Danny and I aren't the best musicians in the world, but you and Barry are *really* good, and we know, after Danny's party, that we're going to have some strong vocals, especially when we add Barry's voice. I mean, we already have a booking."

"I hope Barry feels well enough to do this tomorrow. His dad wouldn't let him miss any school this week. He's still in a lot of pain, but he just keeps taking those pain pills. I guess he's alright with those since his dad is a doctor," Jeff laments.

King walks around and sits at the drums. "Do you know if he bought the Vox Continental?"

"Yes, he did and a Vox Pacemaker amp, too."

"Oh, nice!"

"Danny calls him every day to check on him, and he told me that Barry is going tomorrow to pick up the equipment and bring it straight here. I don't think he wants his dad to see it. Did he ask you? He'll probably just leave it here, if it's OK with your mom."

"Yeah, she won't mind. She's excited about this band 'cause she was a singer on the radio and stuff when she was young."

"Wha-a-a-a? I didn't know that. Maybe she can sing White Rabbit with us?" Jeff says with a sly grin.

"I don't think she fits the image of the band, but she really does sing well. So, how did things end up with Alice after the party?"

"Oh, pretty well. We just rode around in her car and then she took me home. She's a cool girl."

"Do you know any of the songs you want to sing, yet?"

"Yeah, I think so. I really like singing Byrds, so maybe *Have You Seen Her Face* . . . maybe, uh . . . and *Why?* We could all sing *Eight Miles*

High. People would freak out if we did that song. Then, *Dirty Water* and what would you think about doing *Sugar Pie Honey Bunch*?"

"I love that song."

"I guess we could do *Day Tripper*, and we really ought to see if we can do *My Girl*."

"Whew! That will be a lot of work, but I bet we can sing it. All we can do is try it."

"Barry will want to do Doors and *Whiter Shade of Pale*. He was talking about those on the hike, and Danny will do a Monkees song, I'm sure. He could sing *Gimme Some Lovin'* and *Itchycoo Park*, but that has so many effects on it, we couldn't duplicate it, probably."

"We have plenty of songs, that's for sure."

"I better start heading for the game. The traffic has died down, so it won't take so long. Do you wanna go with me? Do you think your mom and dad would let you go?"

"Oh wow! I'll run upstairs and check."

"Ok. I'm going to use your phone and see if Danny wants to go too."

"Far out! I'll be right back." King runs upstairs, and while he is gone, Jeff calls Danny who is home. Danny's dad says OK, and Jeff tells him he'll pick him up in about twenty minutes.

Just as he hangs up, King comes back to the basement a bit dejected. "What's wrong? Your mom won't let you go?" Jeff asks.

"Mom likes you and all, but she said only if Danny is going, too. Do you know yet if he can?"

"Oh, I'm sorry, my young friend . . ." King's face droops. "I called him, and his dad said he . . . could go."

"Oh, you super fink." King throws a fake punch at Jeff for playing with his emotions. "Mom just wants to know when you think we'll be back home."

"Tell her around eleven as long as the traffic is OK. Hurry up though. We gotta go, or we'll miss the game. We need to root your brother on to victory."

King races upstairs, tells his mom that Danny is going, and runs to the second floor to brush his teeth and throw on his jeans and a new flannel shirt he bought at Engel's yesterday. He ties up his Chucks, grabs a navy-blue peacoat out of the closet, and runs back down the stairs. He gives his mom a kiss on the cheek and says thank you as she tells him to be careful. While opening the door to the garage, Jeff gives a tally-ho with "let's roll!" and then "hey, I like that shirt."

King smiles. "Thanks. You should wear it sometime." King replies generously, knowing it's not going to happen.

"There'd be nothing left after I flexed my huge biceps."

King rolls his eyes as they jump in Jeff's mom's car. Jeff immediately pushes in the lighter and digs out a fag.

"I don't believe I've ever ridden in this car before. It's your mom's, right?"

The lighter pops out, and Jeff sits at the bottom of King's driveway while he lights his Camel, then answers while shoving the lighter back into its hole in the dash. "Yep. I've spent some time on the engine and she's running pretty good now."

"When did you get your license? September?"

"Yes, as soon as I hit sixteen, I was at the testing station and aced the test. I'd been driving since I was thirteen anyway, going to Charlie's to get cigarettes for Mom when she had been drinking."

"How'd you buy them, being so young?"

"My mom had worked it out with them. Charlie knows my mom, and he knew it was better for me to get them rather than her trying to drive there. I don't ever want to drink, man. People just destroy themselves with that crap, and they don't care about anyone else but themselves."

"Yeah, I guess so. Have you smoked any pot before?"

"I'm a little scared of that stuff, if you wanna know the truth. I don't know where it will take your mind, and the people I know who smoke it just kinda sit around and do nothing. It seems like your brain turns to mush. I might, sometime just to see what it's all about. The cops are busting the college kids right and left, man. The Appleton boys pull me all the time just to hassle me 'cause my hair is long. They don't want no longhairs in their town. So, I'm not in a hurry to get mixed up in all that. Besides, I hear the cops will plant a bag of grass in your car as they search you and then pretend they found stuff you own. Then, they'll arrest you and take you to jail, just because you have long hair."

"You're kidding. That's heavy." The friends turn right onto Old River Road, fly past Charlie's, and then pull into Danny's driveway. Jeff beeps the horn.

"Howdy, boys," Danny greets his friends while he moves King over with his hip to the middle of the big bench seat. They all wave to Mr. Mosely as Jeff backs out.

"This school we are playing tonight are a bunch of rednecks. So, don't go anywhere by yourself. They will cut you or beat you up in the restroom, if they see you go in alone. We need to stick together, OK?" Jeff asks firmly.

Both the listeners quickly produce their affirmations and stay quiet until King asks Danny if he's picked his songs. "I think so," Danny replies and then proceeds to announce his list of five or so. "*I'm a Believer*, of course, *Lonely Too Long*, *The Letter*."

"Oh, I love that song," Jeff interjects and sings the main line while Danny continues.

"I bet we could sing *To Love Somebody*, don't you?"

"Yeah, I think so. We have to find a PA system so we can hear ourselves," King reiterates.

"Yes, we do, but we can just rehearse with a guitar playing the chords to learn the parts," Danny says. "That would probably be the best way, anyway, so we wouldn't be trying to hear our parts over the drums and all."

Danny looks over at Jeff. "Here, Jeff. My dad wants me to give you two dollars for gas since you're doing the driving."

"Aw, man, your dad is the best. Two bucks, man, that's outasite. My mom will be happy. We'll be able to fill it back up for her."

"So, the rest of my list is *Little Bit O' Soul*, let's see, *Brown Eyed Girl*. You can play that intro guitar part, right Jeff?"

"Yes sir. I learned it when it first came out."

"That doesn't surprise me. How about *Friday on My Mind*? There's some fast playing on that song."

"I haven't learned the whole thing, but I have the intro and that walk down thing. I know I can get it if you want to sing it."

"I can't believe no one has said The Kinks, yet," King says. "We thought you could sing *Gimme Some Lovin'* really well, Dan man. Whadda ya think?"

"I appreciate your confidence in my vocal ability, my friend. I'll try it just because that is one hairy song."

Jeff adds, "I think Barry should sing that Terry Knight song: *I Who have Nothing*. His voice would work really well on The Animals, too. *Inside Looking Out* is *such* a great song!"

The talking stops as WROR fills the air with *Foxy Lady*. Jeff reaches over and turns it up. "Man, Jimi is from a different planet, but Beck is still my man. There's something about the way he attacks the notes that just gets me. Hendrix, though, controls those feedback notes like he's driving a 427. Truly amazing."

King contributes, "I heard he was outasite in Columbus a couple of months ago. I wish I could have gone. He had some band called Soft Machine start the show for him, and I heard the drummer was naked. I hear they were good, though."

"Naked?" Danny questions. "They surely wouldn't let him do that. I mean, things are getting pretty wild, but that's hard to believe."

"Well, that's what I was told anyway. Remember . . . I wasn't there." Jeff directs a pseudo-whine at King.

"Poor baby," Danny says with a pouty face.

King cannot get his mind off of rehearsal. "Did the church let you use the bass, Danny?"

"Yeah, and I can't wait. It sounds so good in the church. I'll just bring it up to rehearsal after work. Is your mom OK with all this?"

"Yes, she's looking forward to it, actually. My dad said we need to be finished with the noise by six o'clock so he can watch the news. He was just kidding about it being noise."

"Outasite! That's really nice of them, and Barry needs to go to work then anyway. It sounds like he needs to hide his new organ from his dad."

"I already told King, and he said his mom would let him keep it in the basement," Jeff speaks up after lighting a Camel.

"That's cool. Hey, maybe you can learn to play the organ, King, since it will be right there. Maybe you could tell Barry he can leave it there if he gives you a lesson each week."

"Aw, he can leave it there anyway, but I'll ask him. That would be really groovy to learn some songs on the organ."

Time flies by as the conversation is non-stop, and the bandmates begin to see signs for Northern. "I brought my shades just in case the red glow from the Northern necks starts burning my eyes." Jeff says with some disgust in voice.

They arrive at the school parking lot, and Jeff parks as close to their school's bus as possible. He would love to walk Alice out to the bus after the game, but they are just not to that point yet. The secret will not last for long though, as they both are getting to the point of not caring what others will think. They have passed letters to each other in the halls at school or shoved them through the air vents of each other's lockers. Their passion to hold each other just burns hotter the less they see each other.

"Ok, boys. Let's stay together." Jeff looks in every direction as he closes his car door and locks it. He is making Danny and King a little nervous but rightfully so. Jeff has experienced, firsthand, the insolent, ruffian minds of the youth in this part of the area. These troublemakers are known as rednecks to all the hippie or more artsy students because their hair style features a very short cut in the back and around the ears. This kind of short haircut did not originate as a fashion statement but a necessity for those who work on farms. Taking advantage of any cool breeze while out in the fields is sought after, and long hair would only prevent airflow. However, the skin on those exposed necks shines red after a long, hard day. Of course, the majority of the Adams County children and teens are well-behaved, but there is a pack of wild ones that like to terrorize their visitors. Flint has a rough group, but they are all preppy, with Princeton haircuts, white Levi's and Weejuns. They heckle the Flint hippies as well, but they would not hurt their own, only make them feel uncomfortable and trip them in the school halls.

The three friends walk closer to the school and see shadowy figures, real and imagined, behind every car. Finally, without incident, the three Pumas pass through enemy territory and have made it to the ticket booth where there is a guard and ample light provided by a flood lamp hanging above the building's entrance. They pay their dollar and get their hand stamped for re-entry to the gymnasium. Leaving and re-entering the building is prohibited, but the stamp tells any school official that the *stampee* is a paying customer.

Just as King is getting stamped, the Flint boys hear voices from the dark outside corner, just on the other side of the entrance doors. "Hello, girls. Are you the cheerleaders?" followed by hysterical laughter from what sounds like four young men. None of the three long-haired Puma boys look at the hecklers and walk straight into the gymnasium, which is packed with faculty, parents, and students. Off-duty policemen guard the doors at both ends of the floor, sending a message to those who want to ruin the sporting event for others by fighting or making inordinate threats.

Everyone knows these two teams hold the biggest rivalry in this area and tensions will be high tonight. There are a few Puma fans that are known for their own kind of aggressive rhetoric, aimed at the other team and their followers, but this particular Adams County school has gotten physical and/or destructive on more than one occasion. Vehicles from the visiting teams and their fans have gotten keyed, windows broken, and tires punctured by misguided, defiant youth yielding hunting knives and tire irons. Now, with un-American hippies starting to wear their concerns for their nation on the outside, the rednecks can spot them quickly and show no mercy toward them.

The rednecks do not hesitate to try and make a long-haired male teen think twice about his protest against his country, with threats of physical altercation and alteration. Because of this legacy, a large number of police will be manning the parking lot as the game nears its end. The problem with this scenario, however, is that there are many on the local police force who went to Northern and who are sympathetic to the student's extreme aggressiveness toward their visiting teams, as well as a hatred for hippie-looking boys. The Northern school students, and some alums, believe they do not have hippies here, and they don't welcome them.

CHAPTER
NINE

I t is nearly game time, and Alice and her cheerleading team are helping to work the Flint Township Puma fans into a spirited frenzy. The decibel level is off the charts with both sides sold out and making a big noise by singing their school songs and chanting whatever each cheerleading team hoists up into the bleachers. King enters first, with Danny close behind and Jeff bringing up the rear to protect the other two. Entering that gym is exciting, and it will be difficult to find seats. The three stroll along the floor looking up at each section of the bleachers, except for Jeff. He is watching Alice jump and dance, shout and sing while hoping she will look his way.

The squad of nine Puma cheerleaders has spread out the length of the entire side of the gymnasium to incorporate all the fans who have made the trip to Adams County. Alice has cheered for so many games that she has learned not to look at individual faces anymore. Tonight though, is her first game since her heart was handed over to Jeff Lindor. Just as she runs across the shiny, yellow floor with pom-poms thrusting to the beat of their chant, Alice's place to stop and turn toward the bleachers turns out to be a beautifully startling five feet from Jeff's grinning face.

Alice almost loses her rhythm when she sees Jeff but quickly produces an Alice Engel smile mid-cheer, discreetly aimed unmistakably at her crush, and it blasts away all the other distractions. If that was not enough to weaken a rough boy's knees, Jeff has no doubt in his mind that the delectable smile ends with a pucker of those symmetrical and irresistible Alice lips: the same ones that have touched his several times.

Danny sees Nick, Hannah, and Adam several rows up. Hannah waves for them to come up and sit next to them. It will be crowded, but that is as good as its going to get at this sold-out game. Danny reveals his find to King and Jeff by hitting them in the chest and pointing, knowing they could not hear his voice without blowing his vocal cords. The swat brings Jeff back to the here-and-now and up they go, stepping over coats that have been shed in reaction to the body heat in the room. Hannah switches seats with Adam so that she and Danny will sit next to each other. She takes Danny's hand as he sits and squeezes it but then releases her grip quickly. Hannah and Danny have attended many church and school events together but never as a couple or what might be considered a formal date. There have always been plenty of friends surrounding them.

"I didn't know you were coming. What a nice surprise!" Hannah yells as Danny gets settled.

"Jeff called me from King's house and invited me. They were both going, so Dad said it was fine with him and here I am. I love basketball in the fall."

"What?" Hannah says.

Danny laughs and waves his hand, and they turn to watch the action and join in with the cheerleaders. King is on Danny's other side, and Jeff just stares at Alice. Down on the court, Captain Sam is warming up his team with a few layup and rebound drills until Coach Fouts calls them all in for a pep talk and play review before the game starts. The two-minute buzzer is loud, and the cheerleaders know to stop for the pre-recorded National Anthem.

The principal of the school appears at the microphone located on a stand positioned on the sidelines at mid-court on the Northern side. He asks everyone to stand for the anthem and introduces a senior girl from the Northern choir named Katy Spriggs. United as Americans, the crowd stands and puts their hands over their hearts as the principal lowers the mic stand and steps aside. A fellow student leads the vocalist to her spot as the room full of Americans become aware at the same time that Katy is blind. The music starts, giving the singer three beats of the five chord before the singing should begin. Having rehearsed this intro a number of times, Katy's powerful alto voice confidently begins the familiar verse, and by the end of Mr. Key's descriptive and moving musical reminder of the cost of freedom, the crowd is cheering. Katy waves, turns, and walks to her seat with her friend at her elbow. Unfortunately, after that moving few moments, the crowd returns to its previously venomous division.

Both teams gather around their centers, the ball is tossed up into the air by the referee and the tip goes to the Pumas. The forward has already reached his position under the basket; he catches a long throw, and two points are made with a bank shot within the first five seconds of the game. The rest of that half is hard fought, and by halftime, the Pumas lead only by four. When the halftime buzzer sounds, Jeff tells his friends that it is way past time for a Camel, but he dreads the chance of a confrontation with a Northern redneck. King grabs Danny and tells Jeff that he is not going without them. Jeff starts to tell them he will be OK but welcomes their friendship and bravery instead.

There should be a few other Puma smokers outside, including some parents, but Jeff knows he will have to move quickly and makes that very clear to King and Danny. Hannah promises to hold their seats as Danny files down the steps, onto the sidelines, and out into the lobby. The main doors are open for the smokers, and there is a sigh of relief when the boys see two police officers standing just outside. No students are allowed beyond the lit area, and as the three Pumas walk out, they see a few more Flint kids off to the left. Jeff and Danny know a few of them, but King is not a sophomore, so he simply follows along. Jeff's Camel is already burning. and his whole body has noticeably relaxed.

Danny begins talking with one of the boys outside, but King makes the mistake of looking around when his eyes catch the gaze of a greasy, pimple-faced Northern student who is not wearing a coat, but only a white t-shirt in the below freezing temperatures. "What are you looking at?" the Northern teen asks between puffs on his cigarette. King looks away quickly, but this kid will haunt King all night, now that he has made contact. The Northern boy continues to taunt King and is joined by two other friends who amplify the first boy's remarks. "They sure do have pretty girls at Flint, but she'd look better in a dress." Jeff leans over to King and tells him to ignore them.

All the smokers hear one of the officers announce that the game is going to start in five minutes. Jeff immediately begins describing his plan of returning to their seats. "When I finish talking, we are going to turn and go back in. Go straight into the gym. King, you go first, and then you, Danny. You are now a target, King, so please watch and listen. Be aware of who is around you. Let's go."

The three stay close together, but the police have gone inside to watch the gymnasium doors as the smokers file back in before the second half starts. About five feet from the gym doors, and behind the officers who have their backs to the lobby, King hears a very hillbilly voice say,

"I'm gonna hurt you after the game. You and your friends." King pushes forward through the people in front of him, including Jeff and Danny. He looks back, but there are any number of faces that look like they could have threatened him. "What's wrong, King?" Danny says.

"That guy got up right behind me and breathed his bad breath in my ear, telling me he was going to hurt me tonight. They can't get by with that stuff!"

King is letting his emotions get the better of him, and he turns around, fists clenched, just to see if he can look eye-to-eye with the hillbilly hoodlum that has threatened him. King wants to confront his antagonist right there where there are witnesses. The more worldly-wise Jeff turns King around and explains that the police would love for him to start even a verbal assault with one of their own model students. That way, they could get as rough as they really want to and throw King and his friends out of the game. At that point, they would be outside by themselves with no protection or witnesses. "Don't let them get to you, buddy. They are redneck morons who have no life. Let's watch the game and be sure to walk out with a crowd when it is over. Hey! Remember, we have rehearsal tomorrow, and can't afford to hurt our precious hands on some ugly Northern creep's bony face."

Jeff's reasoning seems to bring King back to earth, but his mind is spinning with anger. Hannah and friends are right where they were before halftime, and Danny bounds up the less crowded bleachers and flops down hard beside his friend. "Some creepy Northern redneck is picking on King. I feel bad for him, but we do need to be careful."

Hannah shakes her head and puts a tender arm across Danny's back and squeezes him. After the squeeze, she leaves her arm in place and rests her head on his arm while they wait for the game to start and the halftime activity to settle down in her friend and brother in Christ.

Jeff is just staring at Alice as she twists and contorts her sleek-but-shapely body. All the cheerleaders are great-looking girls of various shapes and hair colors, but Alice truly stands out and it is more than simply superficial appearance. As he watches, though, he asks himself if he really wants to get serious with Alice. He knows she will change his life, and he is not sure if he wants his life to change, be it good *or* bad. Life at home is a tragedy, but he loves his friendships and his guitar playing and working at Charlie's. He loves his dad and knows that there will be a strain in both his relationship with his dad and Alice when his dad is in town. He saw that this week already, and he is not even totally committed.

Jeff knows that Alice could bounce his heart off a wall like a rubber baseball if he decides to get serious, and she backs out. He remembers when his mom started seeing Darren and how awful that felt in the pit of his stomach, like an unquenchable fire burning and eating away at his core.

"Jeff!"

"Wha-a-a-at?" Jeff, who is far away from the game in thought, scowls at King who is yelling in his face as the room peaks with cheers and the teams come out onto the floor, again.

"I have got to go to the restroom."

Jeff just stares at his friend until compassion rolls over him. "Yeah, me too. As soon as they make the jump, we'll go." Jeff really wanted to say, *Can't you hold it until we get back to Scioto County?* But he loves his young friend, and he will brave the hillbillies to ease King's bladder.

"If you go out, you can't come back in," shouts one of the police officers at the gym door.

"Just going to the restroom, sir," King says with a mock-serious look on his face. The officer opens the door to the lobby for them, and they quickly walk across a clear lobby. Only the lady in the cash window, counting tonight's money, sees the visitors as they plow into the restroom. There is no sign of anyone who might try to harm them, and each boy finally stands and faces the wall. "You go first," Jeff instructs King. "I feel very unprotected when both of us are in such vulnerable positions." King doesn't hesitate and begins his business while Jeff stands and wishes he could have a Camel. "Jeez, man, you really had to go. Come on and hurry up."

"Almost done. I told you I had to go, man."

As King walks away while zipping up, Jeff moves into place and begins to let nature take its course. Of course, just as King sticks his hands under the faucet for a washing, the door opens, and Jeff cannot do anything but look up at the ceiling. They hear more than one pair of feet, and Jeff readies himself for a crack in the back of the head. Then he hears King say hello and admires his bravery. Jeff breathes again when he hears a small boy and his dad return the greeting. Jeff is finally finished and quickly moves to the sink for his wash up. King stands near the door with his back to the wall and waits for Jeff. Both are relaxed for the first time since their excursion, and King pulls the restroom door open just as a new group of hillbilly faces are pushing the door.

"Whoops! Sorry guys." King wants to get away from this group and back to the gym so badly that he jams up the entrance to the restroom when he should have just stepped back and let the growing group of Northern teens in.

"Oh, I thought we were in the men's restroom, girls. What's your hurry, Pumas?" the boy in the front says to King as he looks toward Jeff. "You two look alike, so you must be together. Why do you guys want to look like girls?" The redneck group of five pushes their way into the restroom and block the door as they form a loose circle around Jeff and King.

"We're just rock-n-rollers, man." Jeff couldn't think of anything else to say and felt stupid after he said it. The honesty turns out to be the best policy because it changed the Northern boy's demeanor.

"Rock-n-rollers?" You play loud guitars? My brother plays mandolin, but that doesn't get very loud. Plus, he doesn't need to have long hair like you two. What do you play, blondie?"

King answers, "I'm the drummer."

"Whoa, now them things get *real* loud. You couldn't hear my brother if you were playin' those things." The Northern boy laughs and looks at King and Jeff as if to say, *You better laugh, too, because my joke was really funny*. King and Jeff could only squeak out a grin.

"Yeah, I guess that's the difference between rock and country music," King says sharply.

Jeff can tell that King's temper is starting to rise. "Well, we're gonna get back to the game, guys. Good seeing you." Jeff tries to cool King down and get him through the door. The dad and young boy, who had come into the restroom a few minutes earlier, finish up their business, wash their hands and start to walk toward the door and through the group of teens. The dad puts his arms over Jeff's and King's shoulders, looks at the Northern boys and says, "Excuse us, friends. We're going to go watch the game now." And out the door the four of them go.

"Wow, thank you, sir," King says as he heads for the gym doors, pulling on Jeff. Jeff earnestly turns, throws his hair back out of his eyes, and nods his head with a smile toward the man and his son as they go toward the Northern side of the gym.

"That was so creepy, Jeff. I am so sick of those guys I could puke."

"I know the feeling. It's almost the end of the third quarter, so we don't have long. This is the only game I ever wished we would lose because the rednecks get redder when *they* lose, and it gets more dangerous. They must carry liquor in their pockets because they really get obnoxious by the end of the game. If we are way ahead, I wouldn't mind leaving before the game ends so we can beat the traffic and the crush, not to mention we will be rubbing shoulders with the Northern people, too, if we leave at the end of the game."

"I'm OK with that, but Danny and Hannah are enjoying each other, and I don't know if we can get him to leave early."

The cheerleaders are gathered in one area on the front bleacher and the boys must pass in front of them to get to their seats. Jeff decides to pretend like he has an immense amount of team spirit and gives all the girls a kind of over-exuberant, handshake-type gesture while he says things like 'go Pumas' and 'we've got this one'. This was all designed to allow him to actually touch Alice and, as he does, he holds onto her hand just two or three seconds longer than the others.

Before he lets go, Jeff looks right at Alice and says, "Rah, rah, sis-boom-bah" with the dumbest-looking fake smile and wide eyes ever. Alice cannot hold back hysterical laughter, and Jeff lets go of her hand and proceeds to lead King to their seats as if Alice is just one of the cheerleaders to him, but they both know differently. While the cheerleader charm is percolating throughout the Flint bleachers, King is successful in getting his brother's attention in between plays.

When Jeff and King return, Jeff sits next to Danny and asks his opinion on the idea of leaving a few minutes early. "I want to walk Hannah out whenever we go. If she wants to leave early, then yes. I'll ask her."

It is loud in the gym, and Jeff only sees Danny's body language. So, he decides to look at someone who interests him more, and she is down on the court. Danny elbows Jeff in the arm and tells Jeff that both he and Hannah want to stay to the end because it is so close. Danny suggests he simply ride with Hannah, Nick, and Adam. "Great idea!" Jeff shouts while giving the thumbs up. "Are you sure? Your dad won't get mad at me for not bringing you home? Well, he never gets mad, but you know."

"Yes, I think everyone will be happy if I just do that." Another non-verbal thumbs up from Jeff to Danny, and he relays the decision to King. King gives an approving nod of the head and then turns back to the game.

Sam is the high scorer with twenty-seven of the sixty-six points on the board. It is sixty-six to fifty-three, but Northern can never be counted out, and Coach Fouts knows it. He and Sam will not let the Pumas get comfortable, and no second-stringers are going in unless someone fouls out, which is quite possible. "Let's go when there are three minutes on the clock, if we have a wide lead."

"Ok." King is into the game, and he enjoys watching his brother control the event. "How is Sam so good at everything?" Sam's little brother laments.

"I don't know, man. He can't play drums," Jeff says.

King turns to Jeff with a sincere "thank you" smile on his face and then turns back to the game.

Buzzers keep buzzing for timeouts called from each team, and Northern has closed in with the score, now a snug seventy-three to sixty-five. This is what makes Northern a top contender as they never seem to tire. You can feel the tension in the gymnasium, and it is exciting. The cheerleaders are relentless, and Sam is fully focused and alert. He knows every player on the opposing team, their capabilities and their weaknesses, and he uses that information to direct his team to either use a full-court press or man-to-man. Though Northern's captain is not as precise as Sam, he knows that they need to force Flint's second-best player, the guard Ted Nichols, to commit a foul because it will be his last for the game. Northern throws the ball in, and Nichols is all over the young man with the ball but tries to be very careful not to touch him.

The ball is passed, and Northern picks up their pace, driving in for a layup that is blocked by Flint. The air ball is recovered by a Northern gun who fakes a shot, goes underneath the blocking Flint player and pushes upward for a bank shot. Just as the Northern shooter lets go, Nichols races in to knock the ball away but hits the shooter's arm instead. It's a foul, and Nichols is out. Surprising everyone, Coach Fouts calls in Terry Baxter, a fiery sophomore who is good enough to make the varsity team. He is hungry to play, rested, and rarely misses a shot in the scrimmage games he has played. Both foul shots are good, and the shot that brought the foul went in as well, shrinking Flint's lead to four points. Flint brings the ball down court; the clock is ticking, and Sam passes to Baxter. who fires a pass to the center as he is rushing in toward the basket. The center grabs the perfect throw but lets it leave his fingers, and the ball spins right into Northern's possession.

The Northern recipient of the lost ball immediately throws a long pass to their forward, who is down-court already. He catches the ball while in mid-stride and dances an amazing fake around a Flint player to drive in for a successful layup and two points. The clock is now under two minutes, and Jeff and King are on their feet cheering the team. They've put away any hope of leaving early, but they will consider all of that at the end of the game. The venue is in a roar and pulsating, the cheerleaders are losing their voices but not their passion, and the fans are responding with great vigor, all caught up in the frenzy. Sam signals his team to try and run out as much time as possible, so the trip back down court starts out slow, but Northern will not allow Flint to relax and go man-to-man. Arms are flying, making it difficult to see who is open for a pass. Sam alley-oops a pass to the Flint guard who begins a drive toward the basket, but not before there are two Northern players reaching in for the ball and causing as many distractions as possible.

Because the Flint ball-handler is being double-teamed, he knows someone is open, and there he is, Baxter. The pass is delivered, and Baxter shoots from the key. The ball hits the rim and bounces not once, not twice, but three times before it falls away from the basket and Northern rebounds. The clock is ticking under a minute. Northern needs two points to tie the game, and as they make their way down the court, the captain sets them up for a play. Passes are made to players who stay in their positions, and then the Northern guard finds himself without a Flint hand in his face. He shoots from fifteen feet, and it swishes in the basket. Sam grabs it, throws it in to his teammate, and takes it back again. There are fifteen seconds on the clock, and Sam seems to find new energy, going into overdrive like Alice's TR3. He holds up three fingers, fakes a pass to the left and then the right. Delivers a bounce pass to Baxter who knows exactly what is going to happen.

Baxter pretends he is shooting the ball and fools two Northern players. While they are still looking up, as if Baxter shot the ball, the pass meets Sam's hand perfectly, and Sam crouches down, fully aware of the basket's location. He makes like a bulldozer and is dribbling at top speed, underneath the radar of the Northern team who is trying to figure out where the ball went.

Just as the Northern team begins to understand what is happening and puts all their focus on trying to stop Sam, the player with all the successful baskets, Sam passes the ball right back to Baxter, and Baxter shoots. The buzzer sounds and for a split second, the room actually gets quiet as everyone takes a deep breath. Northern hands go up to try to stop the arc, but the round, brown ball falls like a meteor to earth through the basket, and the Flint Township Pumas win a hard-fought game.

The Puma fans are going crazy, and the team members are jumping all over Baxter, with Sam clasping his hands behind his head and grinning from ear-to-ear, just standing in the key and watching the sophomore get his due. Sam was a varsity sophomore as well, and he knows how Baxter is feeling. Fans are beginning to file out onto the floor, and the cheerleaders are giving out hugs. Jeff takes full advantage of the exuberant celebratory activities, giving small hugs to a couple of cheerleaders he knows and then grabs Alice, bends her backwards, and gives her a huge kiss while he holds her like he never wants to let go. With his eyes looking directly at hers, he brings Alice back up to vertical and continues to play the part of over-zealous Puma fan, bouncing off toward the team.

The team is being whisked away to the shower room by the coach, making sure no one gets injured in the crushing celebration or by the very unhappy Northern rednecks who hate to lose. There is no way the two teams can line up to shake hands with all the fans on the court. So, the two coaches shake hands and give each other a job-well-done nod and off they go to their locker rooms. Now, it's time to leave.

CHAPTER TEN

The excitement from the close game has receded, and the gymnasium is empty of fans. The janitorial staff slowly enters the gym from the various doors, and the Flint Township cheerleaders sit and wait for the team to come out before they go to the cold bus. Jeff waits for King who has gone into the locker room area to congratulate his brother. Jeff has seen the depths of the depravity in which the rednecks outside wallow, and as casually as possible, Jeff strongly suggests to Alice, via a remark to the entire squad, that she/they make a point of staying close to the coach when they go out to the bus.

"There are some unhappy people out there, and they would enjoy nothing more than to watch fear well up in Puma cheerleader eyes."

"Mr. Lindor, we appreciate your concern, but there is no need to scare the girls. We will be just fine, thank you," Coach Freel says sternly to a startled Jeff.

"Yes, ma'am. Thank you, ma'am. I just want you and them to be safe, you know." And with that, Jeff tells Alice and the squad goodbye and walks away with King across the wooden battlefield and out into the lobby.

Danny has long ago left Adams County with his three friends from church. While peering through the glass in the school doors, Jeff scans the parking lot to get an idea of who is outside the lobby. He sees Puma jackets which create a false sense of security in him.

While opening the school doors, Jeff speaks to King without turning his head. "Let's keep moving, man. I don't want any . . ."

"Hey girls, where you going so fast?" A very hillbilly voice comes from behind the two Pumas' heads.

Without acknowledging the hoods, Jeff directs King "Let's try to stay in this group in front of us." He pulls on King's sleeve and lights a Camel.

"Hey, I'll have one of them, Puma girl." The boys keep moving with the crowd, but Jeff feels something very hard, like metal, in his back. It could be a gun or a tire iron. Jeff tries to move into the middle of the crowd, but someone has the bottom of his coat and pulls him back quickly. "Give me a cigarette."

Jeff tenses up as he swirls around to meet his antagonist. "Here, man. Have a couple."

"I didn't say two, I said one. Don't they teach you math at Flint?"

"Stop hassling us, man. What in the hell is your problem?"

"Queers like you."

King has realized his friend is not with him and turns to go back to help Jeff, but after seeing how many Northern hoods are around him, King thinks he might be able to round up an adult back inside the school, and that is where King runs.

Just as King goes past Jeff, who is surrounded by six or seven Northern rednecks, he sees one of the hillbilly hoods push Jeff and hold something up in front of Jeff's face. This makes King sprint toward the school lobby doors, and he yells for help. King sees the same man and his son who had come to King and Jeff's rescue earlier in the restroom, coming out of the school doors. The outside lights are being turned off as King runs to the man and says, "Please, sir. Some Northern boys are pushing my friend around, and I know they want to hurt him."

"Show me where."

King points into the murky, moist darkness where there are figures moving. "Please hurry, sir."

The man and his son let King lead, and as they come upon the group, the man begins to talk. "Hi, boys. That was some game, wasn't it?" The hoods turn to see who is talking, but do not let go of Jeff's collar.

"We're kinda busy making a new friend, Pastor, if you don't mind."

"Oh, really? That's nice of you boys to welcome our visitors like this, especially when they beat us. I'll be sure to tell the principal about your generosity when I see him in church on Sunday. Arnold, I haven't seen you in church lately. I would love to see you there this Sunday. Do you think you could make it?"

"Uh, I don't know, maybe."

"I'm supposed to see your dad tomorrow when he comes into town. He promised he'd stop by. Will you be with him?"

"I don't know, Pastor. I haven't thought about it."

"Well, please do think about it, my son. I always enjoy seeing you and your dad. Your dad really loves you, and he sure knows his Bible, doesn't he?"

"I guess so, Pastor."

"I hope you do, too. It just takes a few minutes a day. It's a great way to start your day, if you want to know the truth, Arnold. Hey, didn't I see you Puma boys earlier in the restroom?"

"Yes, sir, you did." King has moved over beside Jeff, and Arnold has let go of Jeff's collar.

"There must be something very special about you two. There is always a crowd of interested people gathered around you. I'm really glad you are making friends with our local boys."

The Pastor turns his attention toward the Northern boys. "Boys, we are having a huge youth gathering next Sunday afternoon. It is a sort of pre-Christmas party before everyone starts traveling at Christmas break. Would you all please try to come?" There is a lot of head-down murmuring and shuffling of feet. "It will be really fun, I think, and please don't bring presents. Jesus Christ is the greatest gift we can receive, right?" Again, there is a lot of headshaking, mostly in the affirmative. "Your dad would agree with me, Arnold. Talk with him about it."

"Well, you boys better get home. I'm sure your parents worry about you when you come in late, and there is nothing good happening at this hour. Temptation to do the wrong thing is just waiting for all of us. I'm going to walk with these two Pumas to their car so I can talk with them. I might invite them to the youth Christmas party. Would that be OK with you guys? I mean, to have friends from another school? We are all children of Christ after all, right?"

"Yes, Pastor. Nice to see you tonight." Arnold manages to be civil, and then all seven turn and go toward their highly modified cars. Arnold and two friends get into a cherry red and white 1956 Chevy Bel-Air. The others have similar looking cars into which they have poured their time and money.

"Bye, boys, and I hope to see you Sunday." With backs turned, a few hands go up in an effort to wave. "I'm really sorry, boys, about all of that, and I hope you don't think that behavior represents our community. We have a lot of good kids here. Those guys who were making trouble are good kids too, but they get fed a lot of poison from people who should know better. My name is Pastor Dennis Allen, and this is my son Charles, or Chuck, as we call him. What are your names?"

"I'm King, and this is Jeff, sir, and we cannot thank you enough. That was really something to see."

"I have a friend and protector with me at all times named Jesus, ya know," Pastor Allen says with a smile. "Did you say your name is King, young man? I don't believe I have ever known anyone named King. I mean, Jesus is *the* King, but I don't believe I have ever met anyone *named* King."

"Yes sir, my mom loves Nat King Cole, and she wanted to name her second boy King. My brother is the Captain of the Pumas, Sam Reed."

"Oh, my! He is a great athlete, and I bet you're really proud of him. It's his last year, right?"

"Yes, that's right. He'll graduate in May."

"Oh, that's exciting, and I'm sure your parents enjoy both of you. I bet you would like to get home and please don't let those boys put a bad taste in your mouth about us farmers. I would love for you to come to the youth Christmas party I mentioned. It is two Sundays from now, the tenth I believe is the date, and it starts at five o'clock. I know it's a long drive, but I want you to know you're welcome and bring your friends and family, too."

Jeff and King shake the Pastor's hand and thank him for helping them. The boys get safely inside the car. "Please start it up and let's get out of here," King says. Jeff obliges, and they speed off down the long drive toward the main road. Jeff makes sure he stops at the stop sign so that no lurking Adams County police will have an excuse to pull them over.

Jeff brings the car up to the fifty-five mile an hour speed limit as quickly as his mom's car will accelerate, passing a local police cruiser sitting in the shadows, and it isn't long before they enter Scioto County. It is as if they were holding their breath the whole time they were driving to their county because there was a great release of breath and tension when they crossed the county line.

Jeff pushes the lighter in, pulls out his Camels, and turns up the heat in the car as they both sit shivering. After the lighter pops out, Jeff holds the hot, orange glow to the end of his fag and says "Crap, I gave that redneck two of my cigarettes, and all he did was throw one down and crush it. A perfectly good Camel, too. Can you believe it?" Jeff's humor is like an angel singing to King, and they both laugh, partly because Jeff is funny but mostly because it is a stress reliever.

King turns on the radio, but WROR doesn't reach this far west. So, he turns it off and both boys sit quietly, thinking back over their evening. "You're working in the morning, right?" King makes small talk to purge the sound of Arnold's nasally voice from his head.

"Yeah, and we're getting home later than I thought. At least I still have my face. That Pastor Allen guy was really groovy. He just disarmed all those ugly bumpkins without threats or yelling or anything. He was just really nice to them."

"Yeah, but he knew all their parents and the principal."

"I guess so, but he was like fearless, man. I guess that comes with age 'cause I couldn't do that as who I am right now."

King turns the radio back on and WROR is roaring *Little Bit O' Soul*, which reminds both boys about rehearsal tomorrow. "I'm looking forward to playing my guitar somewhere other than my bedroom. Rehearsal is going to be so much fun."

"I can't wait! The hardest decision will be which song to do first."

"That's the truth. I hope Barry is feeling alright. Please call him tomorrow to check on him, OK?"

"I think I will go over to see him, actually. I kinda worry about him a little. He is *so* stressed around exam time."

"Wouldn't you be if your dad was pushing you as hard as Dr. Meade pushes Barry? I don't know if I could take it."

"Really, man, and after thinking about that, I don't believe I will visit him. I don't want to interrupt his studies. His dad would kill me, and I'm really surprised that Barry gets to rehearse with us anyway. I hope he aces those exams so he'll get a break for a few weeks."

After crossing the ancient Scioto River, Jeff safely arrives at the Appleton city limits where he turns north onto Route 43 and heads for Marigold. WROR is playing some obscure tunes tonight, helping the boys erase the post-game event from their memory banks. The best mind-erasure, so far, is the entertaining and irreverent *Let It All Hang Out* by The Hombres. It always gets the listener's attention from the very beginning, and the boys recite it perfectly, completing the nearly Shakespearian doggerel with their tongues vibrating between their lips and spittle projecting onto the dashboard. King cannot help but to clap along to the rude and unpolished song as they ride up 43, and Jeff honks the horn on beats two and four until he comes to his senses and realizes he might attract Appleton's finest.

Taking the right lane and climbing into the safe and sleepy community of Marigold, Jeff turns right onto the artery and heads up to

Upper Marigold. It is eleven thirty, as King says goodbye to his driver. He runs up the front steps and uses his key to enter his comfortable home, where he finds his dad sound asleep in his favorite chair in front of the TV. King hears Ed McMahon put wise the listener with his reassuring program commencement: "Here's Johnny!" With the band kicking in on cue, King gets close to his dad's ear and softly touches his arm and tells him he is home. Gordon keeps his eyes fully closed so as not to completely lose his slumber and reaches out his hand toward his son. They clasp their fingers for just a second or two. King lets go, throws his coat over the arm of the hall chair and runs upstairs to listen to records and fall asleep on his bed while visions of sticks and drums dance in his head.

Saturday morning comes quickly, especially for Jeff. Charlie wanted him there by seven to help unload Merle Duncan's pickup truck full of butchered meats and that means date money: seven hours at two dollars an hour. The work has to be done early before the temperature rises, and WSAZ says it might get up to nearly forty degrees with intermittent rain on this first day of December. Jeff gets up at six fifteen and throws cold water in his face, dries off, runs a comb through his hair, and lights his first of many Camels for the day.

He throws on pretty much the same clothes as he had on last night at the game, except he puts on a clean shirt. You see, Alice is making her man's lunch and meeting him for his thirty-minute break at eleven. It will be their first public outing, and Jeff is excited – not to mention, he gets to play music with his brothers from other mothers this afternoon. It is a good day to be alive in Marigold, Ohio.

Alice shows up right on time, and they enjoy the food and each other at the picnic table in the back of the building. They part with a short kiss, but there is no one outside on this cold day to witness the affection. Two o'clock comes quickly as two of the three band members make their way to the Reed's house. Barry has been there since one, all wrapped up and ready for a long night at work, not leaving his home until after his dad headed out to do house calls and finish some work at the office. He knows he will probably see his dad at the club later while he bangs out the old familiar songs that everyone loves to hear.

Barry could not wait to hear his new purchase in all its glory and is fascinating his host by playing the instrument as if he had owned it since birth. Barry's intensity and focus seems to unveil a need to rid himself of something, or channel mounds of frustration and other pent-up emotions. As if he has written the songs himself, Barry runs through the intros to *Boom Boom* by The Animals, *Light My Fire*, *96 Tears*, and an incredible take of *Mercy Mercy Mercy* by The Buckinghams on his Wurlitzer portable electric piano, complete with lead vocals on each.

Ellie's voice through the intercom urgently alerts King to the arrival of Danny and Jeff, who rode together in Jeff's mom's car. Mrs. Lindor was kind enough to drive to Charlie's to deliver her car to her son. She walked home so she could get some air and exercise. King runs out through the garage and raises the door to let his friends in with their equipment. Danny has the church's amp and bass, and Jeff lugs his own rig. It is exciting to watch this band come together, piece by piece, and King is like a Labrador puppy, leaping and running ahead of Danny and Jeff opening the doors that lead to the rehearsal room.

Ellie and Gordon go about their normal Saturday routines, although Ellie has baked a German Chocolate cake that she will offer to the boys when they take a break. They both know that their typically halcyon home will soon be shaking to a rock beat, and Sam hopes they begin before he has to leave for a debate team meeting planned to start at three at Fran's. He also hopes to return by five or so to listen to the band's progress before they stop at six.

Jeff and Danny tune their instruments to the new organ and start getting their sounds and volumes set for the comfortable room. Jeff starts a slinky version of *Green Onions*, which was not on anyone's list, and Barry falls right in sounding like Booker T. as much as he can without a Hammond B3 and Leslie tone cabinet. Danny knows the song in his head, but his hands had never played the notes until just now as he watches Jeff's finger positions closely. After Barry finishes his imitation of the iconic organ licks, Jeff immediately rips into a stinging solo that takes the other three by surprise. They had not heard him play his electric for a few months, and he is demonstrating that he spends prudent time absorbing and applying what he hears to his own nervous system.

His choice of notes, rhythm, and tone would be remarkable for anyone, but Jeff's playing is mature, well beyond his sixteen years. When Jeff decides that they have jammed on this song long enough, and he stops abruptly, as if to say, *Let's get on with our real list*, all three of Jeff's bandmates break into a sincere applause. Jeff coolly looks up through his long, dark bangs. "That was fun."

They decide to hand in their five choices of songs to compile the list of twenty and begin real work on shaping their sound and approach. King writes them all down on notebook paper.

LIGHT MY FIRE
TELL HER NO
A WHITER SHADE OF PALE
GIMME SOME LOVIN'
I'VE BEEN LONELY TOO LONG
DEVIL WITH THE BLUE DRESS/
GOOD GOLLY MISS MOLLY
EIGHT MILES HIGH
HAVE YOU SEEN HER FACE
DIRTY WATER
SUGAR PIE HONEY BUNCH
MR. YOU'RE A BETTER MAN THAN I
UNDER MY THUMB
I'M A MAN
GET OFF OF MY CLOUD
HEART FULL OF SOUL
I'M A BELIEVER
WE CAN WORK IT OUT
PUSHING TOO HARD
GIMME A LITTLE SIGN
FOR WHAT IT'S WORTH

They choose these songs in case any of the others did not fit well, or if they just want to keep learning songs:

OMAHA
MY GIRL
DAY TRIPPER
AIN'T TOO PROUD TO BEG
SUMMER IN THE CITY

The four begin with two songs from Barry's list because he knows them so well and is able to point out the places where the chords or the feel might change. *Gimme Some Lovin'* is the first song chosen to refine, and Barry explains to the other three that, though the chords are simple, the feel must be right. No one complained or groaned about Barry's direction because they all know and respect his abilities, and he only wants the songs to sound as strong as they can. As they work on the song, the door opens and in walks Sam. He apologizes for interrupting but sits down to listen until he needs to go. As they work, Sam is impressed by their professionalism and Barry's cynosure, but Sam is most caught and moved by his baby brother's artful gift. King can actually play the drums and play them well.

After some discussion of making a slight change to the approach of how the song is played, they begin *Gimme Some Lovin'* and take it all the way to the end without stopping, even ending at the same time, which is something they had not decided yet. They just all knew somehow, which is something only bands who have accumulated hours of getting acquainted can achieve. As they each sit in the quiet after the song's conclusion, King yells out a huge "woo-hoo!" and they all break into various congratulatory verbal back pats. "That was just incredible, guys, just incredible! I need to go to my meeting, but you are going to be a great band if you keep playing like that. Thank you for letting me sit in!" Sam is thanked by the band, and they wave goodbye to him as he walks out of the playroom door.

While the band is rehearsing, Ellie has made sure she is ironing her husband's shirts just on the other side of the finished wall in the basement so that she can listen to her son and his friends create or emulate the music of the day. It is a bonus that Ellie can give Sam a hug as he goes out into the cold garage. Gordon is outside raking up a few loose leaves that have fallen and making sure the volume of the band does not invade the peace and tranquility of Upper Marigold. He can hear it, but the filter of the house's basement walls makes the volume perfect for Gordon's preferences.

He believes this first song is a bit "thumpy," as he describes the experience to King later in the evening, and he misses hearing the vocals. This will be a perfect time for King to suggest that his dad fund a PA system for the band. He will assure Gordon that, with the acquisition of said PA system, the vocals will be audible and bring a whole new aspect of the band sound to his ears.

For the next two hours, *Light My Fire* is locked in as well as *Dirty Water, Have You Seen Her Face, I'm a Man,* and *For What It's Worth,* which has taken on the band's very own style, considering the distinctive sound of the Vox Continental as opposed to the Buffalo Springfield's guitars. They surprise themselves as they sit with King's old Guild acoustic guitar, an inheritance from his grandfather's estate, and work out the harmonies to the protest song. Giddy, childlike giggles emote from Danny and Barry as the vocals soar through the room. "This really sounds good, my friends," Danny confirms. "I just hope we can sing these parts while we are playing our instruments."

This brings concern to all of their faces, but Jeff is able to bring the plane out of the nosedive. "We will do it, even if we take one whole practice just to perfect the thing." Everyone's head bobs in the affirmative and that concludes the first rehearsal.

"Be thinking of band names, guys. We need to start promoting this beast as soon as possible, and it would be best if we had a name to attach to our greatness." Barry says as he smiles with confidence. "It's OK if I leave this, right King?"

"Yeah. Sure. Is it OK if I play it?"

"That's cool. Just be sure to turn it off when you finish."

"Far out! Thanks, brother."

"Can I have a glass of water so I can take my pain pill, King, please? My ribs are really killing me."

"I'll be right back." King runs upstairs to get Barry a glass of water and meets his mom with a tray full of cake slices for the band.

"You boys really sounded so good, King." Ellie gushes.

"Thanks, Mom. I'm just getting a glass of water for Barry, but go on down. I know they'll love the cake."

King was correct. Each musician grabbed at the baked good practically before Ellie could set the tray down. "Do you want milk or water or pop?" Ellie asks. She takes each of the boy's order and heads back upstairs, meeting King on his way back down. Barry needs to leave soon, but while he takes his pill, Danny asks Barry if he would play organ at his church on the seventeenth. "Are you kidding me? I have played lots of different music, but church music is one area that I have not mined. I don't think so but thanks anyway."

"Come on, Barry. Because it is close to Christmas, you will probably play mostly carols, and if there is anything else, no one sight-reads like you. It will be easy. Please? I would love to hear you on that organ anyway."

"That might be groovy, to be able to play that organ. The seventeenth?"

"Yes."

"Ok, but I want to get in there and practice on that instrument."

"Sure, you can practice while I'm cleaning on Saturday the sixteenth, and we'll be out of school for Christmas, too, so you won't be studying."

"I'm always studying, but that sounds good. I need to split, guys. It was awesome, and I look forward to the next time, whenever that will be. Just let me know."

With that, Barry is gone, and the other three just look at each other. "This is going to be good, guys, really good," King declares.

"Maybe we can play the Two Rivers Festival next summer?" Jeff's gears are turning, thinking of all the possibilities the band has. "While you're packing up your bass, Danny, let me tell you what happened last night." Jeff proceeds to tell the story of the crowd of rednecks who were holding him against his will and threatening him, and King adds his point of view. Danny expressed his guilt for not staying with the other two, but there was a part that excited Danny, the part about Pastor Allen inviting them to the Youth Christmas party.

"Let's go to that," Danny says.

Jeff and King both gasp a *"wha-a-a?"*

"Sure!" Danny continues. "How are we ever going to bridge the very wide gap between us and the rednecks if we always just stay in our yard to play? What a great opportunity the Lord is dropping in our laps, and they aren't going to act the same way at their church as they did at the game. Maybe we can break the ice before they break our necks."

"Now I know you're crazy, boy. I need a fag. I'm going outside for a smoke."

"I really mean it, Jeff."

"I know. That's the problem."

Jeff carries his guitar and amp out to his car and waits for Danny to do the same. King looks at Danny, his best friend, and tells him the Adams County boys will not be friendly to them on their own turf. "That's God's turf, King. If God is with us, who can be against us?" Danny paraphrases the Bible to make his point, which makes King turn around and start diddling on his drums, but Danny continues with urgency. "Don't be afraid, man. God is in control. He will take us when it's our time and not before. I believe these things with all my heart and soul, King, and I pray you will know Jesus someday so that you and I together can face down this kind of fear."

"But, right now, I am not a Christian, Danny. It's not that I don't believe that stuff. I mean, it's just so heavy, man, and maybe . . . I don't know . . . it just isn't for me. Not now." King stops and looks at the floor causing a very pregnant pause in the conversation. "Maybe I will believe it someday, Danny and I'm not saying you are wrong, but I didn't like the way I felt last night, being bullied by those idiots, and it would be hard for me to face them calmly without saying something."

"They were acting like idiots, but we have a chance to show them how to be a bigger person. If you went back and looked them in the eyes with some love in your heart, maybe they could see we are all just humans and not that different from each other."

"I'm *not* like them, Danny. I don't bully people, and I don't want to be bullied."

"You would like to bully them right now, right?"

"I guess I'd like to teach them a lesson, sure, but does that put me in their category?"

"In a way, yes. If you respond badly, then they will too, and then you will, and then they will, and on-and-on. We want our government to stop acting that way so we can stop having stupid wars, right? It has to start with us. You know, love your neighbor, even if they're redneck hoodlums."

Danny is a pit bull when it comes to his friend's soul, even at the risk of pushing King away. While he puts the church's bass back in its case, Danny continues, "Like the Bible says, we have all come short of the glory of God, King. We are all sinners, them and us, and that is the way God sees those of us who have not been cleansed in the righteous blood of Jesus. Sorry, I know that is really hard to get. I'm not trying to hassle you, my brother. I know you're sick of hearing it, but all I'm saying is, if you give your life to Him, God no longer sees your sin, and He will not judge you on that awful day. It's *real* and it's *important* and I love you, King. That's why I mention it so much to you. Hell is real, and I want to hang out with you for eternity."

"I love you too, and you know it, but I really have no desire to see those guys again. You go out there and do the *Lord's* work, but I'm not doing it, Dan."

CHAPTER
ELEVEN

It is dark and cold after rehearsal. Jeff helps Danny take the bass and amp back to church and then drops him off at his house. As soon as Danny closes the car door, Jeff hits the gas and goes directly to the pay phone outside of Charlie's. He has no desire to share his conversation with Darren, knowing Darren would ride him mercilessly. Jeff puts a dime in the slot and calls Alice on her private line in her bedroom. At lunch earlier that day, the two had discussed seeing each other tonight and possibly taking their relationship out into public view. Alice has no reservations, but Jeff is not quite sure.

He feels fantastic when he is with Alice, and during those times together, it is *world be damned*. However, when Jeff has time to ponder the ramifications of announcing this steady relationship with the most sought-after female in the county, he tends to lose his nerve. He starts believing the lie that she is way over his head, and he could never satisfy Alice Engel. Even if it is not true, Jeff wonders how he can persuade himself to stop believing it.

Alice has made no moves away from Jeff. In fact, she is quite bold about it. Any time they are at the Appleton Public Library, not exactly a dark cave away from it all, Alice does not hesitate to walk in holding Jeff's arm or with her arm around his waist, not knowing who they will see as they enter. Jeff knows Alice's affections toward him create new emotions he has never felt before.

He has had a couple of steady girlfriends in the past, but there is something very special about his relationship with Alice Engel, and it is much more than her wealth and beauty. There is something about her heart that lights Jeff up like a Roman candle. As young as he is, Jeff knows that even loving marriages can go sour. So, in Jeff's mind, the feelings he has now, or should we say, the feelings he sees Alice exhibiting for him, can go away tomorrow somehow. Jeff is not sure if he can take being the fool, when all bets are against his success with Alice Engel.

Alice answers the phone and asks Jeff how his rehearsal went. She tells him she stood outside for a while and believes she heard the bass pushing the air up the hill to her house. "I wanted to drive down to the Reed's and ask if I could listen, but I knew it was your first rehearsal, and I would be a distraction." Alice talks as if Jeff is hers.

"Yeah, probably best that you didn't this time. Wait until we get to sounding really good, and then I'll invite you. What do you want to do tonight? A movie or hang out at Fran's or both, if you want?"

"I don't care. I just miss you and want to see you."

"Ok, well, do you want to take our relationship to Fran's for dinner and then go see a movie downtown? Are you ready for the headlines in the news on Monday?"

"Yes, I am. I've thought about it, and there is nothing to fear or hide from. I will pick you up at seven thirty if that's OK with you? The TR3 needs to get out, today."

Jeff looks at his watch and it is six forty-five. He needs to go home to shower and dress and he hopes he has some clean clothes.

"Yes, ma'am, seven thirty is perfect!" Jeff pauses for what seems to be an hour. "I miss you, too, Alice. I can't wait to see you."

Danny had a head start on Jeff with similar plans of his own. As soon as Jeff let him out at home after rehearsal, Danny ran inside and showered. Walter had fixed beef stew for dinner, but Danny is in a hurry and explains to his dad that he would not be joining him tonight. Danny walks the half mile up Old River Road to Fran's, where Hannah is waiting for him at a four-top by the window she was able to wrangle. "Wow, great spot! I figured we would have to stand and wait for a while." Danny says as he leans down and hugs Hannah with his cheek on top of her head.

"Yes, it's fabulous, but I feel a little guilty taking a four-seater for the two of us."

As Danny sits, Hannah can see he is obviously excited, and without any coaxing at all, Danny begins to tell Hannah of the opportunity God has placed before him. It bothered Hannah that Jeff and King were accosted, but she loves what Danny is saying about going to the Adams County church and hopefully meeting the boys who were the threat last night. Before they can plan anything for that event, the waitress comes and takes their orders. Danny wants Fran's meatloaf with mashed potatoes and gravy and string beans. Hannah asks for the grilled cheese and tomato soup, always good on a cold, Ohio night. Each of them asks for a glass of Pepsi and thanks the waitress as she turns to deliver the order to the kitchen.

Danny suggests he take his guitar and that the two of them offer to sing a few Christmas carols and/or a hymn or two if the pastor there would think it is a good idea. Danny will take his guitar anyway, and there is no need for rehearsal. Hannah and Danny love to sing together at church on Wednesday evenings. They work on hymns and two of Danny's songs through the year, but they have been singing Christmas carols for the past month in exuberant anticipation of the celebration of the birth of the baby King, Jesus. They have actually done this since Danny learned to play guitar at the ripe old age of ten, and they have learned to augment each other with accuracy and ease. You could call them a kind of Christian Sonny and Cher.

Hannah listens to Danny as she looks around the room, watching the people cram into the popular restaurant. The door is opening and closing frequently as people come and go. Just before she turns her head back toward Danny, Hannah sees Jeff come in and then Alice. "Danny!" Hannah cuts Danny off mid-sentence. "Are Jeff and Alice a couple?" Danny whips his head around to see them both talking to each other, probably trying to decide if they want to go elsewhere.

"Wow, I guess so. Should I wave them over, Hannah?"

"Yes, please do. I guess God gave me this four-top for a reason."

"Amen, sister," Danny says with a righteous smile as he stands and waves across the room to Jeff. Jeff sees Danny, and obviously points them out to Alice, asking if she would want to sit with Danny and Hannah. Alice pulls Jeff by the hand toward their two friends. Alice enjoyed Hannah immensely at the party.

As Jeff and Alice approach the table, Hannah's voice emerges from the cacophony of voices, dishes and furniture being pushed and dragged over the wooden floor. "I'm so thankful I was given a four-chair table so you two could join us. It was meant to be, and it is really good to see you again, Alice. We had a bunch of fun at Danny's party, didn't we?" Hannah stands and hugs Alice and lightly grips Jeff's forearm at the same time as her way of saying welcome. Danny and Jeff slip each other some skin and sit down at the same time.

Jeff had run out of the house wearing only a sweater for warmth, so he had no need to remove a cumbersome coat. "Man, this place is packed tonight." Jeff points out the obvious, but it is something on everyone's mind.

"I'm glad you two are here," Alice says. "We were just getting ready to leave and go to Frisch's or drive downtown, but this is so much better. Yes, the party was very fun, Hannah, and your dad's barbecue was amazing, Danny. He's so funny and nice too."

Danny is still a bit dumbstruck that Alice Engel is sitting at his table, but he gathers himself. "Thank you, Alice. That guy loves to cook. If you're ever hungry, just come by our house any time, day or night, and Dad will fix you right up." That gets a good laugh all around just as the waitress delivers Hannah and Danny's orders.

"Do you need menus?" The waitress asks Jeff and Alice, getting an immediate affirmative head bob from both. The waitress disappears into the crowd, quickly returning with two lists of daily specials.

"Your meatloaf looks yummy, Dan man. I think I will order the same thing." Jeff looks up at the waitress before she walks away making sure she heard him. He is not one to dally on such things as food orders. The waitress looks over at Alice and asks her if she knows her order yet.

"Your choice is perfect too, Hannah. It's grilled cheese and tomato soup for me as well, ma'am."

Danny and Hannah bow their heads in thankful prayer for their food. Alice bows her head out of respect, but Jeff just looks around the room until he hears an "amen." Various topics of discussion ensue, some among the four and some between each gender. Hannah and Danny eat their dinners a bit more slowly than they normally would, hoping that the other couple's food comes before they finish. Both young women are adamant about hearing the band, but the two band members are just as adamant about waiting until the band is fully rehearsed and have a PA to sing through before their favorite people get to listen.

Alice and Hannah excuse themselves for the restroom, which provides the perfect opportunity to ask Jeff about his relationship with Alice. "So, you guys *are* a couple, huh? Smitty told me he saw you two at the library looking pretty friendly, but I figured I'd let you tell me when you wanted."

"Yes, we have pretty much decided that we are a couple; we just didn't want everyone talking about it yet. This is our first time out in public together, you know, where we figured we'd see friends. I'm glad it was you and Hannah, speaking of couples. Anyway, thanks for not hounding me about it after Smitty told you."

The girls return just as the second food order is being delivered, and everyone seems to be of one mind about the blessing of Jeff and Alice's relationship. Danny and Hannah still have a few bites of their dinners left, making eating for the table guests a little less highlighted. Conversation is easy among the four with Alice and Hannah becoming better friends by the minute. Alice appreciates Hannah's honesty toward the subjects they discuss and overall view of life. Alice finds her simplicity refreshing.

Hannah, on the other hand, can't get enough of Alice's stories of world travel and feels enlightened as Alice provides great detail of behind-the-scenes happenings that tourists never see. Hannah has offered herself in prayer to be God's missionary someday, and Alice's stories have made her feel more comfortable about leaving the quaint and comfortable Marigold. If God calls, she will go, and Hannah believes God has placed Alice in her life to enlarge her worldview, among other reasons.

Danny proceeds to talk about what he and Hannah have decided to do next Sunday, which triggers Jeff to make a restroom run. Upon his return, he finds Alice excited about the bridge-building crusade, and she asks Jeff if he would want to join their friends. "Uh, no, not really. That's not my kind of thing. Maybe some other time though." Alice has heard this tone of voice from Jeff before, typically when he talks about Darren.

With innate understanding and gentle tenacity, Alice tries reason. "It's just a Christmas party, Jeff, and it would be a good olive branch opportunity, don't you think?"

"I'm all out of olive branches right now, but I'll give everyone a firm maybe and then let's leave it alone tonight. Whadda ya say?"

After Jeff finishes his Camel, and Alice her Gitanes, they all decide to go to the same movie, *Cool Hand Luke*, which has been playing for three or four weeks at the Scioto Grand in Appleton. All four had heard great reviews, and the girls were not opposed to seeing a Paul Newman movie. There is no way they can all fit into the TR3, so, they decide to double-date in Hannah's car. When the four walk outside of Fran's, Jeff and Alice head for the TR3 and drive it to Danny's house, where it can sit more safely than in Fran's busy parking lot. After parking in Danny's driveway, the two wait in the cold for Hannah to arrive.

Just a minute behind, Hannah pulls up at Danny's in a well-kept maroon 1962 Pontiac Grand Prix sold to Hannah for five hundred dollars by her grandmother. Jeff loves the car, with its big engine and leather seats, and they find there is plenty of room for the four teens in the Grand Prix. Even though the bucket seats replace the normal bench-style accommodations, the couple in front is well-acquainted with each other and not the car-cuddling kind, and the couple in the back finds a way to stay connected by holding hands.

There is a small line at the theatre ticket booth, but it moves quickly, and after buying their favorite snacks and drinks, the couples find their way into the theatre. Finding four seats together is impossible, and they end up two rows apart. The Marigold kids all settle in, and Alice holds Jeff's hand as if he were getting shipped off to Nam tomorrow. Alice Engel is smitten by Jeff Lindor, and the ice that has grown thick and cold around Jeff Lindor's sheltered heart is slowly melting, drip-by-drip. Two rows down, Danny and Hannah are not being shy about their affections for each other as Hannah's head has found just the right spot on Danny's chest for movie watching. Danny's arm provides warmth and security for his very special friend.

***

Barry is taking his last break for the night in the club kitchen. He idles in small talk with any waitress or waiter who passes and finds himself taking a Benny and a pain pill at the same time. His chest is healing well, but he enjoys how he feels when he is taking the pain pills, and the Benny is taken to make sure he can make it through the night. Doctor Meade had been in earlier with some friends from the hospital. He is sincerely proud of his son's musical abilities and loves to show off his son to his friends and business associates, but his introduction always includes "my future doctor son." He requests *Blue Moon* and *Ain't That a Shame* by writing the song titles on a napkin with a five-dollar bill on top and asking his waitress to deliver it to the piano player.

Barry is a brilliant mess who is very conflicted, and he looks forward to going away to college so that he might have the time and space to actually find out who he is. At the same time, and just about as strongly, he loves Appleton and playing music with his friends. Barry has absolutely no desire to be a doctor. He pictures himself as a Leonard Bernstein character directing the orchestra of some great city in America or Europe, or a Burt Bacharach pounding it out in L.A. But of course, he cannot tell his dad that truth. His dad would tell Barry that he is going to Harvard and that is that. Unless the war ends, Barry has no choice but to go to college, and college life would certainly bring the freedom he yearns for so deeply, but he must figure out how he can change his dad's mind.

The second hand of the clock on the kitchen wall ticks toward the nine o'clock hour. Barry returns to the piano, which sits in the corner of the smoke-stained, worn room, decorated with blue leather and forest green velvet. He has one more set to play. The usual late night party people are gathered at the Club bar with only two of the fifteen tables ordering or finishing food. Most of them know Barry and his award-winning dad and tip him well. They are all professionals, stalwarts in their fields, and share common ground through money and education, which benefits their children. All the *right* connections have been made and treasures invested at their individual alma maters, securing the inherited paths of their pampered progenies.

Wooly-Bully is played, by request, for the second time during this last set, but the room rallies and forms a circle around the piano just before closing when Barry finds his lowest B flat and sings that famous opening line to the Kingsmen hit "Jolly Green Giant." Barry has played this venue enough times to know that any Kingsmen song brings the party out of the last set frat folk, and that means the tips will be plentiful. As he roars out the silly and fun lyrics, Barry moves his head back after each line so that anyone who wants can sing or speak the name of the vegetable of their choice into the microphone.

It is Saturday night, and Barry can sleep late, so the place goes wild when Barry doesn't stop at the end of the song but goes right into the Kingsmen classic *Long Green*. Barry is only seeing dollar signs now and decides to manipulate the wallets and purses of the eternal college students by climaxing the Kingsmen medley and ending the evening with *Louie Louie*, a song that is popular due to its sexual innuendos but is actually a beautiful and tender Jamaican folk song with no sexual connotations. The frenzy produces forty-eight dollars in tips and when you add that to the nightly club pay of twenty-five dollars, Barry will sleep soundly tonight.

Barry thanks the crowd and the venue and closes the lid to the baby grand. Girls hug him, and guys pat his back as he walks past the bar and waves goodbye to Leon the bartender who yells "Good job tonight, Mister Meade!"

Without stopping, Barry continues heading for the kitchen swinging door that leads to the outside. "You're amazing!" Pam the waitress says, causing Barry to smile an acknowledgement. He grabs his coat and opens the back door to find a fair amount of snow falling with huge flakes.

The snow muffles the sound, creating a lonesome but welcomed quiet. Barry stands and listens to the silence before he brushes off his car windows with his coat. He notices people in the distant customer parking lot talking about their night as they find their cars. Barry gets in the Safari and starts up the cold engine. With ringing ears, He lays his head back but does not feel the urge to close his eyes nor turn on the radio. His body is too wired up with Benny and The Kingsmen.

The wonderful peace Barry finds while alone in his very own car allows his mind to drift into thoughts about his sister and how much she means to him. He sees her almost every day, but he does not think about her and he finds himself missing her. He decides he will make time to share with Kay tomorrow, and at the rate it is snowing, they may be sledding down their backyard hill at the foot of Marigold Hill. Barry loves his sister, and he wants to make sure she knows that. Tomorrow will be Kay Day.

Barry puts the car in gear and pulls slowly out of the employee parking area. His destination is the US Diner for a late-night breakfast of eggs, potatoes, and bacon. The cook will probably have it ready for him since this is Barry's usual stop and usual request on Saturday nights after his club gig. His chest is hurting because of the power-singing he did during the entire last set tonight, as well as the secondhand cigarette smoke he inhaled. So, while driving through Appleton to get to the east side, Barry makes the unappealable and irrevocable decision to enhance the cook's breakfast with another Numorphan.

***

Downtown, the double-daters are just getting out of the movies and are also surprised by the snowfall. The boys immediately make snowballs and throw them at the girls, and happy laughter bursts out into the muted city street. Alice has lived on her hill through many winters and knows that a snow like this can mean a difficult and sometimes terrorizing climb home, especially in the Triumph. She conveys her concerns to the others, apologizing for being a bummer on this beautiful night.

"If you think it is going to be dangerous, Alice, you are more than welcome to stay at my house. I live up Hagen Street, which isn't exactly flat, but my big car can make it without a problem. Or, I can probably make it up your hill more easily than your car, so I can take you home. Just letting you know you have options." Hannah provides comfort for Alice as Hannah does so well.

"Wow, Hannah! That's a very nice offer. I suppose we should see what it looks like when we get back out to Marigold, but that is so nice of you."

The four walk to Hannah's car, throwing snowballs made from snow taken from tops of handrails and car hoods. When they reach their destination, they find they need to knock two inches of wet snow off the windshield. Hannah gets in and starts her car and gets the heater running to open up the thermostat, even though it is only pushing cold air until the engine warms. The other three pile in and resume their previous seating arrangement. Hannah heads for Route 43 out of town. WROR is on, but only in the background as the conversation is spirited among the four teens. They talk about the movie, the band, school, and anything else that comes into their minds. As they talk, Alice keeps her eyes on the weather, noticing that the snow has not let up.

It's at least three to four inches as they take the Marigold exit and roll slowly up to Old River Road. As they creep up to Danny's house, they see the TR3 all covered up in white. "So, what do you think, Alice?" Jeff asks.

"Danny, may I use your phone? I think I will call Daddy and see if he thinks I can make it."

"Oh, sure, Alice. Come on in, everyone. We'll see if Dad left us some stew and make a party out of it. Scope is on, I bet." Danny loves having people into his home and Walter never complains, but Danny knows his dad will want to get up bright and early for church, so the party won't go past the Scope show credits.

Danny shows Alice where she can find the phone, and the others find plenty of stew. Walter gets up to say hello and heats up this weekend's dish du jour for his son and guests. He too is surprised at the snow as it had only begun when he went to bed. Walter looks for a minute at his garage roof out the kitchen window where he can clearly discern the amount of snowfall. He washes a couple of bowls never turning to face the three kids who are sitting at the kitchen table. "You kids are welcome to camp out here for the night. I would rather you didn't drive in this weather."

Just as the bowls are being filled, Alice walks around the corner, and Walter gives her a big hug. "Hey, I guess I didn't scare you off the other night after all."

"No sir. I had a great time at the party, and you made me feel very welcome, just as your son does."

"That's nice to hear, darlin'. Stew?" Walter holds a bowl out toward Alice. She stares at it while her gears turn.

"My dad doesn't think I should drive the Triumph in the snow, and he said he would come get me in the truck. What is everyone going to do?" Walter holds the bowl down by his side so that Alice can think and agrees with her dad that she shouldn't drive.

"Where is your car, sweetie?" asks Walter

"It's in your driveway right now, but I will move it out of the way."

"It's no problem. I wonder if we'll have church in the morning anyway? They usually don't call it off, but this is becoming a pretty big snow."

"I think I can drive up Hagen if I leave now," Hannah says confidently. "Why don't you call your dad, Alice, and tell him you're staying with me tonight?"

"Really, Hannah? Are you sure your parents won't care?"

"They would love to have you and wouldn't want you *or* your dad driving in this snow anyway." Alice turns around quickly and runs back to the phone.

"Whatever she decides, she's going to have some of my stew before she leaves," Walter says with extra emphasis and a grin. No more than a minute later Alice returns.

"Mom said it was OK, Hannah. Dad hadn't left yet, so you have a tagalong tonight." Hannah jumps up from the table and hugs Alice.

"Mr. Mosely is not going to let anyone go until he feeds us, so sit down and then we'll make the trip. I'll call my mom and let her know." Hannah exits and Walter happily fills the four bowls.

"You wanna stay here tonight, Jeff? I'll be getting up kinda early for church, but you are welcome to sleep in the downstairs bedroom and sleep in. Just lock the door when you leave."

"Man, how nice is that? OK, I'll call Mom or Moron after Hannah comes back and let her know what I'm doing." The kids snicker at the moron remark, and Walter just shakes his head and turns around toward the sink to hide his chuckle. Hannah returns, and Jeff heads for the phone. The three start their stew without him, and everyone enjoys Walter's cooking.

Jeff returns and eats his quickly. "I'm gonna go out on the front porch and smoke. Would you like to join me, dear Alice?" Jeff holds his hand out to help Alice up from the table just as she finishes her stew.

"I'll move my car while I'm out there, Mr. Mosely." And the two walk out of the room wrapped in each other.

Walter looks at Danny. "My, I had no idea that was happening."

"They seem really happy with each other, Dad. It's a cool thing."

"I'll say." Walter retorts with raised eyebrows.

Alice hands Jeff the keys inferring that he move the Triumph. She gets in the passenger side, and Jeff maneuvers the sports car through the seven inches of snow to the backyard where he knows there is a flat, solid area. Finally, for however short the time will be, they are alone and are able to dissolve into each other's essentia with smoldering desire. Teen lust plays a huge role in their actions, but there is something deeper than either has felt before.

They know that they must stop, and Jeff pulls away saying in a choked-up whisper, "Walter's going to get an eyeful. We'd better get back inside before he does so that Hannah can leave, and the Moselys can get to bed." Alice utters a guttural moan of discontent as she pulls Jeff to her lips one more time. Then, in a frustrated thrust, they open the little car doors and walk arm-in-arm to the back porch and knock on the back door. Everyone is right there sitting at the table, except for Walter who has gone back to bed. Danny reaches over and unlocks the latched door and continues his conversation with Hannah.

"Are you ready to go, Alice? It hasn't stop snowing, right?"

"No, it hasn't and yes, I think we ought to go. It's seven inches deep, I'd say."

They all walk to the front door to say their goodbyes. Danny and Hannah hug and kiss each other lightly. Then Hannah hugs Jeff after he has completed his warm hug and slightly lengthier kiss with Alice. Alice reaches around and hugs Danny and thanks him for his hospitality and asks him to thank his dad for her. He guarantees it and asks Hannah to call him when she gets home. Walter has turned the upstairs phone ringer off so that the kids are free to call each other, if necessary, without waking him.

It is ten minutes after eleven, and several minutes since the girls pulled out of the drive when the Moselys's phone rings. It is Delores Meade asking Danny if he has seen Barry. "He is usually home by eleven, and I am worried because of the snow."

"I haven't seen him tonight, ma'am, but he is probably driving a little slower because of the snow. Maybe give him a half hour more before you go out looking for him."

"Yes, I suppose, but call me if you hear anything, Danny, please."

"Oh, you know I will, Mrs. Meade, and please ask him to call here when he gets home so we won't worry. Don't you worry though. I'm sure he's OK."

"Thank you, Danny, and I'll tell him. Bye-bye."

Danny walks back into the TV room and tells Jeff that Barry isn't home yet. "I worry about that guy, Dan. He's in a different world sometimes," Jeff says somberly.

***

It turns out that Barry fell asleep sitting up in his booth at US Diner and is just now being shaken by the waitress. She wants to close his ticket and she needs to be paid. Barry takes the wad of tip money out of his pocket and gives his waitress two five-dollar bills.

"Sorry for holding you up. Is this enough?"

"It is way too much. Let me get your change."

"Oh no. Don't worry about it. I need to get going anyway. May I use your phone, first?"

"Sure, Barry, and thank you so much for the tip." Barry calls his mom and lets her know he'll be home soon, if the roads are OK. Mrs. Meade dutifully calls Danny, and lets him know that his friend is OK.

Hannah's heavy Grand Prix hugs the snow like a champ as the girls make their way to Hannah's home. There has been very little if any traffic and no tracks where the car tires would flatten and harden the snow, causing slick spots. Hannah is a good driver and guides her car up the middle of Old River Road on her way to the right turn onto Hagen Street. Alice is not saying much, fearing she might distract the driver, but Hannah relaxes as she approaches Hagen. She turns the steering wheel slowly to the right, and the Grand Prix begins the gradual incline toward Hannah's house. She continues in the middle of this road, not expecting any oncoming traffic.

"This evening has been really fun, don't you think, Alice?"

"Oh yeah, I've really had a great time, and I am just so appreciative of you and your family letting me camp out for the night. Do you think you'll have church, tomorrow?"

"I don't know. This snow is pretty deep, and it happened quickly. People didn't have time to prepare. I imagine Mom and Dad will want us to try, and it will be all downhill for us. I suppose we'll take you to Danny's first to get your car, right?"

"Yes, that would nice if you can. I hate putting you out. You know, if I had other clothes with me, I wouldn't mind going to church with you."

"Oh really, Alice?" Hannah almost lets go of the wheel. "You're in much better shape than me, but we are about the same height and all. I bet you could find something in my closet you might like?"

"I don't have my toothbrush or anything."

"My mom has an extra of everything, so I bet she has a new toothbrush put away. I really would love for you to come. I think you would enjoy it. Everyone is so nice, and the chapel is really pretty and kind of serene. That's the Lord knocking on your door, Alice. He might have caused this whole snowfall just for you, to have an opportunity to go hear His word."

"Do you really believe that, Hannah?"

"Yes. I know He is capable, and He loves you that much, but I won't say that I know God's plan for the snow or you."

"I mean, it just snowed, right? There doesn't have to be some big cosmic plan for it, does there? Is that what the Bible says?"

"Yes, it is called providence. We churchy types say that God is sovereign. He made everything, and He knows where everything is all the time. I think He lets nature do the things He designed it to do, but He also uses nature to get our attention or help us. Matthew in the Bible has a verse that says, and this is Jesus speaking, 'Are not two sparrows sold for a farthing? And one of them shall not fall on the ground without your Father.' I'm not really sure what a farthing is, but I'd say it's not much."

"Ok. What in the heck does that mean, Hannah?"

"It means that, back then, they bought birds to sacrifice for one cent, I guess. Very cheap, right?"

"Yeah, I guess so."

"Well, those cheap and plentiful birds won't fall to the ground unless God allows it. It goes on to ask aren't we, the people He created, more important than birds? How much more will God take care of us?"

"Now that's beautiful."

"Yes, it is. In the book of Genesis, a guy named Joseph . . . "

"Oh, I know him. He married Mary."

"Hey, I'm glad you know that, but this is actually a different Joseph who had been sold to Egypt as a slave by his brothers."

"Nice guys."

"Yeah, really. Well, Joseph meets up with those scoundrel brothers of his years later and tells them what they meant for bad, God changed to good. God had allowed Joseph to prosper so that he could do good things for the Israelites."

"Wow, that is a cool story, and you really believe those stories are real?"

"Yes, I do. I believe every word of the Bible, but even if it were a bunch of really wise stories, they would still be good things to follow and model your life after. Archeology keeps finding more and more stuff that proves the Bible stories as well, but Christians have a strong faith for those things that are not seen, as Jesus said. Here's my house. This car is so good. I don't want to try to get up the driveway, though. Are you ready to walk up our hill?"

"Sure. I have driven by here before. I love this house! I love this neighborhood. Isn't there a Little League field right around here somewhere?" Alice asks as they get out of the car and lock the doors.

"Yes, it is down the hill that way. You can see the lights at night when there is a game. They just put them in last year, donated by the West Appleton Electric Company."

"That was nice of 'em."

"Yes, it sure was. Hey, don't let me forget to call Danny when we get in, please."

"I'll remind you because I would like to say goodnight to Jeff."

"What? You two like each other or something?" Hannah says with faux surprise. Looking Alice straight in the eyes and holding her hand, Hannah confides, "I think it's really groovy, you and Jeff being together. Jeff's a cool guy, and you're a pretty cool girl, I'm finding out." That comment warms Alice to the bone. Alice has not had a fun friend to talk with in her life. Aunt Charlene has been her closest friend, but there is a significant age difference, and Charlene is a family member with whom one would not confide too deeply.

They trudge up the hill, careful not to slip and walk around to the back of the house. Hannah's house isn't large compared to Alice's, but Hannah has twin older sisters who are away at Cedarville College. So, the house has four bedrooms and a study that can easily convert into a guest room when needed. Alice will sleep in one of the twin's rooms tonight, but only after she and Hannah have a late-night talk. Hannah unlocks the backdoor, and they enter the mud room where they shed their coats and wet shoes and socks. When dressing for her night out with Jeff, Alice chose to wear her Weejuns with gray tweed slacks and a maroon Lawrence Covell sweater purchased for her by Charlene when she was on a vacation in Colorado. Of all things, the sweater is sporting a white snowflake pattern. Her toes were next to frozen and her soft, black lambskin waist length jacket had not shut out the wet cold.

The girls are greeted by Hannah's mom. "Girls, I'm so glad you are home, and Alice, please make yourself comfortable. I'm sure you both are frozen, so there is cocoa waiting for you in the kitchen when you get settled. What about this snow, uh?"

"It came up so fast, and the flakes were huge, Mom. Hey, just to make it formal, Mom, this is Alice Engel, and Alice, this is my mom, the ever-peppy Louise Birdsong."

"It is so nice to meet you, ma'am, and I can't thank you enough for taking me in tonight. My little car is not made for snow. Hannah, I am embarrassed to say that I did not know your last name. It is beautiful." All three women burst into laughter, and there are hugs all around.

"I laid out some of Hannah's sister's pajamas for you, Alice, and a robe if you feel comfortable wearing one. Some socks, too, to keep your feet warm around the house until you go to bed."

"That sounds lovely, Mrs. Birdsong."

"Come on, Alice," Hannah says. "I'll take you upstairs so you can change."

Hannah takes Alice's hand and tugs toward the stairs. "I'm going to go to bed, girls, so I will see you in the morning. Your dad said we're going to try and go to church in the morning, Hanny. Alice, we would love for you to go with us, but if you don't want to, you can stay here, or we can take you to get your car or wherever you would like on our way. That list includes your home, too."

"Thank you so much, ma'am, and I'll talk with my mom in the morning to make sure they don't have plans for me."

"Yes, that would be wise, Alice. I will see you both in the morning, and Hanny, please turn out the lights down here before you go to bed." Mrs. Birdsong exits the hall in the direction of her ground floor bedroom and the girls run upstairs.

In Hannah's sister's room, the two friends find a soft two-piece pajama set laid on the bed ready for Alice. Hannah shows Alice the bathroom that is located between the twin's rooms for them to share. Just as Hannah predicted, Mrs. Birdsong has a brand-new toothbrush, still in its box, sitting on the bathroom counter next to a tube of Pepsodent toothpaste. "Wow, your mom really makes me feel comfortable. What a cool house. What's your dad do?"

"Thomas Allen Birdsong is an engineer at Appleton Rope and Pulley, and my mom is an RN."

"Oh, neat! I candy stripe sometimes, but I don't remember seeing her, and I'm sure I would remember your last name."

"She'll love you if you're a candy striper. I didn't know you did that. How often do you do it?"

"I try to work one weekend a month, but I can't always stripe that much because we travel some for the store," Alice says.

"Yeah, I loved your stories about going to all those places. It made me feel comfortable about being a missionary after high school. I think I am going to do missions for a year before I go to college."

"Really? Where would you go?"

"Where? . . . Wherever the Lord sends me. I mean, our church sponsors missionaries, and I would see where they need me."

"That sounds really cool, Hannah. What do you do, just leave everything? Where would you live?"

"It varies. Our church has connections with churches all over the world. Sometimes, the accommodations are like dorms, sometimes at someone's house, and sometimes just a room in the church with a sleeping bag on the floor, wherever the word needs to be taught or Christ needs to be known."

"That really does sound exciting, but I don't know if I could do something like that. I'm not sure if I could do without my stuff."

"That's very honest of you, Alice. It is so refreshing to hear people speak the truth. Well, the key, of course, is my love for God, His Son Jesus, and the Holy Spirit, a.k.a. The Holy Trinity. When a person truly loves the Lord, a little inconvenience is not so hard when you're suffering for someone who was nailed to a cross for you. We just kinda put our lives in His wonderfully capable hands."

"No . . . I guess not. Of course, I've never thought of that before now. My dad is Jewish and doesn't believe in Jesus, of course. My mom is not Jewish, though. My dad never practices the faith or talks about religion except when we are in Europe and mentions the Nazis."

"Oh my gosh, Alice! I never even considered that." Hannah does not know how to respond to a real live Jewish person as there are few in the area.

After a short pause, Hannah breaks the silence. "Look, you go ahead and get ready for bed, and I'll do the same. I think there is some makeup remover in that top drawer in the bathroom if you want to use it. In other words, if you need something, just ask me." Alice chuckles and thanks Hannah, and Hannah goes to her room, closing Alice's door behind her. A Princess phone is next to the bed, and Alice wants to call Jeff before it gets too late. She quickly undresses, throws on the very comfy pajamas laid out for her, and goes out into the hall where Hannah's door is open, and the radio is on.

"Hannah?"

"Yes, ma'am. Do you need something?"

"Well, we need to call the guys, and I don't know Danny's number."

"Oh, that's right! Come on in; we'll call from my phone. Hey, those PJs fit you really well. They make me miss my sisters, though." Alice walks through the open door and into Hannah's modestly decorated room. She has a canopy bed but nothing else really girlish. Her Princess phone is gray, and it goes well with her light yellow walls. Hannah picks up the phone and pushes the buttons that ring Danny's phone. One and a half rings later, Danny answers in an English accent. "'Ello. This is the Moosleh residence."

"Hello, is this Nigel?"

"Why, yes. Yes, it is." They both chuckle. "I wasn't worried, but what kept ya?" Danny asks in his normal southern Ohio non-accent.

"I introduced Alice to Mom, and then I needed to show Alice her room for the night. We made it safe and sound though. Are you and your dad going to church in the morning?"

"Yes, we're planning on it. Barry fell asleep at the diner and worried his mom to death. She called here looking for him but then called me a few minutes later to tell me he called her and is OK. I hope he doesn't fall asleep while he's driving home."

"Hey, is Jeff awake?"

"Oh yeah, we've been playing some tunes."

"Please tell him Alice wants to say goodnight, and I'll see you in the morning, Dan."

"Sure thing, dear Hannah-of-the-Birdsong bunch. Sleep well." Danny puts the phone down on the hall table and tells Jeff someone is on the phone for him. Hannah leaves her room, not really knowing where she is going, but she wants to give Alice some privacy. Jeff lays down the guitar and goes to the phone.

"Hello?"

"I just wanted to say good night to you and to tell you I had a truly wonderful evening. Even the snow was fun." Alice says.

"Yeah, it was. I really had a good time too, and let me know if there is anything I can do tomorrow to help get you home. I'll clean your car off if I can get up. The Moselys are going to church, but I get to sleep downstairs in a nice, dark, cocoon style room. I'm sure I'll be up before you arrive. Is your dad coming to get you tomorrow or what?"

"I might go to church with Hannah's family, but I imagine the roads will be clean enough for me to drive the TR3 home."

"You might go to church with Hannah? That's a bit out of the norm, isn't it?"

"Yes, it is, but it sounds nice on a snowy Sunday morning. I'm not going to ask you to meet me there. I know it's not your thing, Jeff."

"You are right about that, but I'll have your car all cleaned up by noon. Isn't that when church ends?"

"Um . . . I'm not sure. Probably. Well, I better go now." They both break into *Go Now* by the Moody Blues ending with a howl of laughter. "I can't wait to see you, again, Jeffrey Lindor."

"Yes, you're a lucky girl."

"You're right, Mister Conceited. I'll see you when I get my car, probably right after church. Goodnight."

"Night-night, Alice. Sweet dreams."

CHAPTER
TWELVE

I f Alice had heard church bells prior to this Sunday morning, they
would have been simply sounds wafting on the breeze that lopes up
from the valley below her house. This morning though, while walking
up the concrete sidewalk toward the sanctuary doors, Alice is hearing
the welcoming bells in real time, and they warm her heart. She is in no
hurry and is feeling an unexpected, solitary calm on the inside while her
brain is buzzing with excitement. Mr. Engel was fine with Alice hanging
out with her new friend but expects her to drive the Triumph home for
lunch if the snow has melted. The forecast says the temperature should
be a balmy forty-one by noon with a light rain that will wash the snow
away even more quickly. It is probably above freezing now, and that
means the Engel driveway and the roads leading to it should be clear
enough for the TR3.

Annie Boggs is greeting people at the church doors this morning and
notices right away that the Birdsong family has grown a new member.
"Tom and Louise, have you been hiding a daughter from us?"

"Annie, this is Alice Engel, a friend of Hannah's and now, a friend
of ours," Louise says with a twinkle in her eye. "You tell your husband
he had better preach a good one today, so Alice will come back with us."
With a huge grin, Annie guarantees her husband will let the Lord speak
for him.

"Alice, we are so happy you are here and please come in out of the
cold," Annie says in a motherly tone, even though she was never blessed
with children of her own, unless you count Danny.

"Thank you, ma'am. I was just admiring your bells. Their sound is so rich and quite welcoming."

"That's very good news, Alice. I'm glad you like them. It wouldn't be a Sunday morning in Marigold without those old things, I suppose. Come on now; all of you get inside. Hannah, I think Danny is up on the platform getting ready to lead worship with Mrs. Harlan and Minister Blanton."

The church parking lot is full, and a senior adult gentleman is flagging cars toward the Boggs' driveway that runs next to the church. When that is full, people will need to park on the street, which is messy this morning after the snow. Not knowing what to expect, Alice walks into the foyer where someone hands her a program and tells the Birdsongs, plus one, where there is an open pew, located right up front. There is no hiding the new girl when you have to walk past everyone from the back to the front of the sanctuary, and the Birdsongs say hello to just nearly everyone on both sides of the aisle. The sanctuary holds five hundred people and it is full, but the church is hoping they can enlarge the building next year to accommodate the growing community. The build will be a community labor of love, with local businesses contributing their time, talent and products, ensuring a glorious place to worship the One, true living God.

Everyone is very nice and neighborly to Alice as she heads to the front, and of course, Alice charms their socks off with her radiant smile and sincerity. While the Birdsongs are still in route, Minister Blanton walks to the microphone, welcomes everyone on this snowy Sunday, and asks the congregation to stand while they sing *Holy, Holy, Holy*. Danny is hitting every chord with Mrs. Harlan and looking the congregation right in the eyes as he sings and plays. As soon as that hymn has been sung, Mrs. Harlan takes everyone into the beautiful melody and lyrics of *Great Is Thy Faithfulness*. The room is righteously alive and buzzing, and Alice is getting chills. The sound of five hundred people singing is like nothing she has ever heard before, and the lyrics are moving. All of a sudden, Mrs. Birdsong turns her head to Alice's ear. "This is what heaven will sound like, Alice."

To watch Danny this morning is like watching someone she has never met. He is in full control and filled with the Spirit, though she is not sure why he is so utterly luminous. As far as Alice knows, Danny is only moderately animated, but this morning, he is earnestly singing every word with a smile that reaches ear to ear. His love shines. A teenage girl takes the platform and asks everyone to bow their heads for a prayer.

Alice is engaged, looking at this person who is her age taking control of the large assemblage, but catches herself and bows her head.

At the end of the prayer, Minister Blanton invites everyone to be seated while Danny Mosely sings *O Come, O Come, Emmanuel.* Mrs. Harlan starts the song with its haunting melody, but it is Danny and his guitar for the first verse, making the lyrics leap off the platform and into people's hearts. The moment is so touching and deep, that Alice doesn't even know she is emotional until she feels a tear on her chin. She isn't sobbing, but the song and Danny's presentation of the lyrics have struck a nerve down deep in Alice, in a place she doesn't visit.

Danny leaves the platform as Pastor Pete walks to the pulpit to begin his sermon on Isaiah 9:6. Mrs. Harlan will play solo as the worship ends. Pastor Pete thanks Danny and Mrs. Harlan and then begins the sermon by reading the scripture. He invites everyone to open their Bibles to the verse and then reads the verse twice for impact and clarity:

> For unto us a child is born, unto us a son is given: and the government shall be upon his shoulder: and his name shall be called Wonderful, Counsellor, The mighty God, The everlasting Father, the Prince of Peace.

Alice does not have a Bible, but Hannah pulls one out of the pew rack in front of them and opens it to the verse as it is being read. Alice's eyes follow these strange words, but when she hears the pastor tell the congregation that the words had been written seven hundred years before Christ walked the earth, she is amazed and confused. How could that be? Alice is determined to ask Hannah after the service is over.

By this time, Danny has made his way to the Birdsong row to sit and offers a big wave to Alice and silently mouths 'welcome' as he snuggles up to Hannah. Pastor Pete's sermon is deep and powerful, and he is good with painting vivid pictures of what was going on in the Middle East and the world around it during the time of Isaiah, juxtaposing it with the time of Christ's birth. All of it was fascinating to Alice, and she could almost place herself in the middle of it, having spent three weeks in Greece and the surrounding area. Israel was dangerous, with so many countries and peoples hating the tiny country, and it was off limits for the Engel family. As he tries to do in ninety-five percent of his sermons, Pastor Pete tugs the glorious and bloody thread of Christ that runs through all of the Bible, as well as life, hoping he will wake the heart of a new listener.

Just down the block, Jeff has opened his eyes and lies in his quiet cocoon of a room for several minutes thinking and pretending. He does not feel the strife at the Moselys as he does in his own home. Darren makes life very trite and repugnant, though Susan does her best to make it a warm place for her son. Susan has matured since her divorce and clings to a dream, one of stability and respectability, not unlike her time with Carl. She has begun to tell Jeff of her dream a time or two, while under the influence of any number of truth-suppressing regulators, but always decides that she does not want to drag him into something that is fleeting and out of reach. Susan has allowed herself to be dragged into mediocrity, simply maintaining a life that bears little, if any, fruit. Life after Carl has produced only a few hours of anything worth remembering.

The temperature is climbing into the upper thirties, and there is a distant, winter sun that uses its rays to slice through the morning haze. Jeff peeks out of the curtains but cannot see the TR3, which is sitting just beyond his sight range from the front bedroom. The Mosely home feels warm and lived in. Things don't change much in this home, and that makes it all the more hospitable. The couch has been in the same place it has been since Jeff met Danny, and the silverware drawer has probably been the same drawer since Beatrice nested the house. It is a comfortable home and surprisingly clean for sheltering two grown males. Before he visits the bathroom, Jeff goes to the kitchen window where he can see the Triumph. Most of the snow has melted and fallen from its sleek lines, but as he looks, Jeff thinks about kissing Alice and just how wonderful that feels.

Jeff makes his bed so that Mr. Mosely will not have to. He puts the same clothes on that he wore last night and waits for the Moselys, who will have Alice in tow from church. He turns on the radio and finds it tuned to a station that is ending a church service. Jeff finds WROR as quickly as possible on the big, round dial. Smoky Robinson is singing *I Second That Emotion* and Jeff sings along with it at the top of his lungs in the empty house. The news begins on the hour, which means it is noon. A heart transplant in South Africa is the lead story, but that is colorless triviality compared to Jeff's musing that it should only be a few minutes from now when he can touch the beautiful Miss Engel.

Just down the road, Alice has said her thank-yous and good-byes to the Birdsongs and promises to return her borrowed clothes, soon. The Mosely car pulls out of the church parking lot, and Walter says with heartfelt veracity, hoping to get input from his two teen riders, "What a great sermon from the Pastor this morning."

Alice takes the bait. "I have to say I was engrossed. I could have listened to him for hours. The history is fascinating, though I'm not sure about the theology. Not that I don't believe it, but that I just have not studied it at all. My family just has had no interest in going to church."

"Well, you were there today, and that is huge," says Walter.

Danny chimes in "I don't believe it was an accident you were there. God is speaking to your heart, Alice. People always want to know what God sounds like, and He *can* use an inner voice that we understand, but He just spoke to you in a big way through the Holy Spirit that filled that sanctuary this morning.

"I really loved your song, Danny. To tell you the truth, I didn't know you are that good at singing and playing."

"Why, thank ya, ma'am," Danny says in a John Wayne drawl.

"Home, sweet home!" Walter proclaims as he turns into the driveway. "And there's the little sports car gleaming in the sun."

Alice grabs her grocery bag of last night's clothes and gets out of the back seat just as Jeff comes out of the Moselys's back door. He practically runs toward Alice and when he reaches her, grabs her up and twirls her around as if he had not seen her for weeks. Alice becomes jelly in Jeff's big arms.

"Man, why didn't *I* get that welcome?" Danny says wryly to his guitarist as Jeff sets his girl down on planet Earth.

"If you don't know, I ain't tellin' ya," Jeff shoots back with his eyebrows high on his forehead, which makes Alice giggle. "Did everyone enjoy their morning?" Jeff asks politely and with only a modicum of interest.

"Yes sir, Jeff, and I wish you would have joined us," Walter says as he walks into his house.

Jeff dodges the church-going reference. "Thank you, sir, for letting me stay last night *and* this morning. I had a great night's sleep."

"I'm thankful for that, my boy. Everyone needs to get good sleep once in a while, and it makes me happy that you found that rest here. Rest is good for the soul, you know. Remember, the Psalm says God *makes* us lie down in green pastures. He wants us to rest."

"Thank you, sir. I will remember that." Walter goes into his house, and Danny asks Jeff if he is coming back in, to which Jeff gives an affirmative head bob. When Danny shuts the back door to the house, Jeff pulls Alice toward him, and they both stand in the driveway holding each other.

"Are you headed home now?" Jeff asks Alice without taking his cheek from the side of her head. He loves the way her hair smells.

"Yes, my dad says he wants me there for lunch. I think he just wants me to touch home plate during the weekend."

"So, did you and Hannah bond last night? Did you stay up late talking?"

"Not very late; maybe midnight, I suppose. She's a cool girl, and her whole family is really groovy. They were really nice to me."

"They should be."

"Why, thank you, my darling. Walk me to my car, please. I better get home." Jeff squeezes Alice before he lets her go, but they walk to the car holding hands. When they reach their destination, which was only fifteen feet away, Alice searches her jacket pockets for her keys, but her efforts bear no fruit. "Where in the world are my keys?" Alice says with a touch of agitation in her voice. Then, in her right ear, Alice hears the sound of small pieces of metal clinking together. She looks up with a puzzled face knowing Jeff must be holding them. "Where were they?"

"You gave them to me last night when I moved the car. I almost forgot I had them too."

"Thank you!"

Alice takes the keys and opens the tiny car door, allowing her to slide into place. The side curtains are on, so before Alice closes the door, she takes hold of Jeff's sweater and pulls him in a downward motion. Jeff knows exactly what this means, puts one hand on the soft top of the car and leans in to kiss his girl goodbye. The kiss is long and meaningful, but Jeff ends it by pulling back slightly and with open eyes telling Alice to be careful, and he will see her tomorrow. She reaches up and touches his face and then puts the car in gear to begin backing out of the Moselys's driveway. She beeps the horn, and Jeff waves as she speeds off toward Marigold Road and the top of the hill.

Jeff sprints back into the Mosely house to find Danny on the phone with Barry. He overhears the conversation, and it seems Barry fell asleep in his driveway as soon as he cut the car off. Luckily, his mom was waiting up for him and had seen him pull in. Barry will sometimes take five or ten minutes to come in from his late-night gig while he lets the buzz of a bar and his own voice in his head soften to a dull roar. Last night, however, his mom had to put on her winter coat over her nightgown and her new Muk Luks just to go out into the snow and wake up her boy. She knows he is beat and almost hated to wake him, but it was far too cold outside for sleeping. Now, Barry is telling Danny all about his night and the progress of his healing. Danny will never forget Barry's bravery on his behalf.

After Danny hangs up, he follows the music and walks into the TV room where he finds Jeff playing guitar. "I don't wanna be in love, Danny, but it's looking like I'm headed that way."

"That's not such a bad thing, Jeff, if you find the right girl. I did when I was twentys" Walter says as he walks through to the kitchen, but he is always welcome, and encouraged to interject wisdom when any of the boys are there. Jeff's comment must bring back memories for Walter.

"Danny's mom?"

"That's right: Beatrice. She was an amazing woman, well, girl when I met her, but I was nowhere near being a man. Even after fighting in the war, I was still not man enough to be a responsible partner. She grew me up, you might say, as any good woman will. The Bible says that women were made to help us men, and I think that meant 'help us become men.'"

Walter leaves the conversation and continues his walk to the kitchen but turns at the kitchen entrance. "I'm sorry to interrupt, Jeff. Look, Alice seems like a very special person, and I think she kinda likes you, too. I know you've had a rough time at home, but don't be scared of love. Just take things a day at a time and *enjoy* it. Don't keep thinking things are going to fail because a person will start building walls around themselves. Your mom and dad are not you, Jeff. *Enjoy* your life, and don't be afraid."

"Yes, sir." Danny looks at Jeff and tells him that his dad hasn't said that much to *him*, his own son, on that topic.

"Dad must see something in your relationship. He is pretty sharp that way."

Danny walks into the kitchen where he finds his dad leaning on the kitchen sink with his head down and tears in his eyes. "You OK, Dad?" Danny asks with tender urgency as he puts his hand on his dad's back. Danny knows what is causing the tears, but he still wants to make sure his dad isn't too sad.

"Oh, yeah, my fine young man. You know, some days, your mom gets front and center in my mind, and I don't really want to let it go . . . at least for a little while. Now that you and your buddies are getting close to the age of when I was falling for your mom, I think it uncovers lots of great memories that I haven't thought about for years."

"I would really like to hear about those times, Dad, if you ever want to talk about them. I'm sure you could shine a light on a lot of things for me if you feel like it."

"Let's do that, Danny. I would love that, but we'll have to buy out all of Charlie Washington's tissues."

Danny chuckles. "Soon, OK? How old were you when you started dating my mom?"

Walter Mosely holds his son and rubs his long hair with his right hand, pressing Danny's head to his shoulder. "You bet, my son. I recall I was about twenty, I reckon."

While they are in full hug, Walter tells Danny how proud he was this morning when he sang his song in church, but then asks for forgiveness about feeling pride right there in the Lord's house. "That was the Holy Spirit singing through me, Dad. I can't even remember much about it, so we have to praise the Lord."

"You're right as right can be, and I love to hear you talk like that. Praise and thank the Lord for the wonderful gift of the Holy Spirit and for using you as His conduit."

Jeff walks into the room and announces that he needs to go home and study for the bevy of tests that are coming up over the next couple of weeks before Christmas break. "Yeah, me too, man. I'll probably get on them in a little while. Sullivan has Ray Charles tonight."

"Oh, you are kidding! That is heavy, man. He is so good."

"I think I would like to see that, too. Nobody can sing like Ray," Walter chimes in with excitement.

"Thank you both again. It was a really fun night last night, and it is always good seeing you, Mr. Mosely."

"Sure thing, Jeff. Hey, when is Carl coming in?"

"Not for a couple of weeks, but then he will be here until the day after Christmas, unless they need a driver. I can't wait."

"He can't wait to see you too, Jeff. Hey, I'm going to cook for him one night because I'm sure he gets tired of eating at restaurants. Maybe you and your dad can come over and help us decorate our Christmas tree and have dinner. Hannah and Alice, too! Anyway, you have a great evening."

"Oh, man, that sounds like a nice evening. He loves your cooking and so does Alice. You guys have a good night too." Jeff opens the back door and heads for home.

The snow is melting so fast that there will be no sledding today, but Barry remembers his pledge to himself to make this Kay Day. He decides to take her into town and spend some money on her. She wants to go to Engel's, of course, and that sounds good to Barry. He is certain to find a few things for himself as well. The Christmas decorations are in full bloom down Main Street, and the windows that wrap both sides of Engel's on the corner will display intricate Christmas story scenes to celebrate the season. Most downtown stores close on Sundays, but starting Thanksgiving weekend, several stores and restaurants not only open at one o'clock through Christmas Eve, but most of them add evening hours to feed the hungry masses of Sunday Christmas shoppers.

Delores is elated that Barry is celebrating his relationship with his sister and is not sure what she will do with herself in their absence. Kay is excited because their first stop is the new A&W restaurant where they order root beer floats. Barry lets Kay order over the speaker/microphone that goes into the kitchen. Soon, a teenage waitress brings out their order to the car, money is paid, and brother and sister talk and laugh while they drink their Kay Day treat. When Barry finishes, he lets out a huge belch. Kay playfully hits him in the arm and tells him Mom would not like that, but then she sits back in the seat and lets out the cutest little girl belch Barry has ever heard. This makes them both crack up laughing as Barry starts up the car to head on to the Christmas frenzy on Main Street.

It is crowded downtown, and the parking places are hard to find. Barry drives around two or three blocks multiple times, having Kay watch for people who are getting into their cars to leave. Kay has gotten used to the streets and their landmarks and loves it every time Barry goes around Engel's block. Suddenly, Barry makes a left turn instead of the infinite right turn pattern he had been making. "Where are you going? You haven't given up, have you?"

"I bet you anything Mr. Klein will let me park in his lot, especially since I just spent a bunch of money there . . . and *please* do not tell Mom and Dad I bought anything at Klein's."

"Is Klein's a music store?"

"Yes, ma'am. The best around. He really has all the best instruments and musical toys."

The term *musical toys* makes Kay laugh. "I won't say anything, but you are a really good musician. So, you should be able to buy things there."

"Thanks, sis. I knew you would understand. Here it is. You want to go in and see all the cool stuff?"

"Wow, you will take me in?"

"Sure, sweetie. You're getting old enough to appreciate nice things, and besides, it's Kay Day."

Barry walks ahead of his sister for a few steps, but only to get the door for her. Kay smiles at her big brother as she walks in and then her eyes get as big as quarters when she sees the drum sets, Vox Super Beatle amps, and a hundred guitars hanging along the walls and in stands. All the salespeople know Barry and welcome him while asking about his little friend. Barry is proud to introduce his sister and Kay does her best to act like a teenager. "Wow, this is really neat, Barry! Look at that drum set. It looks like it is melted."

"Yeah, it's a company called Trixon. It's hard to find drum heads for them I hear."

"What did you buy?"

Barry takes Kay to the keyboard area and there, in the middle on a small riser, is an exact copy of the Vox Continental he bought. "I bought this and that amp over there."

"Oh, how pretty! Where is the one you bought?"

"It's over at King's house where the new band is practicing."

"You have a new band?"

"Yes, and it really sounds good already. It is me and King and Jeff Lindor and Danny Mosely."

"Jeff isn't a very nice boy, is he?"

"Oh, now don't think that about him. He has had some hard times at home and people just get the wrong idea about him. He's a great guy really, and I would trust him with you and that's saying a lot because I don't want anything bad to happen to you."

"Aw, I love you."

"I love you, too. OK, let's walk over to Engel's and shop around."

Kay is floating on air as she walks with her big brother on the sidewalks in the big town. She does not come into town often, and when she does, it is with her mom to buy school clothes on much less festive days. Today, she is with the coolest guy in town, Kay believes, and she watches every move Barry makes until they get to the Engel's display windows.

Each of the ten windows, five along Main Street that runs north and south and five gracing Twelfth Avenue running east and west, present their own Christmas theme or story and are highly anticipated spectacles every Christmas season. Except for the Nativity scene in window one nearest to the main entrance, the mini theatres shamelessly feature Engel's latest fashions and products and no one minds, especially Kay.

Five designers are flown in from France on November first and housed at the Engle's guest house just down the driveway of their home on the hill. They work tirelessly behind curtained panes, preparing for their reveal on the day after Thanksgiving.

The designers return to France the Monday after Thanksgiving and look forward to the Engel family's visit a few days before Christmas, leaving Aunt Charlene behind so that she can manage the sales through Christmas Eve. Her job will change drastically next year as there will be the two new stores in Cincinnati and Columbus and, hopefully, a Cleveland store the following year. After the till is counted, Charlene arrives in Paris on December twenty-sixth and joins the party already in progress. The Engels do not hesitate to celebrate the new year with plenty of Cuvee Dom for family and friends, but they are not known to do any lasting damage to their surroundings or themselves. On January second, the Engels return to America, letting the hung-over American tourists fly on New Year's Day by themselves.

Between Christmas and New Year's Day, there is a quick family day flight in a friend's Cessna 210 to the Engel area of northern Germany. With a rich Jewish and Hebrew origin, Daddy Engel insists the family pay its respects at Bergen-Belsen Nazi concentration camp. Though Bergen was not as brutal as other camps, many Engels died from disease or malnutrition. Markus Engel, Alice's dad and the son of a family who safely fled from Hitler's Germany, wants his family to never forget the horrors perpetrated on their heritage. He does not mention this back home, however.

"Barry! How in the world do they make those puppets look like they are ice skating? That is really amazing!"

"That really *is* amazing, Kay, and I have no idea. Danny Mosely told me Jeff is dating the Engel's daughter, Alice. Maybe that bad ol' Jeff will introduce you to her someday before Christmas and give you a behind-the-scenes tour?"

"The Engels are rich. How is Jeff dating their daughter?"

"I told you, Jeff is a really cool guy, and I guess she just likes him, whether he has money or not."

"Wow! That would be cool to know an Engel."

"No cooler than knowing you, my dear." Kay hugs her brother as they study each window.

After a half an hour, the two go inside where the place is buzzing like the proverbial beehive. Barry says he has sixty dollars to spend on her, which gets Kay's gears turning. She goes from department to department looking for the best deals for the things she really likes. By the end of the spree, Kay has made some great purchases, and Barry is exhausted. He was hoping he could make it through Kay Day without asking Benny for help, but he caves in to his habit and finds a water fountain. He creates a distraction by asking Kay what something is across the big room. As soon as she turns her head, Barry drops a pill on his tongue and bends over the water fountain to wash it down. Kay turns around and says she is not sure what her brother was pointing to.

Barry just brushes it off and asks Kay if she is ready to go back home. "We don't want to keep Mom's dinner waiting. Have you had a good time?"

"I still am having a good time, big brother. You're the best, you know it?"

"I know what you are, so what am I?" Barry leans down and sticks his fingers into a rib or two in his sister's sides. This makes Kay let out a little uncontrollable squeal of delight, but it makes many of the employees and shoppers look their way with concern. Barry and Kay break out laughing, and they start moving quickly toward the door to go back out onto the sidewalk, with bags of love in tow.

***

While his friends have been experiencing human reciprocity on this quiet, post-snowfall Sunday, King is taking advantage of his parents' Christmas shopping trip into Appleton. He knows he must return the drum set to the school band room tomorrow and wants to get the most out of this opportunity while the instrument sits in his basement. Not only is he practicing the songs the new band will play someday soon, but he has a school Christmas concert coming up on Thursday evening, when King will play the set on *My Little Drum* from the Charlie Brown Christmas recording. The song is not difficult, as far as rudiments, but King has learned that the feel must be correct over flash and showmanship, and he wants to lock it into his nervous system before the concert.

There are older, and some might say, better drummers in the school band, but Mr. Newman sees promise in King and wants him to "get his feet wet" with a simple but important song in a live situation. King is not one to stress out about these things or anything for that matter. He enjoys the challenges and does not care, to any degree that could change him, what people think of him. He always gives his best and if it isn't enough, well, so be it.

The little drummer boy has been at it in his basement for at least two hours and is beginning to get tired, physically and mentally. King walks upstairs to see what the day is offering, and he is delighted to find sunshine and shadows creating sharp contrasts between the trees in his backyard. He runs up to his bedroom and moves his artist easel over to the window that looks up the hill that is the backyard. In his closet, he grabs a blank canvas and his paints. Inspiration has been evading the budding Gauguin, but there is something about the lighting today that King believes has to be captured. He needs to express what he sees for no one other than himself. Some people take photographs, some are satisfied with memories, but King loves to make a blank piece of canvas or plywood or a rock become the bearer of a vision. He loves to move colors around so that they become picks and shovels for the mind mine and King is actually quite good at it.

There are voices in the house, but King does not stop. Ellie calls out to see if her boy is home, and King forces out a monotone "upstairs painting." Ellie knows right away that when her youngest says he is painting, it means "please don't interrupt his concentration." She carefully throws out an acknowledgement and goes to the kitchen to heat the oven, which will cook the lasagna she made last night. Ellie changes from her downtown clothes to a more comfortable pair of jeans and sweatshirt. Sam will be home soon from playing basketball with friends at the currently frigid outside courts behind the middle school in Paradise Park. He too must study for exams, and he will, without any encouragement.

King, on the other hand, must be reminded because his mind finds so many other wonderful thoughts he would rather think. There will be no Sullivan unless he studies, and Gordon will monitor his work. Gordon enjoys questioning King on freshman social studies because it was Gordon's favorite subject, and he is very interested in his son knowing how everything works to create the intricate and diverse world in which we live. When he is present for dinner, Sam normally pitches in too, heaving any questions regarding literature and Latin.

Ellie loves to see her family working together and has no problem serving her men as they bond. She has an artist's soul, like her youngest, and is receptive to the idea of just how boring facts and figures can be. Ellie shies away from taking part in any force-feeding of information. School is all very narrow to the sacrificial alto, and she wishes the school gave trophies and medallions for creative thought and expression and celebrated the drama coach as much as the coach of basketball. Of course, Ellie wants King to make good grades, but for her, that would never define his brilliance. For now, though, the sun is once again going down on genius, and King is probably putting his paints away. The time of inspiration was fleeting, but Ellie knows King put something very special on the canvas in his short sprint of time.

***

From her third-floor bedroom that boasts a panoramic view of the Marigold valley and Scioto River facing southwest, Alice tries to study for her exams, but all she can think about is Jeff. She has decided to go with Danny and Hannah to the Adams County church party on Saturday and knows Jeff will refuse her pleas to go. Still, she will ask him because Alice believes the peaceful act of Jeff returning with no fear could change minds and possibly lives. Something that simple could open the minds of the poisoned teens of that area, Alice thinks, and that can only better many lives exponentially.

Then, in a flash seemingly from out of nowhere, the lyrics to the song Danny sang earlier today enter her mind, and they wrap her thoughts up tight like strands of fibers around a core that must be the Jesus she met this morning. The desire of nations; in one; sad divisions cease; and King of Peace. Inexplicably, as she watches another sun set in southern Ohio, Alice Engel receives crystal clarity that a King of peace is what is needed in a world that is unravelling. Is the transformer *a* King of peace or *the* King of peace? Alice is not sure, but she has every confidence that the first step to transformation could be a small but mighty gesture of friendship in Adams County.

CHAPTER
THIRTEEN

Danny, Hannah, Alice, Adam, Nick, and a friend from church named Brenda are headed for the town of Chesterville, home of the church of Pastor Dennis Allen. None of the visitors are sure of the name of his church and ask God to help them connect with this mission of love. "Stop here at this gas station, Danny, and I will ask someone," Brenda offers. She believes that it might be best if she represents the carload of teens instead of one of her mop-topped male counterparts. The fashion of long hair on men has not quite reached this area of the world, even though it is 1967. This sounds like a good idea to everyone and Danny makes the stop.

Danny does not pull the car into full view of the station employees but stops and lets Brenda jump out. The car is quiet as the kids from Marigold watch Brenda walk into the building, but it is not long until Nick begins to recite the "shadow of death" part of the twenty-third Psalm, which immediately breaks the tension in the car. Without any disrespect for the Word of God, those words added levity and a reminder that God is in control. After only a short minute, Brenda comes bounding out of the door in her red Christmas sweater and white earmuffs with a smile on her face and cold breath being generated. "It's close. Just take a right at the next street, and it is up about three blocks. They knew exactly who Pastor Allen is, and they were very nice, old country men."

Danny follows Brenda's directions and soon sees the church with Pastor Dennis Allen's name on the sign at the parking lot entrance. It is a large church, maybe twice the size of their Marigold Christ Fellowship Church building, and with the time being five-fifteen, the parking lot is fairly full and still receiving partygoers. The Marigold kids park near the door in the back of the building, apparently being the entrance to the party according to some signage. King had told Danny to look for a very cool '56 cherry red and white Chevy and to beware if he sees it. Danny just rolled his eyes: a meeting with the car's owner is completely antipodean to the mission. Danny believes, with God's righteous right hand on him, he will face down any fear he might have and bring the love of Jesus Christ to the anticipated powwow.

With all six heads down and hands held, Hannah begins to pray out loud in the car asking the God of creation, the Great I AM to bless their mission of love and that the Holy Spirit will put the words He wants them to say on their lips. Hannah asks that they have no fear and that they glorify Him in all their ways. She closes the prayer acknowledging they come to the throne through The Son, Jesus, and Amen. Alice does not understand exactly what Hannah asked God for, but she hopes that she represents this God and these Christians well.

Danny gets out of his car, leaving his guitar in the trunk, and glances around the lot. He observes several well-maintained rods, but not the one that King told him about. Danny remembers King saying that Arnold is the name of the boney-faced, greasy-haired hillbilly who owns the red and white Chevy and the boy who seemed to not like long hair on the male of the species. All six are now out of Walter's car and walk as a group into the backdoor entrance where they are met with several stares, which quickly change to smiling faces. In a large room full of game tables and padded folding chairs, a record player with a PA microphone in front of its speaker is playing an Elvis gospel album. Several groups of Christian teenagers are gathered in conversation, laughing and listening to each other.

A young woman with red hair and in her mid-twenties waves at the Marigold teens and walks toward them. As she moves closer, she begins to speak. "Hello. I don't believe I have seen you here before. I'm Patsy and welcome." The group thanks the bubbly woman as they are joined by three more partygoers.

"Hey, Merry Christmas, and help yourselves to the food. Where are you from?" Alice steps up and turns on her sophisticated charm.

"Merry Christmas, and thank you so much. We are from Flint Township, and your pastor invited us to your party after last week's game."

"Oh, wow! This is so great! Yeah, Pastor Allen is not shy about inviting people to his church. We are sure glad you're here, and I knew we needed to have name tags. I was voted down as we were buying supplies because we all know each other and didn't figure on visitors. Like I said, I'm Patsy, and I'm one of the two youth ministers here. Jason, the other youth minister, is around here somewhere. There he is. He's the guy who just started serving the punch at the table." Jason looks to be about thirty and has a wedding band on his left hand.

Most of the teens have a country look to them. Some might say "redneck," but no one from Marigold is here to attach negative connotation or pass judgment, and they all know that Jesus leveled the playing field of life. Danny looks at his brothers and sisters in-the-faith, smiling at Alice whom he knows does not read the Bible, and recites, "'There is neither Jew nor Greek, there is neither bond nor free, there is neither male nor female: for ye are all one in Christ Jesus.' The Apostle Paul told the Galatians this truth, and he was really telling all of us. Let's not let go of this while we are here." Alice is fascinated by what Danny said, and she will never forget it. She has been judged as an out-of-touch rich girl, and she has judged others in her own way. She plans to never do that again.

Several new friendships have blossomed over the past hour. There have been games, testimonies, and jokes, but when Pastor Allen visits, everyone gathers around him and pulls up chairs as he sits down. He wishes everyone a Merry Christmas and then looks right at the Marigold bunch and asks them who they are. Alice is quiet and lets the Christians in her group talk to the kind host. Danny introduces himself and tells the story. "Last week, at the basketball game, you met a couple of our friends from Flint Township. Their names are Jeff and King . . . ."

"Oh yes, King. How could I forget that name or those circumstances? Did they come with you?"

"No, sir, they did not. They are not Christians and felt a bit uncomfortable. To be honest, they were not sure how they would react if they saw any of the guys they met at the game. I was excited to hear about your invitation and tried to explain how powerful their visit would be while here on holy ground instead of a school parking lot. I told them that things would be different and that your teens need to see them in a different light, but they did not want to hear it."

"I am really sorry to hear that, Danny. I believe they met Arnold and his friends that night, and they can sometimes get a little carried away. There are a few parents in our community who, unfortunately, speak and spread hate, and I have tried to talk with them about the love of Christ, but they don't want to listen. I would not and have not given up on them, but we need to remember that we are only the messengers and that God does the work. Sometimes, for whatever reason, He deafens some to His Word and please don't ask me to explain it. I talked with Arnold's dad, who is one of our deacons here, just yesterday and reminded him about this party."

Just then, everyone could hear a very loud and powerful car engine pulling up outside, and they all had a pretty good idea who was behind the wheel. "I think that's Arnold now," one of the teens deduces. Pastor Allen does not want the room to be noticeably quiet as Arnold walks in, so he continues to talk, focusing on love and forgiveness.

"Colossians 3:13 says, 'Forbearing one another and forgiving one another, if any man have a quarrel against any: even as Christ forgave you, so also do ye.' I'd say that should be painted on our bedroom ceilings above our beds so it is the last thing we see and think each night and first thing we see each morning. That one verse is just huge. Heavy, you teens would say." The door opens and in walk four tough looking teens wearing sweatshirts and jeans. Danny notices that one has a very boney face. "Hey, Arnold! Come on in, boys, and pull up a seat. We're just having an open discussion on forgiveness, and I would love to hear what you have to say, if you want to add your thoughts."

"Sorry we're so late, Pastor. We kinda forgot about the party, but my dad said I should come anyway."

"Your dad was right, Arnold. Hey, we have some visitors from Flint Township. I invited a couple of their friends last week when we were all talking in the school parking lot after the game. They couldn't make it, but they told their friends, and they decided to come."

Arnold and his friends stop and stand and stare at Danny, Nick, and Adam with their long hair and during the longest minute ever recorded, the party gets very quiet. Danny stands up, which makes the other five stand as well. Danny pushes his chair back and begins to walk confidently toward Arnold and his group with his hand out in a show of peace and forgiveness. Arnold just stands and continues to stare at Danny as he approaches; Arnold's friends are tapping Arnold on his arm as if to ask him if he sees what is coming toward him. One friend tugs on Arnold's arm, signaling him to leave, but Arnold pulls his arm away.

"Stop," Arnold says to Danny, and Danny stops immediately, but he does not take his eyes off Arnold. There is a pause and all of the partygoers, including the pastor, Patsy, and Jason sit in hushed silence. The Marigold group is still standing and is feeling great apprehension for their friend, although they feel comfortable that Arnold would not hit

Danny in the church. Then Arnold speaks. "I don't remember seeing you at the game. Look, I know you think I am some dumb hick, and I am not as cool as you. Maybe you're right, but I don't understand all your long hair and girly clothes stuff, and it really gives me and my friends the creeps. You all look like girls to us, and that doesn't seem right. I think the pastor would agree that the Bible says being queer is wrong, but it's wrong for me to call you names and make you feel scared too. I know it is, but it just seems like the world is going crazy and that people like you are taking drugs that ruin your minds, and you are all having sex any time and with anybody." By this time, Arnold is getting red-faced and stiffening up, but he continues "You protest against our brave soldiers, spit on them and burn our flag, and you just seem like you are against America. What are you doing out here? Trying to turn us into a bunch of hippies?"

With a fearless and calm tone, Danny answers, "No, Arnold. I've seen all those things you are talking about on TV and some movies, and they bother me, too. I grow my hair long because I just like the way it looks. I have never taken any drugs, and I don't protest against our soldiers. I don't support the war because I think a bunch of us young kids are dying for a foolish reason, but I would serve if my country called me. I'm not a hippie, and I have never had sex, with a girl *or* a boy, but I play bass guitar in a band and guitar at my church. I'm just a regular teenager like you, Arnold. You like cars, and I like music. You cut your hair short, and I let mine grow. I'm just hoping I might make the world a little better spreading the love of Jesus, and that is why the six of us came out here. We want to let you know – *you*, Arnold – that we want to be friends with you and hopefully share the love of Christ with you. We were all made by the Creator God, and He loves you and me. My name is Danny by the way. Will you please shake my hand, Arnold?"

Arnold looks at Danny's hand and then back up to his face. From Arnold's left side, a voice speaks out: "I will, Danny. My name is Scott, and I like what you are saying. Come on, Arnold. Shake Danny's hand and let's get some food."

Arnold looks at the floor in thought. The room is as quiet as it has ever been as everyone holds their breath. Finally, Arnold looks up at Danny and says in a peaceful tone, "Welcome to Hicksville, Danny, and please call me Arnie." Arnold looks relieved as does the whole room. The two shake hands and the rest of the room runs up to the boys and pats their backs, and they all praise the Lord. The Marigolders shake all of Arnold's friend's hands and begin a new party in the Spirit of the Lord.

All, except one of Arnold's friends, who turned and walked out the door when Arnold shook Danny's hand.

"What about him?" Danny asks Arnold about the one who left.

"Presley will get over it. He's just like that. So, what happened to the two others who came to the game? Were they scared to come out?" Arnold did not ask this question of Danny and Hannah to deride Jeff and King. He sincerely wanted to know out of regret, a kind of repentance.

"No, they weren't so much scared as they were unsure how they would react. We asked them to come though."

"Well, tell them I'm sorry for the other night, OK?"

"I sure will, Arnold or I mean Arnie, and I know it will change their hearts and minds about everything. King and Jeff aren't Christians, so I think they were more scared of God than of you tonight." They both laugh, but Arnie looks at Danny and admits he is not really sure if he is a Christian.

"I go to church sometimes, and I know the Bible pretty well because my dad raised me with it, but I can't really say I'm saved. I can't shake those bitter thoughts that I have, so it is hard for me to humble myself, as my dad tells me we need to do."

"You know what, Arnie? None of us can, and that is why we need Jesus and the Spirit in us. Our human hearts are hard against God, but when we give our lives over to Jesus, our heart is transformed. Read Chapter Three in Acts and dig how all those people were changed by the Holy Spirit. Jesus can change your thoughts and my thoughts too. We might still have some ugly thoughts once in a while, but we won't be as anxious to act on them, you know? There is an old joke that says 'I'm still a sinner. It's just no fun anymore.'" Arnold's boney face erupts with laughter, and Danny can't help but see the young, innocent boy Arnie used to be as he lets his guard down.

Pastor Allen marvels at Arnold's laughter. "I don't think I've seen you laugh like that in five years, Arnold. What a blessing."

"Hey, I guess these Flint kids are alright," Arnold says with a nasalized hillbilly drawl and a wry grin aimed at Danny.

"We try. We try. We don't have cars like yours, though. I hope you'll show your car to me sometime. Maybe you and your friends can drive over to Marigold?"

"And get killed, man. People hate us over there."

"Aw, there are probably a few who feel that way, but all my friends, including the two you met last week, would enjoy you guys."

Danny gets an idea. "Hey, maybe my band could play at your school sometime? We're really getting good, and that big, dark-haired guy you met is a fantastic guitar player – *and* he loves cars."

"Really?! That's cool. What's the name of your band?"

"You know, we don't have a name yet, but I imagine we will have one this coming Saturday when we rehearse. Arnie, you ought to talk with Pastor Allen about what you were telling me. I'm sure he would be very interested and would help answer your questions."

"What have you boys been talking about?"

"I'll let Arnie tell you, Pastor, when he wants to. Is that cool, Arnie?"

"Yeah, sure. That's fine. I'll talk with you sometime, Pastor Allen."

The party continues for another half hour, and everyone is having a fun time, but at seven o'clock, Pastor Allen takes the microphone from the record player and announces that it is time to end the festivities. "Before you leave or help clean up, let's all hold hands and sing the first verse of Silent Night. It is a Christmas party, if I recall." Everyone joins hands, including Arnold and his friends. Arnold finds himself holding the hand of the girlfriend of the guy he almost beat up last week, but he does not know that. He just knows she is very pretty and has warm hands.

As everyone leaves the party, Arnie is unable to show his car to Danny due to the darkness. After saying goodbye to their new friends, the six teens climb back into Danny's dad's Olds F-85 and point it toward Scioto County. The car is full of the Spirit as they talk about how Danny said the right things to Arnie. Of course, Danny took no credit and gave all the glory to the Holy Spirit who spoke for him. Sitting beside her *friend*, Hannah pats Danny's right leg as she sits close beside him. Adam is on her right side, and all three are watching for the weaving headlights of nighttime drunks. To their right, the ancient Ohio River looks like glass, with the muted light of the half-moon reflecting off its flow.

The six have gotten quiet, looking out the window at the black night. They can barely make out a long barge that is headed toward Pittsburgh, its running lights outlining her shape with their watery reflection appearing to be yellow, insect-style legs. Hannah looks away from the barge and down at Walter's radio. "I wonder what Walter has cued up on his dial? Does anyone mind if I turn the radio on?"

"You make yourself happy, young lady," Adam offers merrily in his most grandfatherly-styled voice.

***

Danny awakes with a jolt. His eyes are crossed and murky as he tries to make out his surroundings. He fights the sheets that are covering him, and he flails aimlessly at whatever is hanging from his left arm. He hears his dad yell for a nurse, and then Danny feels his dad's hand on his chest and can hear Walter saying "sh-h-h-h" close to Danny's head. Danny passes out again and goes limp. When the nurse comes in, Walter tells her his son woke up in a daze and then passed out. He excuses himself to run to the phone just down the hall from the room door so that he can tell Pastor Pete that Danny is waking up. It is Tuesday around noon, and it is the first time Danny has moved since Sunday night.

One thirty in the afternoon ticks by. Pastor Pete and Annie have been sitting with Walter in Danny's room since they arrived at twelve forty-five. They don't so much talk; they are just there as a shoulder for Walter, something he needs. He has slept very little since Sunday night and when he has, it has been in the same chair that he sits in now. Walter is right by the bed, lightly rubbing his son's hand and frequently going into deep prayer.

"Why am I here, Dad?"

"Hello, my boy. We'll talk soon, son. You just rest now."

"What happened, Dad? I want to know."

"Danny, a deer ran out in front of you, a huge buck, and before you could even see it, the car hit it."

"Is everyone else OK?"

Walter pauses. He has rehearsed this a thousand times in his mind, but now that the time to tell the story is here, it seems too acerbic; too harsh for this tender time. With the good pastor's hand on his back, Walter begins "No, son."

"Oh, no, no, no. Where's my Hannah, Daddy?" Danny moans and shouts in a shrill, slurred voice.

"Her shoulder was broken, and some glass in her face. You be still now, son."

"Oh, her pretty, little face. No, no, no."

A nurse enters the room with a syringe and tries to give Danny an anti-anxiety drug called Valium, but he fights the nurse. "I *want* to suffer if Hannah is! Get away from me." The excitement causes Danny to throw up, but Pastor Pete speaks as Annie goes to the nurse's station to ask for someone to clean Danny's floor.

"Danny. Let the nurse do her job. You don't need to suffer, my friend. May I hold your hand while she gives you the medicine?" Danny's eyes finally uncross and semi-focus, looking right at the pastor. Seeing his face alleviates the rigidity in his body, and the nurse takes advantage of the moment and does her job quickly. Knowing it is not the best time to try to get Danny's vitals, she leaves until the doctor arrives.

The drug takes affect with rapid speed, and Danny lies quietly while the floor is cleaned and Pastor Pete continues to hold Danny's hand. "I met Pastor Allen, Danny, and we have stayed in constant contact since the accident. He is a very nice man."

"Please tell me about the others. Please?" Danny tearfully pleads. The Pastor looks at Walter, asking with his face if he should tell Danny. Walter walks over and sits on the side of the bed, rubs his son's thigh and begins.

"Son, it is bad news, the worst, and you are not very strong right now, but I know you need to know."

"What? What happened?"

"Nick and Alice, who were in the back seat, just have minor bruises and a few cuts from the glass. Brenda's injury is somewhat more extreme. The deer that jumped in front of you was about three hundred pounds and when the car hit him, he slid up the hood and smashed into the passenger side of the windshield." Walter conjures up every ounce of courage to finish the story. He pauses and then says, "Adam didn't make it, son."

"No-o-o-o-o-o! God, no!" Danny wails and tears immediately stream down his face. He repeatedly and uncontrollably beats his fists on the mattress in a frustrated and futile fight for Adam's life. His lamentations are heard throughout the hospital floor, but the nurses down the hall at their station, know what has just occurred. With the sudden jolt of blood pressure, the Valium's effects are accelerated and begin diminishing Danny's anguish. The drug strips the young man of his own will until he can only lie tranquilized and sobbing in his hospital bed.

After a few minutes of deep sorrow in the room, the doctor comes in and the nurse follows, taking Danny's pulse and temperature. "Do you know where you are, young man?"

"Yes."

"Where?"

"A hospital room."

"What is your name?"

"Danny Mosely."

"Do you know the people who are visiting you?" The doctor points to Walter, Pastor Pete and Annie.

"Yes sir. That is my dad, my pastor and my second mom." Annie blubbers quiet tears upon hearing Danny give her that esteemed title.

"Your head hit the car door frame very hard, and the blow gave you a severe concussion," The doctor begins. "I want you to stay here through tomorrow, and I will keep a close eye on you. You don't have any broken bones, but you do have a badly bruised chest and left shoulder, so you are going to hurt for a while. I have given your dad a prescription for some pain medicine. You're going to be dizzy for a week or so, and I don't want you to get out of bed without help. Dad, with you holding on, he can get up for the restroom today, and if that goes well, you will want to walk him down the hall and back tomorrow to start returning strength to Danny's legs. If he looks like he is healing, I will release him on Thursday for rest and recovery at home. No strenuous activities for another week. If he is walking without dizziness through this weekend, he may go to school next week, but his teachers should be alerted that he should take it easy."

"Doctor, did you say Thursday? What day is this?"

"It is Tuesday, Danny. Your system was shocked so badly that it naturally shut down and put you into a comatose state. You hit your head really hard, my boy. Please, take it easy. Well hello, Roy." At that moment, Barry's dad enters the room.

"May I speak with your patient, Doctor Perry?"

"Of course, Doctor."

"Thank you. I heard you were awake, Danny. How are you feeling?"

"Sad, sir. Very, very sad. I loved Adam and his family. Oh, what are they going to say to me?"

"They know there was nothing you could have done, Danny. There are deer all over that part of the county, and they cause a lot of damage. I know Doctor Perry told you to take it easy. Listen to him and I will look in on you tonight. Barry wants to see you. Would that be alright, Doctor Perry, if my son comes to see his friend this evening?"

"Sure, if Danny doesn't mind. You'll probably have a headache for a few days, Danny, so Roy, just let your son know that Danny might not be very talkative."

"Good advice, Doctor. I will."

Doctor Perry looks at Danny. "Danny, you take it easy, and I am going to step outside with your dad to give him a few more ideas regarding your care. I will see you tonight, sometime."

"Ok."

Doctor Perry and Walter step outside Danny's room, and the doctor informs Walter that Danny will most likely get depressed, but it shouldn't last for more than a month. "It's never a good time, but Christmas is a considerably harder time of year to accept the sudden death of a friend." Doctor Perry hands Walter a Crisis Counselor's card and suggests Walter use the resource if Danny cannot move beyond the guilt and loss on his own. Walter assures the doctor that their church will surround Danny and will shower him with love and strong shoulders.

When Walter returns to his son, he finds Danny, Pastor Pete, and Annie in deep prayer for Adam's family, Hannah's recovery, and for the others who were in the car who must be feeling the trauma. When they finish, Walter tells Danny that a boy named Arnold had come by to check on him twice since the accident. "God works in the most mysterious ways, Dad. He is the guy that wanted to beat up Jeff at the Northern game. We all had a great time at that party. Adam was so fun and funny that evening. He was telling jokes and flirting with all the Christian Northern girls." Danny drifts off and starts to sob again as the image of Adam's big smile is all he can see.

Walter simply holds his son's hand without speaking and lets Danny release his grief. He knows it will not be the last time he will comfort him. After Danny's tears slow, Walter tries to bring the reality of Christ to Danny's thoughts and gently emphasizes that Adam is thankfully in paradise with the Lord Jesus Christ right now, feeling no pain. "I know, Dad, and I am trying to keep that front and center, but what about those of us here on Earth who miss him like crazy? It hurts so bad."

"You will grieve for a while, and you will always hold Adam close in your heart. When I am thinking about your mom, I find a lot of comfort in Psalm 147 where it says, 'He healeth the broken in heart and bindeth up their wounds.' Matthew 5, too, because it says, 'Blessed are they that mourn: for they shall be comforted.' God won't leave you now, son. He wants you to cling to Him."

The afternoon is quiet with both Moselys succumbing to times of sleep and light activity. After his son's request, Walter walks him to the shower and sits just on the other side of the plastic curtain in case Danny gets weak. Walter had brought fresh clothes on Monday just for this time, but the nurses do not want him to wear anything but an embarrassing gown with an open back. At least Danny is allowed to wear his underwear.

As the sun sets and lamp light is needed, Barry knocks lightly on the door and sticks his head into Danny's room. "Is it OK if King and I come in? Dad told me my buddy was awake, and we want to say hello."

"Is it OK, Danny?" Walter asks. "Sure, but I'm not in the greatest mood, you guys. Thanks for coming though. I do appreciate it. I just don't know if I'll be very talkative."

"Oh, man, that's cool. We'll just sit here with you."

King grabs Danny's hand. "I love you, friend, and so do a bunch of other people. We're all worried about you and miss you.

Barry thinks of a request. "I am supposed to call Jeff later to tell him if you want visitors. Whaddya think? No pressure though. We know you're not feeling great."

"I don't know. Maybe. I wish I could see Hannah." And with the thought of his precious friend all cut up and broken, Danny's tears begin to stream down his face once again. King continues to grip Danny's hand and joins him with tears of his own.

Barry leans over and rubs Danny's arm. "She's home now, and I could go by and check on her if you want. I'll come visit you after school tomorrow so I can give you a full report."

Pastor Pete speaks up. "We checked on her and the Birdsong family. Hannah is in quite a bit of pain, and she must keep her eye shielded from light for two weeks, giving it plenty of time to heal. They say she should recover well though. She'll be fine."

"Oh God, I know this sounds so phony, but I truly do wish it had just been me. A carload of friends makes it so, so incredibly heavy. Dad, I need to go to the bathroom, please."

"Oh, sure, OK. Would all of you wonderful friends please go outside the room for a few minutes?"

Annie closes their visit "Hey, we ought to go, anyway, Walter. Danny, we love you, and we will see you in the morning." Annie assures their friend. As he sits himself up on the side of his bed, Danny raises his right hand and waves and thanks them for coming.

After the Boggs leave, King helps Walter steady Danny. Danny's legs are still weak, and they buckle slightly under him, but Walter and King hold on tightly and get him to a sitting position in the bathroom. They tell Danny to not try to stand on his own and to call them when he is finished.

After Danny is settled back in his bed, he announces he is sleepy and would like to be left alone. "Daddy, go home and get some sleep. I don't want you getting sick."

"I'll sleep right here on this chair this afternoon, and maybe I will go home tonight. I would just be thinking I should be with you if I left now."

"Ok, Dad, whatever you think. Thanks for coming, boys, and tell Jeff I would love to see him this evening if he can make it."

"I'll tell Jeff," Barry replies. "Can Alice come too? I know she wants to see you."

"Oh, man, I wonder how I will react when I see her. I feel so much guilt."

"You didn't do anything wrong. She just wants to make sure you're OK. It would help her too, I think."

"Sure, that's fine. Tell her she's welcome. Maybe they can bring me a Frisch's ham and cheese and chocolate milk shake." Danny cracks a weak smile after speaking his request, and that Danny-style quip makes Walter breathe his first full breath since Sunday night.

Just as King and Barry are putting their coats back on, there comes another knock on Danny's hospital door and in walks Pastor Allen. King recognizes him right away and remembers that Danny was driving from seeing the pastor when the deer jumped out. "Is this a bad time? We saw Pastor Boggs and his wife as we were coming down the hall and they said you were getting tired, Danny, so I just wanted to say a quick hello, and there is someone else who has something to tell you." Arnold's boney face comes out from behind Pastor Allen, and King recognizes him immediately. King stiffens up and stands close to his best friend, but Arnold doesn't even look at King, not for any reason other than he is focused on Danny and does not remember King.

"Hey, Danny. How ya doin'?"

"Wow! Hi, Arnie, thanks for coming. I can't believe you came all this way, especially with all the traffic that is out there." There is a change on Danny's face that shows he has set aside the grief, even if for just a minute. "I'm very sad, Arnie, but God is with me."

"I wanted to talk with you about that," Arnie begins. "After we talked on Sunday and you left, I talked with Pastor Allen about what you were saying, and I gave my life to Christ, Danny." Danny's face lights up and he reaches out to shake Arnold's hand. Arnold reaches toward Danny, and Danny uses both his hands, one on top and one on the bottom of Arnold's, and just holds Arnold's hand firmly while letting out a loud howl of joy and delight.

"God is so good, Arnie, it is just unbelievable what He can and will do. Welcome, my brother, to the family of Christ, and you don't know what a blessing to me you are right now."

Pastor Allen recognizes King. "King, right? How could I forget your name? It is so good to see you again. This is Arnold, whom you met at the game last weekend." Arnold whips his head around, still connected to Danny's hands, and looks at King. King finds himself staring in uncomfortable disbelief. The disbelief is because he is face-to-face with his object of disdain and that this hillbilly bully is friends with his best friend and professing salvation through Christ. Knowing what his friend is thinking, Danny pipes up. "Isn't God amazing, King? How he takes broken jars and makes them whole again?"

"Yeah. Yeah, Danny, that's great. Arnold, that's great. Well, I guess I better go. You ready, Barry?"

"Sure, King. We can go."

King and Barry take their turns leaning over their buddy and giving him a hug. King tells Walter and Pastor Allen goodbye and then looks at Arnold and thanks him for coming to see his friend. After King and Barry leave the room, Arnold confides in Danny and the Pastor "Man, the Spirit is already layin' it on me. When I saw your friend, I just felt bad about what I did. I never feel bad about pickin' on people. It just reminds me of your joke, Danny."

"What, the one about it's no fun anymore?"

"Exactly."

"Well, they say the best jokes are based on reality."

"That one's hilarious then," Arnold says with a boney-faced, toothy smile. "We better get back to Adams County, Pastor, don't you think? Pastor Allen loves to ride in my car."

"That's the truth, Danny," The pastor confirms energetically. "Let's let this young man get some sleep."

"Sure thing." Arnie agrees quickly. "See you soon, Danny, and I am glad you are feeling better."

"Thank you both for coming today. Thank you," Danny says with full sincerity.

The room is finally quiet, and Walter and son agree to close the room door and catch a nap. Walter closes the window blinds, hugs his boy, and pulls his blanket up. He then sits down with a sigh and puts the trash can under his feet as an ottoman. He pulls his coat down from the back of the chair and arranges it over himself as he would a blanket. His body collapses into an unfamiliar relaxed position, and Walter's eyes immediately get heavy because his formerly comatose son is awake and communicating. The hospital chair feels like a motel bed, and Walter quickly begins to drift past an alpha state and right into theta. As he heads toward delta, his last bit of consciousness hears his baby boy sobbing for his friend Adam.

CHAPTER
FOURTEEN

Adam was buried on a bitterly cold and blustery December Saturday, six days after his death. A closed-casket service was held at the church with many family members, friends and supporters. Jeff was there to support Danny and Alice as Danny sat next to Walter on one side and Louise Birdsong on the other in loving support of her daughter and her daughter's friend. On top of torturous and vivid dreams that do not subside until she returns from Europe after the new year begins, Alice suffered a bruised chin and endured five stitches on her forehead. The stitches held together a gash, probably made by the fingernail of a passenger in Walter's now worthless Oldsmobile that still sits cold and blood-stained in the Appleton auto junkyard.

Of the backseat passengers, Brenda suffered the worst. The inertia ran the right side of her head across an antler that had protruded into the car, wrapping her hair around the rack and busting her bottom lip on the back of Adam's head that had been thrust backward by the three-hundred-pound buck. When Brenda's body launched back to her seated position, her entangled hair was ripped from her head. Nick suffered no bodily injury and was the one who flagged down an oncoming car for help.

That next day, Barry helps his friend by playing organ for the church service. Reading the music of the old hymns is effortless for the keyboard wizard, and he enjoys their cadence and arrangements. Barry takes liberties on the Christmas carols, which seem to lift the spirits a bit from the previous day's funeral. The sermon could be preached at Easter as it is all about the victory that Christians have over death, thanks to the resurrection of Jesus Christ.

Alice does not attend the Sunday service and instead spends the entire day into the evening with Jeff. She and her family are leaving tomorrow for France, and this is the first year that Alice is dreading the trip. Alice does not want to leave Jeff, especially during such an odd time of sorrow and upbeat joy. She finds warmth and strength in her relationship with her boyfriend, and they agree that spending time together will be their Christmas present to each other. Carl has returned late on Saturday afternoon, and Jeff is eager to take Alice to meet him on this Sunday morning.

Alice brings all the ingredients of a fantastic breakfast and fills Carl's small apartment with the smell of bacon, eggs, coffee, and biscuits. They all discuss the previous week, including the school Christmas concert and how well King played. Carl is sad about Adam's death and asks several questions regarding Danny's well-being. He is crazy about Jeff's new friend, and after breakfast, he understands that his son needs to be alone with Alice and gives Alice and his son guilt-free hugs and permission to leave, making Jeff promise that he will return by midnight that evening. With a rolled-down bottom lip that would sink a ship, Alice gives her best Brownie Scout pledge to Carl to let his son go by eleven fifty-five. Jeff simply asks the two to stop fighting over him and hugs his dad goodbye. Paris is not exactly boring at Christmas, but after a deeply passionate day with Jeff, Alice dreads tomorrow morning's departure, taking only the physical and mental scars of the week with her to Europe, while leaving her heart in Marigold.

School is out for the holidays and band rehearsals are frequent and therapeutic for Danny. The band name became *Clever Pennies*, a reference to taxes in a George Harrison song that had stuck in King's mind while listening to the Revolver album. Gordon Reed has been enjoying Clever Pennies so much, he can name every song they have learned and will call out song requests on the intercom as he listens upstairs with the newspaper in hand. On several nights at Danny's, the boys would also play acoustically. Walter has salvaged all that was in the trunk of his wrecked Olds, pulling Danny's guitar out, fully intact.

Danny's house is perfect for working on vocals with acoustic guitars, and Barry plays his Hohner Melodica when he isn't singing. Arnie and a Northern friend or two visit the acoustic rehearsals, and he and Jeff have become friends, with souped-up cars in common. Carl visits as well to listen to his son and enjoy a bowl or two of Walter's rabbit stew or whatever is his dish du jour. This acoustic formation of the group would become a useful and lucrative version of Clever Pennies and the one they would implement pro bono for Diana Peterson's birthday party that came in February of nineteen sixty-eight. Her dad stuffed money into King's shirt as they were packing up after the party, and King did not fight the parent's generosity. He also believed that this successful evening was a hint of great things to come.

Christmas Day, 1967, provides a platform for Paul McCartney of The Beatles to ask his girlfriend, actress Jane Asher, to marry him. In Marigold, the day is filled with passion and mixed emotions for each of the Clever Pennies' boys and their families. After the presents are opened at the Mosely home, Danny calls Adam's house and wishes his sympathies and love for all of them. After the call, he excuses himself from his dad and heads upstairs for the rest of the morning.

With his son resting, Walter cleans up the debris from the morning's activity. Danny had given his dad two thick and warm flannel shirts for hunting and a new filleting knife for the walleyes, saugers, and crappie his dad can catch in abundance. Walter gave King money to buy Danny some clothes from Engel's, and King was able to bring back two pairs of wide-rail corduroy bell bottoms, red and royal blue, and a paisley shirt with a high collar. Walter also put a small matchbox car in a big box and told Danny he wanted to go out with his son the next day and look for his very own car.

The 1967 Reed Christmas is a special one. Gordon and Ellie Reed have been so excited with their son's contributions to Clever Pennies that they went to Klein's and purchased a used 1965 blue pearl, double tom-tom Premier 54 drum set for King. The instrument was bright and shining in Klein's showroom and even more so on Christmas morning when it is found sitting under (or next to) the Reed's Christmas tree. Not knowing how to set it up correctly, Ellie and Gordon simply placed all the pieces around the bass drum, but that did not matter to the elated King in the least.

He quickly sets it up in the living room, tunes the heads and proceeds to whack out some beats. This show of jubilation receives mixed reactions as Gordon and Sam remind King that it is a relaxed and serene holiday morning and suggest King wait until later or, better yet, move the new set to the basement. Ellie, however, is fine listening from the kitchen and is a bit disappointed when all three of her men carry the drums downstairs.

Sam's gifts are not as spectacular as his baby brother's, but nonetheless special to him. One gift is a leather briefcase that he had asked for and another, a set of weights with a bench, that will go nicely in his room. Two Italian silk ties and a Timex Viscount watch complete with a mechanical self-wind feature and the date that shows in a small square on its face. Of course, Gordon bought his lovely bride music provided on two albums, one being Aretha Franklin's I Never Loved a Man. Replete with soulful sounds throughout, side one kicks off with a song Ellie had grown to love through the summer called *Respect*. Ellie would sing the "R-E-S-P-E-C-T" part with Aretha and then switch over to the "just a little bit" chant served up by the background vocalists.

The other album was a special Christmas collection of songs sung by Barbara Streisand simply called A Christmas Album. This present was tagged with "Open Me First" so that the morning would be filled with the sounds of Christmas as only Barbara can sing them. King ends the warm and fuzzy feeling after he puts his drums together. It is a joyous Reed Christmas and one they will always remember.

Across Marigold Road is Kay's first Christmas without Santa Claus, and the Meades, as a family, decided to change their traditions. Kay, wanting desperately to act in an adult fashion like the rest of her family, puts a damper on her usual flurry and fury. This year, each family member could wake when they wanted and make their way downstairs whenever the scent of breakfast filled their nostrils.

There is nothing very exciting under the tree, but the gifts are well-conceived and appreciated. Delores receives a set of copper-bottomed Revere Ware and a variety of clothing purchased at Engel's by Roy's nurse, Margaret; Kay is happy to see the riding boots she asked for as well as the albums More of The Monkees and The Bee Gees 1st. Barry is thrilled to receive the albums he requested: Mr. Fantasy by Traffic and Strange Days by The Doors. Borrowing the idea from Walter Mosely, both young adults are given a beautiful Sears Silvertone stereo record player to be kept upstairs for their enjoyment. To Barry's great animus, the good Dr. Meade is excited for his son to open two large packages. They turn out to be very expensive, conservatively fashioned suits to be worn when visiting Harvard in the spring.

Jeff is able to enjoy his dad and vice versa, staying with Carl through almost half of December until Christmas evening when Carl starts his long trip to Washington state. Jeff worked all day during many of the Christmas vacation days off from school, but Carl would meet Jeff at Fran's for lunch. Two of the days though, Carl and Walter went hunting.

After getting up early and spending a cold day in the hills, the two would take their kill to Charlie's to be butchered into venison steaks and ground up burger patties. Walter would normally barbecue the fatty ribs. However, being very conscious of his son's trauma caused by one of the big beasts, Walter chooses to give the ribs to Charlie. He does not mention what kind of meat is being eaten at dinner, even though Danny is very familiar with the taste of venison as he is an accomplished hunter himself.

Jeff spends Christmas Eve with his mom, exchanging gifts that make obvious the divide that has come between them since Darren entered the picture full-time. They do not talk that much anymore, with Jeff dodging his mom's existence unless he needs her car. Jeff is quick to head over to Danny's as the evening with his mom comes to a close. Jeff and Danny talk, watch some TV, sing some songs and then Danny drives Jeff to his dad's apartment.

Carl seems very excited Christmas morning, intentionally waking his son so that they can open presents. Jeff had saved and bought his dad a new and improved CB radio for the cab where Carl spends so much time, but there is a box under the tree with a very familiar shape. It is very poorly wrapped, with Jeff's name on it. At sixteen, he didn't want to seem too anxious, but the little boy in him spews forth, and Jeff grabs and pulls at the box, sliding it out from under the tree until it is in his lap. Carl sits with a large grin on his face and motions with both hands for Jeff to open the big box.

The baby-blue paper, featuring snowmen and snowwomen Christmas carolers, is ripped away, and the Scotch tape takes some of the brown paper box with it as it flies out of range. Jeff slowly lifts the box lid and there, in grand Carl fashion, is a nineteen-sixty-four natty green sunburst, double six Burns of London twelve-string guitar complete with slanted Tri-Sonic pickups. Four of the strings are missing, but Jeff snatches it out of the box, tunes the eight remaining strings quickly and plays the intro chords to *I'll Feel a Whole Lot Better* by The Byrds. Jeff looks up from the guitar just enough to look his dad in the eyes and thank him with sparkling delight in his own.

Carl had received the unique instrument as payback for a favor done for a friend from Cincinnati whose family had worked at the Baldwin Piano Company. Carl's friend knows his son plays guitar and was more than happy to pass this guitar, having been shoved back in a dark closet for three years, along to someone who could and would play it. Jeff does not work the morning after Christmas, knowing he will call the band boys to take him to Klein's to buy a pack of guitar strings for a twelve-string guitar. All three did not hesitate, and though the crash was still fresh in his mind, Danny knows that it is these kinds of happy bonding time that will help him out of his depression and guilt. Barry volunteers to drive, and after spending the morning in Appleton pretending they are a famous band and doing silly Monkee things, they drive back to Marigold and go to Fran's for lunch where they say hello to Sam and his friends. King wants to show the boys his drums and hear Jeff's twelve string on the Byrds' songs they have learned. So, Ellie is thrilled to hear them all roll into the basement in the early afternoon. Gordon is still at work, but he would not have minded.

One of the wealthy former frat boys at the country club loved Barry's entertainment moxie so much that, when he heard him tell Leon about the band, he hired Clever Pennies for his New Year's Eve party being held right there in the country club. The money they make that night is more than Jeff earns in a month at Charlie's, but this first gig is especially hard for Jeff as he is missing Alice deep in his bones. Then, watching the many couples kiss at midnight just makes him think of their own fierce and impassioned kiss while sitting in the little green TR3 at 11:59 in the parking lot of Carl's apartment.

It is not until the first week of January that Danny feels comfortable with the idea of driving. Still, he and his dad find an affordable 1963 Diamond Blue Chrysler Imperial Crown Southampton four-door automatic that an elderly lady, who belongs to the church and cannot drive due to her debilitating illness, sells to them for next to nothing. It had only one hundred and thirty-seven miles on the odometer and features power steering, power brakes, and power windows. The first thing Danny does after taking possession of the blue beast is pick up Hannah to get her out of the house. Hannah has come to terms with the accident and is not apprehensive about getting back out on the road. She trusts Danny, but most of all, she trusts God and knows that riding with Danny will help him move forward.

***

The bloody war in Vietnam escalates through 1967 and into 1968. The so-called TET Offensive on January 31, brought by the North Vietnamese military in coordination with the Viet Cong in South Vietnam, turn a usually quiet national celebration into a destructive show of brutal force. More than 120 towns and cities throughout southern Vietnam are mercilessly attacked. The Viet Cong are able to break through the barricades at the United States embassy, storming the grounds, but the U.S. destroy their own building before the enemy can take it. The carnage goes on for days and is broadcast into every American home. World War Two had purpose and focus, but the bonding fibers that it created begin to fray as staunch American families question if their military leaders are asking their sons to participate in a losing proposition.

Appleton is changing right along with the world as its young go off to college and never return. After growing up in such a comfortable and safe environment, the college grads find freedom and excitement, either in the cities where their schools educate them, or where they drift while searching for themselves. Drugs are beginning to weaken the town's stitch, and the family foundation is dissolving, like a frame house being eaten by termites.

Staunch, married businessmen begin growing their hair and exploring the free love that is being offered by office secretaries and waitresses at their favorite bars – not to mention, the open and willing feminists are usually half their age. Doctors are providing prescriptions for the birth control pill, so the young college educated women feel no threat of having a family when all they want to do is loosen up their boss. There are no strings attached, as the females are no longer objects but participants or initiators.

The men's wives, who are at home raising their children, know what is happening to their husband's, but they do not want what they consider a shameful divorce to scar their children. Religion is for the previous generation, and God is dead to those who want what the television and college campuses are promoting. The housewives smother their loneliness and lack of self-worth with alcohol, Valium, or Librium now that their husbands are showing them no attention. Aunt Charlene has begun experimenting with drugs, but Alice has no interest, and as she helps Hannah mend, finds herself being drawn to the teachings of Jesus. She recalls something Jesus's disciple Peter instructed, and that is for everyone to be sober-minded while waiting for the Master's return.

Still, Jeff is not about to move in the direction of the cross, so he and Alice meet in the middle to protect their relationship that has become so important to them. Jeff will just sleep in on Sunday mornings, and Alice will stay out late on Saturday nights. He is careful not to utter the words, but after she returned from Europe, Jeff knew he loved Alice. It was when Alice was in Europe that she poured out her heart in her diary for her love while in flight back to Paris from Germany. She and Charlene went to The Beatles' Apple Boutique which had opened in early December in London. Normally this would have been a girl's shopping spree, but instead Alice bought twice as much for Jeff as she did herself.

Though Alice and Carl hit it off in a big way, she and Jeff's mom, Susan, had not met until recently. Admittedly Jeff does not want to bring Alice around Darren and subject her to his crude behavior. One evening, however, Darren was working late, so Jeff, Alice, and Susan could all meet at Fran's for dinner. Susan carried herself well but seemed to be slightly intimidated eating with an Engel. She and Alice were very cordial to each other, though, sharing an occasional giggle, and the evening went well.

After Europe, the Engel family knew their baby girl was smitten by someone, and they wanted to meet the young man. A fish dinner was planned featuring lake trout and yellow perch from Daddy Engel's mid-January, overnight, Great Lake fishing charter in Lake Erie. This event is one of Alice's favorites of all the Engel events because she loves eating fish and that it is wonderfully casual. Several of the store managers are always invited and Alice is anxious to share the fun with her love.

Alice believes her dad will enjoy everything about Jeff because her dad does not set many boundaries in his life and neither does Jeff. She fantasizes Jeff and her dad sitting in the great room by the fire laughing and joking about any number of topics. Jeff's wit is never dull and very well timed. Alice does not know that part of the dinner plans this year is that her mom and dad will subtly but rigorously investigate the young man. Friends of the Engels are scattered throughout the area. They are the usual types who want to rub shoulders with, and eat the crumbs of, the rich and powerful business owners of Scioto County.

Some Engel *friends* are in charge of city and school records, and nothing is overlooked or withheld to help Daddy Engel. If Alice is going to bring this young man into their lives, they want to be prepared. Every young man wants Alice, or at least wants into the Engel circle, but this one, who is coming from far outside the circle, has captured their daughter's heart like a stray dog. So, they figure they had better meet him soon in case they find the need to deconstruct the relationship.

On the night of the party, the Engel driveway, looking more like a highway being double-wide so that cars could come and go at the same time, seemed a mile long. It weaves its way toward the Engel home, around trees and benched oasis' until it straightens out into a manicured, open and well-lit front yard. Any visitor is now forced to focus on the bucolic, but turgid Marigold mansion. Alice has invited Hannah and

Danny for two reasons. First, because they have become Alice's good friends and second, because she knows Jeff will need familiar faces as a kind of home plate in the multitude of strangers.

There are employees with flashlights waving Jeff's car toward a parking place along the driveway. Once parked, the three friends stumble out of the car, disoriented by the mere size of the house. This part of the driveway is near the south side of the hill, and the three walk over and look down into the valley from where they came. They conclude that it is King's house, dotted with tiny lit windows, they are seeing about two thirds of the way down the rugged hill. Jeff takes a deep breath, and Danny and Hannah rub his back as they begin to walk toward the front porch. There is a shriek in the direction of the mansion and then a human shape appears to be running toward them.

The shadowy form gradually coalesces into the beautiful Alice, who runs so hard into her man that the force almost pushes him backwards. Had Jeff not been used to base runners coming at him from third and aiming for his rib cage, Alice might have knocked him over, but Jeff's steadfast frame stops the agile-but-fragile cheerleader in her tracks. They hug, with Alice's head buried in Jeff's large chest for at least thirty seconds, marinating in sincere joy at seeing each other. At about second thirty-one, Danny clears his throat very loudly, which lightens the moment and moves Alice's attention toward him and Hannah. Jeff lets go so that Alice can share her hugs with her new friends. Alice's German shepherd, named Berlin, had run right beside his master and watches as she hugs each person. Berlin sniffs the three to get acquainted with their scents and then dutifully walks toward the house with Alice.

After coats are taken and a brief tour of the ground floor is fulfilled so that everyone has first-hand knowledge of the bathroom locations, Alice and her friends enter the kitchen. This one room is larger than the downstairs of Jeff's house and smells like Old Bay seasoning. Various age groups of people shuffle in and out of the room, apparently helping themselves to beer from three different coolers. There is one small crowd who has congregated around a large wooden island about four feet in front of the sink. It seems they are tasting the last three cans of previously frozen salmon roe. A fit woman, bearing a large smile, an exceedingly large diamond on her left ring finger, and an excess of facial makeup, breaks away from the cluster and begins walking in the four teen's direction with both arms open. Alice introduces her three friends to her mom, Abbie Engel, and with great warmth, Abbie pours out a welcome and an invitation to make themselves at home.

Alice guides her overwhelmed friends into the great room where a good thirty people are mingling. A large, rustic fireplace of stones gathered from the bottom of the Scioto River stands twenty feet high directly in the middle of the outside wall that is forty feet across the room from where the teens are standing at the room's entrance. On each side of the fireplace are four doublewide doorways that allow family and guests access to a wood and steel half-rounded deck, hanging twenty feet out and over the valley below. It is painted like a large compass, accurately pointing toward the west. The view is breathtaking, featuring a nighttime sea of the small, twinkling residential lights of Marigold that merge with the stars in the sky. Back inside, from a beautifully carved wooden encasement, a turntable sends the music of The Byrds' Fifth Dimension album to eight theatre-style speakers hanging just above each of the outside access doors, staggered four inside and four outside with separate volume controls.

From the upstairs balcony, a confident and booming voice shouts a big hello to Alice. When she looks up to find her dad, he uses hand gestures to ask if the people standing with her are the friends she promised to invite to the fish fest. She motions for him to come down and meet them. All three friends wave to Alice's dad and wait for him to make his way to their location near the fireplace. Markus Engel is possibly two inches shorter than Jeff and equally stocky with leathery skin and meaty hands that wrap around Danny's and Hannah's. Jeff gives his best grip and locks eyes with Alice's dad to let him know he is sincere and not intimidated. Daddy smiles and then turns his attention to the group instead of only Jeff.

Through the evening, the two exchange glances and salutations, but it is not until the end of the evening that Jeff and Mr. Engel stand together by the fireplace on the deck and converse. There is nothing said that is particularly deep, but Jeff speaks of his baseball prowess and showcases his quick wit and sense of humor, which Mr. Engel seems to enjoy. However, one is never quite sure about Markus Engel's intentions. He is a grand poker player, having complete control over his facial expressions, body gestures, and – unwittingly – over his opponents.

At the end of the evening, Alice's friends give a hardy thank you and goodbye to both parents, and Mom is sure to provide an open invitation of return to all three. Alice leaves with her friends as she and Jeff have decided to make it a late night after they drop Hannah and Danny off at Danny's. On the ride from off the top of the hill, all four talk and laugh about the party. Alice knows exactly how to joke along about some of the people she knows so well, having fun with their obvious quirks and habits, while still retaining her faithfulness toward their friendships. Alice is a master of conversation, and she is sure not to cross any lines into anything that would betray her family friends.

***

As the southern Ohio spring is beginning and the marsh marigold blooms broadcast their yellow hue throughout the damp areas of the hills and valleys, a vibrant fruit-bearing shoot that had sprung up from the vile swamp of racism, is cut down by a thirty-aught-six rifle round. The rights of all Americans are making progress through the sixties, with the creation of the Civil Rights Act of 1964, but on April fourth of this year, the neck of Doctor Martin Luther King, Jr. is pierced in the southern town of Memphis, Tennessee. An hour later, he is pronounced dead.

Riots, fires, and looting flare up throughout the nation for the next few days, bringing death and destruction, and Appleton is not left unscathed. A sizeable group from, what is thought to be, the local Black Panther Party break out windows and throw Molotov cocktails into convertible cars. On Friday night, April 5th, Clever Pennies is playing a prom for Appleton High School. As they carry their band equipment outside after a successful performance, they find their vehicles vandalized, with their windows smashed and tires punctured. None of the boys feel they have any racial prejudice in them and are friends with a local all black band called The Soul Men. It saddens them to see the division and try to understand. They have never thought about racial tensions in Appleton and especially Marigold.

Danny's church congregation consists of several people of color, and Pastor Pete teaches boldly from Galatians 3:28 that there is neither Jew nor Greek, slave or free, male or female because we are all one in Jesus Christ. Jesus Christ leveled that playing field, but the senseless act of killing Doctor King four hundred and thirty miles away is suddenly upon them, and they know they need to search themselves and ask God to cleanse their souls. It is a fallen world and, as Paul the Apostle wrote to the Romans, "There is none that doeth good, no, not one."

Those who became parents after WWII have protected their children from human depravity. The assassination and murder of John Kennedy and Jack Ruby, witnessed on television screens in comfortable homes, unveiled the darkness that parents had hoped was not present in the United States. The four high school friends are growing up at a rate at which they have not been prepared.

Jeff is no longer apprehensive about picking Alice up for dates, events, and Clever Pennies shows. The next time that everyone gathers at the Engel's home is for Alice's birthday party on April 20th when she asked Clever Pennies to play for her guests. She makes sure they are paid well for their time and talent while still allowing extended breaks so that she can walk the grounds with the guitarist. That is, if Alice can pry Charlene away from him. Charlene seems under the influence of some sort of drug that causes her conversations to be filled with non sequiturs. She is entertaining, but sad would be a better description.

This is the first gig that Clever Pennies uses their new PA system. The Vox Metal Clad PA100 Type 4 is yet another Carl Lindor cross-country deal that he was excited to deliver to a Reed basement rehearsal. The band had to buy their own microphones and cables, so they decided to use the money they were going to make at Alice's party. After Klein knocked off ten percent for his favorite customers, they were able to get four Electro-Voice 664 model microphones with stands and cables and still bring home twenty-five dollars each from the Alice party.

Only a few days after the party, tragedy strikes again. This time, the fist that brings the beating is in the form of a terrifying tornado that rips through the eastern suburbs of Appleton. The F5 dances up the Ohio River, splitting the waterway like the Red Sea and throwing large, slimy swaths of mud in every direction. The dark dervish jumps onto the Ohio side of the river's bank gobbling up buildings and homes and spitting them out in pieces, tossing cars and phone poles as if they are toys.

There is a Flint track meet going on at a neighboring high school just east of Appleton. The teams stop their meet as the powerful freak of nature barrels toward them. The swirling, deep green and purple darkness is sinister, and teachers, teams, and families dive for any shelter they can find as light poles become missiles. Sam is there, and he directs as many team members as possible to get inside the cinder block restroom building.

Finding shelter from the multiple projectiles as quickly as possible, seven people pile into a station wagon that soon becomes airborne. The three-thousand-pound vehicle is lifted to a height of ten feet and screaming voices are carried twenty feet over the blacktopped parking lot. The metal tomb spins haphazardly until it is upside down, and as if a giant hand simply lets go, the station wagon full of passengers drops to the pavement. Five of the seven are killed instantly, and then the F5 passes as quickly as it arrived. The devastation lingers for weeks, but the community helps each other dig out of the trauma and life goes on.

The school year is nearly at a close, and testing for the juniors and seniors is brutal. Barry is hanging out with Benny all night, studying so as to not let down his dad. Across the field at the foot of Marigold Hill, Sam, with an easy 3.93 grade average, is accepted into The United States Military Academy at West Point. Gordon keeps a stiff upper lip, but Ellie is heartbroken and pleads to her son not to go. He can have any school of his choice, but West Point is the school of his dreams, and he is going to be the best cadet the school will ever see. His friends understand, but recommend he rethink the decision.

However, it is the ultra-sensitive King who seems to suffer the most, going into a depression. He knows the chances for his brother to die in Vietnam are very high. King cries himself to sleep several nights after Sam's high school graduation and tells the band he will need to miss a show they had booked during the July Fourth weekend, as that is when the family will take Sam to New York. Of course, King's friends understand, and though he was sorely missed, they played as an acoustic trio with the party being held in a backyard.

The May Cream show at Veteran's Memorial Fieldhouse in Huntington is no longer the big date for Jeff and Alice. They are quite close and enjoying each other immensely. All four young men – plus Alice, Hannah, and a very hippie young Appleton female named Cloud, who has been hanging out with King since the Peterson party – bought tickets, loaded up two cars, and hit the road to West Virginia. Diane Peterson was not quite sure why Cloud was at her party or who she was connected to, but she and King hit it off.

King has found that Cloud enjoys a different kind of music which he had not heard, though it feels very familiar. He likens it to Lady Jane by the Stones or Fool on the Hill. He finds later that they are British folk groups with names such as the whimsical The Incredible String Band, Sweeney's Men, Fairport Convention, and Pentangle. King is fascinated by their complicated simplicity and clever poetry. Cloud is also listening to the band that opened for Hendrix in Columbus, The Soft Machine. King loves the drummer, who plays a kind of jazz-rock style and who also sings when there are vocals.

Jeff cannot wait to see the one and only Eric Clapton and is wondering what guitar he will play. They all have to wait to find out due to Cream's late arrival, but the two local bands that open the evening are OK. The more famous Grass Roots do not seem happy and are not pleasant at all.

Also, the long show presents some opportunities that might best have been left alone. Barry, who had driven one of the vehicles, went off into the crowd during The Grass Roots set and was not seen again until the Appleton bunch find him deep into a one-sided conversation with a police officer who is nodding his head and watching the room empty out after Cream has finished their show. Throughout the room, the smell of marijuana is strong, and the smoke is thick, but the police, knowing the numbers are not in their favor, allow the Cream fans to enjoy the show as long as they are peaceful.

Jeff walks over to Barry and puts his arm around his shoulder. The policeman asks if Barry is driving, and though Jeff has no plan, he assures the officer that Barry will not go near a driver's seat tonight. It is 3:30 in the morning by the time Jeff is able to walk Alice to her doorstep in Marigold, and by that time, Danny was already in his bed. He knows he will need to take Barry back to Huntington to get his car later on that day.

***

Good news always muscles through gloom, and so it does for Clever Pennies who gain popularity all through 1968. They are asked to play citywide and are most excited about the Appleton RiverFest engagement in August. The headliners include many of the band's favorite stars, like Mitch Ryder and The Detroit Wheels, The James Gang, and The Lemon Pipers. There are several local bands that play earlier in the day and into the afternoon, but it is Clever Pennies that begin the main stage evening lineup. They are excited to meet the other bands, and Alice is sure to have the Engel's catalog photographer there to take photos for later marketing and press releases. A more sober Charlene has even pitched in, contributing her knowledge of business.

That evening, Clever Pennies, with each member dressed in his choice of Engel's wardrobe, play for over ten thousand people. The crowd had come to line the river levy and watch all the exciting bands perform the songs that they have only heard on WROR and record. It has been very hot all day, but as the sun is setting, a cool breeze meanders up the river. The stage lights have now replaced the sunlight, and they illuminate the boys, making them feel very important and successful as they play three of their own songs, two by Danny called *Rain or Shine* and *Climbing a Mountain* and another called *Stars,* which was written by all four of the band members. They thought it best to include two of their best covers as well. The crowd gives the band a rousing reception after each song, which makes the band entertain its audience, something they had never rehearsed but had become comfortable with over the past few months of gigs.

Their own natural personalities present themselves, and the frenzied throng, containing a wonderful mix of all ages, eat up their spontaneous stage antics. A few members of some of the headlining bands stand just out of view at the side of the stage to watch the young band strut their stuff, possibly bringing back memories of their own beginnings. It is a big night for Clever Pennies and the town of Appleton, and the Appleton Voice give high praise to the band the next morning. Gordon Reed reads his paper every morning, but he was never so excited until the day after the concert. To see King's name in the paper with a picture of the band performing brings happy tears to Gordon and Ellie's eyes as Gordon reads the flattering story out loud. An extra copy of the newspaper is sent to Sam in New York.

To show just how mature the local favorites are when performing, the newspaper prints Danny's lyrics to *Rain or Shine.* With his permission, they are as follows:

Rain or Shine by Daniel Mosely

Don't you know the world keeps turning, rain or shine
And you can bet there's happy laughter when you're crying
It seems to me, there's more to master with less time
So, don't know the world keeps turning, rain or shine. Rain or shine.

I used to think, when I was younger, that I had powers
But now I know I just tune in well to what is ours
So, don't you fret, now, don't you worry; Ease your mind
We're not alone, we're all connected rain or shine. Rain or shine.

I've lost love and it felt like a cold rain from above
But rain brings flowers and it washes right down what tastes so sour
So, I love you. There's nothing more I'd rather do
I'm not afraid. I'd rather lose the game than have never played
I'd rather lose big than have never played

I feel like singing la la la la, wah wah wah
Or maybe singing dee dee dee dee, da da da
So, try and sing a happy song, friend, when you're blue
I'll be the very first to tell you it's not an easy thing to do
No, it's not an easy thing to do

Clever Pennies know they are on their way to some bigger things for the band when WROR calls Charlene. She had given the WROR DJ, whom she had met at the RiverFest, her Engel's business card. The station wants Clever Pennies to come down to their studio and play their songs live on the air. WROR has a powerful transmitter, and the boys know they will be heard in Kentucky, West Virginia, and eastern parts of Ohio. They, of course, agree to play at the station, but they want to wait a week. Before agreeing to play, the boys have all decided to record *Rain or Shine* and *Stars* at a real recording studio so that they can present the 45 rpm recording to the DJ for rotation play on the air. WROR decides not to approve the band's request for a different in-studio performance date because they did not want to lose the RiverFest momentum. However, they do agree to let them mention the recording, and the station agrees to play the record one or more times if the recording is master quality.

The boys are very comfortable on the live radio show, and their personalities shine. WROR fields dozens of calls about the band after the interview and look forward to debuting their single. The next day, Clever Pennies pack up their gear and head to Akron to record, mix, and master their two songs at Akron Recording studios. Their hopes are high.

CHAPTER FIFTEEN

C lever Pennies is recording their first record in Akron and take a lunch break. Three long-haired, bearded young males and three barefoot females are on the street corner handing out copies of a little booklet called The Four Spiritual Laws. No one in the band takes one except Danny. He is intrigued and talks with one of the fellows the whole time the others are eating lunch in a café near the studio. One of the young, hippie-looking men, probably twenty years old or so, excitedly percolates information to Danny about the good news of Jesus Christ and a Christian organization called Campus Crusade for Christ that he had visited in California. The young man on the corner continues to tell Danny that the Bible-based organization is growing quickly and is serving the Lord and spreading the Gospel in several colleges, but Danny is not quite sure how he feels about an organized group of people using a Christian identity that is not the church.

"Yeah, man. One time in California, there were about six hundred members who countered the radical activists at the University of California at Berkeley for, like, a week. By the end of the week, man, there were nearly seven hundred students and faculty who had accepted Christ as their Savior. It was totally far-out, ya know? They called that week the 'Berkeley Blitz,' and Billy Graham preached at the end of the week. Do you know who Billy Graham is?"

"Yes, I do, but I don't know your name. I'm Danny. What's your name, brother?"

"Oh, sorry, man. My name is Martez. It's nice to meet you. Are you a Christian?"

"Oh, yeah! Deeply, every day."

Martez continues. "Me and several other members of Campus Crusade will be gathering at the Democratic Convention in Chicago at the end of this month. You ought to come on up to Chicago and see what we do. We'll need as much help as we can get."

Martez gives Danny his Akron address and phone number and suggests they ride to Chicago together, but if that doesn't work for Danny, he provides his hotel information in Chicago. Martez, sounding very organized, tells Danny he will be working with an offshoot of Crusade called The Christian World Liberation Front (CWLF), a group that will actually infiltrate the radical groups by adopting their looks and expressing an interest in what is being discussed. As they get to know the activists, CWLF will offer crash pads and safe houses for the radicals who are strung out and addicted to drugs. Then, CWLF will find time to take the leaders aside and mention the radical and nonviolent Gospel of Christ. Christ's activities were so antithetical in His time on Earth that the Gospel seems almost familiar to the Yippies and SDS leaders. The Democratic Convention will be one of CWLF's bigger missions, and as Danny is being escorted back into the studio by his bandmates, Martez encourages Danny to come and help.

"What was that all about, Dan man?" Jeff is the first to inquire as he lights a Camel and opens the studio door.

"Whew, my mind was just blown away, Jeff. It's just the coolest thing, a very spiritual thing that seems to be happening in California and other parts of America with people our age, and it is expanding. I mean, I just met that guy on a street corner in Akron. Why? That is so heavy to me! God is amazing, man, really." King jumps into the conversation quickly as he knows Jeff will play with Danny's love for Jesus like a cat with yarn.

"What was he doing in Akron?"

"I don't know. I guess he is from here, but he said he had gone out to California and that is where he heard about the church out there. He called them 'Jesus People,' and it seems like they are doing huge things for the Kingdom."

"Well, let's go back into the studio and do some *huge* things for Clever Pennies." This is all Jeff offered as a retort. Perhaps sweet Alice's growing interest in Jesus has softened him a bit.

The boys finish their 10:00 a.m. session at midnight, and they are all tired but excited. The engineer did not have anything else booked that day until six o'clock in the evening, and that group called and cancelled.

So, the engineer offered the six-hour block of time to Clever Pennies for only an additional one hundred dollars and accepted the boys' promise to send a cashier's check to him from Appleton before the end of next week. With that news, the boys could relax and do better work, as well as take the time to mix the musical sounds correctly, adding reverb and echo and doing an extra take or two for overdubbed solos. Barry's exceptional musical prowess impresses the engineer as he listens to Barry arrange every passage of each song. Barry's brilliant chord voicings illuminate Danny's poignant songs in a way the engineer had never heard, including bands that had been together for years. Barry is Appleton's Brian Wilson you could say.

Clever Pennies record three songs instead of the planned two, adding Danny's *Climbing a Mountain*. This third recording, however, turns the expected release on its head. The performance of all four musicians and singers on *Climbing a Mountain* is superior to the other two. Perhaps, the reason for its brilliance is because of their relaxed state, having finished the two songs they had already chosen for the record. Whatever the reason, *Climbing a Mountain* explodes out of the playback speakers and is about as hook friendly as a radio song can get. As ferociously as they all play the song, starting with Jeff's opening chords slammed out on his Burns of London twelve-string, it is Jeff's solo, dubbed in later, that puts the song over the top.

His performance is a sight to see as well as hear. With his Jazzmaster sitting on the treble pickup and taking full advantage of the studio's Vox AC30 amplifier turned full up and tubes glowing a deep orange, Jeff begins to record his solo. His eyes close and roll up, as if his god is speaking to him through his headphones. The well-crafted string of notes begins to form an incredibly cohesive musical statement. With blistering and masterfully communicated sound saturating the tape, the solo does not stop ascending until the singers re-enter the musical landscape and remind the listener that the character is apprehensive about what lies before him.

At the end of Jeff's solo, the engineer stops the tape. The band and engineer just look at each other with wide eyes, and as Jeff opens the door to the control room where his friends await his entrance, he is greeted with an eruption of whistles and applause for a job extremely well done. This song *must* be their A side now with *Stars* still the B side. This leaves the deep and driving former A side *Rain or Shine* waiting patiently for its release after *Climbing a Mountain* and *Stars* are solidly in the heads of rock radio listeners.

The engineer keeps the master tape and will send the one-inch copy to a record-pressing company in Nashville with which he works regularly. He knows they do quality work and will have a thousand copies of the new 45 record into the band's hands within ten days. There is a form that Danny fills out with song title and songwriter information, and before the labels are printed, the boys need to name their record label. They all agree to call their label *Marigold Records*.

A copy of the master tapes is made, and the boys pack up what equipment they had brought from Marigold and pile back into Walter's replacement station wagon. It is a Ford Fairlane Squire, similar to the old man's vehicle that transported an injured Barry last Thanksgiving, only newer. Walter's new car provides more than enough space. Danny's car was left for his dad's transportation to the oven.

Danny is very tense about driving after midnight on the dark and animal-populated highways and back roads that lead back to Marigold. Jeff and Barry both take over for Danny at different times during the long trip home, and the conversation and cigarette smoke keep eyes open for the first two hours or so. At the end of their junket, just passing Flint High School, the sun is rising over the beautiful hills. The windows are rolled down as the car quickly heats up from the late July morning sun. Jeff is the first band member and valued friend who is delivered to his home. Then, Danny aims for Upper Marigold where Barry and King gleefully unite with their cherished beds and relieved parents.

Walter is taking his time getting ready for work, hoping his son returns, soon. He will finish a warm breakfast for Danny and has lovingly prepared a turned-down bed that waits for him. Walter is locking the backdoor as his son rolls into the driveway. Danny exits the car quickly and excitedly tells his dad all about the session and how well his songs have been received, but he also puts a copy of the Campus Crusade booklet in Walter's hand for his dad to read. Martez had given Danny a handful of booklets to give away in Appleton. He repeats to Walter all the things that Martez had told him. Walter promises to go to the library on his way home to see if he can find any information about the organization.

"You must question these kinds of things and be sure that they line up biblically, Dan. We both know that Satan is no dummy and that there will be lots of false prophets and preachers. Plus, I'm just not sure about an *organization*. I will pray about it, and I know you will too. Maybe, since this interests you so much, you could show it to Pastor Pete. His input might be from a different generation, but the Bible is timeless, and the pastor is a devout man. Son, I'm not saying it's wrong or bad, just be careful."

"I will, Dad. You know I respect your advice."

"Thanks, my boy. I need to go. Just heat up the ham slices, and there is pancake mix that I just now put in the fridge. I guess I'll take my car since it's here."

"Sure, Dad, but please excuse the mess, and the gas is low. There's enough for work and all, but I was too tired to fill it up for you this morning and thought I would do it later today. I love you!"

They hug, and Danny heads upstairs for a morning of peaceful sleep but stops at the hall table to call Hannah. As he did with his dad, Danny skims over the highlights of the recording session with Hannah but provides every detail regarding his talk with Martez. Hannah and Danny are on the same page with their generation hearing the Word of God, and she asks Danny more questions than he has answers. "Do you think we should ask if we can go to the Democratic Convention, Danny?"

"We really need to pray about this, Hanny. How about when I come to your house this afternoon, we discuss it, and pray together with your family. Is that cool?"

"Yes! Perfect! This is exciting, Danny. Get some sleep, and I'll see you tonight."

Danny takes a slow, soothing shower after his hard day's night and then crawls into bed with his window up just enough to feel the warm, southern Ohio breeze being pulled through from his dad's open bedroom window across the hall. With his head swirling with excitement and ideas, Danny has trouble falling asleep, but soon finds himself waking to the comforting sounds of Marigold churning and a cardinal singing "birdie-birdie-birdie" outside his window.

Danny knows it's time to get up and get his day going. He pulls on his cutoff jean shorts and a goldenrod-colored Fruit of the Loom pocket t-shirt, stops at the upstairs bathroom for a teeth and hair brushing, and heads downstairs. He has slept all day and looks forward to his dad's arrival within the hour, but he hopes his dad stops at the library and is successful finding information on the Campus Crusade. Martez seems like someone in a dream now.

Danny sits in the TV room next to the kitchen, picks up his guitar and starts strumming chords. It is relaxing, and it might spark a new song idea. First, he plays familiar sounding patterns like *Magic Carpet Ride* by Steppenwolf, a Canadian band that Clever Pennies has grown to love. Soon, Danny refines his musical patterns until he finds two or three chords that move him or speak to him when played together. Through repeating those three or four chords, changing voicings, and finding new positions on the guitar neck, his very own style of major and minor chords emerges and out pops the beginnings of a new song. His E minor and F sharp minor chords are odd sounding, filled with open strings that drone in an Indian Raga fashion. Then, Danny hears his dad's car pull into the backyard driveway, and in his plain and unpretentious Midwestern patois, Walter greets his son through the screen door.

"There's my sleepy rockstar. How do you feel?"

"Really good. The temperature in my room was just right."

"I don't smell food. Have you eaten yet?"

"No sir, I started playing guitar as soon as I got downstairs."

"Ok. Do you want breakfast again, or lunch?"

"Wow, now that's a good question. My brain says lunch, but my stomach says breakfast." Walter has his hands full and lays everything down in a kitchen chair to hug his son.

"How about brains and eggs with bacon? I'll give you some OJ, now, if you'd like?"

"Perfect, Dad. Hannah and I are meeting up this evening, and we'll get dinner then, maybe at Fran's. Or yesterday was so great that maybe I will take her to that new place that opened in Appleton. It overlooks the river, and I think it's called Gregory's Fresh Catch. I hear they serve the catch of the day, and it's only open Thursday through Saturday for lunch and dinner. You wanna go with us?"

"Sprout, thank you, but I learned a long time ago that three's a crowd. Just tell me about it and maybe Carl and I can go the next time he is in town."

"I think he is here this weekend! Maybe Jeff and Alice could go too. That would be fun."

"That does sound like fun. If you want to call Jeff and set that up, I'll do that. Tomorrow night, I guess, huh?"

"Yeah. We'll probably need to get reservations. I'll call Jeff after I eat. He's probably working though. I'll walk up to Charlie's instead."

"My mind is racing about the Campus Crusade thing, Dad. If I decide I would like to go, would you be OK with me and Hannah going to Chicago in a couple of weeks for the Democratic Convention. Martez said he could get me a room."

"Oh, my. Son, I'm gonna need to ponder that one. I know you would learn a lot, but Chicago can be a pretty mean city. I trust *you*, of course, but you are only sixteen. Plus, I really can't imagine the Birdsongs letting Hannah go, and she would need a room, too. I can't say yes right now; I hope you understand."

Danny shakes his head in the positive and thanks his dad for considering it. Danny's question about Chicago temporarily made Walter forget what he had found on his way home. "Hey! Look what I found at the library."

On the kitchen table, Walter throws down an April 12 edition of the magazine Christianity Today. Inside is a long and informative article on Crusade by Alan Nichols. To the protest of his son, Walter fixes the brains and eggs first and after a short prayer of thanks, begins to read the article aloud to Danny while Danny plows through his ambrosial late breakfast. The article describes Campus Crusade and what they are doing almost identically to Martez's excited portrayal. Danny is captivated and hangs on every word of the article as his dad reads about how the staff gives the students freedom to start their own ministries on their campuses if they promise to stay in touch with their district staff team.

Before Walter can read the last line, Danny blurts out, "I'm going to show this to Hannah tonight and take it to the pastor tomorrow when I go to work."

"Sure, buddy. I understand it a whole lot better now, too. It really is exciting. To think about how God is moving in the world with the youth, and I believe He must be speaking to you, Dan. The Spirit is filling you with this desire and putting people and things within your reach. I say you should follow this, but I still don't know about the Chicago thing."

"Yeah, well, whatever you think about that, Dad, of course it is your call."

"I'll pray about it, and you talk to Pastor Boggs."

"Yes sir. There's just something about this that does feel like it has been put here in front of me instead of me just finding it. I believe this is something I want to be a part of. I'm going to run up to Charlie's to ask Jeff about tomorrow night so we can get reservations. I hope Mr. Lindor will do it."

"I think he will, unless he's really tired, but the man's gotta eat, so he may as well eat with us, right?"

"You have a way with words, Dad, and Mr. Lindor won't be able to say no. I'll be back in about an hour probably."

"You can drive, you know?"

"Yeah, I know, but I need the exercise to keep my rockstar figure."

"Oh brother, get outta here." Walter turns to the sink with a huge grin on his face, shaking his head in mock-disbelief.

As Danny walks out of his front door, he sees King walking down the driveway. This puts a bigger smile on Danny's already lit up face as he greets his good friend. "What's going on drummer man?" Danny yells as King reaches one arm out for a good shoulder hug and begins walking in Danny's direction.

"I just ate breakfast at Frisch's with mom. She was going into town. Where are you going?"

"Headed up to Charlie's to talk with Jeff about something. You want to walk with me?"

"Sure, but why are you walking?"

Danny smiles. "Because it is a beautiful day and my feet don't need gas."

"Far out. Yesterday seems like a dream, but we have wonderful proof that we were there."

"Man! I was thinking the same thing. That was one heavy day, for sure. I can't believe how good that sounds. God is so good, man."

"Yeah. Have you talked with Barry?"

"No, I haven't. Maybe we can call him when we get to Charlie's, but I imagine he has to work tonight at the club, and Hannah and I are getting together, too. Hey, why don't you just hang with me and go with me to pick up Hannah? We're going to go to Fran's to talk church stuff, but we could take you home if you don't want to do that."

"Cool, and yes, you can take me home before you go to Fran's, please because Cloud and I are rehearsing a really cool poetry reading thing at seven."

"Really? That sounds cool."

"It is, I think. I am playing little expressive beats and things on my percussion stuff while she reads or speaks her poetry. I also use that little baby organ I got when I was like, five. Do you remember that?"

"I sure do. I bet that is really neat. When are you going to take it out to the public?"

"Well, they've started a kind of free form night on Thursday nights in a room above Tony's Pizza."

"Wow, far out. I didn't even know they had a room over Tony's."

"Yeah, it was some sort of storage, I guess, but they have some tables up there now. They can't serve alcohol up there, so it's a pretty cool vibe. Nobody is yelling for In-A-Gadda-Da-Vida, if you know what I mean."

"I know exactly what you mean."

"I think you would like Cloud's words. They're like lyrics, you know."

"I'd love to hear what you're doing. Let me know when you're going to do it and Hannah and I will come down there to cheer you on and yell for In-A-Gadda-Da-Vida."

"Great."

"I can't believe we rode all night last night and talked for five hours and you didn't mention it."

"I don't know. I guess I don't think any of you take her seriously, but she's pretty cool."

"Oh man, I'm so sorry. I don't really know her to form any kind of opinion. She's pretty hippy-trippy as far as most people I know, but I will be more open for my wonderful friend. Maybe we can go out after the poetry read or something?"

"That might be cool. I'll check with her, but I'll tell you now, she's an atheist."

"That's cool, man. I'll love her anyway." Danny playfully pounds on his heart and hugs his friend again.

King and Danny walk quietly for a short while, just taking in the day and the pleasure of hanging out like they used to do before they became too busy growing up. King finally breaks the repose. "When do you want to rehearse again?"

"Soon, man, soon. I have a new song called *New Way* that I can't wait to bring to the band. It rocks rather hard."

"Fantastic! I can't wait to hear it. You've gotten good on guitar. Not like a lead guitarist, but a rhythm player with cool chords."

"Wow, thanks King. *New Way* has a really cool tuning, and I think Jeff will tear it up. I'm having a lot of fun writing, and when the best band in southern Ohio starts playing my songs, it is amazing to hear how they blossom. We really are getting good, ya know?"

"I do know, and so do a growing bunch of fans. When *Climbing a Mountain* comes out, I have a feeling we're going to explode."

"I agree, and it kinda worries me a little. Barry's dad isn't going to let him play any more than he is right now, and if he does, Barry will burn it at both ends. It will fry him. He's about ready to lose it, and I think he got a B in Taltenbacher's class. I would imagine that's why he doesn't call us much because he is working on school during any spare time."

Upon arrival, King and Danny find that Charlie's is active, and both boys say hello to Jane the head cashier when they walk in. "Jane, do you know where Jeff is?" Danny asks.

"No, boys, I sure don't. I think he hasn't come in yet. He's scheduled for four o'clock until closing. He was out real late last night I heard, and Charlie let him change his schedule. Just wait fifteen minutes and he should be here, but don't keep him talking. He'll need to get right on the bags."

"Yes, ma'am. I just need to ask him a question and then we'll vacate the premises."

"You boys tell your parents we got a bunch of new TV dinners in. It gives your moms a break, and they'll love you for it."

Both boys thank Jane, and Danny is used to having distant friends talk about the mom he never was able to experience. They see Jeff come in, and he waves as he flicks his Camel out into the parking lot, knowing he'll be the one to sweep it up later tonight. "What are you boys doing here? I didn't see your car in the parking lot, Dano."

"We walked up here from my house."

King jumps in. "Have you seen any 'Lindor is God' signs painted on any buildings yet? If not, you will."

King is referencing the "Clapton is God" spray-painted signs that began popping up in graffiti fashion around London and New York a couple of years back. As he heads for the time clock, Jeff dryly looks at his drummer and simply says, "Not yet." King and Danny crack up laughing at Jeff's perfect timing and delivery.

Jeff says yes to the Gregory's idea, accepting for Alice and his dad without their knowledge. "Alice is bringing me dinner tonight, so I will let her know then. My dad will roll in about five tomorrow morning, and I will tell him after he sleeps. He'll enjoy seeing your dad anyway, so I know he'll go. It's expensive, right?"

Danny responds with little knowledge of the prices. "I hear that it is, but I need to get reservations. I'll call them from here as we leave. Maybe our dads will pick up the tab. I mean, what are dads for?" Danny asks with a fake innocence.

"Danny, you're terrible, and I love that about you." Danny responds with a sideways smile and Jeff gets another laugh as King and Danny say goodbye. They don't want to get Jane's feathers up.

Danny calls Gregory's Fresh Catch and gets a ridiculously early 4:45 reservation for eight. The only other time was 10:30, not exactly prime time for Walter and Carl. King accepted an invitation for two from Danny, hoping Cloud will accept. Walter and Carl won't want to stay out any later than however long it takes to serve and eat dinner anyway, and the kids can find something to do after. Danny wants to take a shower before he picks up Hannah, so he and King head back to the homestead.

When the two arrive, they see Walter has gone out, so Danny tells King to crank up the stereo. King digs through Danny's expansive collection and settles on Music from Big Pink. It is recorded by The Band, Bob Dylan's backup band. It has only been released a short time, and the sound is ghostly, like from another time. The lyrics tell stories, and the instruments are produced with a great deal of intimacy, a drastic change from the rock sounds of Steppenwolf, Hendrix, or The Doors.

King lies on the floor after having moved the speakers to each side of his head. He tends to be transported when good music is being played, and "Big Pink" seems to conjure up earlier America, like a stereograph photo viewer. A song called *The Weight* is especially clever, with singing voices sounding about as slick and pop-laden as depression-era Woody Guthrie, only with better microphones. It takes a mere minute for King to find himself on a freight train with a bandana tied to a stick, riding to California.

Still, with all the psychedelia that is being presented these days, Music from Big Pink actually sounds fresh and bold in its simplicity and its break from the pop fodder that has been trying to replicate an LSD trip. This sound, country-rock, has been bubbling up for a couple of years, with the Buffalo Springfield, The Byrds, and Moby Grape. The Band, however, smartly took their cue from their old boss Bob Dylan and his recording titled *John Wesley Harding*. That collection of songs turned the music of the day on its head as it opened a rocked-up country sound rather than country-rock.

By the time the stunningly impressive organ intro to *Chest Fever* on Big Pink has started, Danny makes his way downstairs after his shower. The August afternoon has produced no breeze, rendering the raised windows in Danny's house useless. Dressed in only his cutoff shorts and a towel around his neck to use for drying his long hair, Danny lightly kicks King's feet that have gone limp with the rest of his body, having drifted somewhere into Steinbeck's Salinas. "Oh, man, did you have to wake me up? I was in such a good place. What a heavy album Big Pink is! I'm kinda diggin' the earthy thing that is happening. It makes me want to start a garden out in my backyard or something."

"That's a bunch of hard work, but I bet it would be satisfying. I'm supposed to pick Hannah up in about 45 minutes. It's just a warning, Will Robinson. Hey, you wanna hear that new song I wrote called *New Way?*"

"Yeah, yeah. Please do. Is it another hit?"

"Ha!" Danny laughs as he grabs his guitar. "I hope so. I really dig the lyrics. They just flowed out of me." Danny tunes his guitar by dropping both E strings to D and the A to a G. His foot starts tapping the beat, and King soon finds a deep pattern with his young hands on the coffee table that fits the feel of the song perfectly. Danny has been down on the F sharp position this whole time while the two musicians connected, but Danny suddenly slides up to an odd position on what is normally the B fret and launches into the most profound lyrics that King has ever heard his friend write.

New Way by Daniel Mosely

The dawn's new summer sun is reflecting light
Off the deep, dark waters of the lake
There is no rest for me. I'm wide awake
Looking for a New Way to live my life

To satisfy some social protocol
Accumulating things I don't need
I'm struggling with a system that I feed
I'm looking for a New Way to live my life

I've read through every book I own
And traveled through that danger zone
It's a soul-felt yearning. A blue fire burning – burning

My search for life's quintessence is a muse
But my spirit's lack of muscle I can't fake
I only hope it's strong enough not to break
While I'm looking for a New Way to live my life

As the writer plays the last chord on his guitar, his friend erupts, "Danny! That is heavy, man. I mean really heavy. Where did those words come from?"

"I'm not sure. For some reason, I feel that the car crash and Adam's death has something to do with it, but like I said, they just sort of rolled out of my head from somewhere. I have been feeling the Holy Spirit pull on me and grieve when I go in a direction He doesn't want to go, which I've done since the accident. Maybe it's just because I'm sixteen and getting more freedom or all the above. I don't know, but there is some majorly heavy stuff happening in my life, and it's hard to just sit still and ignore it."

Danny heads back upstairs to finish getting dressed for his date with Hannah. King plays the Beggar's Banquet album by The Rolling Stones, side two starting with *Street Fighting Man*. He struts around the Moselys's TV room like Mick Jagger and sings every word. Danny, now fully ready to leave, comes downstairs and motions to King to turn off the stereo, but *Stray Cat Blues* has just started, and King takes a begging posture to wait until it is complete. Danny laughs and begins closing the windows in the house while King finishes the song. As the song is ending, Danny opens the backdoor and waits as King puts the album back in its sleeve and turns off the stereo.

As Danny backs his car out of the driveway, King asks a question conversationally or possibly, with genuine interest. "So, what kind of church stuff are you and Hannah going to discuss? It seems like it is really important to you."

"It is huge to me, my good friend. Remember the guy that I was talking to out on the street in Akron?"

"Yeah, kinda. Very hippie-looking with some friends, right?"

"Yes, and a very Christian brother. He told me about a church out in California called Campus Crusade for Christ that is growing like crazy and bringing the Word of Christ to the world. The really cool part about it, I mean it is something I have been talking with Pastor Pete about, is that it is being run by college-aged people. There are adults that oversee everything, but the college kids are the real feet of Christ, *and* they have a band that sings their own songs with Christian messages, or they re-arrange old hymns to sound modern."

"I talked to Pastor Pete about doing that at our church, and Hannah knows about this vision too, but Hannah doesn't know about Campus Crusade. That's what we're going to discuss this evening."

"Is it like that Up with People thing, 'cause that's very uncool, man?"

"I'm not really worried about 'cool,' but no, to answer your question. UWP is cheerleaders for whatever makes you happy, which is nice, but Campus is Christian and all about spreading the good news of Christ. There's a big difference."

Danny pulls into Hannah's driveway and continues up the hill to their backdoor, where he and King find a green TR3 sitting in the paved turn around. He gets out of the car and goes to the door and knocks. Within fifteen seconds, Alice bolts out of the backdoor and hugs Danny as if he is hers. Hannah is right behind Alice and hugs Danny too, and both girls begin to scream, "It's a Clever Penny. It's a Clever Penny!" Alice sees King standing outside of the passenger side of Danny's car and screams, "It's another Clever Penny!" Both girls run over to King and ruffle his hair and tug on his shirt.

King starts laughing uncontrollably, and Danny plays along, standing with his hands in the air. "Hey, what happened to *my* hugs? After all, I wrote two of the songs? I guess King gets all the girls."

The four come together and discuss their Friday night plans. "Alice, I'm going to steal Jeff's thunder, but tomorrow night, you and my dear Hannah, along with King and Cloud and Misters Mosely and Lindor have a 4:45 reservation for Greg . . ." That is all Danny needed to say before the girls start jumping up and down and screaming again.

"Oh, man! I hope I don't forget to ask Cloud tonight. Can we go, guys, so I can get home for rehearsal with Cloud?"

As Danny opens his door and lets Hannah into the front seat, he turns to Alice. "Are you and Jeff going out tonight?"

"Yep. Not really sure where yet, but we'll probably just hang out."

"I'd invite you both to eat at Fran's with us again, but we're going to talk church biz, and I don't think that is what Jeff has in mind for a fun night out."

"I think you're right," Alice responds with confidence and a half-smile. "I'd love to hear what is happening, but I'm trying not to push him about that. I'm enjoying church with Hannah, though."

"Man, that makes me happy, Alice. The Christian life is not easy, but it is truly life-changing and full of fantastic adventure. I pray you give your life to Jesus someday soon, my friend." Alice smiles, showing just a hint of apprehension because she knows that her life will change, and she is not sure she wants that.

Danny pulls his car up to turn around, letting the TR3 head down the driveway and out onto the road to go to Charlie's where Alice will meet her man. King is dropped off at his house, and Danny and Hannah park at Danny's house because there is no parking at Fran's. With Christianity Today in his right back pocket and Hannah's hand in his left hand, the two stroll the half mile to Fran's. Hannah puts her name in at the front service podium, and they find a bench in the outside waiting area with two seats together. Danny sits and lovingly pushes Hannah's hair back.

Danny knows she tends to wear her thick, dark brown, breast-length hair parted in the middle and falling forward over the small, less than noticeable scars created during the car crash. Though Hannah is far from vain, in her mirror she sees a Picasso character, with the most ignominious slices of the artist brush found. In actuality, the scars look to be only lightly sweeping the top of her right cheek, a diamond shaped depression just below her left ear on her jawbone and a shallow line that follows the top of her eyebrow.

Yes, there have been changes to God's artistry, but the new lines imposed by the shards of windshield glass have almost strengthened her features. She looks more mature without looking damaged, and Danny has no complaints. Danny would love Hannah if she had to wear a goalie mask because as pretty as he thinks she is physically, it is her heart and mind that he considers blessings in his life. He feels privileged to know Hannah Birdsong. Being her boyfriend is just icing on his cake.

The bullhorn style speaker, mounted on the building, calls Hannah's name, and the two walk quickly toward the restaurant door. Danny is anxious to talk to Hannah about Campus Crusade and how they could fashion something similar at their church. Danny reads the Christianity Today article to Hannah in between giving their orders to the waitress. Danny reads a paragraph and then they apply what he has read. By the time they have finished their dinners and Hannah has laid the tip on the table, they were feeling very good about their presentation to Pastor Pete.

Danny knows the Four Spiritual Laws will probably sound very simplistic to a knowledgeable Pastor like Peter Boggs, but the more he thinks about it, he believes the simplicity is the key to opening new minds and hearts to Christ and leading them to a deeper, more mature understanding of God's written word. As they are, they are not overwhelming, nor are they archaic sounding. The laws are a perfect sized dose of a life-long medicine that will eventually give a person a purpose to live, hope for the future, and a tried-and-true friend named Jesus.

CHAPTER
SIXTEEN

The radio disc jockeys in the tri-state area have fallen in love with *Climbing a Mountain* by Clever Pennies. King has been given the prestigious title of President of Marigold Records, which really just means he gets to order the records and assign his mom the duty of delivering new copies to the 36 outlets throughout southern Ohio, West Virginia, and northern Kentucky. Because it is fall and school is back in session, Ellie has titled herself Vice President to feel better about doing the work on her own while her boy works hard at school. She doesn't mind and will ask Delores Meade to make some of the closer runs with her, stopping and shopping along the way.

King ordered his fourth batch of two thousand Clever Pennies 45 rpms, and colleges and city venues throughout the area are calling for performances. At first, the boys were asking for payment that just barely covered their travel expenses, but with advice coming from parents, teachers, and WROR, they are charging a hefty fee to play for ninety minutes, and buyers do not hesitate to pay the amount because they know the tickets that are being offered will sell out. The venues and promoters will make plenty of money.

At this point, Clever Pennies only have about an hour of original music, but they realize they need more and have become diligent. Every idea is written down and as much time as possible is being carved out to work the songs into their most listenable arrangement. Also, they are not opposed to throwing two or three of their best covers onto the list. The Beatles's first few albums featured several covers played in their own special way. That is good enough reason for this band from southern Ohio to do the same.

Time, as limited as it is, has incurred a caveat. The good Dr. Meade wants his son to go to Harvard and become a doctor, and he will not budge on that requirement. Barry's grades are slipping a bit. As are becoming B+s, but Barry has agreed to do extra work to bring those grades up to their expected A stature. Barry and Benny have been working overtime to satisfy Dr. Meade, and Barry's health is suffering for it. Barry is sporting dark circles under his eyes, wearing sunglasses much of the time, and displaying gaunt cheeks. Clever Pennies has been playing every Friday and Saturday night since September, blowing right through Jeff's 17th birthday while they performed to a sold-out crowd at the VFW in Vanceburg, Kentucky.

Sweet Alice was able to surprise Jeff by carrying a lighted cake out onto the stage and coaxing the three hundred and fifty fans and other three band members to sing a rousing and rocking version of *Happy Birthday* to the blushing rock star. Articles on Clever Pennies have been written in several city and college papers, but Jeff has been the individual band member mentioned most. Each of the boys contributes masterful and creative musical parts on their instruments and vocals, but Jeff's guitar work is blazing, and it leaps off the records right into the heads of the listeners. Still, the boys appreciate what each one brings to the band, and their friendships are important to them. So, no jealously is raising its ugly, green head.

Arnie and two of his friends have been helping out, doing their best to go along with the band on some Saturday shows to help set up, talk to the girls, take money at the door, talk to girls, and tear down the equipment and load it into the cars at the end of the shows. Arnie and the boys get along well, but Arnie has a hard time communicating with Cloud. She does not attend many of the shows, but when she does, her conversations are never quite coherent as far as Arnie can decipher. For example, Cloud will elaborate on the rotation of the earth while asking if Arnie feels his body is leaning to one side. Arnie has grown a forgiving and gentle heart since beginning his relationship with Jesus, but with Cloud, he just excuses himself and gets busy doing . . . something . . . anything.

All four of the band members are beginning to unravel while they try hard to keep up with their schoolwork and jobs. Even some of their teachers are fans, but when it comes to their class work, the teachers are not merciful. The teachers know that, as successful as the four boys are getting, it could end tomorrow, and they want each one of them to take more than talent into their adult lives. The only plus to working so hard is that King is charging unrealistic fees almost hoping they will be turned down. So far, every venue has paid what the band asks, and the boys have started a business bank account where two sixths of every dollar is deposited. The boys pay themselves one sixth and their personal accounts are bulging as well.

With his wealth, Jeff paid Arnie to soup up his car and then drove it to Akron and purchased the very Vox AC30 amplifier through which his Jazzmaster sang on the record that is selling so well. Barry has bought himself a Hammond B3 organ with a Leslie tone cabinet he found being sold by a church in Cincinnati. King has asked Alice to help him secure some unique pieces of clothing only found in the European market, mainly East Indian in nature. He also ordered a Rikhi Ram sitar from a New York instrument dealer. The unusual and intimidating instrument came with a booklet on how to tune and play it. King has done fairly well at applying what he has learned, being able to play *Paint It Black*, *Love You Too* and following along with some Incredible String Band songs.

After buying his own bass and amp, Danny has squirreled away most of his income. He and Hannah have been working hard on transforming the area of the church that Pastor Pete agreed to, after lots of prayer. Danny loves Clever Pennies, but he has become obsessed with bringing the Gospel to teens and young adults who have tuned out Jesus and the Bible. His obsession has taken its toll on the band, to a not-so-insignificant degree. Danny is focusing his writing talents on songs with Christian messages, and this has opened the door for the others to get busy and put new songs on the table. The new songs are usually composed by more than one writer and are very different from Danny's style. Though many are good songs, none have matched the level of Danny's lyrically.

King is steadily learning the business of music, live and recorded, and is enjoying it. When three high schools and two colleges call for engagements to be booked on the same date, King chooses to tell his *dilemma* to the venue that would be most prestigious and lucrative. He does so with such unassuming reserve, that by the end of the exchange, the buyer on the other end of the line has agreed to top dollar and is willing to throw in lights and sound. King can be relentless when scheduling appearances by booking two shows on one day, if the times work out. One show might be a festival at three in the afternoon, and the next will be the same day but at eight o'clock in the evening on their way back home.

When King hands the band members their monthly calendars that provides all the information for each show that month, the other three complain when they see two shows in one day. Playing just one show can be very draining, but when they are handed twice their usual remuneration after both shows have been rendered, the boys end up patting King on the back and complimenting his abilities. To top off King's business savvy, he has already purchased an old bread delivery truck that will hold all the band's equipment and five people safely and efficiently. All he needs to do is turn 16 and pass his driving test to put it to work for Clever Pennies.

So far, Danny has been able to keep his job at the church, but Charlie's is having a hard time being flexible with Jeff's duties. Charlie has hired someone to work weekends, but the person is not as hard a worker as Jeff and does not have Jeff's strength and stamina for unloading the morning trucks. Barry had been tiring of the Country Club gig before the busy Clever Pennies schedule. So, he gladly handed off the duties to an accomplished pianist and singer he befriended when playing a festival that presented multiple bands. His name is Phil Gregory, son of the Gregorys who own the restaurant, and leader of a very cool psychedelic surf and hot rod band called The Cobras.

Barry has been enjoying sharing the Clever Pennies fever with Kay. Kay will stand to the side of the stage or sometimes stand down front. Barry, being a very protective older brother and fearing a crush of people, asks Kay to stand at the back of the room if she chooses to leave the stage wing and has given her a small flashlight that she is to flash three consecutive beams toward the stage to let Barry know where she is. Also, Arnie watches after Kay when he is able. Most of the time though, Kay loves to sit with Alice at the Clever Pennies merchandise table and help sell records and t-shirts.

Now that Barry has been accepted to Harvard, he will need to leave Marigold in August of 1969. What will happen with his part of Clever Pennies is a mystery, but Phil Gregory's name has been mentioned to replace Barry while he is away. Other than booking them around Boston on occasion, he simply will not be able to continue as the keyboardist for the band and that bothers Barry greatly.

Seeing how hard Barry has been working and how much money he flaunts, the friend at the convenience store near his dad's office, who sells Barry Playboys, has introduced Barry to heroin. No one in the band knows, and actually, Barry has appeared less tense and jittery as the destructive numbing effect of the dark drug blankets the sawlike edge of the Benzedrine. The boys believe Barry must have found some relief, having been accepted to Harvard. He continues to carry a gaunt and skeletal frame around, but everyone assumes his dad, the doctor, would see any problems. So, no one is concerned.

As if a heroin addiction is not a destructive enough Molotov cocktail thrown through the window of deep-rooted friendships, Cloud shared a tablet of LSD 25 with King, and together, they have re-visited the hallucinogen ten or twelve times in the past three months. Ellie and Gordon have noticed a change in their son, but he has always been a bit different, so they think his odd behavior is just a part of his teen years. Danny, however, is very suspicious of King's new demeanor and is planning to lovingly confront his good friend soon. It just seems that none of the boys are thinking clearly or have time to. As success and busyness, desire and obsession slowly penetrate and permeate the four friends, their strong bond is beginning to fray, and it surely would not pass Mr. Doucet's tensile test, if given today.

So far, Jeff is pleased and proud of the success of Clever Pennies and of the hoopla around his guitar playing. His long nights in his bedroom, with his door closed and Jeff Beck spewing stringed profanities at his welcoming ears, have paid off. He needs to decide if he is going to play baseball again, and Carl is on the fence about that touchy subject as well. He loves to watch his son throw out runners at second and protect his plate. However, a new pride has welled up in him about his son's musical abilities. His son could actually make a living at it, too. Right now, Jeff is nearly making in a weekend what he does in a two-week run. To watch audiences of hundreds gather in front of his boy and stare intently at his fingers, while Jeff's digits effortlessly construct short stories to tell his fans, is nothing Carl could have ever dreamed for his son. But what impresses Carl the most about Jeffrey Lindor is that his heart is still kind, and his head is still on the things that really matter.

Two weeks later, just after Thanksgiving, the guitar god decides to put his regal, size-twelve foot down on Alice's church behavior and attendance. Alice has been meeting Jeff at Charlie's for lunch on Sundays after church, beaming with excitement about what she has learned and making it known to her man that she would love for Jeff to come with her some Sunday morning. Jeff has provided tepid support for Alice's church activity at best, especially since the car wreck, but he was not prepared for his smoking buddy to actually start believing all that foolishness. He wants to kill it before it grows.

Jeff loves Hannah and Danny, and he understands that they have their beliefs, but not his Alice. She is doing it just to be nice, right? Jeff feels as if he is now competing with a two-thousand-year-old Jewish guy that seems to have all the right things to say to his beautiful Alice. Jeff does not want to know that what Jesus is saying is for him, too. Jeff can get in bad moods, and Alice has seen them from time to time, but he broke her heart when he told her to stop rolling her lip at him when talking about the Christian crap. He made it clear that he does not want to go to church with her and that he wants her to stop as well.

Right or wrong, Alice has been pampered and protected through her life, and she has never had anyone speak to her that way. Her dad can be gruff, and he gives her orders as a father should, but Jeff is not her father. With a sad and composed anger, Alice rises from her chair in Charlie's break room and pushes her lunch toward Jeff. Alice then turns around, walks outside, starts up the TR3, and has not shared life with Jeff since. That was a week ago, and Jeff is stubborn. He immediately lets the voice in his head tell him that he knew it would go in this direction when it all started. He returns and holds onto that night at the US Diner when he did not believe their relationship would last.

Now, Jeff is quite aware that his bologna and American cheese sandwiches are a dismal substitute for Alice's beef stews and roasted chickens, but bad lunches and the occasional bleak loneliness that try to fill the hole in his heart will not crack this rock. No, he has seen it all first-hand, and he does not want to go down that hellish road like his dad. Jeff tells himself that it is simply better to be alone than to suffer the heartache that love always brings. He sees Alice at school, but he never makes eye contact. Also, she quickly looks away and laughs with her friends. It's all a cover-up for both of them, but each one believes the other is losing interest and finding a satisfying life again without the other.

Alice is trying to sort it all out. She has never faced such a thing before. Sure, she has had boyfriends, and she has flicked some of them out of her life like a ladybug from her Italian Angora sweater. Jeff Lindor is different, though. Alice *loves* Jeff. She is not sleeping nor eating well, and she cannot concentrate at school. Charlene knows exactly what is going on, and she tries to entertain Alice. Alice has not participated in church activities, except for the opening of Danny and Hannah's youth wing, which was a moderate success. Of course, Hannah and Danny pray for it and have hoped that it will grow, but Alice did not stay the whole time, making some excuse about her time of the month, although in reality, she does not experience much change to her emotions during that time of mature femininity.

School did not close for Christmas until noon on the twentieth. The Clever Pennies boys took advantage of the time off and went home to sleep before they had to load the milk truck and drive it to Chillicothe for a private Christmas party. On top of things-as-usual, King had suggested, back in November, the band learn ten Christmas songs for the parties that were already booked. The band loved the idea and proceeded to do their own versions of The Beach Boys' *The Man with All the Toys*, featuring some excellent harmonies that Ellie made sure she sang on while she could. *Blue Christmas* with King on vocals, a blazing guitar propelled *Run Run Rudolph*, and James Brown's *Santa Clause Go Straight to the Ghetto*, a tune on which Barry sings his heart out. Danny was more than happy to sing some traditional songs like *Silent Night* and a very "Jeff Beck" version of *Greensleeves*.

Now, the band is singing their modified Christmas songs in a Chillicothe neighborhood recreation hall that is the size of a basketball court with similar sound quality. Jeff has been in a foul mood all evening. He has flirted with Cloud, which makes her want to vomit because she thinks Jeff is a big sports jerk. He spends his breaks away from the band smoking his Camels and later proves to all the party guests that he has not said no to the spiked punch. Because of his intoxication, he misses musical cues and forgets lyrics. Worst of all, he just about drops his twelve-string guitar which would have crushed him had it been damaged in the least.

The band's last song could not have come at a better time as Jeff is cut off mid-sentence while he rambles on about Darren, of all subjects, over the microphone. Barry is quick to say goodnight and turn off the P.A., but they are all embarrassed and not a little ticked off at their brother. They know what is troubling him, but the other three never want the band to sound bad or get a bad reputation for being undependable. Plus, Danny is elected to pack up Jeff's gear and drive Jeff and his car home, which Danny is sort of looking forward to, since Arnie added a few of his secret touches to the engine.

On the way home, Jeff apologizes in a drunken slur and then falls asleep. Halfway home, however, he bolts straight up in his seat and tells Danny to pull over. Jeff spends fifteen minutes throwing up along Route 43 as the band milk truck, with Barry driving, lumbers past and beeps the horn. Barry had seen it all before, coming home from the club, and has no desire to stop and babysit. After Jeff stops dry heaving, Danny helps him fall back into his own backseat, where Jeff immediately returns to an unconscious state, and Danny gets back behind the wheel.

Ten minutes roll by when Jeff begins talking about Alice, not knowing what he is saying. At that point, Danny pulls into a gas station, takes the car keys, and goes inside to see if he can buy a cup of coffee. The man behind the counter understands the situation but tells Danny he will need to buy a mug from their small, over-priced store. He finds an Ohio State Buckeyes mug and pays the man, takes it to the restroom, and rinses it out. He, then, goes back into the store and fills the mug full of coffee from the man's percolator. Danny thanks the man and goes to Jeff's side of the car where he finds Jeff's head against the window. Danny knocks on the window, stirring Jeff a bit, before he sets the mug on the car roof and opens Jeff's door. Jeff is fairly limp but somehow catches himself. Danny talks Jeff into sitting up straight and then proceeds to help Jeff drink some of the coffee without burning his tongue.

Another fifteen minutes drags by as Danny nurses Jeff back to a place where he can hold his head up. Jeff consumes half of the coffee before he can sit by himself. He starts making some concrete communication and tells Danny he needs to go pee. Jeff gets out of the car and stumbles over to the dark side of the station where he relieves himself in the mud. It is really getting late now, and Danny is dreading getting up for work in the morning. He will most assuredly need to sleep after work before he has to wake up and go to Huntington for another Clever Pennies gig, but he remembers that there is a radio interview.

King has worked with WROR to release *Rain or Shine* tomorrow, the Saturday before Christmas, with the station furnishing much hoopla and teasers as a build-up. The time for the debut has been set for two o'clock tomorrow and the previously mentioned hoopla, that has been blasted in spots airing several times a day, is to include an interview with him and the song's writer, Danny Mosely. The radio station loves the record and has talked up the release and interview all week.

Jeff was supposed to be at work by seven in the morning but did not wander in until nine. Charlie has never had a harsh word with Jeff, but he cannot run a business if *any* of his employees become undependable. He told Jeff to stock the freezer shelves and then go home. By the time Jeff was finished, he was happy to leave the frigid steel box.

Jeff was ashamed of himself as he walked back home, but his pride and pain has taken over and he did not tell Charlie he was sorry. Charlie is also aware of Jeff and Alice's breakup, but he simply cannot afford to let it cause problems with the store. Charlie knows Jeff doesn't need the money with the success of his band, so Charlie has let other teen applicants fill in the schedule, leaving only a few hours a week to Jeff. The sands of life tend to fill in the cracks of one's disregard.

Jeff goes straight back to bed when he gets home and misses listening to the radio interview, but he does not care. His inner struggle has gotten so big and consuming that he has talked himself into being just another victim of love. Deep inside of the over-grown guitar wizard, Jeff realizes how much Alice means to him, but he just cannot call her. That would be giving in, and he was sick of Jesus, sick of being friendly to rich people, and sick of love. He had watched his dad suffer when Carl tried to continue the relationship with his wife, and maybe Jeff wants to suffer a little *for* his dad. He wants to kick in a wall, so he does. His mom, not wanting to upset him, does not make him repair it. So, Jeff has to live with it, which is a constant reminder of his failure. Darren just laughs at Jeff and taunts him, but Carl is coming home tomorrow, and Jeff cannot wait to see his dad.

After arriving, Carl is saddened to see his seventeen-year-old son in such a way and provides sanctuary for Jeff for the week leading up to Christmas. Carl and Walter go hunting, and Jeff sits in his dad's apartment playing guitar, which is the only thing that can take Alice off of his mind. For Christmas Eve, Walter and Danny invite the band and their families to their home for dinner. Walter goes all out with food preparation, and the old house is bubbling with love and joy and thanks to God. Delores and Kay come, but the good doctor has something else more pressing.

Barry has received a low B in biology, and despite several attempts by Dr. Meade to *gently* coerce the young, new teacher into re-thinking the grade, the evaluation remains a low B to this day. Of course, this has no bearing on why the good doctor is not in attendance. The Reed family attends in full, and that includes Sam, as he is home for Christmas break. Sam's grin of pride for his brother's success in Clever Pennies is ear to ear, and he promises to try and get their record played on a New York station.

Jeff did not encourage his mom to attend. You could say Jeff discouraged his mom from being present because he does not want to watch the awkwardness between her and his dad, which would only remind him of his own broken heart. Jeff knows Alice will be leaving for Paris with her family the day after Christmas, and she has shown no signs of missing Jeff. No calls. No notes stuck in the door at his house or under his car wiper blade. It has been so long since Jeff has even seen or heard the TR3 that he is not sure if Alice is even in town. Of course, Jeff could go by the church to see if he spies her car in the parking lot, but there is no way he is going close to that place. It is the reason for all this misery anyway.

In fine Carl fashion, Jeff awakes Christmas morning to a heavy present under his dad's tree. Jeff rips the paper away, and there is a Marshall Bluesbreaker amplifier. As much as Jeff loves his Vox, this is the amp that Clapton used when recording with John Mayall. Some of the most iconic guitar sounds of the 1960s flowed through its well-designed tubes and wires. Jeff has been able to incorporate quite a bit of slide guitar into the CP shows, so like a flash in his mind, he knows he will get himself a Gibson SG guitar, tune it to E, and play slide through the Bluesbreaker.

Carl makes lots of friends and is always on the lookout for what seems to be valuable, especially for Jeff and his band. He has no earthly idea what the big deal about a Marshall Bluesbreaker amplifier is, but the price was right and he trusted the previous owner, who provided some history for him in case he needed to give his gift a sales pitch to his son.

Carl and Jeff spend Christmas day 1968 hanging out in Carl's apartment eating Walter's leftovers and playing poker, but Alice never escapes Jeff's mind. He knows, if she has not left the country already, she is packing and getting ready for France. The darkness of pride and jealousy rolls in and begins to remind Jeff that French men are debonair, and Alice is, well, beautiful and young and wounded. What if she finds a Frenchman, marries him, and lives in France? Isn't that what the old man wants anyway? He has always just tolerated his daughter's relationship with Jeff, hoping she would come to her senses.

Jeff may never see Alice again. He wants to call her, but that call will probably lead to the truth of her dislike for him, or worse, no feelings at all. As it stands now, Jeff can at least pretend he is in control by showing her that he is not going to be bullied into giving in. His dad tried and was emotionally beaten down by his mom who flaunted the likes of Darren in his dad's face. Carl lost the battle, and all that precious time he was with Jeff's mom was lost because of what he thought was love.

Carl has retired for the evening, and Jeff jumps up from his lonely chair. "What's the use sitting here in the dark? I'm going out." Jeff has not had a shower all day, nor any kind of body maintenance, but he heads straight for his baseball friends, where he knows he can find an exit from the pain. Sure enough, there is a party at centerfielder Stewart's house. As Jeff shuts off his car and approaches Stewart's front door, he immediately gets a huge whiff of the unmistakable, pungent fragrance of marijuana, even though the door is closed. A dog begins to bark, and Jeff notices a couple of lights go out inside and the music is turned down.

Just as he raises his hand to knock on the door, there is a clicking sound from the right side of the porch, generally associated with the cocking of the hammer of a large handgun. "Who are you?" asks a voice.

"Jeff Lindor," Jeff obediently answers.

"Crap, Jeff. You should know better than to come up here unannounced. What are you doing?"

"I thought I'd join the party."

"Of course, brother. I'm glad you're here." After coming around from the right side and walking up the porch steps, Stewart pats Jeff on the shoulder. "Why aren't you with your dad, man?"

"He went to bed, and I was sitting there by myself and thought I'd see what you guys were doing."

Stewart laughs. "What aren't we doing should be the question. My mom is gone until Saturday, Barbara and Jenny are here with a couple of their friends, we have ten cases of Hudepohl, two dimes of Jamaican weed that Teddy's brother just brought back from Nam, and tons of music. Maybe even some Clever Pennies, but we aren't really playin' forty-fives."

"I don't need to hear the Pennies, but I'm ready for a beer."

Jeff does not drink with any regularity. Last weekend's blitz being maybe the second time he had more than a taste of hard liquor. You could say he is *not* a drinker, particularly because of Darren. Darren is the poster boy for why one should not consume alcohol in any kind of quantity. If someone's kid is messing with alcohol, just send Darren over for a night or two, and the kid will never drink again.

As Jeff enters the house with Stewart behind him, the whole congregation welcomes him with loud, and mostly slurred, salutations. He hears someone shriek out a recognition of his position in Clever Pennies, and that immediately brings the girls to him. Stewart had stepped away only to return with an open cold beer. He hands it to Jeff and cleans off a place for him to sit. "Who has a doobie goin'? Let's get one over here to our catcher," Stewart barks out his command to his sycophants.

In no less than three seconds, Jeff has a huge marijuana cigarette, wrapped in chocolate paper, staring him in the face. Jeff had been to a couple of places where people were smoking weed. After Clever Pennies played a fraternity gig at Ohio University, the band went to a place called the Lighthouse. Though he did not partake in any smoking directly, he knows his mind was altered just by being in close proximity of the smoke. The change did not impress Jeff and even more so made him wish he could just get back to normal.

"Ah, thanks, man. That was fast." Jeff tries to stall, but everyone is looking at him because he is not usually part of the scenery at these parties and somewhat of a celebrity. Then, like there was someone behind him reminding him about Alice, Jeff takes a big drink of Hudepohl and accepts the weed. His true thought is that he just wants to get it over with so everyone will stop staring, but the gnawing voice, reminding him of his broken heart, wins. He grabs the cigarette and inhales a lot of smoke, which makes him cough wildly. It burns and irritates his throat with the technique being nothing like smoking one of his beloved Camels. The attempt to join the party works, though, because everyone just laughs and then returns to whatever or whomever they were doing before Jeff's entrance.

After about an hour of talking and laughing with everyone in the living room, Jeff stands up to go to the restroom, but when he stands and his shoulders stop, his head keeps going up. He may have had three puffs of the marijuana, but the room was full of the smoke and there was no relief from it, unless you went outside. Jeff is high, and he is not sure what to do with that feeling. He feels a bit paranoid, like everyone is scrutinizing his every move, and he is not sure what move he wants to make next. He hears voices, but they do not seem to be connected to anyone in particular.

Steve Miller's Children of the Future is playing a song called *The Beauty of Time is That It's Snowing (Psychedelic B.B.)* and Jeff finds himself standing there listening, but for how long has he been standing there? Then a voice yells, "Yes!" Jeff whips his head around. Was that a friend? A cop? Maybe it was a voice on the record. The music changes to a cool blues with people talking, but the change of atmosphere did not make sense to Jeff. Had he listened to a whole song or is someone picking up the player arm and dropping it in a different place on the record?

Jeff has walked from the living room, down the hall, and to the bathroom door. He is not sure how long it has taken him to get there, but he opens the door and there stands a short and voluptuous girl wearing a tight, tie-dyed sleeveless t-shirt with, very obviously, no bra. Jeff apologizes and begins an awkward backwards rotation to leave her, but in a very kind and understanding voice, she tells him that it is OK if they share the facilities. "Go ahead and do what you need to do. I'll be gone in just a minute. My name's Candy, Barbara's friend." She proceeds to pull up on her necklace, from between her breasts, which produces a small, cylindrical, porcelain container. Jeff does not really want to pee in front of Candy, but he does need to go, and she does not seem interested in watching him. She pats Jeff's crotch and promises not to look.

Candy unscrews the top of the container, turns it almost horizontal, and from the corner of his eye, Jeff sees her draw out some sort of white powder on a tiny spoon that is attached to the underside of the lid. Candy holds it up to her nose and sniffs very quickly. As soon as she does, she drops the spoon back into the bottle, lets go of the necklace, and grips the sink as if she is keeping herself from blasting off through the ceiling. Jeff is peeing this whole time but finishes and zips up. As he flushes, he asks if he may use the sink to wash his hands. This makes Candy laugh a very shaky laugh and with pupils that remind Jeff of periods on a piece of paper, she offers Jeff some of whatever was in the porcelain vial.

Jeff is admittedly fascinated with what he just witnessed, but the pot is still making him paranoid and being in a bathroom with Candy is making him uncomfortable. "What is it?" Jeff asks Candy.

"Cocaine," Candy says as she digs her spoon in for Jeff's turn.

"No. No thanks anyway. I'm gonna go back out front with everyone." Jeff opens the bathroom door, and as he steps out into the hall, he notices the music is very low and there are fewer voices. He walks back down the hall to the living room where he finds that almost everyone has departed or gone to other rooms. He is not sure where they are, but they are not in the living room. A door he had not noticed, seemingly from the basement, opens and out walks a completely naked female, headed for the restroom.

Jeff opens the door and listens. He hears voices, but they are muted and the lights are low. The marijuana is making his head feel like an echo chamber, but Jeff heads for the basement. As he approaches the basement floor, a naked Stewart hands Jeff another marijuana cigarette and tells Jeff to get naked or go upstairs. Jeff has never experienced anything like this, and somehow through the pot and beer haze, he thinks he sees his pretty Alice's face within the tangled, naked limbs. It is not her, but his emotions and drug-induced imagination is running away with him. He turns to go upstairs and his face meets another naked girl's belly button. In his haste to get back upstairs, Jeff slams himself against the wall in an awkward and over-exaggerated movement to let the girl by.

"Here," Jeff says to the naked girl as he hands her the joint. He spreads his arms out, putting a hand on each side of the stairwell and ungracefully stumbles up the steps. His foot slips once, but he catches himself and makes it back to the entrance to the living room. There is an empty couch where he aims his out-of-control body. Three steps forward allow him to fall over the arm of the couch where Jeff lands and lies there looking up, wishing he was at his dad's apartment. Jeff begins to tear up, reminiscent of when he would lie in his bed at night after his dad moved out. Now, every beat of his heart is owned by Alice. Jeff is tired, and his weed-fueled dreams are melting into his real and comfortable sleep. He is not sure, for a moment, if he is awake or not, but soon drifts into a realm that seems safe, and he stays there.

Jeff wakes up at five in the morning, finding Candy asleep with her head on his chest. Jeff runs his hands through his hair, pushing it backwards and then shakes Candy's shoulder. "I'm leaving. You can have the whole couch," Jeff says to his bunkmate.

"No, please don't go." With that, Jeff lifts Candy's head and left arm up from his chest, rolls out from under her, and hits the floor on his knees. His catcher legs have returned to his body, and he stands up easily. "Now it's cold. You were keeping me warm," Candy moans. Jeff spies a blanket on the back of a chair, grabs it, and gently lays it over Candy. He did not want to treat her badly, and he was pretty sure nothing went on between them, so compassion for the girl kicks in as he tucks the blanket in around her body. Jeff hears a small "thank you" emitted as he kisses his finger and touches Candy's head with it.

Jeff has sobered up now and practically runs out to his car. He lights a Camel on his mad dash out the front door, but a car is parked behind him in the driveway. There is no way he is not leaving, and he stands on the lip of the porch to map out his exit. Jeff starts up the powerful engine, puts it in gear and just misses the boxwoods on the way out. He makes a tight left turn until the steering wheel can turn no further, threads a needle between the back of the offending car and a short stone wall, around to the end of the driveway and, finally, onto the street. Jeff power shifts his Hurst shifter into each gear until he is travelling at a good rate of speed down the hill and finally out onto Route 43.

Out of fatigue, frustration, and a dull marijuana haze, love for Alice begins to fill Jeff until it pours out of his eyes. His pride has been broken, and he wants to tell Alice all about it, but he cannot. She is no doubt taking off for Paris at this very moment. He returns to his dad's apartment, where his dad is still sleeping. Jeff lays on the coach and tries to fall asleep but can't. His heart is racing thinking about how far away, in more than miles, Alice will be. So many things are racing through his mind. The early days of meeting and dating Alice, the TR3 rides, the comfort she would bring after a bad night with Darren, the fun nights with Clever Pennies. Every detail is being played back for Jeff's torment.

What should he do? He has an idea and jumps up from the couch and takes a shower. He fixes himself and his dad some coffee, eggs sunny-side-up, and toast. Jeff is waiting for his bank to open so he can draw out several hundred dollars. After that, he will stop at his mom's house to get his passport, go to the airport and buy a one-way ticket to Paris, France. Jeff knows where Alice stays every year, and he will show her how much he loves her by showing up unexpectedly. He does not care if Alice likes it, nor her family. What does he have to lose except money, of which he has plenty?

CHAPTER
SEVENTEEN

The flight is long and laborious. The time difference is particularly hard on Jeff, but he is running on adrenaline. He does not know one word of French, and the French people are not so gracious and patient with the Yank. They let him role-play his words, like charades, and even let him speak louder so that what he is saying might be more easily understood. Then, in a very French accent, the recipient of the language ignorance directs Jeff and answers his questions in perfectly understandable English.

He has traveled all day from America, but it is now mid-morning in France, which means Jeff has to go through another day before he can sleep. He certainly does not want to take a nap. He wants to see Alice, but he is not able to pronounce the Third District address at Haut Marais on Rue Dupetit-Thouars. Tired and frustrated, Jeff ends up giving the cabby the written version of his destination, which gets a positive response from the driver who tells Jeff that it is a very beautiful area of Paris. The trip takes him by all the great landmarks, like the Arc de Triomphe, Notre Dame, and under the Eiffel Tower. Jeff is young and from a small Ohio town, but he is pretty sure the driver is taking the long way to his destination.

Jeff enjoys the sights, but all his mind can do is run through what he wants to say to Alice. He knows he will get one shot at it, and it must be clear and sincere. Weaving through the streets and up hills, the cab stops, and the driver lets Jeff know he has arrived. Jeff pays the driver, probably too much, and stands on the sidewalk across from where he believes the Engels are staying. As fatigue begins to creep in and weaken

Jeff's psyche, he feels doubt about what he is doing, what he has done, and what he wants to do. Jeff did not plan on staying long, so he carries only one small bag filled with socks and jeans and a sweater. He begins to think that the Engels traveled either yesterday or today and are no doubt as tired as he.

There is a coffee shop near with large windows where Jeff can watch people come and go from the apartment building. In he goes and sits down with a cup of coffee and some sort of sweet-tasting bread. It is relaxing and he can hardly keep his eyes open, but he sets his head into the palms of his hands, with his elbows on the old wooden table, and tries to stay awake. The French waitress is gorgeous, in a very simple way, but that does not matter to Jeff. He knows he loves Alice and thinks about how wonderful it will be to hold her again if that day comes.

After about forty-five minutes, a large black town car pulls up to the apartment building. Cars have come and gone, but this one is special. The back car door opens and out steps Charlene and Mrs. Engle, with Mr. Engel soon to follow. Jeff pulls some amount of money from his front jean pocket, drops it on the table, and runs across the street. Just as Charlene grabs the door handle to the apartment building entrance, Jeff appears and startles all of them. The driver of the town car gets out quickly in defense of the family, but he soon notices that they know Jeff, and they are all speaking American English.

"She didn't come with us because of you, Jeff. Go home," Charlene spouts out in an angry tone.

Jeff jumps straight up into the air, as he has done when Alice is on his mind. He delivers a very Johnny Carson Carnac bow, with a tip of the forehead and a twirl of the hand to whomever is looking at him and runs down to a larger intersection to grab a cab back to Orly. Humans are rocketing around the moon, and all Jeff can think is that Alice, the prettiest girl, the biggest catch in Ohio, could not go to Paris due to her broken heart for him.

Once at Orly, Jeff finds that the next flight to the United States is not for two hours. He buys his ticket, takes his bag and walks to the gate area, where he will sleep deeply. A stewardess has to wake Jeff with strong shakes on his shoulder to tell him his flight is boarding. He thanks her, lights a Camel, pushes his long, dark bangs back with his left hand, and boards. After he gets seated, Jeff could have thought of the current worldwide flu epidemic or the safe return of the three United States astronauts, but instead, he pictures different scenarios of him and Alice reuniting. None actually showing an emotional Jeff. Then he remembers there is no hiding the fact that he went to France, for goodness' sake, to win Alice back. He will need to play it humble.

After landing in Columbus early on Friday morning, Jeff picks up his car from the parking lot and heads south. He slept well on the flight and is anxious to get home. He starts his Arnie-modified car, lights a Camel, and searches the radio until he finds a station that is playing soul music. Off he goes, twisting out of the airport parking lot and making all the necessary maneuvers until he reaches Route 43. There are many small towns on the ninety-minute drive south to Marigold, and his soul music station has faded. He searches for a new station while lighting his fifth or sixth Camel, finally finding a station playing *Cry Like a Baby* by The Box Tops. *Hello, I Love You* by The Doors is next, and Jeff daydreams himself walking up to Alice and singing the song to her. As he passes Chillicothe, Jeff knows he is forty-five minutes away. He plans on stopping at his dad's apartment for a shower and change of clothes. Not fearing family retribution, Jeff will then head up Marigold Road to the Engel house to see if he can find Alice.

Marigold is coming up, and anxiety is welling up in Jeff. He felt cocky when Alice was a day away, but his time to talk with her could happen within an hour or two. He misses her, but his stubborn and damaged heart makes him bristle with pride when thinking about apologizing. He turns left off Route 43 and onto the northern end of Old River Road. He drives up the hill, bends right, and heads south. Along with many Marigold homes, Jeff passes the church building that started this whole thing, and he tenses up. Three streets past Hagen, on his left, is the road to his dad's apartment. Jeff looks forward to a shower which will not only clean his stinking body but wash away the fatigue that he has endured.

There is parking behind the apartment building, and Jeff parks his car. He grabs his bag and practically runs to his dad's home on the second floor. He puts the key in the lock and opens the door quietly in case his dad is taking a nap. "Dad?" Jeff calls.

"Over here, son." Jeff throws his bag in a chair next to the door and turns his head where he hears a voice that is not his dad's. He sees his dad and simultaneously sees another figure next to him. In the millisecond it takes the brain to connect with the eyeball, its calculations tell Jeff that Alice is here. *Alice is here!*

Jeff, in one jump and a slide on his knees, closes the distance between him and Alice, and in a posture that looks very similar to repentant regret, Jeff can do nothing else but lay his greasy head in Alice's tender lap. Carl excuses himself as Alice rubs Jeff's hair back from his face, but her other hand pats Carl on his arm as he stands. "Did you like Paris?" Alice asks kindly.

Jeff's immediate and unprotected, truthful answer is, "Not without you." The two are quiet in this time of forgiveness and reconnection. Nothing needs to be said. Jeff's hands go around and behind Alice's lower body as his arms pull her stomach closer to his head.

More than two minutes go by before Jeff speaks. "Let's not do that again."

Alice is quiet for a few long seconds. "Jeff, you must understand that I love you like I have never loved anyone in my life. I know that now, but you will not ever be my boss. I may serve you, help you, listen to you, enjoy you, and most certainly love you, but you will never be my boss. I have thought about this since the day I left Charlie's, and I am going to leave this place now so you can honestly think about what I have said to you before you answer me."

Jeff looks up from Alice's lap and tries to talk, but Alice looks him in the eyes and puts a loving finger on his lips. "I don't want to hear what you have to say right now. When you have thought about what I have said; when you have chewed on it and chewed on it until you must decide whether to swallow it or spit it out, then call me and tell me which one you have done. I hope that, if you spit it out, you will respect me enough to call me and tell me that. I do love you, Jeff, and please thank your dad for the time he gave me this morning before you arrived. He's a really good man, and you should be proud to be his son." Alice stands up, with Jeff still kneeling in front of the coach, rubs Jeff's back and exits Carl's apartment.

Jeff's first instinct is to run after Alice and have the last word, but something feels very right about what she said and where their relationship presently sits. He has run after Alice, all the way to France and back. Jeff has run her words through his mind several times already, but he has not meditated on them. He has not applied them to his actual life, and in the quiet of his dad's place, he looks forward to his honest time of contemplation. Jeff knows he loves Alice, and he knows she loves him. It is no longer puppy love, nor high school love, nor infatuation. This is life-changing love, and something inside him is telling him to chew on it.

After Alice leaves Carl's apartment, she visits Hannah and asks if she may visit her and Danny's youth class before church on Sunday. Hannah is thrilled, hugs her friend, and welcomes Alice back into the fold.

Jeff, now content that he has not lost Alice, is relaxed and takes a shower. He is looking forward to a nap before he heads out to a Clever Pennies gig in Kentucky. Carl has fixed some coffee, eggs, and toast for the two of them. They sit and talk a while before Jeff excuses himself and collapses into his dad's bed, where he begins his first bite of thought on his relationship with Alice and drifts into a deep three-hour sleep. Carl, a huge fan of love, is happy that someone like Alice loves his son, and he whistles a made-up tune as he washes the breakfast dishes.

After waking, Jeff has some of his afternoon left and decides to change the strings on his Jazzmaster. This is just the kind of work that can be done while watching television or thinking quietly. Carl has gone out to get some supplies for his run that starts tomorrow, and Jeff ponders his life. He thinks that Alice is a real woman, and that if he continues his relationship with her, he will need to grow up to satisfy her. She does not ask much of him, but Alice requires him to make changes. As he honestly adheres to Alice's request to *chew* on her stance, more thoughts begin to excavate and illuminate Jeff's narrow mind, exposing hidden things that have been stuffed away in the darkness.

Jeff will be eighteen in a little over nine months and will be eligible for the draft. Is he going to college on a baseball scholarship? Probably not, but he does have nearly eight thousand dollars stashed away that can fund his higher education. If he goes to college, will he want to continue his relationship with a high school sweetheart or see what is available at Ohio University, or wherever he attends? Does he want to continue focusing on his guitar prowess instead of being a boyfriend, or – as his love is so great for Alice – a husband?

Alice will turn eighteen in April and has everything she needs to leave Jeff and Marigold and live a wonderful life anywhere in the world. Will Jeff be enough for the catch of the county? Maybe now, sure, but what about when he loses his mesmerizing locks and his athletic physique? What about when he is a mill worker instead of a guitar god? Will she replace him like his mom did his dad? And, what about that family of hers that only tolerates her relationship with him? They would never truly accept him as a son, and that must be considered.

The true love constant is the part of the equation that cannot be dismissed nor ignored. The love Jeff feels for Alice holds great sway and shimmers above all the other tinsel of his life, like a glorious Northern Star used to get one's bearings. This exalted love clearly rules royally over the inferior peasant joys of life that live outside its walls. Jeff feels very alone, and uncomfortably vulnerable, trying to make his decision. His dad cannot help without bias. None of his friends are in any kind of a lasting relationship except Danny and Hannah, and they are the last people Jeff wants to talk with. Jeff decides he is a big boy, and he can make his own decisions.

How could he ever look at Alice and tell her that he doesn't want to see her again? How could he ever feel alright about seeing her with someone else? They have experienced deep and intimate times together, times that changed him, and Jeff cannot imagine anything, or anyone, ever erasing those memories.

Not be her boss? Jeff never had a conscious thought of being her boss; he just could not take her new churchy stuff and voiced that very real feeling. He doesn't want to have those kinds of discussions every day. She was not churchy when they met, but she still loves the heathen that he is, even after her new churchy views. He supposes change for humans is inevitable, just as he will change in shape and mind. He knows that the Reds will always be his baseball team, but he might start enjoying football more than baseball or stop wearing bell-bottomed jeans. He might switch to Gibson guitars, so for Alice to have chosen to go to church on Sundays is just her way of changing – of growing. There is nothing to consider with any worry or fear. Perhaps churchdom will be something that will fade, like Elvis.

While dressing for the gig, Jeff decides not to commit to anything tonight. He loves her, and he knows she loves him. Alice loving him gives Jeff some breathing room, and he truly wants to respect her request to think seriously about reuniting. Maybe he could play the odds and tell her no, with the belief she will cave and allow him to call the shots in their relationship. As he says that to himself, while pulling on his boots, he becomes uncomfortable with the idea of playing with sweet Alice's heart and honesty. She was woman enough to say what she feels, and Jeff knows the relationship will be worthless if it is not based on truth and respect. Just look at Darren and his mom. No truth, plus no respect equals worthless.

He jumps in his car and heads off down the street to pick up Danny. King will give the truck keys to Barry, and all, including Arnie, will converge at the event venue. Tonight's gig is a post-Christmas party for a small company of about seventy-five employees plus guests. The money is very generous, but then King knows Christmas is a good time to gouge the buyers because they are in such a merry and giving mood. "'Tis the season to make money, fa-la-la-la-la la-la-la-la" is the song in King's head this time of year. Jeff and Danny talk a lot, and Jeff apologizes again for last week's drunken bumblefest in Chillicothe. They talk about many things, but Jeff does not mention his trip to France nor Alice's ultimatum. He would rather focus on band comraderies and the night ahead.

Knowing Carl's joy in giving his son wonderful Christmas gifts, Danny cannot wait to hear what this year's addition is. A huge grin comes over Jeff's face, and as he takes a long drag off his Camel, he proceeds to give his friend all the details of the amplifier that is in his trunk right now. Danny sits, like a child listening to someone tell him about Frodo's ring, and Jeff tells him his idea about buying an SG and playing slide through his new amp. Danny claps his hands together as he affirms Jeff's auditory vision and asks to join his friend when scouting guitars. Jeff reciprocates his interest in Danny's Christmas, but there is nothing so grand to report. It was simply a nice, quiet day with his dad as they slowly opened thoughtful presents, ate good food, napped, and watched TV.

As the band arrives at the venue, everyone is happy to see each other, and Jeff is happy to show off his Marshall Bluesbreaker among the various stories of Christmas festivities. Arnie pulls up with his Christmas gift in full display. He had worked hard, and with some Christmas help from his parents, he bought himself a 1968 Oldsmobile Cutlass 442. Jeff freaks out and immediately asks his friend if he can drive it around the parking lot. Arnie dangles the keys in front of Jeff, and Jeff does not hesitate to fire up the beast and hits it somewhat hard for a parking lot. Arnie just laughs as he knows he can fix any damage that might occur, or at least he knows Jeff has the money for repairs. He and Jeff know that muscle cars are for driving hard and not just for looks.

The venue is very nice, with a dressing room and theatre lights on a stage that has been built with acoustics in mind. The band sets up, and Jeff blows his new amp until everyone asks him to, please, turn it down. As wonderful as it sounds, Jeff still falls back to his Vox, which makes his Jazzmaster and Burns twelve-string guitars cut like a knife. The Marshall will be perfect for slide on an SG, just as Jeff had heard in his musical mind. Clever Pennies runs through two songs to be sure they can hear each other while getting the sounds they need to perform their songs with all the excitement of their records and the records of the bands they cover.

Through the night, Jeff easily makes up for his poor performance the week before, and the band is rocking on all cylinders. Barry's voice is pristine tonight, and his keyboards ooze with soul and meaning. Barry looks unhealthy, but his mind is fully focused on his performance, and he has a great rapport with the partygoers. At one point, he runs out into the crowd and dances with some of the married women and single girls. Barry is a master of his instrument, and the stage, and he comes alive when he is performing. The stage is truly where he belongs, but the good Dr. Meade will not have any of that nonsense.

King's hair has grown for at least a year, and it is below his shoulders. His parents had to go to the school and present their argument as to why King should not conform to the school rules of boy's hair being no longer than halfway over the ears. Ellie and Gordon convincingly contended that his look is as much a tool of his trade as a hammer is to a carpenter, and there was no argument that his trade was successful and lucrative. The principal had to concur and made an exception for all the boys in Clever Pennies, mostly because his daughters enjoy seeing the band when they can. The whole school loves the band and all the school boys seemed to get a pass from the principal, now, as their hair styles exceed the school length limit.

Still, King continues to take LSD and is becoming less and less a participant in Flint activities. Danny has tried to discuss King's drug use with him, but King just suggests that Danny try some. Seeing his friend diminish is sad for Danny, but he cannot and will not try to control him – only be there for him if and when the need arises. King's IQ is very high, and Danny knows that King will need to decide to quit on his own. Danny just hopes he stops before he destroys his wonderfully fertile source of creativity. Danny makes it clear to his friend that he is there for him.

King is a very lyrical drummer but can lay down a groove when called. It does not hurt him to be as cool looking as he is. The younger college girls, employed by the company that hired the band, love King's hair and Tyrone Power jawline and flirt with him mercilessly at the band's breaks. He will not be sixteen for two and a half more months, but King's behavior has become ageless. He does not see the world as most sixteen-year-olds do, or most people for that matter. Age plays no part in anything he does, except driving, and Ellie lets her son drive to Charlie's when she is in the middle of cooking and running out of a necessity.

Gordon might outwardly be considered a status quo citizen. He is stable and dependable but well-rounded. He can discuss Gauguin and Kruppa with anyone at the library. Now, with Clever Pennies such a big part of his life, he can hold his ground on Jagger and Hendrix if the topic ever comes up in his circle. After all, he was and still is attracted to Eleanor Sparks, and he loves her freedom and how it has rubbed off on both of his boys, shining in their own ways.

At the end of the gig, Arnie begins the process of packing up the equipment, and King pays him well. Having Arnie there allows the boys to talk with the audience and sign autographs on their records, t-shirts that have been purchased and various fan body parts, so he has become a valuable member of the group. After all, to the horse-country folks in Lexington who hear Clever Pennies played many times on their radios, the band may as well be The Turtles or Iron Butterfly and that is still a bit hard for the band to grasp. Because their records are getting so many spins on so many radio stations in the area, King is beginning to receive calls from record labels, but when they find out how young they are, the companies give King their phone numbers and ask him to call in a year. King is not one to rush, so he is happy to continue the band's growth until Clever Pennies is so big, the record companies will need to break the bank to get them.

The ride home is quiet. Jeff and Danny are tired, and they are good enough friends to know they do not need to talk to prove their interest in each other. From time to time, Danny asks Jeff if he is awake and says something silly just to break the tunnel vision that is so easy to fall into this time of night. Jeff introduces conversation about Danny's songwriting, asking about new ideas he has had, but Danny has not been inspired to write anything that would be useful in Clever Pennies. The car gets quiet again, and thoughts of Alice began to emerge in Jeff's relaxed mind for the first time since earlier today. Danny turns on the radio that is already set to WROR, and as the nighttime DJ does so often, he is playing the perfect song for the moment.

Marvin Gaye and Tammi Terrell are expressing love like others cannot, and this time, their vehicle is the magnificent *Ain't Nothing Like the Real Thing*. The lyrics begin to apply themselves to Jeff's own life, and the last line of the bridge of the song hits his heart like a Minuteman III. An excited calm comes over Jeff. He knows what needs to happen.

He and Danny cross the Ohio River and drive through Appleton until they are headed north on 43. Jeff pulls all the way back to the backdoor of Danny's house. A sleepy Danny thanks Jeff for a great night, and they both laugh about how much better the ride home was tonight as opposed to last week. Danny grabs his bass out of the back seat and closes the door. Jeff backs out quickly and heads to his dad's apartment where he will sleep one more night. Jeff looks forward to having breakfast with Carl and leaves a note on the little kitchen table for his dad to see first thing. The note gushes with love from his son, telling him how much he will miss him and that he is looking forward to hugging him when he wakes up.

Carl is up early, reading the paper, but when he hears Jeff closing the bathroom door, he walks over to the kitchen and begins cooking his Eggs Benedict with Canadian bacon. Carl whips up his own Hollandaise sauce and slices a grapefruit that he was able to bring back to Ohio from Florida. Jeff exits the bathroom, drying his hands on his t-shirt and heads straight for the small, well-lit kitchen. It is a pleasant place to start the day and talk about the important and trivial things of life. This morning, Alice is the topic du jour, and they do not stray from it. Carl does not want to sway his son and he is happy to hear what Jeff is saying about her. Carl knows this is an important relationship for Jeff, perhaps *the* relationship that will last a lifetime.

The two talk a good while until there is nothing left but to act on their conversation. Carl stands up, rinses off his dishes in the sink, and announces he will be taking a shower, if Jeff wants to use the phone. Jeff smiles because his wise dad is always one step ahead of him. Jeff grabs his plates and sets them on the counter so he can hug his dad with both arms. Jeff is a big guy, but he looks like a baby while he holds his dad tightly. Carl hugs back, then pulls away and looks at his son and tells him he loves him. He turns and leaves Jeff alone with the phone that sits on the side table next to the couch.

Jeff sits down next to it and gathers his thoughts until his dad sticks his head out of the bathroom door and makes it known that he does not hear any talking. Jeff mockingly lets his dad know he is not talking because he is thinking, and his dad fires right back with a "thinking is not doing" repartee. Carl noticeably holds the bathroom door open until he hears Jeff pick up the phone and dial Alice's number.

After four rings, Alice answers, and with all his rehearsal, Jeff can only blurt out "I love you" and waits for a reply. There are two or three long seconds of silence and then an urgent but soft and tender "I love you, too, Jeff".

"Can I see you after my dad leaves?"

"Could I come there and say goodbye too? I've grown to really care about that good man."

"Sure. I think he would like that. I know I would. That is so cool that you two are friends."

"Ok, then. I will see you in about forty-five minutes. Is that too long?"

"No, he won't leave for an hour or so. I can't wait to see you, my baby." Jeff had not called Alice that for a long time, but it felt right this morning and just came out naturally.

"I can't wait to see you too. See you in about forty-five minutes."

Jeff has showered and dressed rather well for a Saturday morning. Carl has shaved and splashed on some Aqua Velva, the fragrance of which has filled the small home. A small dab of Brylcreem holds back what little hair is left on Carl's shiny head. He sets his travel bag on the kitchen chair where his jacket hangs and tells Jeff that he is thrilled that Alice wants to say goodbye to him. "How nice is that, son?" Carl says with a big grin, mocking himself as he knows his son is sick of hearing it.

"Yeah, Dad. I got it. She's the greatest," Jeff says sarcastically until they are both laughing out loud.

The temperature is nearing fifty on this sunny Saturday morning, which means Alice drives the TR3 with the top off. When the two men hear it, they take turns looking in the mirror hanging by the front door. The car door closes, and then they hear steps up to the door. Carl opens the door before Alice can knock, and Alice is all smiles. "Good morning, sir!" Alice brings the whole morning to life, just with her tone.

"Good morning, my friend. I am so glad you came to see me off, except it makes it hard to leave."

"I can go back home . . ." Alice smiles as she turns to go.

"No, no! I'll suffer the consequences just to gain your presence." Carl bows and welcomes in this lovely human. She hugs Carl and then looks for his son, who is standing off in the kitchen. "Have you met my son, fine lady?" Jeff puts his head down and shakes it in faux embarrassment.

"Yes, we've run into each other at parties," Alice jokes.

She and Jeff meet in the middle of their distance apart and smash into each other and don't let go. "Wel-l-l-l-l, I best be going," Carl announces, as if all of Appleton is listening. Jeff and Alice giggle, and both walk to Carl, giving him big hugs and each a kiss on both of Carl's cheeks. "That's more like it. You two enjoy yourselves and your renewed relationship, and I will see you in a couple of weeks. Do you have a New Year's show, Jeff?"

"Yeah, King has us headlining at the Armory for a big city-wide blowout. There will be four other bands, but we start at eleven forty-five so we can play in the new year. We are getting five hundred smacks apiece, and we're only playing an hour."

"Man, I should have learned guitar so I wouldn't have to drive that big ol' truck."

"Sorry, old man. You don't have enough hair." Carl grins and makes that the last thing said. He grabs his bag and jacket and, with watery eyes, blows both kids a kiss as he closes the door.

The two "kids" stand staring at the closed door and listen to Carl's footsteps trod down the steps toward his cab. Jeff and Alice turn and look very seriously in each other's eyes and fall back into each other's arms. They stay in that position for a while until Jeff releases his hold and kisses his lovely Alice. Alice brings no resistance as she melts into Jeff's lips. "I gave what you said a lot of thought, and it was heavy. I really did meditate on your words, and I believe my love for you is so huge that I can overcome anything that might get in the way."

"Jeff, it seems we are fantastic on everything but church, and that really needs to be discussed. I love you and I respect your views on all that, but it is not something you can dictate for me or anyone else. It is such a personal thing that once a person begins to love Jesus Christ and His teachings, it is hard to turn it on and off, and I don't want to live that way. I won't expect you to walk with me down that path, but I can't be told to turn away from it. Maybe I will turn away in the future, but that will be *my* decision and no one else's. Not even yours, and I love you deeply."

"Have you ever thought about marrying me, Alice?" Though they have been close for almost a year, this has never been mentioned, but it feels like the right time to bring it up.

"Yes, Jeff, I have written Alice Lindor a thousand times on notepads and things. No one has ever made me feel the way you make me feel, and I believe you are the one, and if you turn out half as cute as your dad, I can't lose."

"You would love me with a bald head?" Jeff asks with a sly smile.

"Yes sir, I would." Alice continues, "I don't want you to think I am forcing you to or anything. I know life would go on without you, as Brian Wilson says. Someone would probably come along and fill that void and make *my dad* happy, but I can only picture you as my husband forever. I don't have to fight off any attempts to picture making babies with anyone else." Alice lets go of Jeff and stands back while looking him straight in the eyes. She begins to unbutton her plaid flannel shirt. "Will you make love to me, Jeff?" Without hesitation, he takes her hand and gently leads Alice back to the bedroom.

CHAPTER
EIGHTEEN

After John and Yoko expose their outer selves on the cover of their new album Two Virgins, Richard Nixon takes over as President of the United States. There is no apparent connection. Jeff's favorite team, the New York Jets, wins "Super Bowl III," beating the Colts sixteen to seven, and Mickey Mantle retires from baseball. In the more immediate surroundings, King's sixteenth birthday approaches, and it will be no small event. He and his parents have used many of the contacts King has made with Clever Pennies and created a "happening" of great proportion to celebrate his birthday.

He is not shy about branding the party a Clever Pennies show, as the band will no doubt play a few songs, but the bash will be advertised as a party for the drummer of Clever Pennies, King Reed. WROR will talk it up on the air and will host the gala, playing lots of CP music and presenting interviews on the week leading up to March 7. All the band members are on board and want to support King for this special year.

King has asked Phil Gregory's band, The Cobras, to play when Clever Pennies is not playing. The boys know that The Cobras are a better band, technically, but The Cobras' members are not best friends, and they don't have Daniel Mosely writing songs for them. Unfortunately, Clever Pennies does not have Daniel Mosely writing songs for *them* at the moment. His interests have shifted to writing songs his youth group can sing and use to worship Jesus. Danny has tried to combine both interests, usually using stories he hears at church, and has written some incredible songs that would work for the Pennies. One is a fast rocker titled *I Can't Quit My Ways* about a sinner who cannot control his lusts.

Another is one that burns with passion called *In the New World Sun*, written after hearing a story from a friend. A third song, shown to the band when they were all at his house just watching TV and talking, is called *Another Perfect Morning*. It is a tender love song to Hannah, but the band has not taken the time to work up any of these songs for shows or recordings.

Each band member is finding it difficult to stay enthusiastic about Clever Pennies, even though they are so well received. The rose petals have fallen off, and all that is left is the stem with an occasional thorn. Barry has been struggling to satisfy his dad. His interests are not Barry's, and Barry's grades are suffering. Valedictorian is out of the question now, as Barry has received a C average in chemistry his first two quarters. His health is a mess, and his addictions are becoming harder to hide. His mom found his bag of heroin, but Barry convinced her it was BC powder for headaches. Delores knows better, but she is not a strong woman and would rather turn the other way than face the fact that her son has a problem. Meades do not have problems, especially the men, and there is no telling what her husband would say and do if he knew anything about her finding – and his son using – a white powder.

Barry knows his dad is close to giving him an ultimatum about the band, which Dr. Meade blames for his son's failures. Quit the band or be disowned is the medicine that Dr. Meade will administer to cure the cancer in his family. Barry loves his family and cannot imagine being cut out of its events and traditions, but chemistry and the whole Harvard thing, for that matter, has nothing to do with anything he enjoys. Barry tries very hard to achieve the grades his dad expects, even at the expense of his own health, but nothing helps. As smart and forthright as Barry is, no amount of effort moves the needle on his chemistry grade. So, to stop the frustration and heartache, even for a short time, Barry turns to heroin on top of his addiction to Benzedrine. Benny has become a way of life and a part of Barry's personality. Who knows who Barry really is? Not even Barry knows who Barry is.

Danny has been hearing more about the Campus Crusade for Christ since he subscribed to their Student Action newspaper. Nothing has excited Danny so much, and Hannah is enjoying the paper as well. Together, they talk about going to California and working with CCC, and Danny is considering going to school there. Hannah has not committed to that yet, as her family has talked about her going to Cedarville like her sisters. Perhaps Hannah will go to California for the summer and then return to Ohio for school. As a couple, Hannah and

Danny are secure and could spend time apart while going to separate colleges. All of that is a year and a half away, but the thought that they might be a part of something so important and world-changing causes all other dreams and aspirations to pale in its glow. Danny and Hannah believe Campus Crusade and its imminent adventure is God-breathed, and it only binds them more closely.

There is no doubt that Jeff and Alice have a future together, but it is not apparent what that future looks like. Neither of them talks about their plans after high school, but Jeff has cut his hair for one more year of baseball. He did not even attempt to get a Clever Pennies "hair waiver" because he knew his coach would just look up from his desk over his readers, furrow his brow, and ask Jeff if he is crazy. Instead, Jeff lets Alice cut his nearly shoulder length locks, and she did not do a bad job. She left the top and front long but cut the sides and back so that his hair was acceptable in his hat and facemask. The coach simply said Jeff was "looking good" when he came to practice and nothing else was said.

Jeff was able to give King a copy of his game schedule so that King would not book anything that would conflict. There is only one weekend when both evenings are tied up: the Friday night game at home and then Saturday is an afternoon game at Northern, meaning Jeff could not be available until too late for a gig. Arnie is a second baseman on Northern's team, and Jeff told him that his hits will be aimed right at his head. Arnie was unfazed. "Ain't no baseball hard or fast enough to crack this noggin, so give it your best shot, guitar sissy."

King seems to be the only band member who has not lost his interest in Clever Pennies. He is fully involved and working hard to increase their popularity and bank accounts. All the boys know how dedicated King is, and the reason for their attendance and any effort at all just might be him. They all love their friend and each other, but having started in their fragmented teen years, Clever Pennies is just a part of their lives. Jeff is still excited to play his guitar, but the success of his band was almost too easy. He is not challenged to be great, only to be the guy on the records they make.

King is taking drugs and growing into someone Danny does not recognize. He loves his friend and has great memories of their childhood, but King has become insulated and hard to reach, as much as Danny has prayed and tried to connect.

Through the spring of 1969, Clever Pennies records continue to sell. So, at King's twisting of the arms, the band agrees to travel once more to Akron for more studio time. On this session, they are more careful as they all heard things in the previous recordings that they wish that they had done differently. The band is big in Akron too, and the engineer is able to coerce a small string section from Kent State to perform at no charge for two of the songs they will record. The strings will be used on one song by King called *Over the Moon* and a Daniel Mosely song called *Being You*. King's song is very fun and appropriate for all the moon shots that have made front page news recently, but Danny's lyrics are again deep and poignant.

Being You by Daniel Mosely

(Verse 1)
Why do you try so hard?
Why don't you just let go?
Who must you impress, now?
I would bet everything I have on who you really *are*
Not on who you think you should be
The time you spend on fitting in
Is time you could use being you

Both songs are recorded with the string section executing its parts with finesse and professionalism. The overdubs are scheduled for another day, except the lead vocal for *Being You*. Danny feels that Barry has the best voice for the song, and it is a good call. Barry's fierce and eloquent delivery of the Mosely lyrics is the bright spot of this session. After only one take, Danny's eyes are moist as Barry walks back into the control room for a listen. "That's the one, Barry. I mean it, man. Listen back, but I can't imagine a better take. That was really heavy." King and Jeff agree and Barry humbly thanks his bandmates for their praise.

One of the female string players, obviously enamored with Barry and his abilities, gives him praise as well. As everyone is packing up, Barry, who has nothing to carry back to Marigold because the studio keyboards are more than adequate, continues to talk to the college girl until he turns to the band and tells them he will see them in Marigold. The newly eighteen-year-old Barry opens the door for the cellist, turns his grinning face back toward his friends, and exits the building.

The next day is Sunday when Alice too turns eighteen. Unfortunately for Jeff, the plan is to hang out with the Engels for a lunch cook-out. Jeff has tried to get close to Mr. Engel, to no avail. Markus Engel has no desire to openly welcome this chain-smoking, longhaired rock-n-roller into his well-groomed family, and he definitely does not want to encourage his daughter to continue her relationship with him. Rested from his studio work yesterday, Jeff gives it his best and attempts to talk with different family members except, noticeably absent, Charlene. He is told she is out west at a spa, but the truth is later known that it is a drug rehabilitation sanctuary. Abbie has taken a liking to Jeff, and the two are able to joke and sometimes talk relatively deeply. She will occasionally suggest that Jeff "hang in there" for Markus. "He'll come around," Abbie tells Jeff when her husband is not within hearing distance.

Hannah and Danny are Alice's guests today, but they have become more like church friends instead of band friends. Alice has been going to church regularly since the reconciliation with Jeff, even spending Easter with the Birdsongs. Jeff did meet Alice, Danny, and the Birdsong family at the Moselys's for an Easter lunch but quickly left the gathering after the dining had ended. With all due and sincere respect, there was too much Jesus talk for Jeff's taste, not that he really wanted to go home to Darren.

The Jesus thing is starting to get under Jeff's skin again, but he loves Alice, and they have gotten very close. He wants to be a man of his word, but there is something about Jesus that makes him anxious and almost angry. Danny has used the Shakespearean "the lady doth protest too much, methinks" line with Jeff, but Jeff puts his hands over his ears and sternly tells his friend that he doesn't want to hear any more of that junk. Of course, Danny is simply excited about his life with his Savior and is not inclined to keep his excitement to himself just because Jeff does not want to hear it. Danny does not purposefully try to irritate Jeff, but after much prayer, Danny has stopped holding back speaking of his great love for Jesus.

Barry and the cellist burn through an active and empty night and day, but later that evening, he has her return him to Marigold. Well, not quite into the community. Barry has her stop at the entrance with instructions to drop him off at Frisch's. This is so she does not know where he lives. After Barry says goodbye and reminds his fellow musician to be careful on her five-hour trip back north in the middle of the night, he makes sure she is well out of sight and then calls Jeff. It is very late, with a school day just hours away, but Jeff agrees to leave the house and pick up Barry to take him home. As Jeff is leaving, Darren is cursing at him from his bed about telling his friends to stop calling so late. Jeff slams the door and heads for his car.

On the short trip home, Barry provides plenty of unsolicited detail about his previous twenty-four hours and then jumps out of Jeff's car with a hardy thanks. His mother is frantic when her son enters his home. "Why didn't you call us, Barry?"

"Didn't the guys tell you I stayed in Kent?" Barry does not try to hide his lifestyle from his mom any longer, and that is why she worries more than she used to when she was ignorant of his behavior. She still does not know for sure her son takes drugs, but then again, she is sure of it.

"Yes, son, but I thought you would be home earlier, and I was worried about you."

"Don't worry, Mom. I love you, and I'll be fine."

Clever Pennies has become a shadow of itself, but what does that matter? It is just another rock band, of which the world has many, and this kind of thinking is making inroads into the minds of two band members at least. Setting up, tearing down, signing autographs, commercializing their personal emotions and insights has become passé and meaningless to Jeff and Danny. In the back of all their minds, and sometimes the very front, they know they might be heading for Vietnam one day, if the war does not end or they do not get a deferment. The future and how they live their lives has become very important at a young age. The generation before them was called to a war that was changing millions of people's lives for the worst. Nam, though the lives of its people are important, has little relevance to the salvation of the world and those living in Marigold. Communism must never flourish, but the boys are sure that a cruel, godless government is not a concern in America.

Barry loves to perform and strives to raise the bar of whatever music he is playing. Contributing his exceptional talents and abilities on the keyboards and vocals is something he lives for. King, the one who outwardly portrays the artist life, is actually the savviest businessperson in the CP organization and the only one who cares to capitalize on the Clever Pennies brand. He wants the band to continue and be known around the world for life-changing music and lyrics. It has been done before, and King believes Clever Pennies can reach that acumen. He and Barry know that without Danny's songs, the band is less likely to attain world popularity. If The Monkees had not been singing the songs that had been written for them, they probably would not have made much impact on the rock music scene. Success is in the song.

But the real bond of these four boys, the life that flows through their cumulative walk, was etched years ago when adults did not listen to their ideas. They listened to each other, supported each other, and provided a place where their thoughts could be important enough to consider.

Walter has always been a supportive figure in Danny's life, as well as his church family. Ellie and Gordon and the Meades nurtured and took great interest in their young children's lives, and even Jeff received lasting love from his dad. It is a natural process for parents, good and bad, to not have the mind to speak and think like a ten-year-old. Therefore, the four boy's adhesive is a blend of love and respect for each other that they could not find anywhere else.

Why these four, out of so many school acquaintances and neighbors? Is it because of something like Edison's one thousand attempts to invent the light bulb until the final combination formed something meaningful? Did their relationships take great planning, like the carving of Mount Rushmore? Purposeful social engineering with their parents creating playdates and making sure they were going to the right schools to meet other children like themselves? These children's backgrounds and personalities are too diverse for that to have been successful. Of course, there are many who would consider their union providential, and why not?

⁂

"Who's ever heard of a river burning? They put a man on the moon, can't they clean up the rivers?" Barry asks this apt question, for any band member ear to hear, while traveling with the band to a gig somewhere in Ohio. He's speaking of the Cuyahoga River in Cleveland, which is so polluted, it caught fire. He knows they have all discussed it before, but it still weighs heavy on Barry's mind.

King answers with another unanswered question, "Why did Brian Jones have to die? He was the most important Stone, I think." Hoping that King might apply the truth about Brian to his own life, Danny reminds him that the story is that Brian had been out of it on drugs for years. He didn't die of a drug overdose, but he was just not functioning properly and could not save himself in his own swimming pool. King does not reply.

"Who's going to that festival in New York next month? It's called Wood-something. Woodbine? Woodburn?" Barry asks.

With a freshly lit Camel between his lips, Jeff says he and Alice had talked about going, but he hadn't bought any tickets. He figures if they go, he'll just buy the tickets at the gate.

"I think it's called Woodstock because it is in a town called Woodstock." King contributes. "It is sort of near West Point, and Sam said I could stay around there and use his car. He has no interest in going. I was thinking I would get a motel and just drive to the festival every day."

Jeff tells King that he probably cannot get a motel room because he is only sixteen. "We were going to drive up in the TR3, but I'll drive if you guys want a ride."

Danny says he is not going, so that means there would be plenty of room in Jeff's car. "I have a fake ID for a motel, and can Cloud go?" asks King, who is driving the bread truck today.

"Sure. There's room for everyone, especially if Danny isn't going. Are you sure you don't want to go, Dan man? You and Hannah, maybe?"

"Yeah, I'm sure. We have a lot going on, and I hear there might be a hundred thousand people there. I just don't want to get into all that. Thanks, though."

"I think you can camp out. It's in a big campground or something, so I'm just gonna take my sleeping bag and get my ticket when I get there, too," Barry says as if he has thought it out already.

"Do you need to cancel any CP gigs, King?" Jeff asks.

"There is one that pays pretty well. It's a fraternity in Columbus that wants to get the year rolling with the boys of Clever Pennies, but I haven't signed a contract, and I'll just see if The Cobras want the gig. I'm going to Rugburn or Woodchuck or whatever it's called." The boys erupt with laughter at the idea of a festival called "Rugburn."

Barry's mind is still on current events. "Has anybody heard that Nixon pulled some troops out of Nam? Maybe he's going to do what he said he would do? After LBJ's lies and throwing American boy's lives at his little problem over there, I hope so."

"Really?" Jeff says with his eyes as round as quarters. "Oh man, that would be so heavy, man. No more war to worry about. I want to go to college, but I'd like to be able to maybe take a year away from school before I start again, but I have to have a damn deferment instead."

"I know; I worry about you guys. Surely the war will be over before I turn eighteen. Surely," King says with dread and doubt in his tone.

***

After making all the necessary arrangements, the Marigold bunch head for New York. The path to Bethel, New York, where the festival is actually taking place, is decorated with small towns, turnpikes, and good food. After they leave Ohio, they find that the bigger highways across Pennsylvania provide the most efficient travel. For some reason, they have been followed by the local police through every small town, like a rear escort, until they are out of town.

Alice and Jeff decided they will camp out at the festival too, so there is a guitar in the backseat for playing songs on the way up to New York and for use when camping in the quiet nights at the festival. "Why didn't you book *us* at Rugburn, King?" The funny name has stuck for all the kids, and they have renamed the festival for the next four days.

"I wish," King says, but he and Cloud have taken some sort of drug, making them mostly non-communicative. Cloud has braided King's hair as it is past his shoulders now. He finds that he likes it braided because it is keeping him cooler on this hot August Thursday.

Alice started driving somewhere near Pittsburgh and on the eastern side of Harrisburg, the traffic is getting heavier. The scurry of vehicles is forcing Alice to stay more alert to unfamiliar traffic patterns and some very bad drivers. They are starting to see an abundance of hitchhikers, male and female, holding signs for Woodstock, and most are young with tie dyed shirts and long hair. It is time for a pit stop so that Alice can give the driving duties back to Jeff, and the car needs a fill up anyway. Alice takes an exit off the Pennsylvania Turnpike, and the change in speed wakes Jeff. He is awake, but he has only opened one eye as he watches Alice pull into a gas station.

While there, Barry buys a New York map, and they all discuss whether they should keep going or get a room and finish the trip tomorrow. Jeff is wide awake since his nap and believes he can drive the rest of the way. Besides, there are three other drivers, including Cloud, but Jeff knows how high they are and does not want to risk his or Alice's life. As well, he shies away from any chance of damage to his new pride and joy, a nineteen sixty-seven, Arnie-fied, Chevy Impala Super Sport SS427. He will persevere!

The oil is checked, and the tank is full after contributions from all the passengers, but King tells everyone to put their money back and pays for the gas himself. After observing King's booking skills, the band agreed to pay King ten percent off the top of every gig he books, so he is carrying a lot of money and, because of his love for his friends and state of mind, King shares the wealth. As the car pulls out and heads for the entrance to the last bit of Pennsylvania Turnpike, Jeff lights a Camel and asks Alice to find a radio station. She turns the knob slowly until she gets to seven seventy, and ABC Music Radio 77 out of New York City is blasting Creedence Clearwater Revival. It's *Green River*, and the whole car explodes into air instruments, singing, and seat dancing.

The station plays great song after great song: *Touch Me* by The Doors, *Everyday People* by Sly and the Family Stone, and a powerful song by The Temptations that mesmerizes them called *Can't Get Next to You*. The music does not stop through the night, which helps Jeff stay awake. After getting off the turnpike, they are headed for the New York Thruway, but as they drive farther north, with New York City to their right, the traffic gets slower and slower. Jeff assumes there must be a bad accident ahead, but the traffic never stops. On the northern end of New York City, they enter the Thruway, and it is bumper-to-bumper.

The Weight by The Band is the soundtrack music for this hazy Friday morning sunrise, and all Jeff can see is cars. Why are there so many cars? Everyone else in their car is asleep except Barry, who has been talking about all the different bands that will be playing at "Rugburn." He has named them all, Jeff believes, delineating every detail of every member in every Woodstock band and every song they have ever recorded. Fascinating, yes, but it would have been pleasant if the flood of trivia had slowed to a trickle, even if just for a short time. Jeff knows that Barry is either on or off, and there is no in between. Nonetheless, Jeff feels he is on some great conveyor belt being pulled toward a large grinder or compactor. Maybe a huge, fat, bald man gobbling up cars and trucks as they drive into his mouth.

After realizing what he was thinking, he knows he had better take the next exit to throw some cold water in his face and fill his car up again. As he moves to the right lane, Alice wakes up and asks, in a whispery morning voice, if Jeff is doing alright. He smiles and tells her some of his wacky thoughts, validating his desire to get off the road for a few minutes. Jeff pumps gallons of gas into his SS, and Alice asks if he would like for her to drive. He shakes his head no while he is looking down at the entrance to the tank and then, lays his head on her hip.

"Are you looking forward to the festival, baby?" Jeff asks Alice.

"Yes. I'll be glad when we get there, but it should really be fun. I can't imagine seeing a hundred thousand people all in one place. I bet the musicians are excited."

"That would be far out to play in front of that many people. Clever Pennies could rock the farm, I think. Can you imagine hearing *Climbing a Mountain* blasting out of a bunch of speakers? I'm sure they have to have a huge sound system for a hundred thousand listeners."

Barry walks up to the couple from his trip into the building. "The guy inside said all this traffic is for Woodstock. He showed me some back roads we can take on this map if things get hairy on the Thruway."

"If it gets any worse, we just might need those."

Everyone is back in the car after freshening up for the rest of the trip. It takes Jeff a good twenty minutes just to get back into the Thruway Traffic. To small-town Jeff, the atmosphere seems harsh, and the bridges and buildings look unfriendly in the dark and dawn as they pass Philly and Newark and finally the New York City area. The radio is now playing Mr. New York himself, Frank Sinatra. He is passionately emoting his masterpiece *My Way*, and as the car slowly moves north, the terrain is looking much more like home. Trees and houses have replaced warehouses and metal structures. The radio is talking a lot about the festival and telling drivers how slow the Thruway is moving.

Jeff is now boxed in by a day-glow painted VW bus with about fifteen hippies from New Mexico in it and a nondescript maroon Chrysler, probably just trying to take a salesman to his next customer. Jeff is going fifteen miles an hour when he asks Barry to start figuring out another route to their destination. Barry has already been studying the different ways his gas station attendant friend provided and believes he has an alternative to the Thruway. He tells Jeff that he should exit in about ten miles, which at this speed, should be about forty-five minutes from now.

The traffic is entertaining for those who are not driving. There is just about every state in the country represented, and each car seems full of crazy, happy characters. Alice puts on her cowgirl hat for the first time since she received it from Charlene after a Colorado trip. Of course, she wears it perfectly, and the whole car loves it. Jeff brought his Flint baseball hat to keep the sun from beating down on him at the festival, and Cloud has a floppy farmer's hat that she has stuffed in her backpack. She, too, is waiting for the festival before she wears it.

They are all getting excited now because the radio won't stop talking about Woodstock and playing songs by most of the bands that will perform. "I cannot wait to see The Incredible String Band. Mick and Marianne love them, The Beatles love them, and so does King Reed."

"My, you've put yourself in some pretty grand company there, old boy. I'm sure they won't start until you arrive." Jeff tries to playfully bring King down a peg or two, but it is no use. King looms large in his own mind, and his parents and Cloud back him up.

Music77 continues to surprise and delight with more great music from Blind Faith, Country Joe and The Fish, Canned Heat, Joni Mitchell. There is a commercial, allowing everyone to talk until the speakers pulsate with Neil Young's *Cinnamon Girl*. "Far out!" Jeff exclaims. "Listen to that tone. How does he get that tone? That's so heavy! It almost makes me want to start playing a Gibson."

Some of the back roads prove beneficial while others are just as backed up as the Thruway. Still, the scenery is better when they are off of the beaten path, and the friends from Marigold are actually able to talk to other young, musically astute people when the traffic is stopped, and everyone gets out of their vehicles to mill around. It is hard not to notice the frowns on the town's people's faces, as well as some one finger salutes. There are those who are sitting in chairs in their front yards as if they are watching the circus come to town on State Route 178. Some are helpful though. The traffic stops again, and a man in a bowling-style shirt and a beer gut walks slowly out to Jeff's car. With a heavy New York accent, he asks how everyone is doing and if they would like a soft drink or water.

Barry requests a glass of water, and the others accept the soft drink offer. He has root beer and Pepsi-Cola, and they each make their choice and thank the man. "If I were you" the man says to Jeff, "I would park my car right here and walk the rest of the way to the festival."

"How far is it, do you think?" Jeff responds as he lights a Camel.

"It's about six miles up this road, and I have been watching this traffic all morning. I bet you that it won't move forward anymore. I went up there this week while they were building it, and their parking lot can't hold all these cars. I'll need to charge you ten dollars for the weekend, but I'll keep a good eye on this beauty. It'll be better than moving up a mile, then having to leave it on the side of the road."

Jeff likes what he hears but turns to everyone and asks them what they want to do. They all let Jeff decide, so he gives the man ten dollars and parks in his gravel driveway. Everyone gets their belongings, thanks the man, and wishes him well until they see him again. "That was really nice of him," Alice starts a conversation with anyone in the group while putting on her backpack. She is a smart traveler, bringing only what she will need.

For this weekend, she has a pair of long bell-bottomed, hip-hugger jeans, a jacket, two t-shirts, and a thin, cotton India-style shirt, four pairs of undies, a hairbrush, and a toothbrush. She's wearing cutoff jean shorts for the hot day that is expected. "This thing feels good already. I just feel free or something." Alice twirls around and runs headlong into Jeff for a hug, which he is happy to provide. Jeff is saddled with the tent and his backpack, but he had gone to the Army-Navy store for easy travel versions before they left Ohio, so his burden is slight, and he does not notice anyway.

The Marigold five have never seen so many people moving in the same direction, and they are happy to meet some kindred spirits along the six-mile walk. A group of kids from Sandusky spend some time with them and tell the Marigolds they have heard Clever Pennies on their radio station. Everyone is amazed and flattered, and the kids from Sandusky ask why the band is not playing in Woodstock. As if rehearsed and on cue, Jeff and Barry look at King at the same time with overly dramatic scowls on their faces. King just gives a sheepish grin and raises both hands up as if to say he is sorry, knowing they were joking.

The six miles goes quickly, feeling like a part of the festival rather than simply the way there. People are sitting on top of their cars playing guitars, and small 50cc motorcycles buzz by with two or three guests somehow on board. Artists are selling their wares, and LSD is plentiful. Jeff and Alice stop frequently to wait for King and Cloud as they seem to want to talk with everyone they see. Some of the hippies talk about Jesus, which is alright with King, but Jeff takes Alice's hand and walks on toward the farm.

People are shoulder to shoulder walking toward the entrance to the site, and Alice holds tight to Jeff. They are close enough to start getting their tickets ready, which Alice has stuffed away. Jeff looks around to make sure everyone from Marigold is close. Jeff waves his arms to gather, and the three oblige him. "Let's meet right here at nine o'clock Monday morning. I'm going to need a good night's sleep before we head back. Is that cool with everyone?" Heads bob. "Just please don't be late. I'm sure we're not going to be able to stick together in all of this, and I don't want to get stuck here. I'm not going to leave anyone, ya know." All three shake their heads in an understanding way and follow Jeff and Alice to the entrance.

When they get to the entrance, there is no one there taking tickets. Alice politely asks a couple of people who are coming from the entrance area where they give their tickets. The two hippie college students just laugh and tell Alice that they do not need a ticket anymore. That it is a free concert now. Everyone just looks at each other and smile in disbelief. It is about five thirty in the afternoon, and they can hear a band with someone on acoustic guitar and someone playing congas. The band stops and then a thunderous roar of approval comes from a crowd, the size of one that these southern Ohioans have never experienced, not even at a Buckeye football game.

As the group make their way further into the venue, everyone wants to set up their tents and dump their backpacks so they can groove to the music and fun. They find a spot far from the stage but pleasant, and there they put down stakes. Jeff grabs Alice and falls with her onto his sleeping bag. He is tired and just wants to lie there and hold Alice for a few minutes. The others tell them goodbye, and Jeff and Alice continue to just enjoy each other for twenty or so minutes, even though there is a parade of footsteps near their heads and voices in their ears. After their rest and cuddle, they decide to venture forth into the sea of bodies and get closer to the stage.

They make their trek through the mass of bodies until they can see the stage, clearly. A man in an ankle length shirt is playing guitar with a bass and conga player. He's very rhythmic in his style and sings with a husky but pleasant voice. There is no way they can get any closer to the stage. Jeff hears someone in passing say that fifty thousand people were at the site yesterday before it started, and the stream of music lovers has not slowed. "I can't imagine where this many people will go to the bathroom, Al. I've never seen anything like this."

The singer/guitarist is finishing his set and his name, Richie Havens, bellows across the grand sea of humanity from the enormous speakers. Alice and Jeff look at each other as if saying "never heard of him" and walk toward the merchandise tents. It looks like food and water has been depleted, and Jeff asks Alice if she brought any food. She had brought some cheese and crackers and a couple of candy bars. Jeff had bought ration-style food at the Army-Navy store and put it in his backpack, just in case the car broke down along the road. Neither of them dreamed that the event would not serve some sort of food.

From the top of the hill, Alice and Jeff can hear someone speaking. They see a string of platforms with people sitting on them, the person speaking on the highest platform in the middle. They listen for a minute and then Jeff can hear that the man was talking about religion. "Crap, I thought this was a music festival. Clever Pennies would be tearing it up right about now." Alice agrees with him about Clever Pennies and chooses not to take on a religion conversation. Everything feels too good for disagreement, and they have both learned to choose their battles. The music returns, and Jeff sincerely enjoys Ravi Shankar, but the master sitar player from India, who influenced George Harrison and Brian Jones, had to stop due to rain.

As well as it started, the weekend is fraught with rain and some hunger, but the spirit of the people is upbeat and peaceful. Everyone makes the best of the rain, and Jeff, Alice, King, and Cloud all enjoy sliding down the muddy hill on a path that had been shaped by others doing the same. King thought he had missed the Incredible String Band, but due to the rain, they are now scheduled to play on Saturday instead of the scheduled Friday time slot. Somehow, after listening, King did not enjoy them as much as he thought he would. There had been other acoustic acts playing earlier, but when the ISB played, people were wanting to rock, and they were far from that. Still, he was glad he saw them, just because their appearances are scattered and rare, and he may not get a second chance.

By the third day, people are freely walking naked through the fields and crowds. Many are leaving even though the performance schedule is far behind, and many bands are yet to be heard. The two couples are thrilled when they see Barry at a campsite near the pond across the street. He is playing a harmonium and harmonizing with others who are playing instruments as well. They all seem very skilled, but Barry shines and carries whatever song they are playing. Both King and Jeff agree that they are proud to know and be associated with such a brilliant and accomplished musician.

When the Marigold group try to have a conversation with their friend, however, he seems distant and, frankly, high as a kite. He is communicative but does not respond to questions regarding what bands he has seen, as if the question has no relevance to what is happening now. Barry simply turns away from his friends and finds an entrance into the current musical groove. The four stay and listen for a short time more and then tell Barry they will see him at nine in the morning, as they turn and leave. Alice states the obvious concern for Barry's health, mental and physical, but the discussion does not go much further than that as they all know that their brother's condition is getting desperate.

The fearless four watch Sunday's bands, separating from time to time from each other. The Band was all four's favorite act so far, but Jeff wants to hear Johnny Winter before he calls it a night. Jimi Hendrix was supposed to play, but the schedule is so far behind, he is sure Jimi will not appear. Jeff knows he will need to drive the first leg of the trip back to Ohio, and he wants to try and get some sleep. He is disciplined that way, perhaps because of his sports background or maybe because he does not want to wreck his SS. Johnny Winter does not disappoint, and the four are able to get fairly close to the stage. Jeff watches every stunning note that Winter plays and files them away in his mental repository for later use.

King and Cloud are camped next to Jeff and Alice, so Jeff is semi-comfortable leaving Alice with the other two while he trudges back to the tent for some sleep before they leave in the morning. He has gotten used to going to bed hungry and sleeping while the peaceful madhouse is happening on the other side of the canvas. As Jeff feels the absence of his loving tentmate, his comfort level for leaving Alice practically alone in the middle of it all is quickly dissipating. Normally he would have gone back to be with her, but she was still interested in seeing the bands, and he is not her daddy. As he thinks about Alice and listens to Blood, Sweat & Tears, he drifts into a deep sleep.

Jeff wakes with a jolt and immediately looks over to where Alice has slept. She is there, breathing quietly, muddy, and beautiful. Jeff, wearing only a pair of cutoff jeans, opens the tent curtain and heads for a tall bush. He is not sure what time it is, but he hears a familiar guitar sound playing the Star-Spangled Banner. "That sounds like Hendrix, but it is Monday morning. Surely not." He zips up and runs back to the tent where he finds Alice standing outside the tent reading a piece of paper and crying. "What's wrong, baby? What is it?" Alice hands Jeff the handwritten note that simply reads:

> *Jeff and all. I will not be meeting you this morning. I have left the festival with some people I have befriended and I won't be coming home. Please tell my mom and I love all of you. P.S. Tell Kay I love her and not to worry about me. Don't waste your time looking for me because I am gone. Barry.*

CHAPTER
NINETEEN

I t is a sunny September Saturday in southern Ohio, the kind of late summer sun that feels hotter than an August sun, more direct and with less moisture to soften the rays. The Mosely house is stirring with Walter making a breakfast of crispy venison strips, rabbit brains, and eggs. Walter loves to drink buttermilk with his breakfast, but Danny always sticks with black breakfast tea and honey. The smells wake Danny, as they have done all through his seventeen, nearing eighteen, years. This morning seems extra-special, though, for whatever reason. Danny never discounts these feelings, however, because he believes God is guiding his life and that the Holy Spirit will pique new discernments and enlightenments along Danny's sanctifying journey. These new revelations and mindfulness help Danny grow as a Christian and prepare him for what lies ahead, which is unknown to him.

The high school senior takes a shower, dresses, hops down the steps as he did when he was six, and heads directly for the kitchen. The sun is well over Marigold Hill to the east, blasting sunlight throughout the Scioto County river lowlands. The leaves have dropped enough to where the river is visible from the kitchen window, and the light sparkles off its surface. The air is clean outside and beckons both Moselys to come out and enjoy. Danny suggests he and his dad go fishing after he returns from his service at church. He has provided this work for no pay since his income has just about matched what his dad makes at the mill after thirty long years of early mornings and grueling heat. Walter was smart enough long ago to tell Danny that the Moselys were taking the word *fair* out of their vocabulary. They both know that it is a relative term and one that becomes unimportant when we realize we are all here by the grace of God anyway.

"That sounds good, my son, but I have been getting really tired in my old age. Let's see how I'm feeling after your work today. I'm tired right now. It's kind of frustrating because I have so many things I want to do, but no energy to do them. This getting old thing is a bunch of bologna, and I will be giving Adam and Eve a piece of my mind when I get up yonder."

"As if we're any better than them, huh? Just take it easy, old man. I gotcha, at least for now. Hey, I have kept in touch with Martez from CCC. He says it's active and growing. He said it is like an awakening or something. Really beautiful. So, I'd really like to hear your thoughts on me going out there after high school and taking religion at USC while I work with Crusade. USC will protect me from Uncle Sam too."

"Dan, I think it's a great idea except I will miss you like crazy. Just pray about it, and I will too, but we need to apply soon."

"Yeah, you're right. I'll see what I need to do to get that going. The school counselor has all those kinds of answers. I hope you're not getting sick, Daddy. Let me know if I can help you with anything, OK?"

"You are the best son ever, my boy, and I am so thankful for you. I'm sure I'll get over it soon. If I still feel puny on Monday, I'll call Doc Giddings for an appointment."

"You better eat some of your own fantastic breakfast. You've told me all through my life to be sure and eat to keep up my manly strength. So now I'm turning the tables." Danny wags a finger at his dad.

Danny cleans up the kitchen before heading for church while Walter finds his comfortable spot in front of the TV. As Danny opens the back door to go, Walter asks for the Pepto to get some relief from a very active stomach. "Don't be suckin' on this all day, Dad. I look forward to your doctor visit on Monday so you can get some relief. I know ol' Doc Giddings will fix you up. I'm leaving unless you need me."

"You get outta here before you're late. Ain't no reprobate teen coming from this house. I love you and have a great day. I'll probably just take a bunch of cat naps today."

"Love you, Dad. Call me at church if you need me. Since we're not fishing, I think I'll call Hannah and see if we can do some singing together after work. So, call me at the Birdsong's if you need me later on."

"Well, that explains the guitar in your hand. I'm glad you have the weekend off. King must be slippin'."

"Ha, I'm happy too. I'm truly blessed to be in that band, but it is becoming a job, especially since Barry left. Phil Gregory is doing a good job, but it's just not the same, you know? Also, there are just so many other things that I want to do."

"Hopefully Barry and his dad will work things out, and Barry will let his family know where he is. They have to be terrified and miserable. That will be our prayer for the day, for the Meades. Now, get outta here!"

"Yes sir, sir, my dad, sir," Danny replies in his best Peter Tork impression.

As soon as he hears the car back out, Walter lets out a rather unworldly sound from the pain in his lower stomach. He is having such a pain in his gut that he didn't want to worry his son with the twisted and unmistakable grimace that would have certainly startled his son. With Danny's busy schedule, Walter has been able to fool him so as not to burden him in his spirited youth, but Danny is home tonight. Prayer is where Walter goes, but instead of asking for healing for himself, he asks for God's will to be done no matter the outcome and that he may accept it and glorify God to the best of his ability. There is a reason for the pain, he knows, and hopefully it is just some bad venison, but it has been going on since July, if not before, and it's not getting any better.

After work at the Birdsongs, Danny wants to call his dad, but he's afraid to wake him if he is napping. Hannah fixes them both a beautiful lunch, and they sit in the kitchen talking for an hour before beginning their work. The two love to take old hymns and change the music and arrangement to fit a more modern sound. For this Wednesday's youth group, they have chosen *Nothing but the Blood of Jesus*, *It Is Well With My Soul*, and if anyone wants to come forward, they have chosen *Come, Ye Sinners, Poor and Needy*.

These are all deep and theologically sound songs and that is what Danny and Hannah want to present to their fellow youth. The two do not want to lead a group of people and leave them wanting. Those who have not had sound theology at home need to know that Jesus died for all of them and was resurrected to free them from sin and death; that God loves them and wants to share eternity with them. It's not a club they have all joined. The youth that Hannah and Danny lead *must* know that the message of Jesus Christ is about life and death.

King and Jeff have driven to Akron to overdub some guitar solos, vocals, and percussion onto their latest recordings, which includes Danny's *New Way* and *You're Not a Failure till You Quit*. A couple of Reed/Lindor compositions have been recorded showcasing a very poetic

251

lyric by King called *A Bird of Passage*, written about southern Ohio. The recordings were made prior to Barry's abrupt departure, and the three original band members have no desire to scrub them and replace them with Phil's parts. Not to discount Phil's abilities and efforts, but the three are all hoping Barry will return soon, alive and healthy.

Barry's dad is being very detached about it all, going on about his day as if nothing has happened. Dr. Roy Meade does not fail, but Barry's desertion from his family has the entire community talking and wondering why. Most know how strict the doctor was on his son, and some do not blame Barry. They may even be happy for him, and that group includes a few teachers. Delores and Kay have suffered the most, with Kay crying herself to sleep on many nights.

Danny cannot get his dad off his mind and asks Hannah if she would mind shutting down the rehearsal for the day. Hannah immediately takes both of Danny's hands in hers and bows her head in prayer for Walter and Danny. At the end of the prayer, Danny pulls Hannah into his body and hugs her like he has never hugged her before. More agape than romantic this time. "I think there is something really wrong with my dad, Hannah. I love him so, so much."

"I know you do. You two are a shining example of what a father and son should be. It's a fallen world, Dan. Sin is in everything, but our God gave us an eternity that will wipe away every tear, praise the Lord. Please call me tonight and let me know how he is doing, OK?"

"Of course I will. I love you, my sweet Hannah, and I thank God for you."

"I love you too. Go see your dad."

As Danny drives back down Old River Road, he is dreading what he might find. He asks God to please let everything be alright and to heal his dad from whatever is ailing him. The backdoor is locked, telling Danny that his dad did not want any intruders while he was sleeping. Danny and Walter's friends are pretty much free to come and go through that back door, but crime is beginning to raise its ugly head in Marigold. A man grabbed an old woman just a few blocks away as she was getting into her car to go to work. She was able to close and lock her car doors before the ski-masked creep could get a full hold on her. The elderly lady backed out of the driveway and went to Charlie's and called the police. The assailant was never found, but the story and a sketch from the lady's description made the newspaper.

"Daddy? Are you in here?" Danny bellows with some guarded anxiety. There is no answer and then he hears the most hideous of sounds coming from his dad. Danny rushes to the middle of the house and finds his dad on the landing of the steps completely doubled over in agonizing and constant pain. "I'm here, Daddy. I'm going to call the ambulance. Hang on for me." Danny runs to the phone and calls the number in the front of the phone book that neither he nor Walter hoped they would ever need to call. He is thankful it is there, and after calling, an ambulance is at the house in no more than five minutes. Danny puts a blanket over his dad and talks to him softly, saying things like it will be alright and God's got this.

Danny hears the ambulance pull up and sees the colored lights filtered by the living room curtains. He assures his dad that he will be feeling better soon. "I will ride with you, Daddy. Don't worry. I'll be with you all the way. The ER doctors are fantastic, I hear. Hang on, Daddy. I'm going to open the door for the ambulance people."

Four young and capable men enter the room quickly with a rolling gurney. "Where do you hurt, sir? Can you talk to us?" Walter squeaks out the origin of the pain, and the four young men provide their professional assurance that Walter will feel much less pain soon.

One of the four pulls Danny aside and asks about his father's symptoms. Danny admits that his dad has probably been concealing them from him for some time, but he knows that his dad has no energy and has made Pepto Bismol a large part of his daily diet. "While you are putting my dad in the ambulance, I am going to make a call and lock up the house. It will just take a few minutes, so please don't leave me. I want to ride with my dad. We're really close."

The responders abide, and Danny calls Hannah with the news. He then gets his jacket and a book and turns on a lamp in the living room, locks the front door behind the men, and exits and locks the backdoor. He runs to the ambulance just as they are ready to close the backdoors and off they roar, with lights flashing and siren blaring, to Scioto Memorial Hospital. It is a quick five-minute trip, especially at speeds of ninety miles an hour while going south on 43. The emergency room has been notified, and a bevy of nurses and doctors are waiting to rush Walter off to an operating room.

The team has been given all of Walter's vitals and personal information and begin to talk with Walter as they wheel him into position. They cut off his jeans because Walter cannot stop folding himself in half, but he is able to plead with them not to cut his shirt because his son gave it to him.

It is a struggle, but a kind team member honors Walter's request and unbuttons the plaid, flannel shirt and pulls it off his arms. "I will put your shirt in a safe place, Mr. Mosely. Don't you worry, sir." Walter meekly thanks the young lady and then he is sedated with morphine.

Danny tries to read a magazine in the waiting room, but he cannot concentrate. His eyes go up and leave the page with each person's footsteps that come from the location of the ER, and there are many. Several people are wheeled into the emergency room check-in area. Some are escorted by Appleton Police, showing signs of a failed attempt to break the law. Danny imagines that he is watching himself and his friends being carted into the same emergency room. Not everyone made it then. Will his dad make it now?

"Mr. Mosely?"

"Yes, ma'am!" Danny jumps up from his seat and answers the nurse.

"I am Nurse Peebles. Your father is having intense pain in his abdomen, as you probably already know. We have relieved the pain for now, but we will be keeping your dad for a few days as we run some tests. We are not yet sure why there is pain. We do not believe it is his appendix because the location that seems most sensitive to your father is not near the appendix, though we don't rule out appendicitis yet. There are rare occasions when the body feels the pain from the infected area in another area, but we still do not want to operate on him for appendicitis at this time. He is lucid, and you may go to him to provide some comfort, but he may drift in and out of conversation due to the drug. Would you like to see him?"

"Oh, yes please."

"Great. Please follow me. It's Danny, am I right?"

"Yes, ma'am."

"He has mentioned you many times." This puts a distorted smile on Danny's scrunched and concerned face as he follows dutifully behind the nurse through two big double doors and down a hallway to a room with several recovering patients separated by curtains.

"Hi, Daddy," Danny says with a soft, quiet voice. "How ya doin'?"

"Well, I'd rather be hunting, but better than when I came in this place."

"Yeah, you weren't doing so good a little while ago, but you sound a whole lot better now. Hannah and her family have been praying for you, and they send their love."

"They are some nice people. I bet you marry Hannah and that would be OK with me."

"Wow, Dad. Tryin' to marry me off, are ya? Well, she'll be the first girl I ask when I feel like making that leap."

"She'll say yes. She couldn't find a better man. More attractive, maybe, but not a better heart."

"Nice, Daddy. You *are* feeling better throwin' those zingers at me." They both laugh, which is good medicine.

"I think they're going to keep me in here a few days to poke and prod me until something shows up. I know you'll be fine by yourself, but please eat well and be sure the house is all locked up when you're not there. Check the locks before you go to bed, too. I know you'll come see me, but please get your homework done and do the things that seventeen-year-olds do. If Hannah wants to come, she is surely welcome."

"That's nice of you, ol' man. You know Hannah, it wouldn't matter if you minded or not, she will place herself right here by your bed to talk with you."

A nurse comes in and begins taking Walter's vitals and suggests Danny leave the patient until tomorrow. "You should see Doctor Giddings in the morning, Mr. Mosely. I'm going to take some blood now for testing, and then I want you to sleep if you can. Unfortunately I'll probably need to wake you through the night right about the time you get comfortable, but please know it is for your good."

"Daddy, I guess I will go. Pastor Pete will want to visit after church, but I will be here early. I am going to ask Hannah to lead the Youth by herself in the morning. She'll do a great job. She doesn't even really need me, ya know."

Walter chuckles. "Well, you two make a great team. I'll be fine, so come visit when you can, my fine young man."

"Please rest easy. I will see you tomorrow morning."

"Ok, my boy." Danny leans over his dad and rests his face on his for a few seconds, then turns and gives his dad a kiss on the forehead.

"Goodnight, nurse. Please take good care of him. A bunch of people love that ol' guy, probably just because he cooks for them." Walter laughs out loud and tells Danny one more time that he loves him as Danny walks out of the room.

Over the next two days, Walter receives several visitors: Pete and Annie, the Birdsongs, and some of the boys from the oven come as well as the band and their families. They all offer help in any way while Walter is down, and they all make sure Danny understands that he can call at any time, night or day. Carl will not be in town until the weekend, and Walter looks forward to seeing his hunting buddy the most. Their friendship would surely pass Mr. Doucet's test with ease.

The morphine has become less effective as the pain increases with each day. The doctors inform Walter and Danny that they should be able to make their diagnosis on Wednesday morning, and Danny is there at six to pray with his dad, read the Bible, and hold his hand. Pastor Pete has arrived early, as he has other members of his congregation to see as well. It is Walter and Danny he sees first and will stay with until the doctors have visited. There is anxiety this morning, and Pete's calming tone is welcome.

Footsteps are heard coming down the hall. Dr. Giddings enters Walter's room first followed by two more doctors. "Hi, Walter, this is Drs. Jansen and Higgins. Good morning Danny and Pete. Walter, we have your results. Is it OK if Danny and Pete are here or would you like to hear the diagnosis by yourself?"

"Hello, doctors. If they want to be here, it is fine with me."

Dr. Jansen nods. "Mr. Mosely, there is no easy way of telling you this, but after several tests, we are certain that you have pancreatic cancer. The tumor is so large that it is the source of your pain, and it has now spread to other vital organs. Mr. Mosely, we estimate that you have six weeks to two months to live, and it will be painful. I am very sorry, of course, and I do wish I had better news."

There are audible gasps and weeping as the doctor continues, "We will dismiss you later this morning with a prescription for morphine tablets. They will be very strong, and you can easily overdose if you do not keep up with how many you are taking. I recommend that, by week five or six, a nurse administer the drug intravenously in your home, or you may choose to be hospitalized. The constant drip would allow you some steady relief, but we leave that decision up to you, sir. It is the least we can do in such a vexing time. I will leave you with your family and friends now; I am very sorry."

Dr. Jansen turns and excuses herself, and she and Dr. Higgins walk out while Dr. Giddings stays. Danny is already lying across his dad and hugging him, probably tighter than he realizes. He sobs uncontrollably, and Walter rubs his back. Walter does not say anything because it has all been said. After a moment or two, Pastor Pete asks if he can pray, and Walter nods his head yes, with a pleasant smile. The pastor proceeds with a peaceful prayer about the comfort and protection that only God can provide. At the end, they all say a unison "amen," and Dr. Giddings leaves with a verbal assurance that he will do anything he can to make these final days more bearable.

Over the next few days, Danny and friends help comfort Walter. Danny purchases a Zenith television that can sit on top of Walter's dresser for when he does not feel like coming downstairs. When Carl arrives, he makes sure Walter gets out of the house, even if for short walks. Danny follows suit and takes his dad to a park where they enjoy light fishing. On that day, Walter decides that this is the time to tell Danny all about his mom, Beatrice.

WALTER'S STORY OF BEATRICE COLLINS MOSELY

Beatrice Collins was seventeen years old when she found herself falling in love with a handsome young war veteran named Walter Mosely. Walter worked hard at the steel mill and would come into the luncheonette where Beatrice worked nearly every day. Usually, Walter came in with two or three of his boisterous and funny friends, but sometimes, he came in alone and those were the times that Beatrice enjoyed the most. She could actually hear what the twenty-year-old young man was saying, and he would say more to her on those days when he was alone.

Beatrice finds Walter to be very sensitive, tearing up when talking about his time in the war. He had seen things no one should ever see, especially for someone Walter's age, but Beatrice is sympathetic to the young man's stories and listens intently. Her complete captivation only fuels Walter's desire to tell his stories and more than once causes a reprimand from the owner of the diner. Beatrice would be jolted from her enchantment by a harsh reminder that she has other tables. She quickly looks around at the owner in fear and then apologizes to Walter profusely for interrupting his dialogue.

After a few weeks of talking and enjoying each other's company, even though it was during work hours, Walter asks the seventeen-year-old if she would like to see the movie *Easter Parade*, starring Judy Garland and Fred Astaire. She explains that her mom may not let her go out with someone so much older than she, but Beatrice gives Walter her phone number and tells him to call her that night after she talks with her mom. Walter presumes that Beatrice does not have a dad but does not pry and looks forward to calling Beatrice later that evening.

Walter goes home, fixes himself some dinner, turns on the radio and waits until the agreed time of seven o'clock to call Beatrice. As

Walter dials the number given to him by Beatrice, he finds he is nervous with fingers shaking. The last number is a zero, and it seems forever for the rotary dial to spin back to home. One ring . . . two rings . . . three, and a voice answers; it does not belong to Beatrice. An older woman with a raspy voice says hello. Walter says hello and asks if he may speak with Beatrice Collins. The raspy-voiced woman asks if this is the old mill worker that has been harassing her daughter.

Walter is a bit shocked but manages to respond by clearly stating his name and assuring the woman that he has never harassed her daughter. The woman, presumably the mother of Beatrice, proceeds to tell Walter that he is too old for her daughter and that he had better stay away from Beatrice. She tells Walter not to call again and hangs up the phone. Walter sits with the phone still up to his ear. He listens to the tone of disconnect for what seems to be a minute while he gathers his thoughts about what just happened. There is not much he can do at this point, and he does not want to call again for fear of aggravating an already-strained situation. The only thing Walter can do is wait until lunch the following day to speak with Beatrice about the phone call.

The next morning, seeing Beatrice at lunch is all Walter can think about. He manages to get through his work morning without hurting himself or others due to a lack of concentration. When the lunch horn blows, his protective garb comes off, and he flies out the door to the diner. Once inside, he must stand in line for a seat, but as he peruses the interior, Walter does not see Beatrice. She is usually quite visible as she scurries from table to booth, but there is no sign of her today.

With squinted eyes and furrowed brow, Walter turns his attention to that part of the kitchen he can see to no avail. Beatrice is not working today. Is she sick or has her mother gone so far as to require she leave her job? Walter is beside himself and taps another waitress on the shoulder, asking her if she knows Beatrice's whereabouts. The waitress is busy and just tells Walter she did not come in today. Being a World War Two veteran, Walter will not be detoured in his pursuit of Beatrice. He spies what seems to be the manager or owner of the diner standing at the kitchen door.

Walter pushes through the crowd until he reaches the owner and asks her if Beatrice is OK. The owner looks at Walter and sees obvious panic on his face and with all the waitresses she has employed through the years, quickly recognizes a dog in heat. She tells Walter that Beatrice is out due to illness and will hopefully return soon. She offers Walter a seat at the bar for lunch, but Walter thanks her and admits he is not hungry as he turns to leave. He turns back to the owner and asks her if she could tell him where Beatrice lives, but the owner frowns and apologetically reminds Walter that she is not permitted to give him that information.

Walter spends the rest of his day in a frenzied, frustrated mood. Upon arriving at his apartment, he picks up the phone book and looks at all the Collins' that are listed. There is a Thelma Collins on Third Street that matches the number he dialed last night. It is still early, and Walter is determined to see Beatrice, if for no other reason than to let her know that his interest in seeing her has not been impeded. He respects her mother, but Beatrice is old enough to make this decision.

After work, Walter eats a quick dinner, having not eaten lunch, showers and shaves and puts on his best khakis and shirt. He jumps into his new Chevrolet Stylemaster and heads for Four-Thirteen Third Street, as the phone book had revealed. He parks his beautiful automobile right in front of the house so that *Thelma* can see that he is responsibly employed and able to treat her daughter well. The house is showing signs of disrepair, with old paint peeling and the white picket fence now a light gray. It is a stately house, but as Walter reaches the front porch, he sees missing and warped floorboards.

With absolute determination, Walter knocks on the door. There is no answer. Walter knocks again and hears footsteps coming toward the door. He sees the curtains move in the window near the door and then the door opens halfway. A disheveled woman, looking older than her years, appears "What do you want?"

"I am Walter Mosely and I would like to see Beatrice, ma'am."

"Are you the man who called last night?"

"Yes, ma'am, I am."

"Look, buddy. You ain't gonna have nothin' to do with my daughter. You don't look very old, but I know you were in the war and all you guys only have one thing on your mind. I ain't havin' it!" The door is abruptly shut in Walter's face.

Walter knocks, again, on the door but no one answers this time. Walter knocks more loudly. The door swings open and there stands Beatrice, barefoot, in a flower print cotton dress and her hair down, not pulled back in her usual waitress bun. With a distressed look on her face, Beatrice says "She is not going to let me see you, Walter, and I don't want her to be mad at me. I don't know what to do. I want to see you, but I just can't."

Walter hears Thelma yell to Beatrice, *"Close the door!"*

"I'm so sorry, Walter. I should be back at work, tomorrow, and I will try to talk with you, then. Go, now, please."

Attaching hope to any part of this encounter, Walter turns from the door and walks back down the broken steps. He looks back to find Beatrice in the window watching him. He raises his hand to wave and Beatrice waves back; then she drops the curtain. Walter knows it will be another long night, and after seeing Beatrice in her natural state, his longing for their next meeting has been amplified to a large degree. The Stylemaster turns right over and off Walter rolls. He just wants to drive around for a while to think.

Walter drives along the Norfolk and Western railroad tracks and then turns north onto Route 169 toward Paradise Park. It is a nice evening for a drive with the windows down. Walter has not yet driven over the new Marigold Hill connector that was finished last year, so tonight is the night. Saunder's Creek Road has a pothole here and there and features a skunk, an opossum, and a stray dog all dead along the stretch before the new road starts.

The new pavement is noticeable with clear lines painted down the middle and on both sides. Walter turns on his headlights as afternoon turns to dusk on the eastern side of the hill, and he downshifts the Stylemaster to start his ascent. His new car obeys with vigor and up the hill he roars with great excitement. He had scaled the Alps in Government Issue trucks, so this was not threatening, but the connector was a welcomed addition to Appleton area life, and Walter was enjoying the clever and precise workmanship.

At the top, Walter could see the newly designed Marigold community with lights flickering and one or two tiny headlights heading up the main artery, Marigold Road. Walter slows his speed so he can take in the beauty of the evening and vows to experience this with Beatrice someday soon. But he knows he must first win over Thelma. It is time to descend into Marigold, and Walter keeps his car in low gear so as not to burn up his brakes. The road is well-designed, and each snaky curve is banked so as not to let the momentum of the gravitational pull take the driver off the edge of the road.

Soon, he is driving down the east to west ribbon he saw from above until he comes to its end. Walter figures, from the top of the hill to this stop is about three miles. There, he finds he must turn north or south on a road call Old River Road. He decides to go north, away from Appleton, as Walter is still not ready to go back to his apartment. He knows he would just lie there on the bed and think about Beatrice.

About a half mile up, Walter sees a friendly looking new building called Charlie's Market and Pharmacy. After hearing on his car radio, three times this evening, that Pepsi-Cola "hits the spot," Walter is compelled to drink a bottle of the brown bubbly and pulls into Charlie's gravel parking lot. He gets out of the car and heads directly for the cold soft drink. Sure enough, up by the cash register, is a washing tub full of ice with Pepsi bottle necks sticking up. Walter pulls out a bottle by the neck and reaches into his pocket, fetching out a few coins. He picks out a quarter to pay for the drink and a candy bar found conveniently at the counter. The man opens the Pepsi-Cola for his customer, Walter thanks the man and returns to his car where he satisfies the thirst the radio announcer told him he had.

From the parking lot, one can see the Scioto River, and Walter takes a few minutes while eating his candy bar to simply enjoy the glimmer of the slow-moving current of the water way. It is right then that Walter dreams about leaving his apartment and moving out to this serene little cocoon of a neighborhood. He has plenty of money in his savings account, earned while serving his country, and it is just waiting for the right house that suits Walter. He wants to have a family one day and hopes to become a manager at the oven in the future, so a house would be a good investment.

Walter gets back into his car and leaves the parking lot. He continues north for only another half mile when he sees a house under construction on the other side of the street, with the back of the house facing west and a "For Sale" sign in the muddy front yard. The address is 2310 Old River Road, and Walter pulls his car into the mud driveway. It's dark now, but he sits looking at the humble abode with his car lights shining on it. It will be a two-story dwelling, with a front porch and a garage in the back at the end of the driveway. The lot looks lovely, with plenty of room to watch his wife and seven kids play badminton and croquet.

As he leaves and drives farther north, there are other houses being built on both sides of the road and a pretty church with a tall steeple rising high into the air, topped with a cross. There is a large brick elementary school that sports several sets of swings, teeter-totters, and sliding boards. Walter pictures his children going there and imagines them on the playground equipment during recess. The road takes a sharp turn to the left and leads into Route 43. Walter points his Chevy to the south and heads for home, full of dreams and a plan to try and meet the builders of the house at 2310 to discuss the price.

At lunch the next day, the diner's dish of the day is roast beef, but for Walter Mosely, it is Beatrice Collins. Walter made sure he sat in Beatrice's section, forcing a conversation between the two. Beatrice says, "Hello, Walter. I'm really sorry about last night. My mom was really mean to you. She just simply thinks I am too young to date a twenty-year-old war veteran. She knows that war vets took advantage of their popularity with every pretty girl while you were in Europe, and her Beatrice is not going to be just another one of those pretty girls. I don't think you're like that, though, but that's what she thinks."

"You're right, Beatrice!" Walter exclaims. "I wasn't like that in Europe and I am not like that now."

"Well, you need to convince my mom, not me. I would really like to go out with you, but it wouldn't be right to sneak around on my mom. She'd have you arrested. No, you need to convince Momma, somehow."

"Don't you worry! Before it's all said and done, your mom will love me. I promise, if it's the last thing I do!" Beatrice sees the manager looking at her and quickly leaves the table without Walter's order. She writes up one for roast beef, hoping he will like it.

The next day is Saturday, and Walter is up early. He dresses for work, grabs several of his tools, and jumps into his car for a drive out to 2310 Old River Road. As he comes upon the address, Walter finds the lot bustling with carpenters, plumbers, and electricians. He asks one of the men who he can talk with about buying the home, and the man points to the only person wearing a tie. Walter walks through the debris of two-by-four pieces and introduces himself to the gentleman in the tie. "When do you think this house will be complete?"

The realtor answers, "Two weeks, I would say, if the brick layers can get here. There's building going on everywhere, if you haven't noticed."

"You're right about that. What is the lot size? Does it go all the way to 43?"

"It's an acre, but not all the way to 43. No one would want to own that mess. Why, are you interested?

"Maybe. How much are you asking for this house, sir, and I guess it is going to be brick, then?"

The realtor quotes an inflated price to the twenty-year-old, but Walter is aware of the realtor's ploy and just laughs as he shakes the man's hand and turns to walk away.

"Hey, kid. How much are you thinking you can pay for a brand-new house in this beautiful new community?

Walter cannot argue with either of those attributes, but he reminds the realtor how far he would need to drive every day to work or to see a movie. The realtor tells Walter he has a point and asks him again how much he is willing to pay. Walter tells the realtor that he is going to head up the street to look at the other homes under construction. This disregard secretly flusters the realtor who did not expect the young man to be so sharp a negotiator.

Sustaining composure, the salesman takes out his business card, writes the house address and purchase price on the front, hands it to Walter and says, "Look, when you are serious, you call me." Walter asks the man for his pencil, turns the man's card over, and writes his phone number on the back with a price one thousand dollars less than the price the realtor quoted.

The realtor smirks and says "Friend, I will sell this beautiful house, on this beautiful lot, in this beautiful new neighborhood, at *my* price before the close of next week. If you really want this place, I wouldn't mess around." Walter tells the realtor he will keep that in mind and says thank you. Walter, then, smiles, turns and walks to his new Chevy Stylemaster, knowing the car would tell the man that he has money to spend.

Walter's next stop is the hardware store, where he buys some eight and sixteen penny nails, a scraper, sandpaper, three gallons of white exterior paint, and two paint brushes. One is wide and one is small for edges and small spaces. Walter then drives directly to Four-Thirteen Third Street. When he reaches his destination, Walter removes all his tools and painting supplies. He knocks loudly on the door until Beatrice opens it. Fear, mixed with delight, takes over her face when she sees all the paint supplies, and in a whisper asks Walter, "What in the world are you doing?"

Walter confidently replies, "I am here to paint your house. Is white OK?"

Thelma pokes her head out between her daughter and the door, which stiffens Walter's body a bit, but his moxie kicks in and he repeats his plan with even more confidence this time. Thelma shakes her head and walks away. Walter is not sure if she is going to get a gun, but he looks at Beatrice and she gives him an unsure gesture to go ahead and start his work.

Beatrice dares not go outside with him, however, but as Walter works diligently through the day, Beatrice walks by the window and waves or sets glasses of cold water outside the front door. At noon, she seems comfortable serving Walter a ham and cheese sandwich with a glass of milk. She stands and talks with him for a few minutes but tells Walter she does not want to make her mom angry and goes back inside. The odd thing is, Thelma has not said an angry word, and Beatrice is not sure if her mom is accepting Walter or is just happy someone is painting her house for free.

Just before the sunset, Walter stands back and looks at the work he has completed, that day. He has scraped the entire front of the cottage-style house and has painted two thirds of it a very snappy white. His plan is to purchase and apply a blueish-gray color to the shutters, if it meets with the owner's approval. Walter has also replaced various pieces of one-by-six planks throughout the porch floor and used the same to fashion stronger, safer steps twelve inches wide, using two planks side by side. The porch is going to get the same color as the shutters if approved. Since Thelma has not made any effort to look at Walter's work, he is not sure from whom he would get the approval, but it is time for him to leave now. He thinks it best not to require a meeting with Beatrice for his day's work, so, Walter leaves his tools and materials in a corner on the porch, making it very clear that he will be returning.

Walter paints Sunday and Monday afternoon after work, finishing his job like Jacob for Rachel's hand. As he packs his tools into the trunk of his car and cleans his hands with thinner, Thelma walks out from behind the house, careful not to tread on her newly painted porch. She strolls ever-so-slowly to the sidewalk, near Walter and his car, turns and looks at the house. After a minute, Thelma lights a cigarette and, while continuing to study the work Thelma says, "That's a real good job. I appreciate it. Walter, right?" And with that, she turns and looks Walter in the eyes with a kind face this time.

"Yes, ma'am."

"Walter. Beatrice is my baby," Thelma confesses. "She means everything in the world to me and I want her to have a good life. Better than mine. You seem like a decent guy, Walter, but you're just too old for Beatrice. She is a senior in high school, do you know that?"

"Yes, ma'am, I do, and I understand your concern. I really don't have anything but good intentions. You have raised a very special girl, and I would like to spend time getting to know her better. I will treat her really well, ma'am."

Thelma's eyes become moist, and she tells Walter that he can take Beatrice out to someplace public and only in the day. This Saturday would be fine if he can offer an acceptable venue. The fading sunlight accentuates the deep and plentiful distress lines on Thelma's war-worn face. Excitedly, Walter thanks the haggard woman and tells her he will pick Beatrice up at one o'clock Saturday with an appropriate destination in mind. He finishes loading tools into the car, thanks Mrs. Collins again, and drives off tired and elated.

Weeks of trust are built, with Walter towing Thelma's line. The more Walter offers his help around the house and returns Thelma's baby to her on time and unharmed, the more Walter is welcomed into Thelma's life. However, as more time is spent at the Collins house, it becomes more evident that Thelma has a problem with drinking. When drunk, usually beginning at six in the evening, Thelma is not so discreet about the men she brings into the house late at night from the bar up the street. This troubles Walter most of all because it would not take much for Beatrice to become the target of one of Thelma's drunk partners. This only makes Walter visit even more evenings, taking Beatrice out away from the sad and unreliable carousel.

One warm, April day when Beatrice turns eighteen, Walter picks up his date for what Beatrice thinks is to be a long day of picnicking on the levee by the fast-running Ohio River. She is surprised when Walter turns north up Route 43 and tells her he has a birthday surprise for her. She is excited and surprised when he takes the Marigold entrance which leads them up onto Old River Road. Beatrice is not very familiar with this new area as they pass the intersection with Marigold Road and then Charlie's Market. After passing Charlie's, Walter drives a short distance and pulls into a driveway of a pretty home on the western side of the street. Walter stops his car and gets out to open Beatrice's door for her.

Beatrice asks Walter who lives there and why she has not met them, yet. He takes her by the hand and walks up onto the large front porch that holds a swinging bench that is bolted into the ceiling. Walter takes the door knocker in his hand and raps on the wooden square that absorbs each knock. While he is facing the door, Beatrice looks out at the road and when she turns back around to see if Walter's friends are home, she sees the door being pushed open with a key in the doorknob. When the door is open, Walter turns around and says, "Beatrice, this is my house, and I want it to be ours. I love you, and will you marry me, my dear Beatrice Collins?" Walter kneels onto the welcome mat.

Beatrice is shocked and confused and then bursts into tears while blubbering a soft and beautiful "yes. Oh, yes, Walt. I will."

Walter slides a beautiful half carat diamond ring onto her long and slender left ring finger and then stands up quickly and picks up his bride-to-be into his arms. He carries Beatrice into their new home at 2310 Old River Road and stands her down in what will become the sitting room for proper meetings. He shows her a downstairs bedroom, a full bathroom with a tub and shower, and a TV room that sits just off a very modern kitchen.

They then walk up the stairs where Beatrice is delighted to find a full bathroom at the end of the staircase, in the middle of two large bedrooms. Walter jokes that at least four of the children can have the upstairs bedrooms while they sleep downstairs. Beatrice already knew of Walter's desire to have a large family, so, she rubs Walter's back and assures him that it all sounds wonderful to her.

The two tour the rest of the property including the garage and backyard. Beatrice loves the backyard and suggests that her husband-to-be build a large grill so that he can cook his venison and duck for all their kids and friends. That idea animated Walter, as he walks to an area where he thinks it could be built. His arms are waving out the shape to give Beatrice the full picture, and she laughs with excitement.

Though Walter open-heartedly offers to provide the most decadent of ceremonies, neither one of the newly engaged want a large wedding. As a matter of fact, they both think saying their vows at City Hall with a party at their new home the following night sounds like the right thing for them. Walter wants to build that backyard grill first and will have it finished and ready for dinner within two weeks. Giving themselves those two weeks, plus a week to buy a few pieces of furniture, their wedding date is settled for April twenty-ninth at City Hall. A party with their friends would take place in their new home the following evening on April thirtieth with Walter at the grill. They were as giddy as two children on Christmas Eve.

Beatrice had saved some of her diner money, but Thelma would find where her daughter would hide her income and use it for an array of needs, most frequent of which being the acquisition of fifths of Southern Comfort. Some of it did go for the electric bill or car repairs when Beatrice's estranged father did not pay the alimony and child support that was due, but Thelma could justify any expenditure when necessary. Therefore, Beatrice has little to contribute to her and Walter's new home, but Walter did not ask her for anything, anyway. As their date grows closer, he gives his Beatrice three hundred dollars to buy furniture for their home on the condition that she spends it the next day so that Thelma does not take it.

Walter gives Beatrice the furniture money on the night before he knows she will not be working the next day. That way, she can wake up, get dressed, catch the bus and go downtown to shop without giving Thelma the opportunity to find it. The plan works and the next morning, off she goes, on a beautifully brisk spring day, to Kemperline Furniture, where she has window-shopped many times while dreaming of a day like this. The salespeople are very helpful, and Beatrice is able to purchase a double bed and a Simmons Beautyrest mattress, a dresser, and a kitchen table with four chairs all to be delivered on April twenty-eighth.

After Kemperline's, Beatrice walks three blocks over to the new Engel's Department Store where she purchases sheets for the bed, dishes, glasses, and a small set of silverware. She splurges on a grand set of knives for Walter to use when cooking, serving and eating his venison and fish. Last, Beatrice cannot resist buying a man-sized apron with the words "Come and Get It!" painted in cursive on the front. Oh, she loves her man and cannot wait until she is Mrs. Beatrice Mosely.

Engel's agrees to hold her purchases until she and Walter can return that afternoon to pick them up and take them to 2310 Old River Road. Walter loves what his bride-to-be bought and enjoys watching her find places to store or display them, knowing her home life had not offered these opportunities.

Their marriage ceremony is quick, but nonetheless special and full of love and happiness. The couple is able to have Thelma and Walter's supervisor, Stockman, attend the blip of an event as witnesses. They sign their names, hug and shake hands with the new Moselys but leave quickly afterward as Stockman had to return to the furnace and Thelma went back to bed. The happily married couple leave City Hall walking on a cloud. They climb into Walter's car and, with Mrs. Mosely clinging to her husband's arm so tightly that it made his veins bulge, drive up Route 43 to their new home.

They immediately make a beeline for their brand-new bed and just lie there on their backs in disbelief and excitement. Dreams are shared and developed through the afternoon, as well as tender exploration. The Moselys remain in their quiet, safe, soft and amatory room until hunger sets in later that evening. Beatrice is first to leave the bed, as Walter lay sleeping. The downstairs bathroom is next to their bedroom and easily accessible to the homeowners as well as visitors.

In the downstairs bathroom, Beatrice is first to enjoy the new plumbing. The hot water reaches the shower head quickly, and Beatrice steps her naked body behind the curtain that kept the water from flooding the floor. As she washes her hair and enjoys the warm stream of water running down her back, Beatrice takes in the beautiful design of the camo-green tile that is outlined in medium gray that not only lines the shower walls but is featured throughout the bathroom. Complimentary wallpaper, displaying a faint lake scene with tall green grasses and birds in flight, rise waist up everywhere in the room but the shower. It is stunning craftsmanship that sends Beatrice into humble disbelief and thankfulness for her husband.

Through the rest of 1949 and into 1950, the couple slowly decorated their home and enjoy little surprises for each other. In February, Walter surprises Beatrice in a very big way, with a week-long trip to the Surfcomber Hotel in Miami, Florida. Walter calls it their honeymoon, but Beatrice does not care what Walter calls it as long as it is half as beautiful and warm as she has heard from friends and she shares the time with him. By the time the newlyweds leave after work on February tenth, the southern Ohio winter is dragging on, and Beatrice cannot wait to bask in the hot sun of Miami Beach. Walter wants to see a race at Hialeah, and they both want to see the flamingos that adorn the lake in the middle of the track.

Walter works hard, pulling as much overtime as he can, to be sure he can provide for his family to be. He starts a savings account, and with Beatrice's tips and wages, they accumulate a hefty balance. Thelma visits their home only once in 1950 before she finds a new boyfriend, who takes her away to live in New Jersey. Not before selling Beatrice's home and leaving with its profit, however. Beatrice receives a postcard from her mom around Christmas of 1950 that displays a picture of the Empire State Building on the front and a note on the back telling her daughter that she is having a great life with Lou and for she and Walt to visit when they can.

By 1951, Beatrice has not become pregnant, and that is of some concern to both Beatrice and Walter, but they enjoy each other and savor their life as it is. Their life changes, though, in mid-April of 1952. Beatrice sets up a date for her and Walter to meet for dinner in Appleton. Beatrice has not been feeling well, and she had gone to the doctor at the beginning of the week. That night, Beatrice announces to her husband that she is about five weeks pregnant, and Walter explodes with excitement. In honor of the news, he orders the very best dishes on the menu and gives their waiter a very large tip.

Walter is ecstatic and makes sure his wife and future mother of his child is comfortable and happy. He cooks for her every night until

Beatrice finally starts beating him to the punch, having dinners ready for them when Walter comes home from work. They buy a bassinette, planning to have the baby sleep in their room for the first few months of its life, but Walter is anxious to set up the baby's room. Beatrice is able to talk her husband into waiting until they know if the baby is a boy or girl so that they can decorate appropriately.

That glorious-but-trying day when they discover the gender begins at around two thirty in the morning on November twenty-fifth of 1952 with strong contractions. Beatrice bleeds heavily, and Walter is distraught with the fear of losing his precious Bea, but at eight ten that evening, after a long and brutal labor and delivery, a healthy, beautiful seven-pound eight-ounce boy is born. Beatrice and Walter have both agreed to name a boy Daniel after Walter's deceased brother. So, Daniel Wayne Mosely (Wayne Hill was Walter's best army buddy) is brought into the world under harsh, surgical lights and men and women in masks.

Beatrice is kept in the hospital for seven days to be sure she is not going to hemorrhage and to build up her strength before going home. Walter is at the hospital every day after work, staying until late into the evenings until Beatrice and Danny are released. Beatrice has not been able to nurse, no doubt due to anxiety, but a concentrated infant formula had been approved by the FDA, and this allows Walter to feed his boy in the evenings, giving his wife a break from her daytime duties as a new mother and helping her recover.

Though he fights off any suspicions of change, Walter cannot help but notice that his wife is not the same as she was prior to having their son. Beatrice, Danny's once child-like and spunky mom, seems very sad after Danny's birth and cries and begs Walter to take the baby and leave their dark bedroom where she stays most of the time. He complies with his wife's unnatural request and takes Danny out of the room and into the living room where there is sunlight and outside sounds of life. Walter would bundle up his son and sit in an oversized wooden rocker near their wood-burning stove, used on the coldest winter days, and rock Danny while singing to him.

Walter is good with Danny. He knows how to fix the bottles and change Danny's diapers without sticking Danny or himself very often with the diaper pins. Walter's favorite songs to sing, with Danny in his arms or laying him snuggly in his bassinette, are *Glow Worm, Jambalaya*, and Al Martino's *Here in My Heart*. He used to sing Martino's lyrics to his Beatrice, but Danny is getting the full show since his birth. Walter believes Danny gets excited when he sings, but he also realizes it might just be a touch of gas. The house needs a little fun, so "excitement" it will be.

Walter knows he cannot leave his beloved Beatrice alone for an extended time while she is feeling so sad, but his vacation time from the furnace is ending tomorrow and he has to return. Walter has missed his friends and the smell of the melting ore and the teamwork it takes to get the job done each day, but Beatrice is his love, and Walter is worried about her. He begs Bea to go to her doctor, but she will not guarantee that she will do that. She tells her husband that she will be alright.

When Walter goes into work the next morning, he talks to Stockman, who understands his friend's predicament but is very direct when he tells Walter he cannot be away any longer. Stockman knows Walter has no family in the area that can help while Beatrice recovers. The closest relative, living in Kansas, has to care for their own family. Walter thanks Stockman for his patience and assures his foreman he will not miss any time, but when Walter returns home after work, it is glaringly clear that he absolutely cannot leave Bea alone with Danny. He finds Danny screaming in the living room with a soaking diaper and the same bottle in the Frigidaire that he had made that morning before he left.

"Don't cry, my sweet baby," Walter coos to Danny. "Daddy will make you a new bottle and change your wet ol' diaper. You must be miserable, my sweet boy." Walter has a natural kindness toward children, and that kindness is magnified by one hundred for his own son. He fills a pot with water and puts it on the stove. Then, while the pot is heating, Walter takes off Danny's soaking diaper and washes the day-old urine off Danny's soft-but-red skin with a warm, wet cloth. This soothes Danny somewhat, but he breaks out into fierce cries for food while Dad stands the refrigerated bottle down into the not-quite-hot water in the pot. "It's almost ready, my good boy," Walter tells Danny with a comforting, soft voice.

After he feeds Danny and makes sure he knows he is loved, Walter has no choice but to call Stockman at home and ask him if he can work half days for a short time. Stockman firmly, and without hesitation, tells Walter that their coworker Larry is going to be out for a week at least, after having had his appendix removed the day before. He tells Walter he understands his problem, but he has a mill to run. "Be there tomorrow, Walt . . . all day, or I will be forced to let you go. You know I don't want to do that but try to find some help so you can work." Stockman abruptly hangs up.

Walter stands staring at the wall behind the phone table. His mind is racing, and he has no answers as he starts running through every face he knows that might be able to help. The neighbors either work or are not people who seem very trustworthy. The church up the road has a playground. Maybe they might take Danny, but Walter is embarrassed to ask. Still, this is bigger than his pride, so Walter takes out the Yellow Pages and begins looking for the phone number of the church. What kind of church is it? A Catholic church? Methodist? He isn't sure, so he begins looking at church's addresses on their street. There it is! Marigold Christ Fellowship Church.

Walter frantically dials the number with a shaky finger, and when he had dialed the last number, he can hear the phone ringing. Once, twice, "Marigold Christ Fellowship" announces a female voice.

Walter blurts out "I live down the street from you. Uh . . . I don't go to your church, but I need help. I mean, I need someone to watch my baby tomorrow from six thirty in the morning until about three thirty in the afternoon. Is there *anyone* there who can help me?" Walter says with high-pitched desperation in his voice.

There is what feels like an eternity of silence. "What is your name, sir?"

"Walter Mosely, ma'am," he says somewhat meekly, like a little kid talking to his teacher.

"And you said you live near the church?" the lady on the other end of the phone asks.

"Yes, ma'am, not more than four blocks away, I bet. Our house sits right on Old River Road at 2310."

"Ok. You are close! I believe the Blankenships are your neighbors. Mrs. Blankenship is going to have a baby in February," she says with a comforting friendliness as if to tell Walter, in her tone, to relax and not worry. "I am the pastor's wife, Annie Boggs, and I could come down there at six thirty in the morning. Will the baby's mother be there?"

"Well, Mrs. Boggs, my wife is ill, and that is why I need help."

"Oh my!" the Pastor's wife exclaimed. "What is wrong with her, Walter?"

"She just hasn't felt well since she had the baby just over a week ago. She kinda . . . well . . . she just doesn't have much energy. Beatrice, that's her name, she just sort of sleeps a lot and stays in bed, Mrs. Boggs. She's just not real interested in the baby, I guess you could say."

"I will come down tomorrow morning at six thirty, Walter and spend some time with your wife. Did you say her name is Beatrice? That's a pretty name."

"Yes, ma'am, and ma'am, do you think you could be here by six fifteen? I want to introduce you to Beatrice and make sure she is comfortable before I leave, but I have to leave by six thirty or else I'll be late for work."

"Sure, Walter. That will be no problem. I will see you at six fifteen, so you won't be late." Mrs. Boggs says in the kindest, warmest voice that Walter has heard since before Beatrice had Danny.

"Oh, thank you, ma'am, and I guess, God bless you," Walter gushes. He is a bit timid about the "God bless you" because he is not a churchgoer, but he's heard others say it, and that salutation seemed appropriate under the circumstances.

"Thank you, Walter. God bless you and have a good evening."

The relief Walter feels is incalculable, and his eyes fill with tears because he has never known a stranger be as kind and understanding as Mrs. Boggs. He can actually sleep tonight. Walter turns from his phone call and goes into the gloomy bedroom, a place where there was once passion and silliness and conversation about the future. He asks Beatrice how she is feeling. She is sobbing but is able to ask Walter if he will get her a glass of water. "Of course, I will, Bea, and can I fix you some dinner?"

"Dinner?" Beatrice says with sluggish surprise.

"Yes, baby, it is almost eight o'clock at night," answers her husband.

"I'm not very hungry, Walt. Just some water, please."

"Would you like to see Danny?" asks Walter with the slightest tone of hope in his question.

"No, not right now, but thank you."

"He sure is a beautiful boy, Bea. He looks a lot like you."

"That's nice, Walt. Please get me some water, OK?"

"Sure, baby."

Quickly, Walter leaves the room, goes to the kitchen, pulls a glass out of the cupboard, and fills it full of cold water. He returns just as quickly as he left because he knows his wife must be thirsty. He sits the water on the bedside table and asks, "Are you sure you don't want to eat, baby?" Walter prods one more time.

"I said *no!*" Beatrice's voice sounds unworldly, like it came from someone else deep down inside her.

"I'm going to go into the living room, Bea. Call me if you need me, and Bea, a nice lady from the church up the street is going to visit tomorrow and help with Danny while I am at work. I think you'll really like her, and you'll be able to sleep and get well," Walter whispers, putting all the hope he can muster in his voice.

Danny is eating about every two hours, so Walter does not get much sleep through the night; mostly camping out on the couch with Danny's bassinette pulled up close. At five a.m., Walter begins preparing the house and Danny for Mrs. Boggs. Beatrice makes a bathroom trip around six, and Walter reminds her that they are going to have a visitor. Beatrice acknowledges what he is saying and actually brushes her hair, brushes her teeth, and puts on her robe. Beatrice has lost weight and strength, but she props herself up in the front room chair with her head in one hand while they wait for the nice lady from the church.

At exactly six fifteen, there is a knock on the front door. Walter has just finished making his lunch, throws his ham and cheese sandwich and thermos of tomato soup into his lunch box, and sprints to the door. When he opens it, there stands Annie Boggs, just as she promised. Of course, she is not at all what Walter had pictured her to look like as they talk. Short and rotund with wire-rimmed glasses was his vision, but she is about as opposite of that as one can get. Mrs. Boggs is tall, slender, and about thirty-five. Her hair is cut short, but with natural waves, and she wears no makeup. Mrs. Boggs is not necessarily stylish, but she dons a very smart wool Balenciaga coat stopping about mid-thigh, obviously meant for warmth only on a cold December morning.

Walter is excited that he already feels comfortable with Mrs. Boggs as he invites her in, sliding her coat the rest of the way down her arms. "Bea," Walter says softly. "Please meet Mrs. Boggs, baby." With her head still in her hand, Beatrice moves her hand to under her chin and looks up through squinted eyes that are surrounded by dark, deep circles.

"Hello," says Beatrice in an unaffected tone. "Just help yourself around the house and thank you for helping me today." Beatrice stands up with wobbly legs, smiles, and slurs, "I'm not feeling well, so I think I will go back to bed." And that was that as Beatrice closes the bedroom door behind her.

"Mr. Mosely, she does not look well at all," Annie states with sympathetic concern. "I think you should take her to her doctor soon. How long has it been since Beatrice has had anything to eat?"

"I'm not really sure, Mrs. Boggs," said Walter as he looks at the cuckoo clock he brought back from Germany that, now hangs on the wall. "Anything you can do will be greatly appreciated, but if I don't leave now, I will be late for work and then we'll really be in trouble."

Mrs. Boggs smiles and tells Walter not to worry. She assures him she will take good care of Danny and Beatrice as she shoos him toward the door to go to work. Walter says, "Thank you," and goes through the kitchen and out the back door to his car.

Normally the early bird, Walter just barely makes it to work before the morning shift whistle, but Stockman is friendly and tells Walter to get his ass inside. That is Stockman's typical morning greeting, so it was music to Walter's ears today. All the way to work, Walter thought about what Stockman would say if he was late. So, Walter just smiles a thankful, toothy smile as he passes his Foreman and friend on the way into the furnace. His family is being cared for, and his foreman is being nice. It is a grand morning!

Not so grand for Mrs. Boggs, who is in a strange family's home caring for two people she does not know. She is a strong woman, though, with great faith in the Lord. She has seen much worse conditions on mission trips with her pastor husband, Peter, or Pastor Pete as he is fondly known to his congregation. Still, Mrs. Boggs is worried about Beatrice and pays close attention to her when she isn't caring for little Danny. Having Beatrice eat something substantial is her top priority, but the pastor's wife starts with simple but tasty treats. While Danny is sleeping, Mrs. Boggs prepares a small plate of cheese and crackers, grabs her Bible that she always keeps in her purse (she does not see a Bible anywhere in the house), and opens the door slowly to Beatrice's room.

When Mrs. Boggs walks in, the room is dark and quiet except she can tell Beatrice is crying. "Hello, my dear," says Mrs. Boggs in that soft, reassuring voice that had won over Walter the night before. "I have some cheese and crackers for you and a pot of hot tea. I brought a book, too . . . . my Bible. May I read to you while you eat?" Through her heartbreaking fast breaths and sniffles, Beatrice turns her head toward the voice of the lady in her room.

"Will you help me sit up, please?"

"Of course, I will, honey." Mrs. Boggs wants to jump up and down with excitement that Beatrice asked to sit up, but instead, she smoothly sets her tray of snacks, tea, and Bible on the dresser; leans over the frail new mother; and scoots her up just a little. She lets Beatrice adjust, and then lifts her again. Mrs. Boggs is excited but contains herself, takes a breath, and helps Beatrice sit up all the way. In nurse-like fashion, Mrs. Boggs fluffs and arranges the pillows for maximum comfort.

"How does that feel, my darling? Are you comfortable?" Beatrice nods and asks Mrs. Boggs if she may have a cracker and tea. "By all means," Mrs. Boggs exclaims, and she quickly but gently turns around, puts a napkin from the tray in her palm, picks up two cheese crackers, places them on the napkin, and lays them on the lap of Beatrice. "Are you able to pick one up, Beatrice?"

"Oh, yes. I'm tired but not helpless." As soon as she reaches down and puts her thumb and finger on the parallel edges and begins to lift the treat all the way up to her mouth, Beatrice drops the cracker sending little white cracker chards all over her lap, which is covered with the top sheet and thin bedspread.

"Oh, no!" Beatrice grunts with great disdain for the whole situation. "I don't want to eat now, please."

Mrs. Boggs is not deterred. "Nonsense. I will help you. You need something in your stomach, and we need to read Bible stories." Mrs. Boggs cleans up the mess and creates a place where she can sit on the edge of the bed right next to Beatrice. Mrs. Boggs put two fingers on each side of the second cracker with cheese and lifts it right up to Beatrice's mouth. "Just take a little nibble, sweetie. Why, I make the best cheese and crackers in town." Mrs. Boggs touches the cracker to Beatrice's dry, withered lips and is surprised to see teeth and a tongue. "The tea isn't quite as hot as it was, but I think it is a good temperature for drinking. Would you like milk or sugar, dear?" Beatrice just shakes her head no, but she already seems to show a bit of life in her that has been missing.

Mrs. Boggs reads the story of the Prodigal Son, Adam and Eve, and a bit of Noah's Ark before Beatrice lifts the covers off her. She slowly throws her skinny legs over the side of the bed, and meekly announces to Mrs. Boggs she will return soon from the bathroom. "May I change your sheets while you're gone and open your drapes just a bit? It's always good to allow some light in or else you'll stub your toe."

Beatrice thinks that is humorous and whimpers out the slightest chuckle. "Sure, go ahead. The sheets are in the hall closet right outside the bedroom."

As soon as Beatrice is clear of the bed, Mrs. Boggs starts stripping off the sheets, pillowcases, and bedspread. The sheets smell of urine, and they are musty from not being changed. She tosses them into a pile in the hall, grabs the fresh sheets, and on the bed they go. With apprehension, Mrs. Boggs pushes back the thick, floral curtains and lets the sunny day saturate the room. There are clothes and old, used tissues strewn on the floor, a cup and saucer and a part of a sandwich at least three days old. This is not because of Walter's negligence but because his wife does not want him in the room, and Walter does not want to excite Beatrice. The kindly lady from the church up the road picks up the mess and goes to the kitchen to throw away the litter.

Over the next few weeks, Mrs. Boggs helps Walter and Beatrice as much as possible, and they have formed a strong relationship. Even Mr. Boggs, the pastor, visits on occasion and enjoys talking with Walter. Beatrice has gained some strength and is able to care for herself, but she is still not enthusiastic about her baby. She has gone to her doctor once, and he prescribed an exercise and vitamin regimen. He assured Walter that, if followed diligently, the prescription will bring the lovely Beatrice back to her former self.

After Walter had received the glorious news of Danny's impending birth, he knew his wife would need her own transportation. It was not a week after he was told the good news, that Walter had a 1951 Nash Rambler two-door station wagon – a soft, sunny yellow in color to match Beatrice's personality – delivered to their home. She had been thrilled, of course, and Walter had to pry her arms from around his neck so that she would climb in behind the steering wheel. Beatrice's five-foot six-inch frame fit perfectly behind the wheel, and she could not wait to drive it. Walter gave her the keys, and Bea backed it up and down the driveway. She soon passed her State of Ohio driving test and received her license.

For the weeks after Danny's birth, when Beatrice did not go out, the car just sat in the garage. As Beatrice gained strength, though, she would drive to Charlie's Market or the dry cleaners about a mile down Route 43. Those drives were infrequent and sporadic, but Walter was thrilled that his love was getting more active. Mrs. Boggs was able to get her life back to normal, only checking in on Beatrice once a day by phone.

It is a very hot July afternoon, just before Walter will be leaving work, when Beatrice decides to drive her cool Nash station wagon into Appleton. Without looking in the mirror, she puts on a lightweight sun dress with sandals and combs her hair. Beatrice grabs her keys that hang next to the back door, jumps into her car, and heads south on Route 43.

Walter arrives home after coming straight from work and notices Bea's car is out of the garage. He walks inside his home through the backdoor that has not been locked. He calls out for his wife, but there is no answer. He thinks she probably just ran up to Charlie's without thinking she needed to lock the door for such a short trip. Walter takes his work shoes off at the door and proceeds to the bathroom where he showers off the day's work. He throws his clothes into the clothes hamper, sets the water temperature to a setting that will cool him down, and begins to get clean. He cannot wait to see his family, but he is all for

Beatrice getting out and, hopefully, buying something for a tasty dinner. His shower is short and invigorating, and he dries off before heading for his bedroom for clean clothes.

Before he finishes combing his hair, he hears something that petrifies him. Danny is crying! Walter runs into his room where the bassinette is, and there lies Danny, kicking his legs and saying, "Da." Walter tells Danny he will be right back and then searches every room in the house for his wife. He looks out front and then calls for Beatrice out the backdoor. By this time, Danny is crying again, and Walter scoops him up from his bed and holds him while he prepares a bottle. He also opens a jar of creamed peas and a jar of creamed carrots.

Setting Danny in his highchair, Walter is shaking a bit out of anxiety, but he manages to feed Danny his peas and carrots. He then grabs Danny's warmed bottle, picks him up out of the highchair, and lays him in his bassinette with his bottle, which Danny can handle by himself. Finally, Walter calls Annie Boggs and asks her if she had talked with Beatrice that day. Annie had talked with her around two o'clock and reported that Beatrice had sounded very lively and happy. Beatrice told her that she had cleaned the house and had had a good day with Danny. Nothing sounded out of the ordinary except that she sounded so peppy and happy.

Walter tells the pastor's wife what he had found as he came home and said that he was going to take Danny for a drive and look for his wife. Mrs. Boggs assures Walter that she will help if needed and they hang up. Walter changes Danny as he is finishing his bottle, puts him in a carrier he and Beatrice had fashioned out of a basket, and then sets his son in the big car seat beside him. Walter is not sure where to start, but he decides to look at Charlie's parking lot and then go off in any direction hoping to get lucky in his pursuit.

He and Danny drive for two hours all around Marigold and then into Appleton. He feels as though the whole force would laugh in his face, but he stops at an Appleton police station. Walter lifts Danny from his basket and goes inside to ask if there have been any reports that involved the Nash or his wife in particular. The officers are nice enough but did ask if they had been fighting, etc. Walter mentions that his wife has not been the same since the birth of their son, and this concerned the officer. He asks Walter if he wants to file a formal report, and Walter gives an emphatic affirmative response, practically pleading. Walter fills out papers, and the officer comforts Walter, telling him he will make sure all his officers will be on the lookout. The officer tells Walter that he should go home and be by the phone in case his wife calls. Walter agrees and goes on his way, heading for home while driving slowly and keeping an unblinking eye on every road he and Danny pass.

That evening, July seventh, 1953, at ten thirty-four, the police call and ask Walter to meet them at a park where the Scioto River empties into the Ohio River. Walter is shaken and calls Mrs. Boggs to please come watch Danny. Of course, she agrees to Walter's request and is there in fifteen minutes with her husband who drives Walter to the location after seeing how nervous Walter has become. As Pastor Boggs approaches the scene, it is eerie, with the police cars' search lights on a Nash station wagon that fits the description of the one owned by Beatrice. It is off the Park's parking lot, facing the Ohio River and abandoned with the driver's door open.

Walter's face is frozen with fear, and Pastor Boggs stays close to his friend. The officer in charge walks to Walter and asks, "Is this your wife's car?"

"Yes, I'm sure it is," Walter answers.

The officer holds up a sun dress and sandals "Do you recognize these garments?"

Walter screams, "Yes!" and grabs the officer by the arm asking him what is happening.

"We are not sure, but it appears your wife drove to the river or had been abducted, disrobed or was disrobed, and possibly walked into the river or was discarded near this area. This has not been confirmed, as no body has been found, but that's how it appears at this time." Walter is beside himself, but the officer says he cannot give him any more information until the morning when there is better light.

The night is long, and Walter is at the sight at sunup. Pastor Pete and Annie had stayed with Walter, and Pete, again, had driven for Walter. Walter is running on adrenaline and coffee and has nothing to say. He knows that his wife is gone, but he just needs to get close to where she might be. When Walter and Pete arrive, the Detectives on duty ask for their identity and then proceed to tell Walter that there was no apparent struggle. Nothing torn, no blood. There was nothing questionable or intoxicating in the vehicle, but they did find muddy, shoeless footprints leading into the river. The Detectives take Walter to that area where he can see for himself. Without a body they cannot be sure, but the police report will state that Beatrice walked into the northern side of the Ohio River from the western bank of the Scioto River. The motive is not certain, but it was either for a reckless swim, or Beatrice committed suicide.

THE END OF WALTER'S STORY OF DANNY'S MOTHER

Danny is in quiet tears, more for his dad than for the lady he never knew. He helps his dad stand and puts his right arm around Walter, practically carrying Walter to the car. Walter's weight, on his five-foot ten-inch frame, is a mere ninety-six pounds now, but Danny would have carried his dad ten miles at full weight. After hearing the story of his mom, he knows how well he was cared for by the man in his arms, and he will never forget it. Danny is fully aware that this humble, caring man has only weeks, if not days to live, and Danny will be by his side until Walter Mosely's heart beats its last. Danny is who he is because of the choices his dad made all through his life.

CHAPTER
TWENTY

Walter had done a thorough job of making sure Danny would not want for anything after his death. The house at 2310 Old River Road is now Danny's, paid in full, and a large insurance policy payout is tucked away in Danny's bank account. Walter did not want to finish his life in that house. He was afraid Danny would attach his death to the address that had been so full of life and love, prayer and praise. So, he instructed Danny to take him to the hospital where the nurses administered large amounts of morphine to subdue the cancerous torment, according to Dr. Giddings's direction.

Of course, Danny would give it all away if it meant he could have his dad, if he could hear his voice and smell his cooking. If he could just feel one more, warm daddy hug and hear him say "If I had to design a son, he would be just like you, my boy." Danny knows he is blessed to have heard it even once, but all through his life his dad would continually reaffirm his love for his son, and Danny will carry that always. These days Hannah frequently and lovingly cooks for Danny using Walter's pots and pans on Walter's stove, but there is a huge, indescribable void that no person can or will ever fill.

Pastor Pete visits Danny every other day or so. He not only visits out of obligation to his friend Walter, but because Danny is like a son to every adult in the church, and Danny loves the Lord. Danny's faith is so strong, it lifts up the pastor, and as the good book says, "Iron sharpeneth iron, so a man sharpeneth the countenance of his friend." At the end of one visit from both Annie and Pete, the pastor notices "Vincit qui patitur" burned rather neatly into the hardwood trim above the back door. He recognizes it right away as the Puritan motto roughly translated "He who suffers, conquers." As Danny stands rinsing dishes in the kitchen sink, Pete acknowledges the work and tells Danny, in a lovingly taunting tone, that he is happy that Danny is *finally* getting some use out of the wood burning set that he and Annie had given him on his tenth birthday.

Danny has been suffering and wrestling with Satan; make no mistake about that. The old reptile wants Danny to break. Oh, what a prize that would be for Satan, who wants this fine example of Christianity to show the world, or at least Marigold, that God is not always there when you need Him most. Danny thinks about The Screwtape Letters and wonders if it is Wormwood who speaks to him late at night when he is sitting alone in the quiet, empty house. Danny would give anything to have his dad back, but he knows that, if he gives his soul to Satan and denounces God, he will never see his dad again. Then, he reminds himself that Christ will never let go of him. Satan has no power over Danny.

The faithful Christian is in prayer much of his time at home. The crystal-clear Word of God speaks right to him, and it is His sword that defeats Satan's attempts, attractive as they are. Danny's pain is so deep soon after his dad's death that he did think of suicide, but only in passing. His credo has deep roots, and he believes that the God of all creation sent angels like Hannah, Pete, Carl, Charlie, Annie, Nick, Pastor Allen, Brenda, Arnold, Jeff, Alice, Barry, and King to remind Danny that he is still very blessed.

School resumes in January of this new decade, and Danny's grades suffer for a short time, but his dad's voice is still strong and unimpeded. Walter's smooth tenor timbre is as present to Danny today as it was just a month ago when he instructed his son to not get behind and to always do the very best that he can do. Danny had heard that wisdom a hundred times through his life, but he now understands why his dad hammered that truth into his brain. Walter knew that he would not always be there when his son needed encouragement, and he wanted Danny to be able to access his advice on demand. Walter was right, and that reassuring trust of foresight helped pull the young Christian out of his dark place and catapult Danny back to all As. The immense effort that was needed to come from behind actually created a comfortable perch from which Danny can now consider the other important aspects of his life, like his relationship with Hannah.

Danny is thankful for Nick who selflessly took the wheel and helped guide the youth group with Hannah. As far as Danny's role at church, he will play guitar with Mrs. Harland if needed, but he has not sung solos because he knows he is unable to get through the lyrics without sobbing. His dad would sing the hymns around the house sometimes, when he thought Danny was asleep. Walter knew that some music, not just any music, but the kind with a message that urges one to put their best foot forward, was all his son needed to wake up without complaint. Danny knows that those memories will flood his mind if he were to sing them now. The whole church staff knows that Danny will be leaving for college in just a few short months, and Nick has promised to continue with the youth. Nick sings and plays guitar and piano and is a lover of Jesus Christ. These attributes are what is required to take the youth into the future, and Danny and Hannah rest easily, as they plan their departure.

Danny is writing songs again and shares a new one with Pastor Pete after the Wednesday night gathering. Pete cannot imagine what will be said in the lyrics after Danny's heart has been so brutally broken, but he knows it will be sincere. Danny announces the title of the song as *He's with Me All the Time*, which piques Peter's interest immediately. Will the deep and brilliant young man be singing about his dad or Jesus or both? Danny sings the following words in a very powerful, lilting fashion:

Some days the Christian walk is hard
I reach out, but God seems so far
It takes all of my faith
To think I'll ever win the race

But then the Spirit comforts me
I recognize His voice, He speaks so quietly
He tells me not to fear and
Reminds me that God's always near

He's with me all the time
He has me by the hand
And when I fall down flat
He picks me up, again
There's nothing in this world
On which I can depend
He's with me all the time
He's Jesus Christ, amen

When the lust of life crowds my mind
I feel the war within; my soul is on the line
I can't win on my own
The victory is in Christ alone

He's with me all the time
He has me by the hand
And when I fall down flat
He picks me up, again
There's nothing in this world
On which I can depend
He's with me all the time
He's Jesus Christ, my friend

There's nothing in this world
On which I can depend
He's with me all the time
He's Jesus Christ, amen

After the song is sung, Pastor Pete's office sits quietly while it absorbs the words and emotions that just permeated its nooks and crannies. Knowing what this young man has been through, Pete is nearly in tears. Grabbing a tissue from the box on his desk and giving a quick blow of his nose, the pastor clears his throat. "It's not exactly the style of music we normally present in a service, Danny, but I believe everyone would love to hear this powerful message from you. Let me know when you want to sing it, and we will make it happen."

Danny has begun to get out some, meeting friends at Fran's and going to movies. All the while, though, his mind has been on southern California and the apparent Christian revival that has been going on there. Danny wants to be a part of it. Without the comfort of his very stable home life with his dad, Danny's raw nerve-endings are keeping him fully focused on leaving Marigold the day after graduation from Flint. His home is not the same, but he is not so much running away from his sorrow as running to a deeper relationship with Christ through fellowship and greater purpose.

King continues to book engagements for Clever Pennies and is currently securing the May dates. The money and the venues are better than ever, but without Barry's essential contributions to the group's sound, Danny is not excited about Clever Pennies. He is accepting the shows that King has booked but has been very clear that he is leaving at the end of May. Of course, Danny loves his Marigold band brothers and appreciates the effort that Phil Gregory has contributed. Phil is quite talented, and he wants to fill the chasm created by Barry's departure, but Phil is not Barry and the band is firmly in Danny's rearview mirror. His passion to grow as a Christian, bring others to the Lord Jesus and to help others grow in their faith is all consuming. The toothpaste is out of the tube. King knows this and has not decided how he wants to proceed without half of the original band.

Jeff is catching for Flint for his last season and has earned a baseball scholarship, in conjunction with higher-than-average grades, from Ohio University, Kenyon College, Kent State University, and Bowling Green State University. He is happy about that but is not really sure he wants to go to college right away and is hoping the war will end. He is not sure if he will continue playing guitar and singing for Clever Pennies or start a new band or become a guitar-slinging sideman for a touring band. He might just have to attend one of those colleges, though, which would not be his first choice of how to live for the next year or so.

Alice has not had her period this month, an event as regular as her dad's end-of-day glass of Lagavulin single-malt Scotch. She has not revealed this new development to Jeff or anyone else, hoping that her body has simply changed due to maturity and there is no reason for panic. Having provided only a half a dozen opportunities to introduce the elements necessary to instigate mammalian creation, and the long shot that must occur even with all the players in place, a bullseye seems ludicrous, preposterous. However, Alice's mother's voice, telling her that it only takes one time, prevails and sobers up the young adult. Alice knows the truth and has begun the phrenic, and sometimes audible, rehearsals of her speech that will hopefully cut a clear path toward her announcement.

She is nearing nineteen years of age but is still her parent's baby. Jeff, the other half, has not cinched his future and has no big desire to think much past tomorrow. What will he say? How will he react? He has never shown harsh anger toward Alice or anyone else, but every person has their breaking point. Jeff was not clueless when taking part in the miracle of cell division, but he does not think like that. To him, the occasions were beautiful moments with someone he loves very much. Jeff does not like to think ahead because when he does, the end results always look gloomy or unachievable. So, he does what he does when he does it and did what he did because it seemed to be the right time.

On a cold, early February evening, Danny and Hannah leave church together and head for Fran's to discuss the future. They both know that God has His plan for them, and after an abundance of prayer, Danny believes he has been led by the Holy Spirit to attend Biola College so that he can engage in the southern California Revival. Danny's dream is a bold step in the name of Jesus, and everything about the journey deserves deliberate consideration. This is heavy and Hannah knows that, over the next few weeks, she will be deciding if she is really on board for this approach to serving Christ and the Kingdom or if she is just following someone who she loves deeply. Though not equal, either reason holds significant merit in young Hannah's mind.

Before this brainstorm meeting at Fran's, the Birdsongs planned a special dinner with Danny and Hannah to discuss the pilgrimage so that they could express their views and concerns. What they offered was support of Danny's dream and a blessing of their daughter's westward adventure. However, Hannah must return at the end of the summer. The loving parents wanted to articulate and deliver their decision while in Danny's presence because they know how excited and consumed he is about his southern California trip. The Birdsongs are aware that Danny's full immersion is his way of dealing with his recent grief as well and know his method is honest and principled. As a matter of fact, they do not find any fault in his dream and want to help.

On the flip side of the coin, Tom and Louise have invested in Cedarville for years and believe in its leadership and want Hannah to follow her sisters. The Birdsongs love Danny and know that he will be an ethical and level-headed summer partner, and they are not ignoring the love between the two: Danny may be Hannah's partner for life. Together, Hannah and Danny are a powerful force for the Kingdom and that is eminently important to the world wherever they dig in, but Tom and Louise believe that at least one year at Cedarville will be good for, not only them, but Hannah and Danny too. A school year apart will be a bona fide test of their love and godly aspirations.

Fran's is buzzing as usual, but Danny and Hannah do not hear anything other than their own enthusiastic voices. As they munch their french fries, Hannah writes notes, outlining the trip, and Danny gushes thought after thought, step by step. Danny will give Pastor Pete a key to his house so that he can drop in twice a month or so to be sure there are no broken pipes or windows. The day after they both graduate with Honors, Danny will drive to the Birdsong's house and eat breakfast with the Birdsong family. After breakfast, he will load Hannah's things into his car, give everyone very big hugs, and leave Marigold with their daughter. He hopes to catch Route 66, the *Mother Road* as John Steinbeck named it, somewhere along the way. The Interstate system of highways has created bypasses that have taken most of the business away from the old American trail.

Though Hannah and Danny are both anxious to start working with the Hollywood Presbyterian Church, they have decided to interject some sightseeing into their pilgrimage. They have enjoyed poring over maps to see what sights are on their path. They will head toward Nashville and then Memphis, where they will spend their first night. They hope to hear some authentic blues live on stage and listen to some country on WMPS radio, loud and clear. The station Danny wants to hear the most, though, is KAAY out of Little Rock, Arkansas. This is the station where Danny first heard James Brown's *Licking Stick* just two years earlier, late at night while he lay awake in his bed. The bass part for that song is what inspired Danny to begin learning the instrument, along with Peter Tork's character.

After taking in The Great Plains, Santa Fe will be their next stop. Hannah has spent a great deal of time studying the American Indian and is excited she may possibly experience the great Navajo and Apache Nations in New Mexico. Of course, the grand prize will be the Grand Canyon, in all its glory. They will not make the mile hike to the bottom, but to see its expanse will be breathtaking. As far as Los Angeles, they are not sure what to expect. Tall palm trees and fancy cars are all they can come up with. The Beverly Hillbillies, Dragnet, Adam-12, The Monkees, and some skits by Johnny Carson – these TV shows, which they have watched for years, are where their ideas of the sprawling city come from, but they know it is something else.

Danny's heart is not necessarily yearning for L.A. as it is Hollywood where the church is located. Danny has corresponded with one of the pastors of Hollywood Presbyterian Church named Don. The Pastor has spoken at length about how much there is to be done in the way of helping addicts and wayward runaways, and Danny cannot wait to roll up his sleeves and get involved. Because Hannah will only be there for the summer, her ideas are not as far reaching. She does know that she will be playing a large supporting role with church and Campus Crusade activities and will help Danny get settled into his school life there.

Danny and Hannah will not share the same motel room along their route to California, but once they arrive, Danny will set up his pre-arranged off campus abode. According to his Hollywood Pres contact, Neil, Danny's rental accommodations only offer one bedroom. Though marriage has been discussed and passion has not been a stranger, neither of them wants to at best create a child or at worst disappoint the God they worship and love. With those convictions firmly in place, Hannah and Danny believe they can room together through the summer without crossing the invisible line of respect for each other and God's will for them. If they do get married, they want to be virgins on their first night together in the same bed.

Several friends come by the couple's table while they talk, but no invitations to join them have been uttered. Danny may as well already be in Hollywood, and all his friends know that. Still, his friends love him and enjoy Danny's deep thoughts and soft humor. They know that this is a rare evening when Danny does not have to play with Clever Pennies, and his time is valuable with Hannah. His friends probably do not know that Danny has a hard time at night in his house without his dad. Danny's grades are way up, so a school night at Fran's, until he is tired and able to sleep, has become an acceptable deterrence from his grief, and Hannah walks those hours with him as much as she can.

Danny and King are going to get together tomorrow night, maybe just in King's basement. They have not talked with any depth since Clever Pennies became so active, but Danny knows that King has taken a much different path than the one they were on together as young boys. King's involvement with psychedelic drugs, LSD in particular, has caused a false separation between them, and Danny hopes the drug has not damaged King's mind. Cloud is no longer a force in King's life, and Danny looks forward to just being two friends again, talking about fun and funny things. Danny would never have tried to come between King and Cloud. That is always the kiss of death to a friendship, and Danny loves and highly values his friendship with King. Danny has put his friend on the top of his prayer list and makes it a point to lift King's wellbeing up to the Lord on a daily basis, and the Lord has blessed Danny with the gift of time tomorrow night.

On his way to King's house, Danny plans on stopping in at the Meade's home to check on their mental and emotional wellbeing since their son exfiltrated, not that they will be honest with him about those things. Danny has not and will never forget that Barry saved his life at the waterfall and Barry's wellbeing weighs on Danny's mind as well. No one has heard from Barry in five months, and Danny knows the whole family must be beside themselves with fear and guilt. Even the good doctor must be shaken by his son's desertion. Dr. Meade's dream for his son has been expunged, and he has no way of changing the outcome. Barry is out of his dad's shouting range and is no longer susceptible to the incapacitating barrage of guilt-ladened reminders of who he is and from where he came.

If culpability has set itself free from the rusty, old shackles of the good doctor's suppressive Freudian catacombs of emotion, it has not yet entered his purview. He believes his son will show up any day, and at that time, Dr. Meade will grab his son by the scruff and put him on a plane to Harvard and a better future, for his own good. A bitter medicine can turn one's life so sweet. This is the motto by which Dr. Roy Meade lives his life, and he expects his family to adhere.

Late at night, Kay will occasionally cry herself to sleep, wishing she could just talk with her brother. He always encouraged her and made her laugh. Barry would climb onto Kay's bed, sit upright with his back on the headboard, hold her with her head on his stomach, and sing quietly until she fell asleep. His song of choice was usually *In My Life* by The Beatles.

How could he have done this without telling her, without saying goodbye? She doesn't cry every night, but there are those nights when she thinks she hears brother downstairs playing lightly on the piano, perhaps Satie or Chopin. She then reminds herself that the big, beautiful instrument just sits closed up, like the rest of the family, waiting for the day the beautiful music returns.

Danny is prepared to be a punching bag, a sounding board, and a shoulder to cry on. He understands the pain of loss, but to not know Barry's whereabouts is on a different level and that is actually good therapy for him. Danny is missing Barry, but caring for his dad before his passing, and his passing, overshadowed any normal reaction he would have had regarding his good friend and bandmate. Danny thought Barry would come home after a month with either his tail between his legs or a new ferocity protecting his freedom and individuality. Of course, it was right around that estimated-time-of-arrival that Walter began to stop hiding his illness from Danny, and from that point on, all of Danny's emotions were completely concentrated on and dedicated to his dad.

Tonight, though, he is with his beloved Hannah, and she is with him. Hannah has taken two pages of notes, and they are ready to pay their dinner bill. Fran's has thinned out on this Wednesday night after youth group, and it is time for Danny and Hannah to call it a day. Hannah's car is back at the church, which is only about the length of a football field away from Fran's, but Danny will drive Hannah back to her car.

After he makes sure she is safely on her way home, Danny will head back to his house and do his homework. He just bought an album that was recommended by Clever Pennies guitarist himself, Jeff Lindor. It is called The Allman Brothers Band, and what he has heard of it so far has absolutely blown Danny's mind. Jeff had stopped in at Danny's for a few minutes on Sunday evening just to play one song for Danny before he and Alice went to the movies. The name of the song is called *Dreams*, and it seemed to float on a bed of B3 and slide guitar. The singer was gruff sounding but about as sincerely passionate as Danny had ever heard. He rushed out on Monday after school and bought his own copy so that he could hear if the rest of the record was as powerful as that song.

Danny enters his house, pats the motto burned into the door jamb above, and closes and locks the back door. He walks right over to the record player, tears the plastic off the cover, pulls out the album, and places it on the turntable. An instrumental opens the album, and Danny turns his birthday stereo all the way up while he goes upstairs and changes clothes. When he returns, Danny grabs the album cover for a good once over. The band is standing in front of an old, southern mansion-looking place. They have long hair and a black guy in the lineup.

The album cover opens and in all their glory, the entire band is naked in a creek, some standing and some sitting down in the water. No private parts are showing, and though startling at first, the picture automatically presents a fraternal impression of the band, as if they have no secrets from each other or from their fans. The cover is colorful, and the pictures were taken when it was obviously warm. One can feel a warm southern breeze, as if the cover is a window into another world.

As the songs play, the sound is very bluesy, but there is a new power to it. Like the Grateful Dead, Danny reads that The Allman Brothers Band has two drummers and two guitarists, but the musicianship is on a different level; the arrangements are much tighter, and all the parts of the song work together like a Swiss watch. This precision sets up a perfect bed for masterful improvisational soloing on the two guitars. The musical foundations allow the singer to sing from the heart and not the mind. He does not need to worry about leading the band astray. The back cover has the band standing in front of, what looks to be, a Jesus-like statue. Danny assumes it is one of the band members.

This album is so fresh and new sounding, it is difficult for Danny to finish his homework. He will finish it before he leaves for school in the morning. He lets *Dreams*, the last song on the album, finish before he heads for bed. He brushes his teeth and shouts a sweet "goodnight, Daddy" to the dark room across the hall before he climbs into his bed and stares at the ceiling. Sometimes his dream of service to Christ feels like a sacrifice. When he hears music like what he was just listening to, he is reminded that he is currently in one of the best bands to come out of southern Ohio. The musicianship is superior to most, and there is love among the band members. Audiences get excited about them, and they have fun while making a whole lot of money.

Service to Christ is always sacrificial because Danny knows he is a flawed human who was born selfish. As a human, he knows that we would rather do anything than be the world's welcome mat, but when one has the power of the Holy Spirit dwelling in him or her, natural instincts are replaced with the supernatural of God. It is the most remarkable thing and Danny knows that, if it were not for his gift from Jesus, he would be going to school at Cedarville with Hannah and playing weekends with Clever Pennies. Not a bad life at all, but God has put this pilgrimage on Danny's heart, and there is no turning away. Nothing on Earth can compare with what will be. Jonah tried to run from God, and God let him spend three days in the belly of a large, smelly fish and ended up being part of its barf on the beach. Jacob wrestled with God in the flesh, possibly an early incarnation of Jesus Himself, and his hip was thrown out of place to be used as a reminder. Danny knows, when God calls, you go.

***

King is excited that his friend is visiting tonight and watches the Meade's driveway for headlights while he thumbs through the February Rolling Stone magazine. John and Yoko are on the cover, but the text on the front seems to make a point of saying they have a "private" talk with John. To King, that sounds like the magazine is saying they have wrangled John away from Yoko for ten minutes, and he speaks without any other input or distraction. The best part, though, is the ad for a story about Woodstock that is coming to theatres soon. He wonders if he might end up in any of the photos or film taken at the venue.

King looks up to see car lights coming down the Meade's drive. He gets up and opens the front door. Danny crosses Marigold Road and then makes his way into King's drive and parks next to King's new Econoline PopTop camper van. With Danny in hearing distance, King asks him what he thinks of his new purchase. Danny gives a thumbs up, and King tells Danny that he just had to have it after Woodstock. He plans on going to other festivals, and it will be great for the band to ride to gigs in while the bread truck goes ahead to the venue with the equipment. Danny just chuckles, knowing he won't be there, but he looks forward to travelling in the PopTop for the next three months.

The two friends hug, and King ushers Danny in from the cold. Mrs. Reed comes out of the kitchen and gives Danny a hug and welcomes him. "I hope you are hungry, Dan. I have a roast in the oven with your name on it, honey."

"Oh no, ma'am. I didn't come for dinner. You shouldn't have fixed anything just for me, although you know I love your roasts."

"That is why you are going to eat with us, or you boys can just take it to the basement, if that is where you are going. I also made some peanut butter cookies, Danny. Does that sound good?"

"Wow! I remember the first time I came up here to visit King. You were making peanut butter cookies then, and you asked us to help you by crossing the tops with a fork. Those were so good."

Ellie just smiles, and King confirms that they are indeed headed for the basement and asks his mom to let them know when dinner is ready. The two boys flop down on both of the comfortable couches that face each other in front of the basement fireplace. King wads up five or six pages of old newspaper and begins to build the bed of what will be a roaring fire. He gathers a few thin sticks that are in a bucket and sprinkles them on top of the newspaper balls and then lifts two medium sized split log halves and throws them on top. He grabs a match from the urn and lights the newspaper. In no time, the kindling sticks catch fire which produces enough heat to combust the logs. Voila! Radiant heat on a cold, southern Ohio evening.

"How ya doin' without Cloud, man? You two were together for a year or so, right?"

"Yeah, it's OK. Nothing lasts forever. She was sort of sapping all my energy, you know? By the end of our relationship, I was just following her around while my head was going in a different direction. She's cool and all. She showed me a lot of new music and opened up my mind, in some ways. I'll love her always, but I just forgot who I was and had put away all the things that I like to do. I stopped painting and writing poetry. I didn't lie in bed in the mornings and just enjoy. I knew she was always waiting for me to call so we could begin our day. I mean, you and Hannah are a couple, and a really cool one, but you each have your own lives too."

"That's probably what I love most about Hannah. She is loving and tender, but she doesn't *need* me. She chooses to be with me and to sacrifice some of her time for me, and that feels so much better than something like John and Yoko. I would suffocate with someone like that. We have gotten really close since Daddy passed away, though. She's an angel, and she knows I won't abuse that gift she gives me. As a matter of fact, we had dinner with her parents, and they want her to come back here, from California, at the end of the summer and start school at Cedarville."

"Oh, wow! That's heavy, man. Is that OK?"

"You know, when I first heard that, I felt possessive or something. I could feel her absence already. As the evening went on, though, her mom and dad said that the separation will be a true test of our love. I get that now. I love Hannah, whether she is right here beside me or two thousand miles away. We don't sleep together or anything, so that won't be something that we would miss. I will concentrate on school and Campus Crusade, and she can focus on her first year of college and be close to her family. I am so focused on the Campus thing that she would probably get sick of me anyway."

They laugh, then sit quietly and watch the fire. This quiet time lasts for two or three minutes, just enjoying the comfort of the other. Finally, Danny breaks the silence "Have you heard The Allman Brothers Band?"

"They are incredible, man. The drummers tear me up with all their polyrhythms going on. Pennies couldn't do their stuff, I don't think, with the double guitar thing and the drummers. Jeff is certainly good enough to play the parts, but it would never sound like the record."

"Yeah, I guess so. The bass parts aren't easy either. The musicianship is ridiculous, but you could probably sing it. Their singer is very bluesy, and you sing Eric Burden, so you could sing the Allman singer. Is the black guy singing?"

"No, man, he's one of the drummers. The kid-looking guy with the blond hair is singing. His name is Allman, Gregg, I think."

"Well, I've never really heard anything like them. The Dead are similar, but the Allmans are a whole different level. A different approach, ya know? Every note and beat matters. The Dead just seem to meander sometimes. I guess it's the drugs that I hear they take while they're playing. Sometimes their music goes places that no one has ever gone, but for me, it can be excruciating getting there. Everybody seems to have fun at their concerts, though, so what do I know?"

Barry's Vox Continental sits in the corner of King's basement like a good dog waiting for his master to return. Master has not returned, however, and King finally decided to play the instrument when the urge hit. He does not think Barry would mind. As King and Danny sit at the organ listening to King play with comparative mediocrity, King asks

Danny how the Meades are doing. Danny turns his body toward the fire and admits that he can tell they are stressed and uneasy about discussing their runaway son. Little Kay seems the saddest, Danny observed. "She can hardly talk about her brother without welling up."

King stops playing and turns off the organ. He walks to the fireplace and puts another log on the fire and the two friends move back over to the couches. They discuss Danny's departure from the band and his relocation. King is excited about the Clever Pennies "Farewell to Danny" night, but right now, Danny just wants to get to California with Hannah. "Are you going to keep the band together without me and Barry?" Danny asks his friend.

"I'm gonna try. Neither one of you guys is easy to replace, and I am sure our songs will not be up to your level, but I want to keep playing and Clever Pennies has a name now, even if I have to live off of your songs." King says with a big grin.

Ellie calls the boys upstairs for dinner, and they do not hesitate, making their way back up to the first floor and into the kitchen. Ellie has Andy Williams on the stereo, and she is singing along with Moon River. King joins in for a third part, and they sound good enough to be the next big thing. Well, at least one of the better Upper Marigold trios. Ellie tells the boys they can load their plates and go downstairs, if they would like to, or they most certainly are welcome at the dinner table.

"Can we watch Pat Paulsen, Mom?"

"Well . . . I would like to watch Family Affair, please. That Paulsen guy isn't very funny to me." Both of the boys begin talking like the comedian with very deadpan faces. "See? That's what I mean, except you two actually make me laugh. I think you better go watch it downstairs if you find that funny." They all laugh, and Ellie tells them she loves them as they disappear to the basement.

The weekend Clever Pennies shows are both sold out, and one place holds about two thousand people. It is a corporate gig, but there are more daughters and cousins in the mix than usual, and they camp at the front of the stage all night. Jeff is intense and plays like a demon, possessed. Phil handles the keyboards and some vocals better than he had, as he is getting more comfortable with his role. He is starting to be himself instead of Barry's replacement. Losing Barry's voice and keyboard brilliance is a detriment to the hardcore CP fans, but for those who have only heard three or four songs on the radio, Phil works surprisingly well.

Without Cloud being there, King is more of a showman and flirts without end. He is good at it, though, giving only the occasional glance and then giving one to the girl next to that one. That way, there is a competition to get more eye time with the drummer, almost elbowing each other to be the one in King's best view. Danny is singing well and playing helps him keep his mind off his dad and California. He does not look burdened and dances around with Jeff when Phil is soloing.

It's a two-hour trip back from Dayton, and Jeff is driving himself and Danny back to Marigold because the camper van, or "PopTop" as they have begun calling her, is going to stop and get a room instead of driving back tonight. Jeff is smoking like a fiend, and he is more quiet than usual, though he is not a *talker*, per se. Still, Danny can tell there is something on Jeff's mind, and he is sure of it when he sees Jeff wipe his eyes and sniffle his nose.

"You OK, man?" Danny asks sincerely.

"Not really. I want to talk with you about something, but I don't want to hear a bunch of Jesus stuff. I just need to talk to you as a friend, you know?"

"Sure, I am your friend in either style of conversation. Let me hear it."

"I really do *not* know what to do. You gotta promise me you won't mention this to anyone else, and I mean Hannah or anyone. Can you do that?"

"Of course, Jeff, if that's the way you want it, I'll respect that."

"Alice went to the Appleton Clinic last week."

"Why, man? Is she OK? Why the clinic?"

"Because she didn't want to see the family doctor."

"Whoa. I have a feeling I know where this is going."

"You would be right if you have guessed that Alice is pregnant."

"Oh, wow. That is super heavy, my friend. Wow. How far along?"

"About two months."

"Hey! The baby will be born around your birthday!"

"Yeah, real cool, except I don't know if I want her to keep it."

There is a long, deep quiet after Jeff admits that he might prefer an abortion. Danny just sits and looks out the window as the dark world passes by. He is sure what he wants to say, but not quite sure how to say it. "Jeff, that is your son or daughter, man. I don't want to blast you, and you know I love you like a brother, but 'that' is a human being. It is a gift to you and Alice. I know you, and I believe you and Alice got together out of love and not *just* lust, but either way, the baby is a human being who wants the chance to grow up and be someone. Maybe even a great guitarist."

"Come on, man. It is so much more complicated than that. If we keep the baby, she and I have to tell her parents, and I can tell you right now, they *do not* like me. They tolerate me and hope I'm just a fling, but they do not want me to be their son-in-law. Plus, the fun doesn't stop there. If we keep the baby, we will have to give up a lot of things that we have talked about doing. I can't even take care of myself, much more change a crappy diaper. I'll have to get a job at the railroad or the oven so that I can have insurance and stuff." Jeff pauses. "My kid will have to know Darren." They both explode with laughter, along with some teary eyes and runny noses. The thought of Darren babysitting is scary but still funny to imagine.

"Have you and Alice talked about that option yet?"

"No. I'd say she is kind of happy but scared."

"That's good! That's a healthy reaction!"

"Right, but when we start talking about telling her mom and dad, she just turns around and walks away. I love her, Dan. I really do. I want to marry her because I want to marry her, not because I *have* to marry her. You know what I mean?"

"Of course, and that is very honorable and dare I say, sweet of you, big guy. I know you love her, since the first time I saw you with her at my sixteenth, I knew. There is nothing like that chemistry. Some people dodge it, you know, run from it because, once it gets hold of you, a person knows there is no use looking any further. It's a beautiful thing, and the baby is a product of that love. It's just a little early, that's all.

"I won't go Jesus on you, but I really do believe that God has put that baby here for a reason, and who are we to question that? Her parents may hate you, but they will love that baby, which means they will end up loving you one day. That's as long as you don't grow into some kind of ass, but I don't believe you will."

"I don't want to be Jeff Engel, you know? They'll bring all their money around, and my railroad money won't mean anything. I'll never be good enough unless I write some hit song and make a few mil from it."

"Well, not that you couldn't, but that probably won't happen. You just need to face things and put the baby's wellbeing up pretty high. Jeff, I just think killing a baby, your baby, so that you don't have to face the truth, will haunt you for the rest of your life. You will always wonder who he or she would have been. I wish you would take that option off the table and figure out how you want to stand up and welcome that little one into the world. Two loving parents and you know there will be two loving grandparents. And don't forget Darren." Jeff laughs and turns up the radio. Enough has been said tonight.

CHAPTER
TWENTY-ONE

Danny checks the locks on his doors and windows. He goes back upstairs to make his bed and sit on his dad's bed for a few minutes before he heads to the Birdsong's house. He opens Walter's closet and smells that familiar smell of someone who loved him like no other. Danny is not so melancholy anymore. He is anxious to go to California, and he is very sure he will see his dad again, someday when the good Lord chooses.

With only one suitcase, Danny packs light bringing three pairs of shoes, his pillow, and his guitar. The Charles Causley books from his dad are tucked inside for comfort and inspiration. Danny decides to leave his stereo so that *he* will be compelled to make the music, and besides, he is going to reside in Hollywood California. If he can't hear other music there, then "God didn't make little green apples". Plus, Danny hopes he will have an opportunity to play with the Salt Company Band that he has read about. They play the kind of music that Danny has been playing for his youth group, taking old hymns and putting electric guitars and drums to the chords or singing new songs of praise and worship in the style of Bob Dylan, Joni Mitchell, or Barry McGuire.

He takes his belongings out to his car and comes back in for one last look. The thermostat is set so that the furnace will not run until it gets below fifty in southern Ohio. Pastor Pete has promised to keep an eye on it through the winter months because Danny does not plan to come back for holidays, but plans can change. He hopes to be immersed in his work with the church out west and taking breaks, holidays or not, seems unlikely when helping addicts and runaways. They don't take breaks.

Everything is ready. Danny bows his head, thanks the Lord, and prays deeply that God keeps his head and heart pointed in the right direction, in a direction that pleases Him and helps others. With an amen to close his prayer, Danny reaches up and touches his indelible life motto, leaving his fingers there for just a few seconds more than usual, as if the etching might burn itself into his soul. He walks out of his house and out of his childhood. His mind immediately goes to 1 Corinthians 13:11-12, which says:

> [11] When I was a child, I spake as a child, I understood as a child, I thought as a child: but when I became a man, I put away childish things. [12] For now we see through a glass, darkly; but then face to face: now I know in part; but then shall I know even as also I am known.

Danny locks the deadbolt and knob lock, walks out of his back porch, and checks his garage doors. It is seven o'clock on a beautiful May morning in southern Ohio and it is hard to believe he will be hundreds of miles away by tonight, thankfully with someone whom he loves dearly. Danny has wondered how well he and Hannah will govern their new freedom. Will she see things in him that she will not like? Will the changes in environment and lifestyle change them? They will grow; Danny knows that without doubt, but will he and Hannah grow apart? He puts that and everything else in God's capable hands, turns the car on, backs it out of 2310 Old River Road, and points it toward the Birdsongs for breakfast.

All the women are home with Mr. Birdsong. The smell of bacon is wafting through the air as Danny walks in through the backdoor. Each family member gives Danny hugs, including Tom Birdsong. "Are you ready, my dear?" Danny asks Hannah.

"You bet." She rubs her palms together and answers enthusiastically.

Mr. Birdsong asks Danny if he is ready to drive such a long distance, and Danny shakes his head yes. "I feel great, although it is strange that this day is now really here."

"Are you ready to be cooped up with Hannah for hours and hours?" Hannah's sister Elizabeth says with a look on her face as if she had just smelled a skunk. Louise tells her oldest daughter (by two minutes before Lydia) to not be mean while Hannah punches her in the arm.

Louise sets a fine breakfast table, and Tom Birdsong says a prayer before the crowd begins to eat. There is fruit, sausage, bacon, scrambled eggs, yogurt, and orange juice and milk to drink. The talk is mostly about the dreams and ambitions regarding the trip. Hollywood Presbyterian was able to secure an apartment for Danny near the church for a reasonable monthly rent. There is only one bed, but Danny assures the Birdsongs that he will be on the couch. There is no snickering or innuendo about how Tom and Louise feel about the two living together for the summer. The conversation is straight-forward, and the subject of temptation is not ignored.

Danny opens up. "I haven't said a lot of what I'm about to say to you, Birdsong family. Not even to Hannah, herself." There is a pause before Danny takes a deep breath. "I love your daughter. She is my best friend, the one person I can open up to in this whole world. I love her for her beauty, inside and out. I love her for her sense of humor, her kind heart, and the way her hand feels in mine. Hannah is someone I respect, and that includes her walk with God. I am but a sinful man and she is quite a beauty, as you know. I just want you to know that there is no way I will allow myself, or her, to defile her wedding gift simply out of convenience or comfort or even lust. I can wait and I believe she will wait, too. I won't lie, it may be a struggle, but we both recognize the struggle and we are ready to put on our full armor as we will be serving God and will not let sin defile our work, as well."

Hannah sits blushing and a bit slack-jawed, and the sisters' eyes are filled with tears. Tom and Louise's faces remain parental but have softened. Danny has that effect on everyone. His quiet demeanor is disarming, and you do not realize that your heart and mind have changed until he has moved on to another topic. That is what happened to Arnold. He could not resist Danny's kindness and tender tone.

"Tommy, please tell them what we have for them," Louise says to her husband, satisfied with Danny's promise. Tom reaches under his place mat, pulling out two envelopes.

"Danny and Hannah, we were not sure what we wanted to give you as graduation presents, so we decided to give you dirty ol' wadded up money as it will probably be most important over the next few months." Tom hands the envelopes to Danny and Hannah and tells the two graduates to open them when they get settled in Los Angeles.

"Thanks, Mom and Daddy," Hannah says with sincere surprise in her response.

Danny's mouth falls open. "Oh gosh, you guys. You really didn't need to do anything. Thank you so much. What a blessing, speaking of the gift *and* knowing you and your family."

After all of Hannah's bags are loaded into Danny's trunk, Tom Birdsong prays over the two pilgrims as they all stand in a tight circle. Everyone is emotional except Danny. He is drained of emotion, but his hand rubs the backs of Elizabeth and Lydia as if to say, *We will be OK.* He hugs Tom and Louise and opens the door for Hannah before he jumps in the driver's seat. Danny starts the car, waves one more time, and backs down the long driveway. The four remaining family members follow the car to the front edge of the house and all wave as the car pulls away, literally pointing west toward California.

After a serpentine foray through Kentucky, north to south, the travelers find themselves only forty-five minutes from Music City, Nashville. It will be the perfect stop for lunch, and they will take their time to find just the right souvenirs. Music City is not as big as they pictured it, looking like a lazy southern town. Their jaws drop as they drive past the Ryman Auditorium, home of the Grand Ole Opry. Danny finds a parking place, and they get out and walk the downtown streets of Nashville, taking pictures in front of the Ryman, Tootsie's, Earnest Tubb's Record Shop, and standing under famous street signs. They ask for directions to Music Row where all the Country hits are written and recorded and then head up Broadway until they can make a left over to 16th.

Once on "The Row," they get pictures in front of the RCA studios where Elvis and Dylan have recorded, among many others. It is a fascinatingly low-key area that simply looks like a bunch of homes. Inside of these houses, though, is where so much magic is made, contracts are signed, and new sounds are created. It is so quiet and plain, just about four square blocks, that it doesn't seem possible.

Back in the car, Danny and Hannah study their map and find that Route 70S will take them to an entrance onto Interstate 40, west of Nashville. It looks more scenic than jumping on Interstate 40 just down the street, and they are hoping to get a better feel for the Nashville area. Hunger has taken over their thoughts and dreams, though, and Hannah has accepted the responsibility of being the lookout for a restaurant.

After passing Vanderbilt and Peabody colleges, they enter a lush green area with houses built on big lots, similar to the upper Marigold area. There are a few churches, but one stands out to them, Woodmont Baptist Church. Its architecture, the way the bricks are laid and the huge windows are set, somehow, exudes the loving hands that built it. They drive on through the budding hills until they reach another suburb called Bellevue. Very hungry now, they are happy to see several restaurant choices. They decide on burgers and pick a friendly little place called Archie's. The food and service are great. Everyone seems so friendly, and the locals do not hesitate to strike up a conversation about Nashville or where Danny and Hannah are from and where they are going. Danny pays the bill, and the two climb back into the car. They get their covered wagon filled with gas and the oil checked, and Hannah finds the entrance to the interstate. Next stop is the "Home of the Blues", Memphis.

The drive is a long and boring two hundred miles, with nothing but farmland and forest on either side of a fairly straight Interstate 40. It is beginning to get dark in Central Time, and the young adults are tired from their first day's travels. They have been energized by the radio, though, as the dial is filling up with great music of all genres, and they both cannot help but seat dance all the way into the legendary city. Hannah sees a sign for Holiday Inn, a safe and clean chain of motels that they later learn started right there in Memphis.

Danny pulls in under the carport overhang and goes into the motel to secure two rooms. People in the south have not taken to long hair, and Danny's has certainly grown long. After securing two single rooms next to each other, the lady at the desk asks Danny why he grows his hair so long. He is not quite sure what to say, but a friendly "Jesus had long hair" comes rolling off his tongue and that seems to satisfy, or at least, quiet the lady at the front desk.

"Do you want 105 or 106?" Danny asks Hannah.

"Five, please." She answers, after considering the choice for a second or two.

"I really wanted to see some cool music being played, but I'm whipped. Right now, I just wanna lay on the bed and watch TV. You better call your mom and then let's watch some TV *together* before we call it a day."

"Sounds like a great idea, sweetie, and it is lie, not lay." Hannah was always playfully correcting the word-meister on this little gaff of his, and Danny would always respond with, "How would *Lay Lady Lay* sound as Lie Lady Lie? Huh-h-h?"

Danny parks the car in front of the two rooms and the two just sit, looking out the windshield, out of fatigue and a bit of disbelief. Hannah reaches over and softly holds Danny's hand, which triggers Danny's natural reaction to turn his head and look at the lovely young lady who has blessed his life. He breaks his right hand loose from hers and reaches over Hannah's shoulders and pulls her to his side. They sit there quietly, and Danny lightly rubs Hannah's right shoulder. They are not in Marigold and will not drive its roads or see their friend's faces for many months. It could be years for Danny.

Danny breaks the silence and speaks in a broken whisper, "Let's say a prayer, thanking our Lord for our blessed lives."

"A wonderful idea from a wonderful, godly man."

With great thought and sincerity, Danny begins, "Dear heavenly Father, we do not deserve the wonderful lives You have provided for Hannah and me, together and individually. We are in awe of You and Your Son, dear God, and we thank You for the Holy Spirit as He guides us every day. We are putting our lives in Your capable hands, dear Lord, individually and together. Teach us, Lord. Fill us with Your lovingkindness and wonderful truth. Give us strength to fight the fight and to stay on the path that You have set for us. We love You and we pray this in Your Son's Holy, beautiful name, Jesus Christ. Amen."

"Amen."

They share a sweet kiss and then head to the trunk of the car, where they each grab a night bag and go to their separate rooms. Hannah freshens up and changes her clothes, needing to relax in something less constricting. Not quite pajamas, but close, although Hannah knows that she will need to walk that parade for her man this summer. She has no qualms about Danny's integrity, but she does not want to be his temptress. They both know they are hundreds of miles away from their childhood but never closer to God, and that is Who they want to impress.

Danny brushes his teeth, but hunger has set in and he wants to get something to eat before he settles down. He goes next door and knocks. Very quickly, he hears Hannah ask if it is him, and he answers her. The door opens and Hannah, with hairbrush in hand, lets Danny in. Hannah's TV is on, already, just for some background noise and to see if they can get any idea of what Memphis is like. Danny does not sit and tells Hannah he wants to get something to eat and asks if she would like to go. Hannah declines, but she assures Danny that anything that he would like to bring back for her will be A-OK, as they say in outer space. She thinks it will be fun to eat in the room and watch TV together.

Danny picks up the phone and asks the front desk what is good and close. The man on the other end of the line gives Danny a couple of choices, fried chicken or burgers. The fried chicken sounds good, so Danny goes out to the car and heads off in the direction he was given by the gentleman at the front desk. There is a Colonel Sanders not more than a mile down the road, and it is fairly busy for seven o'clock at night.

Danny parks his car and goes in, but his wait is not long, and he is able to order quickly. His eyes are much bigger than his stomach, and along with the bucket of chicken, Danny buys mash potatoes with gravy, some biscuits, and baked beans.

Danny's mouth is watering while he drives back to the motel. The car is full of the good food smells, and when he gets to Hannah's room, he cannot wait to get in and make himself a place to eat. He knocks again, and Hannah plays it safe and asks if it is Danny. He says it is Elvis, and she opens the door. "Of course, I will open the door for Elvis," Hannah tells Danny, and they laugh. "Wow, Dan, that food smells wonderful. A bucket of chicken is perfect. What else did you get?" Hannah asks as she rummages through the bag.

"I didn't get any drinks at the Colonel's 'cause I saw a drink machine right down by the office. I stopped there and got you a Sprite, which is the South's version of 7Up, I hear."

There is a bottle opener screwed tightly to the bathroom door frame, and Hannah opens her Sprite, and she opens Danny's Coke. Hannah had already created a little eating area for them in front of the TV, and they both settle in for an evening of winding down with the TV and maybe, a little conversation. Danny eats and throws away his trash. He then stretches out on Hannah's bed, pulling a pillow out from under the bedspread. He props it up and lays his head back, situating the pillow until it is holding his head in just the right way for maximum simultaneous viewing and comfort.

Hannah goes into the bathroom for a minute or two to wash the chicken off her hands and lips. When she comes out, not more than three minutes later, she finds her man fast asleep in his TV-watching position. She just stands and looks at Danny, much at peace and without his usual drive and passion for life. Hannah thinks she can see what he looked like when Walter would tuck his son into bed after a long day of play. She loves him even more now, getting a shot of excitement about the summer with Danny and how close they will become.

Hannah thinks to herself that she would not feel strange simply sleeping next to Danny. It is the alternative to waking the sleeping boy and asking him to go to his room. Hannah putters around the room a bit, looking in drawers and closets, and then sits in a chair facing the television set. They are in the central time zone, and the nightly news is coming on at ten o'clock. She watches politicians making speeches, stories about babies, shootings, local interest, the weather and then sports, which talks mostly about baseball.

"Hannah, baby. Wake up, Sleeping Beauty," Danny whispers softly to her as he kisses the top of her head. "I'm going to my room now. It's about one in the morning."

"Oh wow! I didn't know I was asleep. Aw, we're both so tired. We should feel good in the morning though. I love you, and I hope you go back to sleep quickly. I know I will," Hannah says with her eyes half open and a sweet smile.

"I love you too. Sleep tight," Danny says and closes the door while walking out into the humid heat of Memphis at the end of May.

After checking out the next morning, Hannah and Danny fill their hungry tummies with eggs, bacon, and biscuits at a restaurant called The Buntyn. Hannah has coffee and Danny drinks hot, black morning tea with honey. It is a wonderful place to start the day and talk about today's map. After much discussion, they both believe they can make the seven hundred or so miles to Amarillo, Texas. They will drive through Arkansas and Oklahoma before they even touch Texas, and then they still have a ways to go before Amarillo. It is a big bite out of the American landscape, but they are very hungry travelers.

As they discuss their friends back in Marigold, the two speak lovingly about Alice and Jeff, and they pray for good and godly decisions to be made, as well as understanding by the Engels. Danny is sad that he will not see their baby, maybe for years. "Sometimes I wonder why I have chosen to go all the way out to California when there is so much work to do right there in Marigold and Appleton. A town is only as good as its inhabitants, and it feels like the Appleton fiber is unraveling from its core." Danny looks out the restaurant window. Hannah rubs his arm and assures him that God has called him to California, and he must trust in what God is telling him. It may not make sense now, but God sees the bigger picture of Danny's life, and He will not lead him astray.

The drive is short to the Lorraine Motel, which gives them both chills and resurrects their broken hearts. It has only been a little over two years since that ugly day in history and one that Danny and Hannah will never forget, as they loved Doctor King's nonviolent approach to racial problems and his passion at the pulpit. Danny and Hannah know that it is, after all, a problem with people's hearts and the good news of Jesus Christ is not brought with a burning cross. It seems so simple, to just judge a person by their character instead of their color, but the poison of racism has been pumping through the veins of the Old South for two plus centuries, and it takes time, intense work and sometimes, life itself to eradicate the cancer. With great embarrassment, the hideous stain has been uncovered, and just like they defeated Adolf Hitler for Europe thirty years ago, the United States is now facing racism head-on, determined to end the madness, even if it takes generations of transfusions.

As the children of southern Ohio leave Tennessee and cross the *muddy* Mississippi River on the Hernando de Soto Bridge into West Memphis, Arkansas, Danny sings the song *Route 66* several times. He focuses on the part of the song that talks about winding from St. Louie, and through Missouri and all the way to Amarillo, where Danny hopes to stop, today, before Hannah reaches over and turns on the radio, only half-jokingly. As Hannah looks for a station, she lands on 1090 and KAAY, the station Danny hoped to hear. They listen to great song after great song, but they did not seem as cool, as underground as the ones Danny heard on his old Admiral radio by his bed. The reason for that is the show he listened to late at night was Beaker Street with a DJ named Clyde Clifford.

KAAY is so powerful, the government used it to broadcast American rock and roll and anti-Castro propaganda into Cuba after the revolution there and during the Bay of Pigs. The music is good, but Hannah and Danny want to try to experience the feel of the South through a radio station. Hannah moves the dial to 1070 and out pops *Didn't I Blow Your Mind* by The Delphonics on WDIA. It is wall-to-wall soul music, just what the doctor ordered. *Turn Back The Hands Of Time*, *Sex Machine*, *Express Yourself*, and the coolest sound Danny has heard since he discovered the Allman Brothers Band.

The very familiar voice of Eric Burden of The Animals is singing a hypnotic song called *Spill the Wine* with a band that is as soulful as you can get. Uniquely, they have incorporated harmonica as part of the horn section. The band behind Eric has a looser, more relaxed feel than James Brown, but their syncopations are dizzying. This sound is not Philly soul, but it has a more earthy sound with Cuban style percussion. Earthy urban is the only description that comes to Danny's mind. As it fades out, the DJ tells his listeners that it is Eric Burden and War. Just fantastic.

After a long morning and a quick lunch in Oklahoma, Hannah looks at the map and announces that they are smack dab in the middle of the lower forty-eight states. Without saying anything, she glances back on the map at Ohio and then quickly looks away. Reminding her of Lot's wife, Hannah knows that if she looks too long, she will get homesick, and that would not benefit her or Danny. The traffic really slows down, as they are on the beginning edge of afternoon business traffic, and then suddenly Danny sees nothing but red taillights and has to stand on his brakes. Danny's protective right arm goes out in front of Hannah, but she slides under it and into the front floor.

While Danny and Hannah sit still on the interstate due to a bad accident about a mile up ahead, their friends in Marigold go about their lives. Knowing Danny would be on his way to California, thus creating a financial shortage, Jeff has resumed his job at Charlie's. He takes steady work and finances more seriously because of the baby he and Alice have accepted. At this point, Alice and Jeff are living at Carl's apartment because he is not there much, and he loves them. The Engels love their daughter, but they were so adamant about an abortion, Alice stormed out no matter the cost.

If Jeff takes advantage of his scholarships, he plans to go to Kenyon, but it is the end of May and he has not decided. This is typical Jeff, and Alice would like to know his plan. The tension in their life together is not slight; Jeff still struggles to accept the fact that he is in a relationship with a female that could continue for the rest of his life. The baby will make the inevitable change of mind and heart a nasty tug of war that cannot end, and as the time of birth gets closer, Jeff's fear grows.

Alice is physically uncomfortable and sad about her family's decision to demand abortion or nothing at all. Jeff stockpiled a great deal of money while playing with Clever Pennies, but he comes nowhere close to equaling that income at Charlie's. Alice does not call her parents, and they do not call Carl's phone. Alice and Jeff love each other, but things have gotten so complicated so quickly that their heads are still spinning. This is not the life that either of them, individually nor together, pictured when they talked about the future. The future seemed so free and attainable. Now, there will be someone else to consider with every decision.

Up the hill and to the right, Barry has not returned, nor has he communicated with his family. Kay rides Precious and spends a lot of time out in the barn with her horse. She stays very somber and has been that way since Christmas when it truly hit home that her brother was gone, and she doesn't even know where. She can hear her mom crying at night, which only makes her sadder and angrier. Kay is old enough to understand why her brother ran away, and she has lost love for her dad, a man she had once adored.

On the other side of Marigold Road, King is working with a new bassist named George Russell. George has played with some great bands in Appleton and is a couple of years older than Jeff and Greg. George is well prepared for their work today, and King is pleased. He knows the Clever Pennies songs as if they are old rock standards, and the cover songs that were on the "to learn" list are all very familiar to George. The booking that is coming up this Saturday is not a concert, per se. It is a three-set corporate gig that will require playing about thirty-five songs, and granted, the band will jam many minutes on Van Morrison's *Gloria* and get the room dancing for nearly half a set with Sly Stone's Thank You *(Falettinme Be Mice Elf Agin)*. With all that Danny brought to Clever Pennies, and as good of a bass player that he had become, George makes this grooving bass part sound as if he had written it.

***

After two tow trucks pass, going fifty miles an hour on the right shoulder of the road, followed by two more Oklahoma City police cars, Interstate 40 finally starts moving again. They are way behind schedule now, and they are hoping to get out of the city traffic soon. It does die down quickly, as city turns to even more ranch land and oil derricks, and Danny *extends* the speed limit as much as he feels comfortable doing.

They have lost at least an hour, putting them in Amarillo at eleven o'clock, barring no other accidents. The sun is directly in front of them on its way to California, and it will remain that way until it says goodnight with a slow descent into its next destination. The terrain is interesting, but after about ten minutes, there is nothing for which to strain one's neck. There are ranches and cattle and wheat fields and ranches and cattle and wheat fields. The giant sun is setting, like a fat man getting into a bathtub, and the bright light casts beautiful and odd shadows on everything.

Danny's sunglasses are barely doing the job of staring down the sun, and Hannah is asleep, with her stationery and pen still in hand. She will send letters written about their trip twice a week until she returns to Marigold, she promises herself. Texas is coming up soon, as they fly past Texola, Oklahoma. Danny's dream of Route 66 has come to fruition with Interstate 40 being sporadic, jumping from the massive four lane highway to sometimes two lanes of the legendary route. There it is! *Welcome to Texas* the sign says, and Danny puffs up a bit with whatever pride a non-prideful person can muster. He is finding it hard to believe that he has driven this far away from Marigold.

Just then, as the sky grows dark, he begins to feel quite insignificant in such a boundless and open area of America. The Panhandle seems small on a map, compared to the rest of Texas, but boundless is the only word the lyricist can think of to describe this area. The sun has disappeared, and Danny sees new kinds of animals in his headlights: skinny dogs with long legs that he imagines are coyote and little creatures that scurry across the road, looking like opossum with a suit of armor.

Danny tunes in a new station on the radio and lands on *Band of Gold* by Freda Payne. Hannah is still asleep, confirming her status by producing a sweet, little girl snore. Danny hears the words to the song on the radio and wonders if he and Hannah will get married. She may get sick of him by the end of the summer and find a new, more stable young man at Cedarville. Maybe he will get tired of her after seeing her every day from morning until night, at least through the summer. *Alright Now* by a new band named Free breaks Danny's train of thought with its great sound and catchy hook.

"I need to stop at a restroom when you can, sweetie." Hannah is awake. "Oh, I love that song. Who is the band, do you know?"

"Their name is Free, and yes, I agree. It is a great song. Did you sleep well, beautiful dreamer?"

"Sort of. I was kind of in and out of consciousness, but I think I went deep for a little while. Hey, there's a gas station that looks open. What time is it?"

"Just after ten; I will stop there and fill up the car." Danny reaches his hand over to Hannah's and lays his palm in her open palm and then mingles his fingers with hers and squeezes. Hannah squeezes back and leans over on Danny's arm while he negotiates getting off Route 66.

After pulling into the first gas station they see, Danny asks the attendant where they are and how far to Amarillo. The teenager tells Danny they are in Groom and Amarillo is about an hour away, give or take. He asks Danny where they are headed, and Danny tells him a bit of the story behind the trip. The boy has heard of the Crusade and asks several questions about the organization and what is happening in California. Hannah soon joins the two and enters the conversation. After introducing themselves, Danny and Hannah tell the sixteen-year-old, named Butch, all about their lives in the church community, as well as their church family back in Marigold. They witness to Butch and in twenty-five minutes of candid and forthright questions and answers, Butch gives his life to Jesus.

Hannah and Danny are ecstatic, and Hannah wants to baptize Butch. She opens the door of the car and reaches in and retrieves her Bible. As Danny is telling Butch about baptism, Hannah quickly turns to Acts 8:34-39 and reads the Spirit-filled text to Butch. Butch begins to cry and pleads to be baptized. Butch runs inside the station and fills a bucket full of water from a hose. "Baptize me, please," Butch implores, and he drops to his knees in front of Danny.

"Dear Lord, like those first disciples who had little training and education, I too am not worthy except that I am filled with the Holy Spirit and directed by the words of Jesus Christ. Butch, do you confess that you are a sinner in need of a savior and that Savior's name is Jesus Christ?"

"Yes."

"And, do you want, with all of your heart and with all of your mind and with all of your soul, to make Jesus Lord of your life and have a relationship with Jesus Christ for the rest of the life, the life the good Lord in heaven gives you?"

"Yes, I do. I really do want to be saved from my sins and follow Jesus."

"Then, as a disciple of the One who saved me, Jesus Christ, I baptize you, Butch Twilley, with Hannah Birdsong as our witness on this blessed evening."

Hannah holds one of her bandanas over Butch's nose and mouth and lays his head back, placing her right hand behind his head as a brace. Danny pours the bucket of water over Butch's head and guides the act by saying it is death to the old Butch. Soaking the top of Butch's gas station shirt, Butch's arms go out straight from his body as if to embrace all of heaven at once while Danny empties the bucket telling Butch that, just like the resurrection of Jesus, he is a new creation. Butch weeps like a baby for minutes, and Danny and Hannah kneel beside him, hugging and petting Butch at this most tender of moments. Butch is finally able to hug back and then he stands up and skips around the parking lot, like a grievous weight has been lifted off his shoulders.

"Can Hannah and I write to you, Butch? It is important for you to find a Bible-strong church and to keep investing in this moment, right here. You are saved now and Satan can never take that away, but that filthy old demon will talk in your ear because he would like nothing more than for you to doubt your salvation. Just remember in John Chapter Ten, I think this is where it is, Jesus says that no one can snatch His sheep out of His hand. Love the Lord now, Butch. Get yourself a Bible and read it every day. The Lord will bless you through His Word. Well, my brother in Christ, we better be going. Do you know of a good motel where we can stay?"

"Uh, yeah, but we have a little ranch house out behind our house where you could stay, if you want. It is not far, and I should close the station now anyway." Danny looks at Hannah with his shoulders up and a look of "what do you think?" on his face. Hannah shrugs, signaling that the decision is Danny's.

"Hannah and I are not married. Will it sleep two separately?"

"Oh yeah. It has four bedrooms. Come on, I would love to say goodbye to y'all in the morning instead of right here. You'd be like that guy Philip, disappearing from the Eunuch, if you go now," Butch says with a laugh.

It is nearing midnight and feeling like Eastern Time more than ever, but Danny and Hannah agree to go to Butch's house. "I'm really whipped, Butch. Will we be able to sleep in a little? Not late, but not early, please."

"Sure 'nuff. Sleep as late as you want. It's pretty quiet back there. Daddy will come here to the station at six, but you shouldn't hear him at all."

"Ok. I'm going to hold you to your Christian word, my new brother. We'll be in our car waiting when you are ready."

"It will just be five minutes max. I don't want Daddy fussin' at me tomorrow when I come in for not closing down correctly."

"Do what you need to do. We'll be fine."

Butch closes out the station and climbs into his 1957 Ford F-100 pickup truck. This old road-warrior has seen plenty of Texas life on the range and is very beat up on the outside, but she purrs like a kitten and the bench seat is black leather, rolled and pleated. After the two vehicles travel a mile down the dusty road that runs perpendicular to the north of Route 66, there is a collection of building silhouettes off to the west dwarfed by the wide-open, starlit night sky. Butch turns his truck toward the buildings and Danny follows, seeing only one light on which illuminates the side of the house that sits in the front of the other structures.

Butch leads the two travelers to their home for the night. He opens the door and flips on the lights. Two yellowish, striped scorpions stand still and face the sound they hear and then run for a safe place to hide. Butch admits it is difficult keeping the little pests out this time of year due to the rising heat. He tells Danny and Hannah to just be sure and wear their shoes whenever they are up walking around tonight. They will be off in some cool hiding place during the day.

This is not comforting news to either of the Ohioans, and Hannah squeezes Danny's arm until he rubs her hand as security. Danny is about as nervous as his loved one, but he will play the knight in armor against the vicious little two-inch foe. Butch shows them their rooms and pulls down the fresh bedding in each to make sure the bed is scorpion-free. They are and he assures them the little critters will not bother them. Even if the worst happens and a striped bark scorpion stings them, they will just need to put some ice on the swelling. It hurts some, but it will go away in a couple of hours.

Wearing their shoes, Danny and Hannah try to relax after Butch leaves, but their eyes are constantly searching. "I have got to get some sleep, my dear," Danny confesses to his partner. "It's gonna be a long drive, and I don't want to be noddin' and drivin'." Danny checks between the couch cushions and finally lays his head on a pillow. Hannah does not want to fall asleep yet and sits dutifully at Danny's feet as a watchman so that her driver can sleep; she can sleep in the car tomorrow.

CHAPTER
TWENTY-TWO

S urviving the threat of scorpion sting and having enjoyed a farm fresh breakfast of steak and eggs served by Butch's mother and one of his two sisters, the two Ohioans have traveled far enough that they are nearly ready to stop for lunch and a little sightseeing in Albuquerque, New Mexico. Danny slept well, and Hannah has been asleep since they left their new convert and his generous and friendly family. The conversion of Butch last night excited the two pilgrims, and they are anxious to apply their love for Jesus to the lost in sunny southern California. Before he left Marigold, Danny had read as many newspapers as he could find at the newsstand that could tell him what life is like in Los Angeles. He found the cultural news to be a bit grim.

It seems as if LSD and Mescaline have not been devastating enough to the teenage mind, harder drugs like heroin and crystal methamphetamine are quickly working their way into hippie life, bringing an even more seedy element to the playground. What was once simply a false feeling of idyllic euphoria has been replaced with sunken eyes and overdoses, but when people become that lost, many times that is where Jesus meets them. The Christian "Awakening" is a witness to the lost coming to Christ in a big way and a reminder that Christ is bigger than any problem.

Hannah is fully awake after a solid three hours of sleep on the uneventful road to Albuquerque. Danny is glad she is awake so that he can bounce his three hours of contemplation and dreams off her, but Hannah is not yet ready to reciprocate deep thought. They are beginning to see sizeable hills that look like mountains off in the distance. The scrubby brush that has dotted the flat floor of the Texas Panhandle and New Mexico east of Albuquerque is beginning to be complimented by the more substantial Ponderosa and Pinyon Pine trees. The unfamiliar landscape is a lovely sight, but the air is not getting any cooler.

The two are hungry, and Hannah sees signs for more and more places to purchase authentic Navajo and Apache pottery and jewelry. They find a perfect diner on Central Avenue in Albuquerque, with a view of the only tall building around, a bank office. Most of the passersby look like anywhere USA, but occasionally a Native American in colorful garb walks by. After a shopping spree, they get back on the road to Flagstaff, Arizona.

Radio disc jockeys are playing a wide array of what has been offered this year by new and established artists: *Bridge Over Troubled Waters* by one of America's very best songwriters, Paul Simon, with his other half Art Garfunkel; *Fire and Rain* by newcomer James Taylor, who got his start through The Beatles's worldwide offer to produce anyone for their new record label Apple Records Corp. *Make Me Smile* by Chicago Transit Authority, who shortened their name to Chicago after threat of a lawsuit, is powerful through Danny's car speakers and *The Rapper* by The Jaggerz is as fun as pop rock music gets.

Cactus is beginning to show up in the landscape, and the scenes outside Danny's car windows are breathtaking. After a pit stop in Gallup, the Ohioans cross the Arizona state line, and the canyons and high ridges are more frequent. The sandy soil is red, and cactus, pine, and scrub offer little shade in the hot sun. They have agreed to try and meet the sunset south of Flagstaff in an enchanted area called Sedona. Danny has heard there is a seventy-foot cross built there, something he would love to see, but the natural, God-given beauty of the red and orange sandstone rock formations at sunset is why they will make a left at Flagstaff.

A quick gas fill-up garners authentic Indian ware next door. Hannah buys a silver and turquoise bracelet and an ornate coffee mug with a funny-looking little Indian playing a recorder while carrying a sack on his back, painted onto the two sides of the mug. After the purchase, Hannah finds out that the character's name is Kokopelli and he represents fertility. That does not necessarily mean babies but a bountiful life. Hannah is not one to be taken in by folklore, so she simply enjoys the art and looks forward to her first cup of coffee in the vessel.

Another couple of hours have passed since Gallup, and they watch closely for signs to Sedona. If they don't get lost or get tangled in a traffic jam, their timing should be just right. The landscape is especially beautiful and so different from Ohio and Marigold Hill that they feel they have landed on a different planet. The temperature is getting hot, making Danny watch the thermostat on his car. He remembers being with his dad on a church trip when the church bus overheated. It was not fun, and Danny has no idea where the next gas station is located, although they are very near Flagstaff.

Just past Canyon Diablo, under a sign announcing how many miles to Sedona, Danny sees an old man sitting beside a car with a flat tire. Danny quickly moves over two lanes to pull off the road and help the old man, who apparently has no spare. The sun is going to set within the hour, but Danny will not leave the old man stranded. Hannah knows her man and this act of selfless kindness is a huge reason why she loves Danny. Hannah knows they will miss the Sedona sunset, but that is the high cost of loving Daniel Mosely and following Jesus Christ.

The old man is hot and tired. Danny checks to make sure the car jack is properly engaged, grabs the tire iron, and takes the tire off the vehicle. Hannah watches Danny talk with the man for a moment and they both start walking toward Danny's big, blue Chrysler. Danny opens the back door for the exhausted gentleman who was very appreciative of Danny's kindness. Danny introduces Mr. Banders to Hannah, and Hannah offers the man a bottle of pop out of the cooler she keeps by her feet. Mr. Banders takes the cool drink without prodding and drinks half of it before he takes a breath.

There is an exit at Winona where they can get the tire repaired. They pull into the station, and the old man gets out. After showing his tire to the attendant, he finds out that the tire cannot be repaired because the hole is on the side of the tire and not the tread. When the man finds out it will be forty-two dollars to buy a new tire, he pleads with the attendant to lower the price. The attendant cannot, but he takes Mr. Banders behind the station, with Danny in tow, and shows the man a pile of used tires. The attendant looks at the size on Mr. Banders' damaged tire and points to the tires that could be replacements.

Danny finds a good one for ten dollars. There is a fifty-cent charge to put the tire on Mr. Banders' rim. While that is going on, Danny, Hannah, and Mr. Banders all go into the restaurant that is attached to the station. Hannah is not hungry but asks for a Pepsi-Cola. Danny echoes Hannah's order, but Mr. Banders will not order. Danny asks his new friend "Do you like cheeseburgers?"

"Oh, no, no, but thank you." Mr. Banders waves off the question, trying to not be embarrassed by the fact that he does not have the money for such a treat.

Hannah turns to the waitress and says, "One cheeseburger with fries for our friend, Mr. Banders, please."

With a huge smile and moist eyes, Mr. Banders thanks the couple and eventually enjoys his meal.

After the filling station feast, the three leave Winona and head east to whatever exit will allow them to journey back to the ailing car, sitting on a jack with only three tires. Canyon Diablo allows them to return to their western route, and they soon stop to put the used tire on the old man's car. There is still a sliver of sun straight ahead producing just enough light for Danny's project. It is Mountain Time, and both Danny and Hannah are very tired after their not-so-peaceful night at Butch's. Danny tugs at each lug to make certain each is snug and will not ring off. Hannah watches Danny through the windshield as Danny is in conversation with Mr. Banders. He puts the man's car tools back into his trunk but does not close the trunk and apparently, asks Mr. Banders to leave the truck lid up.

Danny walks back to his trunk, where he had put Mr. Banders' new used tire before leaving the Winona filling station and walks past Hannah's window back toward Mr. Banders. Danny reaches Mr. Banders' trunk and Hannah sees Danny throw another tire in and close the lid. Mr. Banders is waving his hands, as if to say no, and starts to open his trunk again. Danny hugs Mr. Banders around the shoulders and trots back to his car where Hannah sits with tears on her cheeks. "Did you buy him a spare?"

"I did."

"I love you, Danny."

"I love you, too."

The two decide that their day has been long enough and head straight for a motel in Flagstaff for a good night's sleep, foregoing the beauty of Sedona. Tomorrow will be their day to enjoy the Grand Canyon, and they want to be rested so that they can do as much walking as their young legs can handle.

The following morning, the sky is clear on this twenty-eighth day of May, and the air is comparatively cool at seven thousand feet. While walking in the town, looking for a restaurant, they notice that Flagstaff has seen its better days. Except for two or three, most of the buildings look as if they have replaced the previous buildings that suited the environment. Mundane, sufficient facades cover many of the older buildings that have survived demolition and nondescript rectangle boxes have replaced what was probably picturesque but not modern enough places of business.

However, one look north, and the awesome beauty of Humphrey's Peak takes your breath away, and it is that direction the Ohioans will travel today. The restaurant they choose is of no significance, and the menu offers nothing unique, but they are excited to see one of God's greatest natural wonders. They lean toward driving to Williams and taking the train, but the waitress favorably describes the scenic drive up Route 180 that she often takes when she is not working, and the pilgrims are sold. They will drive to the South Rim of the Grand Canyon, but first, they are told to stop at the Museum of Northern Arizona. It is there, they are told by their most informative waitress, that the easterners will get the real story of this magnificent part of the world.

After showering and checking out of their rooms, Danny and Hannah get into the car and head toward Route 180 and the South Rim of The Grand Canyon.

The ride is not so interesting. It is scenic and very different from southern Ohio, but the ponderosa pines line each side of the road, which block the view of any snow-topped mountains. Every so often, the pines suddenly stop and there is an immense clearing with the San Francisco Peaks looming in the distance. It is all very gorgeous, and it is a perfectly beautiful day, but Danny and Hannah are hoping for sensory overload when they gaze upon the Grand Canyon.

On the way, Danny fiddles with the radio until he tunes into a station that is playing Norman Greenbaum's *Spirit in the Sky*. On cue, Danny recites his disdain for the lyrics of the song, as Hannah looks out the window and mimics every word that is flowing from Danny's mouth. "I don't know if I've said this before, but I love the sound of this song, but it is so wrong theologically. 'I'm not a sinner'? 'I've never sinned'? Who does he think he is, Jesus?" Hannah squeaks out a "No kidding," and the song rocks on until Van Morrison takes over the playlist with *And It Stoned Me*.

There is a line at the entrance to the South Rim and the temperature has reached eighty-four degrees, just before noon. It is very dry, with the humidity at about fifteen percent and Hannah decides to buy them each a canteen for water at the gift shop. The canteens are not true hiker or camper quality, but she does not want to invest that much, anyway. She fills them with cool water from the fountain, and they both take long drinks and re-fill before they venture out.

The canyon is glorious, and their heart rates may have risen slightly, satisfying their sensory overload expectation. It is truly magnificent and, to be very cliché, breathtaking. The day is refreshing and scenic, but by three o'clock, Hannah and Danny are hungry and their feet hurt. After finding a table in a restaurant, Danny finally breaks the silence. "I don't want to rain on the parade, but I am really itching to get to L.A."

Hannah does not say anything at first. "Me too." Their food comes, and they quietly eat while looking out the window.

"Would you like to leave soon, little darlin'?" Danny says in his best John Wayne voice.

Without hesitation, Hannah replies, "I love it here, and I am very happy we decided to make a point of coming, but my feet hurt and if you would like to leave, I am ready." They finish up their late lunch and walk to their car. It's at least a three-hour drive to Williams, which would put them back on I40 West at around six thirty or so. Danny believes he can make Needles, California tonight, where they can get a good night's sleep before they make their way across the Mojave Desert and on to Los Angeles.

They may need to spend their first night in Los Angeles at a motel because Danny told Neal, his Hollywood Pres connection, that he and Hannah would probably sightsee through the West and arrive on Saturday. In his mind, Danny decides to cross that bridge later. Right now, he has a long drive from the South Rim to Interstate 40 and west to Needles. So, he finds a friendly radio station that is playing country music. Buck Owens, to be exact, lighting up the two tired travelers with his hit *I've Got a Tiger by the Tail.*

They stop for dinner in Kingman and then drive some more. It is not very late, but Needles will be their stop so that they can get the rest and sleep they need for their trip's final destination. It is exciting to think about. Neal will hopefully be able to get them into Danny's apartment near Hollywood so that they can unpack and meet some people at the church. Hannah and Danny are very eager to start doing some Kingdom work, and they know there is plenty to do.

The sun has set, and it is very warm outside, even for this time of night. Needles is not far, and Danny will be sure to have all his fluids looked at when he fills the car up with gas in the morning. The Mohave Desert area could sit at over one hundred degrees for most of their drive tomorrow, and the last thing Danny wants to do is break down in that kind of heat. Danny sees a sign for the Colorado River, and there it is. As soon as they cross that wild river, they are welcomed to San Bernadino County, California, the Pacific Time Zone, and both Danny and Hannah give out a loud "Ya-hoo!"

A short ways up the road is a funny little booth where they have to stop. It is a California Agricultural Inspection Station, and Danny is asked if he has any produce not found in California that might infest local agriculture. Hannah and Danny graciously open their cooler and trunk to prove they are clean. The inspector thanks them and flags them on. "That was strange. They must really have a problem with their fruits and vegetables, I guess," Danny says with a half grin but some sincerity.

Needles is coming up, and they are glad. While in Kingman, they were told that the Mojave will be very hot at midday, and they should drive either early morning or after sunset. So, with that bit of no-nonsense information, Danny and Hannah have decided to leave at nine o'clock Pacific Time. After all, tomorrow will be only the fifth day since they left their lifelong Eastern Time Zone, still making nine in the morning in Needles a very comfortable noon for the sleep habits of the two Ohioans.

Barstow is two hours from Needles and where Danny will catch Route 15 headed south toward Los Angeles. Just talking about their day tomorrow has generated a nervous energy in Danny, and Hannah wonders if he will sleep well tonight. They leave the interstate and follow Route 66, or West Broadway in Needles, where they easily find a beautiful and large inn named Overland Motel. Both young adults can see from the street that it has a pool and restaurant, the latter making it the perfect stop as they can more easily make their exit in the morning. "I am going swimming tonight." Danny says to the world with just a hint of defiance. "Would you, please, join me for a nighttime dip, my sweet?" Danny saw the pool, and it called him like the Sirens in Homer's Odyssey. After a hot and dusty day at the South Rim followed by a long drive, his body was screaming for some TLC.

"Oh, wow! I think that would feel wonderful! Good idea, Dan. I kinda like hangin' out with you anyway."

Danny pulls into the well-lit office area where business is done for the giant trove of rooms; he rents two near the pool. They are in their swimming suits and in the water within fifteen minutes, and the feeling is nearly medicinal. The two young Christians just lie back, covering everything but their heads with water, and stare up at the stars. It is bliss and could not have been timed any better. They both know that God is providing some rest and peace before they start their final leg of their journey tomorrow.

"I am going to call Mom when I get back to my room," Hannah says in a quiet voice.

"That's a good idea, and please tell them I said hello and I miss them." Neither one of them turns their head when speaking, but Hannah takes Danny's hand in hers and that is how they relax for five minutes. "I'm actually getting sleepy." Danny, in a whisper, breaks the silence.

"Oh, that is good news. You really need to sleep well tonight and sleep as late as your body tells you."

"Yeah, I'm excited though. It is really hard to believe it is finally here. I do wish I could share it with Daddy."

"I know you do. What a great man he was, and you are a strong, articulate, and kind product of his loving care. He was always proud of you, and I am thankful I know you and knew him."

Danny pulls Hannah over to him and kisses her gently as a thank you for her kind words. She lays her head on his bare chest, and they stay that way for another five minutes before Hannah says it is time she call home. The rooms are ground floor and pool-side, and Danny walks his love to her sliding door and asks her to stop by after she talks to her mom. Hannah promises and their fingertips slide out of each other's grasp. This is a good love, God-ordained. After she finishes her call to a thankful family, Hannah's visit to Danny's room is short, as he has already fallen asleep and she does not want to wake him.

Morning comes quickly, and Danny is refreshed. He takes his car for a fill-up and check-up and he purchases cooler treats and drinks for Hannah. Danny buys a map of Los Angeles and talks about their destination with the attendant, who gives Danny a few tips on the trip there. The attendant has never been to Hollywood, but he has gone to a couple of Dodgers games. Danny tells him he is a Reds fan and looks forward to seeing a Reds vs. Dodgers game in Dodgers Stadium. They part with a handshake and a wave, and Danny returns to the motel. Hannah is sitting out by the pool when Danny arrives, but quickly returns to her room and grabs her bag.

They are in the car and back on the interstate in minutes, and they get their first daylight look at their surroundings. Bleak but beautiful is Hannah's description, and Danny does not try to improve on such a perfect summary. There is nothing but scrubby bushes throughout a very flat desert, with mountain ranges off in the distance, and this is their panorama for the two hours through the south end of the Mojave. They stop in Barstow to unleash their recycled coffee but quickly get back on the road and find Interstate 15 South that will take them to Interstate 10 West and the 101 to Hollywood.

As the traffic gets heavier, the AM radio stations fill the dial with every kind of music. Sinatra, Sonny & Cher, Stevie Wonder, Bach, Little Richard, James Taylor, The Temptations, Merle Haggard, Van Morrison, Ray Charles, Kris Kristofferson, Tammy Wynette, Dylan. Hannah stops scrolling the airwaves when the antenna finds the signal of a station that is playing a song called *The Blood Will Never Lose Its Power*, featuring lush harmonies and a prominent bass guitar part that catches Danny's ear. The lyrics are deeply spiritual and speak of Jesus, making Hannah and Danny look at each other with open mouths. They have heard bluegrass and country religious music on the radio in the Ohio hills, but this was soulful, rockin' blues with an incredible melody, and on a Friday.

It is music bliss for Hannah and Danny as the excitement level is going through the roof. Danny is having a hard time driving because he wants to sightsee at the same time. Just the highway signs are exciting, with so many familiar names and locations, recalling a Johnny Carson skit that makes them laugh out loud. Hannah points out the Hollywood Freeway, and Danny moves over to head toward their destination. This is it, the last leg. They will be on the west coast, and Danny will get to see if his Marigold style of Christian songwriting will reach the hearts and minds of the many big city lost.

The Santa Monica Mountains, sprouting beautiful homes that seem to all be painted white, are everything the two pictured. It is three o'clock on a Friday, and the traffic is heavy, as well as the smog which produces a yellowish haze throughout. Exit 8C should put them about a block away from the church where they will try to contact Neil. They pass Exit A and Exit B and just before they take Exit C, they look to the right, and there is the famous Hollywood Sign that has become an icon for the movie industry and the town.

Instead of delight, however, their hearts are filled with a woe that they feel in their guts. The icon is unkempt, falling apart and missing chunks of the huge letters that once stood stately along the shape of the hill, according to the pictures they have seen. Hannah and Danny wonder out loud if the deterioration is an omen or a prosopopoeia of the life below, which returns their minds to the reason why they are there in the first place.

The exit is long and takes them to North Gower Street. Following Neil's directions, Danny turns left and drives underneath the Freeway on the divided street, and as soon as they come out from under the eastbound Freeway above, there is First Presbyterian Church of Hollywood. It is a magnificent building, and again Danny has a hard time watching the road as his eyes gaze up at the stately tower that lifts the cross of Christ high above North Gower Street and Carlos Avenue. Danny turns left, again onto Carlos Avenue, drives just past the church, and finds a place to turn around so that he can pull right up in front of the place that he and Hannah will call their church for the summer.

"Danny?" a male voice from behind startles the Ohioans. They turn around quickly and there stands a young man, maybe twenty-six years old, with dark, wavy hair and a mustache. "Hello, I'm Neil. I was just picking up some flyers to hand out at the coffeehouse tonight and on the streets tomorrow morning. I saw your car with Ohio plates and just kinda guessed that the two people gawking like they've never been here are my new friends."

"Yeah, Neil, you guessed correctly. It's great to put a face to your handwriting. This is my girlfriend Hannah, and yes, we just got here. I was going to go inside and call you since I made it sound like we weren't going to be here until tomorrow, but now I don't need to worry about that. Very cool how God works, isn't it?"

"Indeed, it is, my friends." Neil says as he gives Danny and Hannah welcoming hugs.

"Do we need to get rooms tonight, or is the apartment ready?" Danny asks Neil while the three stand at the concrete corner in the heat of the southern California afternoon sunshine.

"I think you can get into the apartment tonight, but come on in the church with me while I get my flyers. I'll introduce you two to whoever is in there this time of day. Probably just some volunteers and Marjorie, I would imagine. She knows everything about First Pres, and I know she would like to meet you. I have mentioned you to her already. You know, that you were going to help out and work with us while you go to school. Come on in."

Neil leads Hannah and Danny into the building and shows them the incredible sanctuary with its huge organ pipes scaling the walls behind the staging area. Then, over to the office, where Marjorie sits behind her desk, Danny and Hannah immediately find out that she has boundless energy and a smile that could illuminate the Hollywood Sign. Marjorie says hello to Neil and hands him his flyers while she welcomes the newcomers. She asks Neil if he is taking them to the apartment tonight and invites Hannah and Danny to the Salt Company coffeehouse for some great music and fellowship, if they are not too tired. Danny and Hannah look at each other trying to quickly discern the other's facial expressions, and then Danny looks at Marjorie and tells her that they would have to see how they feel after getting settled. Marjorie laughs, seeing the fatigue in their eyes and reminds them that, if they miss tonight, Salt will be open tomorrow night too.

The three leave the building and return to the sidewalk next to Danny's car. "I think we can get into the apartment now. I'll be on my Vespa, so just follow me," Neil tells the tired travelers. They make a left onto N. Gower Street and drive about four blocks, crossing Hollywood Boulevard to Selma Avenue. They make another left and go up half a block. On the right is a very California-looking building that is in a "U" shape with a concrete walkway up the middle. Danny parks on the street and follows Neil, who has the apartment key. There are only three apartments on each of the three sides of the "U," and Danny's apartment is all the way back and on the right side of the three apartments at the bottom of the "U".

Neil puts the key into the lock and turns it. "They were supposed to clean this, this week. We'll soon find out." The three walk in and find a clean and naturally well-lit living room with an open kitchen to the left and a short hallway down the middle leading to a nice-sized bathroom on the right. A bedroom door is open at the end of the hall and sunlight from the French doors on the very back wall, streams into the room. The French doors lead to a small patio that is incased by decorative block and a gate that locks. It appears safe enough and seems to be an inviting area where one might sip their morning tea and read or do homework. This place will be Hannah's home for the summer and Danny's for the next four years, until he finishes his studies at Biola.

After Danny spends the next morning working the kinks out of his back from sleeping on the living room floor, he and Hannah spend the rest of Saturday going to thrift stores, looking for various furniture pieces. They find a five-drawer chest of drawers for the bedroom and a couch, chair, and center table for the living room. Danny will get the top two drawers in the bedroom, and the living room couch was picked specifically to be his bed for the summer.

They find a Safeway grocery store where they stock up on food and dish cloths. The apartment furnishes silverware, a can opener, pots and pans, and a heavily used coffee percolator, but they find some glassware and buy four milk glasses and four mugs for their coffee and tea. Danny did not see a tea pot, but he will settle for hot water from a pot for now, unless one is hiding somewhere on the shelves. Danny is not exactly sure how he will get the furniture to the apartment, but he believes Neil will know where there is a truck. Neil just seems like the guy who can pull things together.

After shopping, Hannah and Danny use their new products to take showers, and Hannah fixes them a healthy dinner consisting of baked chicken, fresh fruit, and a salad. It is six o'clock, and they are refreshed and excited to go to the Salt Company coffeehouse and see in real life what Danny has been reading about for the past year. Of course, Danny relayed every story he could remember to Hannah on their drive from Ohio, so it is fresh in her mind as well.

The Ohioans walk the five blocks to the church and find the coffeehouse is packed and busy. They are warmly greeted at the door downstairs and are told to just follow the music, and they do. Sweet harmonies and rock and roll guitars supporting the good news of Jesus are on the menu as they walk upstairs and into the coffeehouse. Danny's heart starts racing while wondering if he will ever get a chance to play in the band or on that stage. There is no place to sit, but Hannah sees Neil across the room at a table with friends.

Danny and Hannah do not try to get Neil's attention as he seems to be deep in conversation. It is not long before Neil sees the two, and they watch him get up from his seat and come over to where they are standing. "Wow, I am so glad you came!" Neil shouts over the music.

"We're glad to be here, Neil. This is far out!" Danny replies without too much conversation. He is not exactly sure what to say because Danny and Hannah have been leading their youth for a couple of years in a similar way. This scenario was not foreign, but he had never seen it so robust and active.

People are squeezing by and bumping the three, but there is no aggression about their actions, only effervescence. The lyrics that the band is singing are unashamedly about Jesus and what He has done in their lives and what He can do for the listener. For whatever reason, Danny leans over to Neil and nearly yells his question "When do we get to work?"

The question seems too professional-sounding to Danny as soon as it leaves his lips, but Neil did not hesitate to lean his head back to Danny's ear and say, "We are working – right now."

CHAPTER
TWENTY-THREE

The summer of 1970 is non-stop for Danny and Hannah, and it is a time that initiates much growth in their relationship, with each other and Christ. Working together and apart only strengthens them, as they help the many lost hippies and street people of the day. There are the fun days at Venice Beach and witnessing the ocean baptisms at Newport Beach's Pirate's Cove, but the hard nights on Hollywood Boulevard, talking someone down from a bad acid trip or simply being a lap on which a weary head can rest or cry on, are, in many ways, more satisfying.

First Pres and various evangelicals own several houses throughout Los Angeles where junkies, trippers, runaways, prostitutes, and searchers come to spend the night. The needy receive food and comfort and the good news about a way of living that answers many of the questions they are asking. Some people quickly, or eventually, hear what is being said and turn to Jesus for help, while others return to the lives they have learned to endure and, in some cases, enjoy. They wake up each day and dive right back into the "pond of despair" of which they are so familiar. Most are thankful for their caretakers, and their gratitude is always directed right back to the One who provided the healing salve of the blood of Jesus.

Some nights are quieter than others and some are an ungodly hell, with people writhing in unnatural pain as the dissipating heroin clings to their veins and their souls. To Danny, they remind him of his dad's last couple of months before the Lord removed his earthly shackles. Of course, neither Hannah nor Danny has ever seen anything like this kind of self-inflicted woe on such a large scale. The flow seems to be endless, with familiar and new faces every night. The word was out, that there was comfort at these houses, and the hosts stand with open arms.

When in downtown Appleton, Hannah's mom would always point out the lone junkie that would roam the streets and make sure her daughter knew what caused the man's troubles. Hannah's father and his friends had many stories about their war buddies tasting evil in Asia, and the white powder did soothe their physical pain and mental torment, but only for a short time until the poppy grew thorns. Danny and Hannah know that the good Lord has placed them here, in Los Angeles, and they look to Him for the strength it takes to help their fellow humans, their fellow sinners. It is power draining, reminding them of Mark 5:30 when the bleeding woman simply touched the robe of Jesus, and He immediately felt a portion of His power drain from Him.

The Appleton junkie was one of those war casualties. Before he went off to the East, he was becoming a gifted watchmaker with steady hands, able to place the smallest of gear or jewel in its place inside the casing so that the timepiece provided accurate time for its owner. While cleaning up Japan at the end of the war, he became friendly with some of the locals who had potions that brought him instant euphoria. It was something he needed, and he became consumed with the faux bliss and hated the feeling of real life. His addiction destroyed nerve endings and synapse paths until he could not stop shaking.

With all the opportunities laid before them, the summer moves along very quickly. Danny has been able to play a few of his songs at The Salt Company on off nights and was asked to sit in on bass on one occasion. On the last Sunday before Hannah is to leave, the Cincinnati Reds are playing a double-header at Dodger Stadium, and Danny buys two tickets. The Reds have been playing really well this year, especially compared to last year, when their pitching staff left little to be desired. Danny and Hannah want to see their favorite players beat the Dodgers. Rose, Bench, Concepcion, and Perez are all outstanding players, but the Dodgers are not far behind in the standings, so these games will surely be exciting.

Game day is another beautiful day in southern California, except for the smog, which is thick as dust. Danny and Hannah arrive at the field and have prepared to buy some Reds trinkets, although they have so much already; they actually buy a few Dodger items. They find their seats along the third base line where they can clearly see the great Maury Wills at shortstop for the Dodgers, and that is exciting enough, but they wear their Reds hats proudly.

Neither fan was able to see a game at the new Riverfront Stadium before leaving for California because the first part of the season was played at the old Crosley Field where The Beatles played a concert four years earlier. It was not until the end of this past June that the Reds played the Braves at their new field, but Hannah and Danny were deep into introducing people to Jesus in Dodgerville by that time.

The day was a win, but the Reds lost both games miserably. The Dodgers are so far ahead by the seventh inning of game two that the sojourners gather their programs and trinkets and venture back to Selma Avenue before the start of the eighth inning. Their trip back to the apartment provides time to reflect on this being summer's end and time for both Hannah and Danny to prepare for school. They have tried very hard not to dwell on this day, with some success, but last night, Hannah had to ruminate as she packed her bag. The reality of leaving in the morning and the meaningful, servant life they have followed together brought recalcitrant tears to Hannah while Danny was at the grocery store. Danny has just buried his dread in his work, forcing First Pres to suggest he slow down and take a break. The baseball game was the result.

Though their last night together compounds their desire to be intimate, they warrior through the temptation with only snuggling each other in front of the TV. The two Christians successfully remain virgins, although the writing on the wall was clear as they became more comfortable with each other and their arrangement, as adults and partners without parental supervision. God has a way of saving the day, though, and they know that it is good that one of them leaves before the overwhelming and natural temptation to make love turns to sin. They hold tight to the supernatural.

The next morning, it is a quiet drive to LAX, but after they park, Danny holds Hannah's hand as they walk through the terminal. There had just been a serious plane mishap in San Francisco when a Pan Am flight had to make an emergency landing, but Hannah is not scared and looks forward to seeing the earth from way up there. They are a little early, so they stop and get something to eat and talk about their summer and the year that is ahead of them. Danny looks forward to getting mail from Hannah but confesses that he may not write back that often. He is hoping to be very busy with school and continuing his work with the people on the street but declares that he is not one to correspond in any prolific way.

The two pilgrims hear the boarding announcement over the airport loudspeaker and quickly toss the meals they did not eat into the trash.

Danny grabs Hannah's bag, and they walk just about fifty yards down the corridor. Hannah shows her ticket to the uniformed woman at the gate and then, after she is approved for boarding, turns around and steps out of line while pulling Danny's arm toward her.

Hannah stands still and looks up into Danny's eyes. "I believe in you, Daniel Wayne Mosely. Our Lord God is using you in a mighty way, and I will never keep you from the work He has for you. Please, don't you ever forget that I love you deeply and sincerely. I have no idea what the future holds, and I won't even speak it, but I will always keep you in my heart and miles and months will not change that. Let's both just open ourselves completely to the Lord's calling, and if He wants us to be together through the rest of our lives, then there is nothing in this world that will keep us apart. Anyway, how much better will our lives be with His blessing rather than trying to make something work that wasn't His plan? I need to board, Dan-my-man. I love you."

A tight and feeble voice, broken with the passion of the moment, exposes Danny's heart as he hugs Hannah tightly. He buries his face in her hair. "I love you too, and I will miss you so much." With mutually watery eyes and quivering lips, Hannah smiles, touches Danny's wet cheek, takes her bag from Danny's shaking hand, and walks toward the plane, turning and waving just before she disappears.

As usual, Danny makes himself busy through the rest of the day, visiting the church to accept any needs that must be met and a bus ride to Biola for last minute familiarization. It is late afternoon before Danny returns to his apartment, and for the first time, he feels strangely vulnerable. The sun has passed over his dwelling now, and he turns on the radio to hopefully get his mind off of the quiet loneliness that hovers inside his home. Danny lies down on the couch that has been his bed for the past two and half months and drifts into a sleep full of images as the radio station is playing music from the forties and fifties.

An hour or so later, Danny slowly wakes without opening his eyes. Perry Como is crooning a song followed by Jo Stafford singing *You Belong to Me*. Miss Stafford's song tugs unfairly at Danny's guarded heart, but God chips away the wall when Danny hears the lyrics of the next song. It is the song Walter Mosely sang to his precious boy throughout his childhood, and Danny no longer hears Al Martino's voice on the radio, but his dad's. Without any hesitation or imagery, Danny's dam of heartache bursts into rivers of tears, and with no one to witness or interrupt his grief, he stays that way for a good thirty minutes.

Wasted, Danny cries out to God, asking for mercy and strength and to not let the loneliness and heartache of missing his dad and his best friend steer his mind into places it should not go. Danny knows that Satan loves to whisper in his ear when he gets weak, but Creator God never lets the rebel angel sift His chosen soldier. However, this is God's apt, providential time and unimpeachable way to break down the wall that Danny has built around his heart. Full worship of God is clear in Exodus 20; there must be no other gods, and we must not put any idols before Him, and that includes Danny's dad. That wall, the one that has been protecting cherished memories and keeping out the pain of great loss, has to come a-tumblin' down.

Stone by stone, Danny's load lightens, as if he just dropped at the cross of Jesus, every worldly possession and emotion he had been carrying around for almost a year. When he read *The Pilgrim's Progress* at ten years old, Danny did not understand why it took Christian a prolonged amount of time and many events to lose his worldly trappings at the cross, after having entered the gate so long before. Now, he looks back and realizes that the sanctifying walk with Jesus is lifelong, and it is clear to him that he needs to make that trip to the cross often, if not every day, because Jesus does not want us to carry the weight. The phone on the kitchen wall rings, and it is Hannah letting Danny know that she has arrived home safely and that she loves and misses him. Her voice is soothing to Danny, but he is able to hang up the phone without hesitation, once the short-but-expensive conversation ended.

Danny is now free to do The Father's work without worldly restraint. The first thing he does is head to the coffeehouse where he hopes to find Neil or someone else who will enjoy going down to Hollywood and Vine. Danny feels a great need and an even greater strength to help the lost tonight. Once Danny reaches the coffeehouse, he listens to the singer/guitarist for a short time while thumbing through a *Right On!* Newspaper, and he says hello to a few friends he has made over the summer.

Everyone asks about Hannah, but no one is eager to go with Danny. So, he decides to visit His Place, owned by a pastor named Arthur, with the serendipitous last name of Blessitt. This devout man carries a huge cross over his shoulder while walking the streets. This "City of Angels," where Danny will live for at least the next four years, is surely not Appleton.

As Danny walks down the stairs, coming up at the same time climbs someone with whom Danny and Hannah enjoyed several outings from afar. Danny puts his hand out to the very large young man and introduces himself. The young man smiles broadly and tells Danny his name is Israel Jones, but everyone calls him "Tippy-toes." Danny's face immediately twists into a furrowed human question mark, subconsciously wondering why someone so large, as big as any middle linebacker he has ever seen, would be called Tippy-toes. Tippy-toes just laughs out loud and tells Danny that his facial expression is the look he always gets when he introduces himself.

"Where are you going, Danny? Things are going to get rollin' upstairs soon."

"Well, Tippy-toes, God has laid on my heart a huge desire to minister to and evangelize the lost down on Hollywood and Vine tonight. When God is speaking this clearly, His direction is impossible to confuse, refuse, or ignore."

"Hey, cool! May I go with you, my brother?"

"You're literally a godsend, sir. I would love it if we went together to fight ol' Satan. He might just be scared of you," Danny says with a grin.

"Nah, that rascal would make mincemeat out of me if I didn't have Jesus right there with me, fighting my fight."

"Amen to that."

The two divulge their backgrounds to each other as they walk into the heart of Hollywood, contributing to a couple of beggar pots along the way. Tippy-toes is from Macon, Georgia, and he played high school football until he bent his knee backwards. He always caps that story with "you should have seen the other guy." While he was out of commission and on crutches, he had the time to go with some friends to a church, and on the second visit, decided to hand his life over to Jesus. He jokes that it took three men to immerse him in the Ocmulgee River and bring him back up. He got his nickname from an opposing quarterback who told the school paper that Israel must sneak up on quarterbacks on his tippy toes because you never hear or see him coming until you are flat on your back.

Hearing that Tippy-toes is from Macon, Danny quizzes him about The Allman Brothers Band. Tippy-toes tells a story of hearing them play a year ago, when he was home, at a park called Central City Park. They had two great guitarists and two great drummers, and the lead singer was very bluesy and powerful. Their songs could go on for fifteen or twenty minutes, but it never got boring. At least when he heard them, they didn't.

His sister would go to an old downtown bar called Grant's Lounge where she would see different members of the Allmans come in and jam with whatever band was playing that night. She would talk about them all the time. Danny shakes his head in agreement the whole time Tippy-toes is telling his story and interjects his tale of when Jeff brought the album to his house. They agree that there is something very special about that group of musicians.

Being refreshed and renewed, Danny feels a new commitment to his mission. Tippy-toes seems to enjoy the task at hand as well, and together, they bring God's word to The Strip in a dynamic way. They get to the hearts of several people and escort or direct two or three strung-out hippies to a CWLF house for some food and comfort for the night. Sometimes, the Word of God lands on fertile soil, and Danny gets to see a familiar, formerly distraught face, restored with the hope of Jesus. Mostly, though, he never sees the person again. Both Tippy-toes and Danny know that they are to only plant the seed and help water and leave the rest to God.

They run into a large group of excited people who are coming from an entertainment venue named The Troubadour. Tippy-toes remembers that someone named Elvis Jones is or was playing there all week. Neither one of the missionaries had ever heard of Elvis Jones, but they deduced that he must be extraordinarily talented to do so well at one of the better venues in Los Angeles. They will have to look at the newspaper tomorrow morning to see if there is any information. Tippy-toes hopes he is family, having the same last name.

A young female is lying in an alley off Hollywood Boulevard and when Danny and Tippy find her, she is out cold. They check to see if she is breathing and if she has a pulse. Both checks produce positive results, so they sit her up as straight as possible against the wall of the building behind her. She is limp, but Tippy-toes flips her palms with his middle finger that is positioned by his thumb. She moans and groans and slurs out, "Stah – Stop it!" Tippy-toes knows not to stop or else she will fall right back into her sleep state. "Damn it, I said to stop it. That duzzunt fill vay goo!"

Danny holds back a chuckle and then asks the girl what her name is. "Go away! I'm sleeping!" Danny asks her name again, and her two eyelids open, exposing two crossed eyes.

"Come on, we want you to walk with us," Tippy-toes says to the girl as he lifts her from her seated position with ease. She does not fight but rests on Tippy-toes' large arm that is firmly around her tiny waist, holding her up. When they shuffle out of the alley, the bright lights of a passing car make the girl squint and feel pain, but the shock gets her blood flowing. So much so, that she pushes Tippy-toes' massive arm away from her waist and stands, with wobbly knees, in front of Danny and Tippy with her hands on her hips and arms akimbo.

"Who are you jerks?" she utters with some strength and clarity.

"I'm Danny, and this is Tippy-toes, and we found you passed-out in that alley. We couldn't just let you lay, er . . . lie there."

"You're such a dumbass. I have slept in that alley many nights. That is why I am there, because no one bothers me, until you two idiots, that is."

"Are you hungry, Miss?" Tippy-toes tries to change the subject to something they all have in common, but the girl flips them the bird and starts heading down Hollywood Boulevard until her knees buckle, and she falls sideways into some parked cars.

Danny and Tippy-toes quickly walk to her and help her up. "Please have something to eat with us, OK?" Danny asks.

"Will you leave me alone if I do?"

"Yes, sure," Danny responds.

"Ok, OK. Some food would not be a bad idea, but then you have got to go. Both of you!" Her cross-eyed glare broadens from Danny to include Tippy-toes too. Both the boys shake their heads profusely in the positive, making sure the girl understands they agree with her rules.

The three soon find a diner, go inside the air-conditioned building, and sit at a booth. A peppy, gum-chewing waitress comes to their table and asks the three what they would like to drink. They all order Pepsi-Colas and then sit quietly for a moment, waiting for their drinks and just taking a break.

Danny sits up a little. "What do you think you would like to eat, Miss?"

"I don't know yet. I don't have any money anyway. Are you two paying, since you brought me here and all?"

"Of course, Miss," Danny says. "Get whatever you want. We've got the bill." Tippy-toes shakes his head in agreement.

"I'm going to the restroom. Please don't follow me in there."

"Miss, we're not forcing you to be here with us, we just want to help you out," Tippy-toes blurts out before the girl climbs out of her booth bench and disappears into the door labeled "Ladies."

"Man, she is so messed up," Danny says. "I hope she doesn't use while she's in there, man. Please pray with me that God will work through us to help her." Tippy-toes lowers his head, as does Danny, puts his big hand on Danny's right shoulder, and reaches out to the God of the universe for help and strength. They ask that God would open the young girl's heart and eyes and cut through her drug-muddled mind so that she will see His love for her. That she will allow Him to heal her and become part of His Kingdom.

"Whaddya guys doing? Having a huddle to see who jumps me first?"

"Um, not sure what you mean, Miss. We just couldn't stand seeing you sprawled out unconscious in a dark, dirty alley," Danny speaks directly, in his naturally calming voice, to the girl who seems to have washed up a bit in the restroom. "We just wanted to see if we could help you get some food and wonder if you have a place to stay. If you don't, we know of some really safe and comfortable places where you can get a good night's sleep and wake up to quiet and breakfast, if you want."

"How 'bout birds chirping and crap like that? Give me a break, man. You're some weird-ass guy."

"Well, I don't mean to be weird. It's OK to care about people, and I care about you, that's all."

The waitress delivers the food, and the girl sits and picks at it, taking small bites. The three are quiet until Danny finally asks the girl what her name is. "Julie," she says. Somehow, Danny and Tippy-toes know that that is not their guest's name, but they go with it.

"So, Julie, are you from L.A.?" Tippy-toes asks.

"Nope," she says with a mouthful of food, her bites getting larger with her stomach.

"Are you going to school here?"

"I have no money, idiot. How would I do that?"

"There are scholarships and that sort of thing. If you want to go, there are ways."

"Look, you guys shoveled me up out of an alley. How well do you think I would do in school? I have a little problem, and it won't go away, so sitting in classes would not be the best use of my time."

"If you don't mind my asking, how bad is your problem?" Danny asks.

"Again, you found me passed out in a dirty, stinky, rat-infested alley. You figure it out, clown."

"Yeah, OK. I get it. Don't you want to quit?"

"Buddy, look. You're a cute little guy, probably from some sappy little town in the Midwest. Don't you want to quit being like that? I ought to take you back to the alley and introduce you to the city."

"My life is exciting enough, but I enjoy talking with you. Where are you going to sleep tonight?"

"Oh . . . here we go. Do you want me to go home with you?"

"Nah, that's not what I'm asking. Do you have a safe place to sleep?"

Julie pauses for a few seconds. "I stay in a house with a bunch of people. There are mattresses on the floor, and usually I can find one to crash on. I get high, and I sleep. Oh, and don't forget about sex. Plenty of that, too."

"Well, if you want to just get a good night's sleep and would like some help with your little problem, here's my number. Call me anytime. I don't have all the answers, but we will figure it out." Danny writes his phone number down on a napkin while Julie wipes her mouth on another. Danny slides it over to her, and Julie stares at it for a few seconds. Then, her right hand grabs it, scrunches it, and stuffs it into her worn out and slime-caked, hip-hugger back pocket.

Julie scoots to the end of the booth to leave, but pauses, just for a second, before turning and looking Danny in the eyes and thanking him. Julie jumps up and disappears again, but this time she goes out the front door and onto the street. "Man, she was far out. It's going to be a long night for her, Danny," Tippy-toes laments.

"I hope she remembers that my number is in her back pocket."

"Well, I don't think you need to worry about her washing it. I don't think those jeans have been washed for a month."

The two street missionaries go to His Place and help until three or four in the morning. Tippy-toes lives near UCLA, so Danny offers him a couch at his apartment, since Danny is looking forward to his first night in his bed. Tippy-toes agrees, and they make the long walk back to Selma Avenue. When they get there, Danny tells Tippy-toes that he is welcome to watch TV and announces that he will return to the front room in a few minutes.

In his bedroom, Danny gets his guitar and begins writing a song that has been in his head all day. He is pretty sure it will be called *No Time for Jesus*, but he may find some other title as the words flow. Tippy-toes locates the bathroom easily and then accepts Danny's invitation to watch the tube while his cohort strums away in the other room. However, at four in the morning, there is only an educational farming show, which Tippy-toes actually watches for the thirty minutes while Danny is in his bedroom.

Tippy-toes is impressed with what he can hear from Danny's room and when Danny re-joins his big friend, Tippy-toes asks Danny if he has played any of the coffeehouses. Danny tells him about the few off nights, but he hopes to play more. "Are you writing a song?" asks Tippy-toes.

"Yes, I have the first verse, and I think I wrote the second verse while I was in there."

"Will you read them to me, or do you not like doing that before it's complete?"

"No, I don't mind. This is what I have so far:

No Time for Jesus by Daniel Mosely

Verse 1
There's no time for Jesus. That's what they say
That He's in the way; He's so passé; He's not what's happening today
But I really love Him. He's been my friend through thick and thin

Verse 2
There's no time for Jesus. There's too much to do
So many opportunities for me and you
But He's been the one Who's kept me strong
When the day was long

"Oh my goodness, Danny. Oh my goodness! Those are actually really good, like professionally good. Really heavy. Do you write songs a lot?"

"Thanks, man. I have written a few, but I kinda feel like I am just starting."

"Man, you need to show this to somebody when you finish. Show it to Bob."

"Oh, man, he's not gonna want to hear this. I'm sure he has plenty of his own. It's not finished yet anyway. It needs a bridge. I may butcher it by the end."

They both chuckle and then agree to get some sleep. Danny digs out his blanket and pillow from his summer of couch-sleeping, puts on a new pillowcase and hands the bedding to his friend. "Do you need to wake up at any certain time?"

"No, not really," yawns Tippy-toes. "I can sleep in. How about you?"

"I have a three o'clock class and that's it for Tuesdays."

"Nice! OK, then, I will see you sometime tomorrow."

"Sure, man. I hope you rest well, and I enjoyed serving with you tonight. Say a prayer for Julie."

"Same here, my new brother, and yes I will. Goodnight."

"Goodnight, and if you leave before I wake up, please make sure the door is locked." And with that, Danny walks to his room, shuts the door, and flops down on his bed that still bears a slight scent of Hannah. He misses her and tells her goodnight as if she could hear him through the airwaves. Maybe she can.

Danny and Tippy-toes become good friends over the next few months and flourish as servants of God. They become familiar faces at all the crash pads throughout Los Angeles and are loved because they not only plant the seeds but water the soil by continuing the relationships they start, if possible. Young, drug addicted hippies and hate-filled, radical Yippies have seen their lives become peaceful and filled with purpose because Danny and Tippy-toes, and those like them, show true caring and love for the lost when their families and so-called friends did not.

Hannah has written Danny almost every week from Cedarville, and he has responded a whopping three times, but those three letters were replete with love and good stories. Hannah misses LA but is growing accustomed to college life and meeting lots of new Christian friends. Danny stays in Hollywood through his birthday and Thanksgiving, but he makes it home over Christmas. Every night, he fills Walter's house with old friends, music, and cooking. King contacts an Appleton venue and books a Clever Pennies reunion. They tell WROR on Wednesday the twenty-third, and the Saturday night show, the night after Christmas with bitter cold temperatures, sells out. It will be played with Greg on keyboards, as Barry has still not been heard from since Woodstock.

Danny gets to spend some quality time with the newly formed Lindor family. Baby Elska Lindor is as beautiful as her mother and born on her father's birthday. Her name is Nordic and means "love." Jeff holds her any time he has a free arm, and Alice is usually under Jeff's other arm. They are a close and beautiful family – yet burdened by Alice's parents. Though he is the father of their granddaughter, Jeff is not completely welcome in the Engel family. Markus offers Jeff supervisory level employment at the store, but Jeff believes he would become more Engel property, and he will have none of that. So, after a relentless sales pitch from a recruiter and without asking Alice, Jeff has enlisted into the Marines and will head for Parris Island on the Monday after Christmas.

Carl comes by and visits Danny as well and tells him how much he misses Danny's dad, providing funny and poignant stories of their short but robust relationship. It is bittersweet to Danny but still a welcome remembrance. Danny is with Hannah and the Birdsongs from morning until night but still spends a lot of time with Pastor Pete, Mr. Blanton, and Nick. With great love and desire, Danny sings a song for his church the Sunday after Christmas. Oddly, after hearing the story of his mother's death just before his dad died, Danny makes a point of going by himself, after church, into Appleton and to the spot where Beatrice presumably entered the Ohio River.

***

Back in Hollywood, Danny brings in 1971 with someone else's vomit down the front of his shirt. Tippy-toes will not return for another week, so Danny decided to just go it alone. He takes small breaks on side streets and in alleys to pray to God for more strength and a clear mind and then returns to Hollywood Boulevard to see who might need help. It is now after midnight, and the celebratory minds of the thousands of local hippies and tourists who have been smoking and drinking all day should be spinning.

Danny slides down the wall of a building where a young man with very long hair and a thick beard sits with his head laid back on the window sill. "Are you OK, brother?" Danny asks the hippie.

"Sure I am. I'm just diggin' the groovy lights, my man. What's your name?" Before Danny could answer, the young hippie vomits almost straight up, but the skinny kid only throws up liquid.

"I know a really groovy place where they are serving hot food and coffee tonight. You wanna go with me?" Danny asks.

"I'm trippin', friend. I don't think I want to eat right now. Thanks, though. Are you an angel or something? Hey, dig it! It's the City of Angels, right, and you must be one."

"No, friend, I'm pretty much like you. Just a poor sinner who needs Jesus every day."

The two just sit and watch the people walk by. There is a lot of music all around, coming from music venues and cars. A guy with a guitar is busking at the end of the block, and occasionally, Danny sees an acquaintance or two walk by while talking to someone about Jesus. They wave to each other but continue the Lord's work, planting seeds and hopefully bringing some comfort to people who should be productive and full of life at their young age. Drugs are rampant and robbing young people of their identities.

The young man beside Danny doubles over in pain, and Danny knows that he has taken LSD that has been combined, or "laced," with strychnine, a rat poison. A small amount of the poison is supposed to give the acid a bite or edge to it while you hallucinate. It certainly does that, and if not mixed correctly or if you are undernourished, it can rip up your stomach and cause great pain and discomfort. "Come on, man, let's go get some good food." Danny pulls the boy up while the boy is laughing and crying at the same time.

They go to a large house nearby where they find people serving hot soup, milk, coffee, scrambled eggs, and lots of love. A cross hangs on the wall, mimicking the Arthur Blessitt house. Reverend Blessitt has enlarged his ministry and no longer presides over his crash pad, but his and others' ideas to communicate with the hippie generation has spread throughout the world. It is wonderful to watch God work, but Danny is starting to see, possibly, too much structure from man. Danny thinks he may be seeing the heart of the movement slowly becoming the mind. He prays for them often.

Danny decides to take a break and just sit with the young man and help him down from his high. The young man cries and laughs with Danny. He tells stories of his sister running off to join a cult and that the last time he saw his parents, they kicked him out of the house because he was tripping. He tells Danny that he lives all over town, wherever he can crash for a night or a weekend and has been doing that for at least a year. Danny begins to tell him about Jesus and how He is a solid rock on which one can stand. That the world shifts and changes and the struggle to stay upright and focused is extremely difficult without Jesus at the helm.

"Yeah, I've heard of Jesus, man," the kid confesses. "He was kinda like a hippie way back then, with long hair and sandals and stuff, right?"

Danny chuckles and says "Well, Jesus certainly was a rebel to the Romans *and* the Jews, but we don't really know if He had long or short hair. Sandals, yes.

"Was He a good guy or a bad guy?"

"A bunch of people hated Him and wanted Him dead, but He was a friend to many and helped people. He claimed to be the Son of God who had come to earth to save the world."

"Wow, that's far out. Why did people hate Him, then?"

"Jesus sort of messed up people's lives because He told the truth. Some of the Jewish teachers who were in charge of their people were really snobby, and He showed them that they were far from where God wanted them, when they thought they were perfect. He was the Messiah, or Savior, that the Jewish Bible told them about. Most of the Jewish leaders should have recognized Him, but they were all pretty much wrapped up in themselves and didn't want to believe that a carpenter from Nazareth was the one who was going to save them from Rome."

"How did He know?"

"Because Jesus was and is the Son of God, and God gave His Son the power and authority to represent Him in every way." This topic causes Danny to lean forward with intensity as he continues, "Jesus came to Earth for one reason, and that was to tell us that we don't have to die in our sins and go to hell, if we just believe in Him. Jesus would give sermons, and His first one is what we have come to call the Sermon on the Mount." Danny begins to recite the Beatitudes to the young man, and the young hippie is transfixed on Danny, as if Danny is glowing.

After Danny recites all of the Beatitudes, he settles back into his chair and asks the young man to tell him his name.

"Samuel," the boy answers.

"Samuel! There is a very important man in the Bible with your name."

This interests Samuel, and he and Danny talk about Samuel's biblical role while they eat and sip coffee.

It is now four o'clock in the morning, and Samuel finally yawns and tells Danny he better get going so he can find a place to sleep. Danny tells Samuel that there are beds upstairs and that he is welcome to crash there tonight. They walk up and find a soft bed with a pillow and blanket in a room that is quiet, calm, and dark. Danny suggests the boy get cleaned up in the bathroom down the hall so that he will sleep better. That sounds lovely to Samuel, and Danny says he will stay by the bed so that no one else gets it.

Samuel is gone for about fifteen minutes and then re-appears with the puke cleaned out of his beard and off the front of his shirt and pants. "Man, I was a mess. Thank you for talking with me tonight. I really enjoyed hearing about Jesus and Samuel and King Saul. Blessed are the sleepy for they shall have sweet dreams." Danny chuckles as Samuel gets under the covers. Because he has always had a difficult time trying to find a pen to write his number for those he meets, Danny had actual cards with "Danny loves Jesus" and his phone number printed on them. He always wants to be a dependable resource in a lost person's life, and tonight was a perfect time to dig one out and give it to Samuel.

"I'm going to go now, Samuel, but call if you want to talk some more. Here is five dollars for tomorrow, and they will have free breakfast here when you wake up. You sleep well and dream about Jesus, alright?"

"That sounds good, man. Thanks again. I don't know why you spent your New Year's Eve with me, but I'm glad you did."

"The Spirit of God is strong in those who believe, and I get my strength and desire from that very Spirit. I know you won't understand this now, but the Spirit counsels me, directs me, and helps me to do the right things in life. If not for Him, I would be barfing on the sidewalk too, probably. I know this sounds trite, but I cannot express strongly enough to you that Jesus loves you, Samuel. He really loves you and wants great things for you, but you have to let go of the worldly things you are holding onto, and I know that can be scary. It's like skydiving, but you trust the God who created you instead of a manmade parachute or LSD. I look forward to seeing you again, Samuel. Sleep well."

Danny begins his long walk home but feels like Samuel understood and that God opened his heart to the Word. Danny also feels the Spirit leading him to another house. The dwelling is a little off the main path but hosted by some of the godliest hearts Danny has met in Los Angeles. Danny knows they take those who have the worst addictions, and though very tired, the Spirit drives him there. He finally walks inside and sees Josh, who owns the house, and he welcomes Danny with open arms.

"Danny, my brother in Christ! Happy New Year, and it is so good to see you! We have a full house tonight, my brother. What a wonderful way to bring in '71, I think. We are here by the grace of God, and He sent you here for a reason. He will show us what that is, I'm sure."

"Yeah, man. The Spirit put some pep in my tired step and turned me in this direction as I was walking home. What can I do for you, Josh? I'm sure you could use a little help."

"There is a young lady in that room who is tripping, but I think Cindy, you know Cindy, right?"

"Yep. What a wonderful Christian."

"Well, I think Cindy has calmed her down a bit, but you might stick your head in and check. Then there is a guy who is pretty much a regular, twice a week probably, in the other room down here on this floor. He's really lost, man, heroin at least, along with twenty other various drugs, probably. You seem to be able to cut through to them. God has made you his scalpel, I guess. The others upstairs seem to be quiet now."

"I'll take a look, and then if I don't see you, I will head home. You have my number if you need me."

"Sure thing, Danny, and thank you for doing God's work. You are an inspiration."

Danny walks past the front room and turns right, where there are two bedrooms. He sticks his head into the room where Josh told him Cindy was with a tripper. The tripper's head is asleep in Cindy's lap, and Cindy waves to Danny and blows him a quiet kiss. This puts a smile on Danny's face as he backs out of the room and pulls the squeaky door to where it is open about an inch. Danny laughs to himself and thinks of Jim Morrison as he "walks on down the hall".

Danny opens the next door, where he finds a body in a bed facing the wall. It is a male with long, matted hair and filthy-but-expensive clothes. There is a pair of gold-colored leather boots on the floor, and as Danny leans down to make sure the young man is still breathing, he inhales quite a stench. This guy hasn't taken the time to bathe in a few days. The high is more important. Danny's heart softens, though, as Danny's heart can do. He lifts the man's feet up from the mattress on the floor so he is able to grab the blanket that is under them and starts to pull the blanket up over the guest.

When he does this, the young man stirs and rolls over with his nasty, very long hair lying over his face. This posture has created a sprawling body, and Danny gets a full view of badly bruised arms where needles have damaged the skin. His arms are skinny and frail, with no color and little muscle. The addict raises a hand and brushes his matted hair from his face with a moan. Danny finishes covering the man's body with the clean blanket and finally gets to see his face in the light provided by a small wall plug night light. With no control at all, Danny falls to his knees as tears fill his eyes and flood over onto his face. He lays his head on the filthy concave chest. "Oh, thank you, God!"

There, under Danny's healthy head, is the beating heart of Barry Meade. "Oh, God, I love you. How can I ever thank you enough, Lord? Please give me the strength to help him, Lord. Please, Lord, help him." Danny lies right down on the floor next to his old friend, who had saved his life once, and tries to calm his system so that Barry can continue to rest. "Thank you, God," Danny repeats under his breath until he drifts off into a wonderful, Spirit-drenched sleep. Tomorrow is going to be a busy day.

— *Fin* —

RESOURCES VIA THE DUCKDUCKGO.COM SEARCH ENGINE:

Thesaurus.com. Wikipedia.com, History.com, Freedommag.org, calendar-365.com, Ultimateclassicrock.com, Blessitt.com, Merriam-Webster.com, Biblegateway.com, Biblehub.com, LAWA.org, Nature.com, The Farmer's Almanac, thepeopleshistory.com, YouTube.com and various medical, geographic and topographic websites.

FOLLOW RS PERKINS ON:

 @perkins_RS

 RS Perkins

 RS Perkins

RS's Newsletter at **rsperkins.substack.com**